David Densmore

The halo

An autobiography of D. C. Densmore. Vol. 1

David Densmore

The halo
An autobiography of D. C. Densmore. Vol. 1

ISBN/EAN: 9783337120429

Printed in Europe, USA, Canada, Australia, Japan

Cover: Foto ©Raphael Reischuk / pixelio.de

More available books at **www.hansebooks.com**

Yours truly,
D. C. Densmore

The Halo:

AN AUTOBIOGRAPHY OF D. C. DENSMORE.

*"There are more things in heaven and earth, Horatio,
Than are dreamt of in your philosophy."*
SHAKSPEARE.

VOL. I.

BOSTON:
VOICE OF ANGELS PUBLISHING HOUSE,
5 DWIGHT STREET.
1876.

PREFACE.

Tiiis volume is intended to be a truthful autobiography
of the author, so far as pertains to experiences and thrilling
adventures which are believed to be more *exceptional* than
representative. It is designed to illustrate Spiritual philosophy ; or, in other words, to demonstrate the fact that
our friends in spirit-life attend and act upon us while we
inhabit material bodies ; and that they frequently influence us for good, watch over us in the ups and downs
of life here, are cognizant of our every thought, cheer us
when desponding, and give us hopeful words of encouragement when misfortune assails us. Also when we are
ready to sink amid conflicting emotions and trials, not
knowing which way to look for succor, they come to our
rescue, and assist us with cheering words, bid us look up,
and infuse fresh courage, fresh aspirations, and renewed
vigor to battle valiantly with all the severe vicissitudes
and disappointments of life ; and, if they cannot give us
all that we may desire, they give at least assurances of
their loving presence and sweet sympathy.

To the struggling, discouraged men and women of the
world, to those bent down with sickness and cares, this
volume is respectfully dedicated ; and if the perusal of
its pages shall gladden the heart of some wayfarer, in his
gloomy pilgrimage through the world, with fresh hopes,

one great object of the author will be fulfilled. It is not expected that the volume will meet the tastes of all classes ; for I do not possess nor claim any literary qualifications for the work here undertaken. My object is mainly to help some who stand in need of Spiritual truths, and encourage them amid the arduous duties of life. Every step of the author over the rugged hills of this world has been guided and aided by his spirit-friends.

It is customary, I believe, when one is writing out his autobiography, to relate most of the incidents and accidents pertaining to his course from birth on to and through manhood ; but, as this history is intended chiefly to set forth a series of scenes made interesting by their intimate relation to the Spiritual philosophy, I shall, in the main, adduce only such prominent ones as in some point obviously connect with the higher life ; and show, in a marked manner, the care and guidance of my spirit-guardians, from my earliest recollections, on through many succeeding phases of a life full of thrilling events.

THE AUTHOR.

5 DWIGHT STREET, BOSTON, Feb. 25, 1876.

CONTENTS.

AUTOBIOGRAPHY OF D. C. DENSMORE.

CHAPTER I.

CHILDHOOD.

I WAS born in the town of Bowdoinham, Me., on the banks of the Kennebec River, the 10th of April, 1813. While I was an infant, my father purchased a tract of wild land in what was then called the town of Harlem (but subsequently named China), where he erected a log-house, cleared off a few acres of land, and commenced getting a livelihood in our forest home. There was no other habitation for miles; and here, amid wild beasts and screeching owls, my dear mother, with health impaired, was compelled to endure a toilsome existence for a few years. She being naturally of a very sensitive nature, her life was one of continual anxiety, from fear that she should be unable to procure the necessaries of life. Here we lived until I was two and a half years old, when father purchased another farm some little distance off, on which was a frame house partially finished.

In this house I passed the earlier part of my life; in fact, I made it my home until I had grown to manhood. Our family increased nearly every year by a new-comer, until the children numbered sixteen boys and girls. Among them were eleven boys; making the family circle, in round numbers, eighteen human beings; all the children from the same father and mother. It was a beautiful sight to see us all sitting at the table at one time. This I witnessed only during a few weeks; for generally some of the children were away from home. Of course it required tact, with industry and strict economy, to feed and clothe so many; and consequently all who were able to had to contribute their quota to its maintenance. Here I passed a happy portion of my life; yet although I had a harmonious, contented disposition, I was uneasy under the restraint I was constantly compelled to submit to in working on the farm, a kind of labor which I very much disliked; my mind would be running upon the building of mills of various kinds. At one time, when father had gone away for a few weeks, instead of working on the farm faithfully, I got it into my head to build a miniature saw-mill; and, with the aid of some of my younger brothers, managed to construct a dam across the brook, a stream running through our farm. After the dam was completed, I made a flume, with an apron for the wheel to run the machinery. After a good deal of difficulty for want of tools, I constructed what millwrights call a " breast-wheel." I had got the lower part of the mill completed, and the wheel running, before father came home. As it was located in the " alder-bushes," I was so screened from observation that no one knew what was going on, until I had the wheel set, or hung, in its place. Although it is over a half-century since the operation, I remember how pleased I felt when for the first time I hoisted the gate, and let the water on. The wheel was four feet long, and about fourteen inches in diameter. I was so elated at my success, that farm and every thing pertaining to it was quite forgotten.

After I had the lower part of my mill completed, and the wheel running, I changed my mind about building a saw-mill, as there was so much machinery attached to it, and I had no suitable tools to work with. I concluded to make a turning-lathe instead, similar to one a neighbor had, with this difference: he worked his with the foot on a treadle, while mine was to be run by water-power. After overcoming incalculable difficulty, for the want of proper tools to construct my lathe, I got it completed. With the belt in its proper place, I hoisted the gate, and set it spinning; how grand I felt at my success! Now, to prove its efficiency, I must turn out something. Not having any turning-tools, I went to the house, and got the butcher-knife, the end of which was quite round and very thick. I got a piece of green poplar-wood, such as spools are made of for winding yarn for weaving, and turned out one, which looked as perfect as those I had seen mother use. With this trophy of my success, I ran as fast as I could to show it to her. She said it was a nice one, but there was one objection to it: it had no hole for the spindle, which deficiency I had quite overlooked. When I told her I did it myself, she thought I had been down to Varney's, and turned it in his lathe; but when I told her I had built a lathe myself, and it run by water, she was quite astonished, and rather questioned the truthfulness of my assertion. To prove what I told her was true, I persuaded her to accompany me to my field of operations, which she did. After we got to the mill, I hoisted the gate, and turned out another spool. She seemed pleased with my ingenious turn of mind, but feared "father would not like it;" but, when he found it out, he was not displeased with me, but rather encouraged me by suggesting some improvements. A long-continued rain caused a freshet, before I had finished my works, and swept the unfinished mill, and every thing belonging to it, down the stream; which so discouraged me that I never attempted to rebuild it. This little boyish operation has no particular importance beyond showing what hard work and perseverance under difficulties may accomplish.

I used to work on the farm with the rest of the boys; and, when called to our meals, it was a common saying with them, that I must put a stick down where I left off hoeing corn or potatoes, to know where to begin again.

My mother, before and at the time of her marriage, belonged to the society of "Friends," or "Quakers." My father was a Methodist in good standing. The Quakers don't allow any of their flock to marry other than their own denomination. As a matter of course, my parents could not marry according to the ordinances of the Friends, unless father renounced his Methodism, and allied himself with the Quakers.

This he did not or would not do at that time; and, as they wanted to get married, they were joined in wedlock in accordance with father's religious belief. For this act of disobedience to her church, mother was hauled over the judicial coals, and was either compelled to say she was sorry for what she had done, and publicly condemn her act in the monthly meeting, or be "turned out" of the society. Whether she was ever really sorry, and condemned the practice, or not, I never heard her say. At all events, she chose to say so, and thus regained her standing as a good and exemplary Quaker, and kept it as long as she lived. When both parents belong to this church, the children are born members, thus obviating the trouble of joining it after they have gained their majority. Since mother, at the time of my birth, was under the ban of her Christian friends for "marrying out," as a matter of course, I was neither a born Quaker, nor a Methodist. However, when I was four years old, father determined to leave the Methodist persuasion, and join the Quakers. In the mean time, mother had been "dealt with," as they call it. But, after due consideration by the Friends, after she had confessed repentance of the disobedient act, they took her in again. By some process, which I never comprehended, they have a way by which minor children, when both parents belong to the society, no matter if neither belonged to it when the children were born, to take them into the church without their will or consent, and compel them to conform to all the requirements of the society ever after. When I was four years old, father became convinced that the

Quaker religion was the surest and shortest road to heaven; and like any other sensible, thinking man, felt justified in taking the shortest cut and the safest boat to cross life's tempestuous seas in, and therefore renounced his Methodism altogether, and joined the Quakers. After he had got firmly fixed in the church, they, the "meeting folks," went through some process by which we children were all taken in as good members of the "society." After this, as father and mother belonged to the society, all the children born afterwards belonged to the same before they ever saw the light of day.

I have been subject, from my earliest remembrance, to strange prophetic dreams, or visions; and one or two of the earlier ones I will relate, to show that I was subject then to unseen influences, which I now know were really and substantially my guardians, who have been controlling me in all my movements through life; also some experiences of hearing voices telling me in distinct and clear words what to do to relieve me when in embarrassed circumstances; but not until all hope of relief had forsaken me would such put in an appearance. These voices, or impressions, or whatever folks may choose to call them, have attended me from my earliest childhood; and not until the advent of modern Spiritualism had become a fixed fact in my mind did I realize from whence they came. Before that, although I hadn't the slightest faith that there were unseen spirits, either good or bad, yet I paid the most profound respect to these strange interferers in my business affairs, and treated their advice with the courtesy and consideration that I would give to the advice of a valued friend, in whose wisdom and ability to guide and direct I had the utmost confidence.

The first distinctly remembered dream or vision of coming events, which I could not have otherwise known any thing about, occurred when I was about nine years old. I dreamed, that while the family were taking breakfast, I with the rest, a flat-iron fell from the mantle-piece, and broke the handle off. When it occurred, mother said, " How sorry I am! what shall I do?" (being in straitened circumstances, the repair or replacing of this was quite a draft upon the slender means), when father said, " Never mind, mother: I have a broken axe, and I will send David out to Bragg's, and get them both mended." (This Mr. Bragg was a blacksmith, living some three or four miles from us.) I did not know that the axe was broken, until I heard of it in my dream. I saw father put the iron in one end of a meal-bag, the axe in the other, put the bag across the saddle, adjust the stirrups to correspond with my short legs, and start me off. The axe was on the left, and the flat-iron on the right side, of the horse. This dream did not occur to me when I awoke. While partaking of our breakfast the next morning, Louis Bean, a domestic living in our family, in moving something on the mantle-piece, pushed off the flat-iron, which broke the handle. When mother saw the accident, she repeated the same words that I dreamed she did; and father consoled her misfortune in precisely the same words I heard him use in my sleep; and he put the broken articles into a meal-bag, the axe and iron on the same sides of the horse that I saw in my dream. It was not till I heard father's consoling remarks to mother about sending me out to Bragg's to get them mended, that my dream came vividly to my mind.

Sometimes in later life, as well as in boyhood, these dreams would relate to things that had previously occurred, or were transpiring at the time I dreamed them, but under circumstances that precluded the possibility of my knowing any thing about them in the usual way; one of which I will relate: —

In 1860, when in Birmingham, Eng., engaged in experimenting on some patents, and selling others, I arose one morning, dressed, preparing to go to the shop; but, it being rather early, I thought I would lie down a few moments, not thinking of going to sleep; but I did lose myself, although I don't think I was in a sound slumber. When I aroused from my lethargy, I remembered very distinctly of going home, and finding Helen, my oldest child, very sick. I thought I told my wife what to do for her, and then came out of my trance-like sleep. This was the sixth day of August; and, the dream getting a strong hold of me, I could not resist an inclination to write. I did so, and described the disease, and told them what to do if she was no better when my letter arrived. On my way to the shop I mailed it. When I arrived at my place of business, I told Mr. Edwards, the proprietor of the building, my dream; remarking, at the same time, that by due course of mail I should receive a letter corroborating in every particular Helen's illness.   He laughed at my credulity, and left me.   I had told Mr. Edwards, before this, some of my experiences in relation to spiritual matters, more particularly to clairvoyance, &c., all of which he ignored as fanatical and positively absurd.   I felt just as sure that I should have my dream corroborated, as that I had dreamed it.   Time passed ; and, being very busily engaged in my business, I quite forgot my dream, till one morning Mr. Edwards came into the shop, swinging a letter over his head, saying, " Here's a letter all about Helen." My letters came to his care.   His remarks put me in mind of my dream.   I sat down at once, and read it, he watching me all the while to hear the dream corroborated.   I read the third page, which wound up by saying, " We are all as well as usual."   There was not a word about Helen's sickness.   I told Mr. Edwards that for once I was mistaken ; when he whirled on his heel, and went up-stairs to his office, laughing at my credulous disposition.   I sat there wondering how it could be possible that I was mistaken, when, in doing up the letter to put it back in the envelope, I saw on the fourth page a postscript dated the 8th, in which wife said, " Helen has come home very sick to-day ; " and there was given a description of her case in precisely the same words that I had used when writing home.   The letter was dated the 6th of August, the same date of mine to them ; but they did not close it until the 8th.   I went immediately up-stairs, and let Mr. Edwards read the corroborating testimony of my going three thousand miles to diagnose a disease, and back again

2*

in a few moments. He looked astonished, and finally told me I was a "wizard," and playfully said he "wouldn't have me on his premises."

The facts of the case were these; Helen being five miles away, teaching school, was taken violently sick with diphtheria; but the folks with whom she boarded thought she would soon get over it, and didn't consider it necessary to carry her home; of course her mother, who was five miles away from her, knew nothing about it until two days after she was taken; but I, though three thousand miles away, knew it (as I heard afterwards, calculating the difference in time between the two places) the moment she was taken. This proves that there is no limitation to the range of spirit, whether in the physical form or out of it. I could relate many others of similar nature in my experience, but this must suffice for this time. As I go along in my history, I shall have occasion to refer to many similar experiences, especially about the time when I commenced the investigation of modern Spiritualism, which will show how and why I became convinced of its profound truths.

From the time this occurred, that is, the first dream related above, when I was about nine years old, there was nothing of note transpired until the spring when I was eleven years old.

CHAPTER II.

PRECOCIOUS SHIPBUILDING.

My father was a farmer, and, to enhance his income, annually peeled hemlock bark for tanning purposes, which when properly dried he would haul to a market, and exchange for money, or household commodities used in the family. The last of November, 1824, he had a large load of this bark ready for transporting to Pittston, on the Kennebec River, some sixteen miles from our farm. He had intended to start in company with a neighbor by the name of Estes, Uncle Jonathan as he was familiarly called, who had a load of the same material ready loaded. In taking large loads of any material to market, it was customary for two neighbors to go together, so that they could "double up the hills," as they call it, when one team assists the other; by this process each can carry a much larger load than if alone. After father had made all his arrangements to go in company with this neighbor, some business matters coming up which had to be attended to, he made up his mind to defer going till another day. While we were taking our supper, Uncle Jonathan came in to inquire what time father intended starting. He was told that he couldn't go at all, father giving his rea-

sons.   Uncle Jonathan said he must go if he went
alone, in which case he would be obliged to leave a
part of his load behind.   After a few minutes the
old man says, " Why can't thee let David and Henry
go?   I will do the selling and buying, and I can
have thy team to assist me up the hills."   After a
few minutes' reflection the proposal was favorably
received; and so it was settled that Henry and I
should go to the great town of Pittston, where we
should see so many new things.   For us, who had
never been over five miles from home before, to go so
far was quite an event in our secluded lives.   After
we had finished our evening meal, we were told to
go to bed immediately, as we were to start at twelve,
midnight.   The idea of our going to sleep with such
prospects ahead of us, was simply ridiculous.   We
lay and talked, and speculated in a suppressed tone
about what we probably should· see; and, as new
thoughts constantly came before our excited minds,
sleep was getting farther and farther away from our
eyelids.   We had no means for knowing the time,
but at last the joyful word came, to " get up."   We
were not long in getting our clothes on, and ourselves
down stairs, where mother had provided a bountiful
breakfast, steaming hot, to which we did ample justice.   While we were eating, father was yoking up
the·oxen, and getting them ready.   Before we had
finished our early meal, we heard Uncle Jonathan
drive along, and by the time father had our team
" hitched up " we were ready to start.   Mother provided us an ample lunch to eat the next day.   All
things being ready, the teams were started, Uncle

Jonathan taking the lead. Father attended us a short distance to see that all was right, when he retraced his steps, and we were fairly under way on our first journey to a distant town. We trudged along by the side of our team, and that was about all we had to do ; for the cattle followed the team ahead, and seemed to know they were on their own " hook." Towards morning there was quite a shower of rain, but about daylight the clouds broke away, and before sunrise not one was to be seen. We arrived at our destination about eight, A.M., tired, foot-sore, and hungry. After the teams were disconnected from the cart, chained to the wheels, and eating their " cornstalks," we ate our cold breakfast sitting on a log, our eyes all the while wandering all " over the lot," scanning critically every thing ; for every thing was new to us. What attracted *my* attention more than any thing else was what I subsequently learned was called a topsail schooner. She lay tied up to the wharf just below where we were sitting. After we had finished eating, and while Uncle Jonathan was hunting up a purchaser of the bark, I went down to the head of the wharf to inspect more closely the " ship," as I thought every thing that sailed on the ocean was called. At this time all the sails were hoisted up to dry, having got wet from the rain of the night previous. Of course I knew nothing whatever about a vessel of any kind, not the names of the different sails or rigging, or, in fact, any thing which went into the make-up. I thought she was, and in fact she was, the grandest thing I had ever seen ; and I contemplated her with the greatest possible interest. I inspected critically her hull, masts, and rigging, also the sails. The vessel was " light; " that is, had no cargo in her hold, consequently there was but a small portion of her hull under water; and, judging from what was above the water-line, I was enabled to determine very near how the part under water must be formed to correspond with the portion above. After my inspection of the vessel was through with, it seemed to me that I had the whole of her, sails, rigging, and hull, within. my comprehension. How to ascertain the proper proportions of the length of the masts and spars to the length of the vessel somewhat puzzled me: to get this important knowledge I went up to the head of the wharf intuitively, and compared the length of the masts with the length of the vessel, and found, as near as I could tell, that the masts were very near as long as the hull of the vessel, which conclusion I subsequently ascertained was very near correct. From the first look at the vessel, I got a longing to build one myself; and, by the time I had got through with my inspection, I had fully determined that I would, and that I would sail her over a large pond on our farm. Exactly how this was to be brought about, I hadn't the slightest idea, for father was decidedly opposed to my " foolish notions," as he was wont to designate my architectural proclivities; but somehow or other I couldn't disconnect the conviction from my brain that I should build a vessel some way. I said nothing to my brother about my plans until nearly half-way home, when I told him of them, or rather of my determination to build a ship the ensuing spring, but enjoined the strictest secrecy.

There was but a solitary chance for me to accomplish any thing in that direction. In early spring father usually went to Bowdoinham on the Kennebec River, his native town, and from there went a-fishing three or four weeks; seldom more than three, but occasionally he would prolong his visit to four. He might *not* go this spring, which was the only formidable hinderance I had to fear. I had told my brothers over and over again through the winter what I intended to do when the snow was gone, all the time cautioning them to the profoundest secrecy. I told them if father found it out "the fat would all be in the fire;" assuring them that if they kept it to themselves, and would assist me, they should all have a sail in my "ship." They promised compliance with my wishes; and I don't think there existed a doubt in their young minds, but that I would build one, and that they would have a sail in her. This confidence was greatly enhanced, I think, by the fact that I was forever building dams and mills, or making something. They evidently thought me a superior genius; and hence, when I desired the dear confiding creatures to assist me in my works, they were always ready and willing to comply.

There was a piece of uncleared land about half a mile south-east of our house, which went by the name of the "Pine Woods." It was once covered with great white pine trees, the most of which had been made up into shingles; but there were many parts of logs still lying on the ground. I had often passed through this land with the cattle, and I remembered part of one large log which, if sound, would do for the hull of my miniature ship. I had often spoken of this to my confederates through the winter; but, as the snow was deep, I had no way of examining it until the snow left. Some time about the middle of March, the snow had so far gone that I could prospect pretty well. I did so, and found that if that log was sound I could have a "ship" over twenty feet long. Its soundness I could not tell until I cut it off, which I had as yet no opportunity of doing without risking my secret. "Hope deferred maketh the heart sick," it is said, and it did in my case. Up to this time father had said nothing about "going fishing:" at least, I hadn't heard him. Time rolled slowly on, my patience pining, till one Thursday evening, just before we were sent to bed, I heard father tell mother he was "going down river next week." Now, thought I, in a few days I shall commence my enterprise.

I lay half that night thinking over my project, and wondering where I should find a log suitable, if the one I was thinking about proved unfit.

Father got away on the 10th of April, my birthday which made me twelve years old.

The day previous to his leaving, he took me out into the "Pine Woods," and informed me that he was going to "clear up" a part of it; and, as there were many remnants of old pine-trees scattered all over it, he wanted us boys to cut them up for "summer wood" while he was gone. To encourage me he said, "If thee'll be a good boy, and see that the rest work well, I'll bring thee home something." I readily made most faithful promises, my feelings being intensely aroused by my good luck in being placed right where of all others I most desired.

Here I could carry on my works without exciting the suspicions of mother or any one else as to what we were up to; and, if the great log I had selected was only sound, I was all right. Before father was out of sight I had the boys, four of us, on the spot, when I told them, that, if they would work hard enough to make up for me, I would get up the ship, and they should all have a sail in her. They promised to do so, and all went to work, they to chopping wood, I to cutting off the big log. Oh, with what vigor I worked until I had got it off! To my intense satisfaction, I found it was as sound as a nut. I cut it off twenty-one feet long : my rule for measuring was the axe-handle. I had no tools to work with except a broad and a narrow axe, drawing-knife, one and a fourth inch auger, and a one-inch chisel. With these tools I commenced forming the outside of the hull. I seemed to know just how to begin to save work; and to-day I couldn't begin and carry on the work by any better system, with such tools as I then had, notwithstanding my lifetime experience, than I did in that operation.

In the first place I hewed what I intended for the top side of the boat, then shaped the outside as I remembered the vessel looked that I was modelling from.

After I got the outside to suit me, I commenced "digging it out;" and it was several days before I had the inside completed, I intending to have the sides and bottom about an inch thick. At length the hull was complete. The next thing was to make the masts and spars (sticks, as I called them then), which I soon accomplished. I set her upright on some blocks, secured so as not to topple over. I remember with how much pride I looked on the hull, with her masts standing, and she sitting upright on the miniature stocks.

We used to go and come from our work as regular and steady as old men. Mother told me in after years, when referring to my boyish freaks, that she thought then that there was something special that kept us so steady to our work. We were called to our meals by mother's blowing a horn. I had to keep ever lecturing my confiding brothers " not to tell," and grew more earnest the further I had got my ship along. I was fearful that they might be overheard talking about it; but they proved remarkably reticent, for no one else ever knew that a ship was being built in that section of the country, until she was finished, and had made several voyages across the " big pond."

The next trouble to overcome was the rigging. Where was it to come from ? For without that I could do nothing. I remember, while making the masts and spars, that once or twice the rigging came into my mind ; but, as I never anticipate trouble, I threw thoughts of them away, preferring to wait until I came up to need of them. I used to do my main thinking after everybody was abed and asleep. The night after I had finished the spars, I lay thinking what I could do to get the rigging, when a bright light flashed through my brain, and in a moment I saw a way to surmount the difficulty. Directly over where I lay, on a shelf supported by the collar-beams, were two large balls of doubled and twisted twine, which mother had prepared for making harnesses for weaving cloth in a loom. I determined at once to appropriate them for my use. This being settled, I went to sleep. Soon after daylight I was up, and got the twine down, ready for carrying it out to our shipyard. I had to use some little tact to get the twine away from the house unobserved. While "doing the chores," I had an opportunity to tell of my luck to my brothers, and the plan I had adopted to get the twine out to where I wanted to use it. I selected Philip to do the express business. He was instructed, after breakfast, to wait at the east end of the house; the others to proceed to their work as usual. I was to go up stairs, as though I wanted to get something there, and watch for the signal agreed upon, to know when the "coast was clear." Directly I heard it, — a low whistle, — and out of the little window went the two balls of twine. The barn was due east from the house; and, as arranged, Philip scampered as fast as he could, got behind the barn, and then kept the barn between him and the house until he got abreast of our working ground, when he could cross the field at leisure, and none in the house would be the wiser; all of which he executed remarkably quick. Now I had got the material, but it must be made into a small rope to be useful. To do this I improvised a rope-walk. One of the boys I set to carrying an end away, until I thought the ball was half unwound: then I fastened the "bite" to a stump; next I took the ball, and started for the other end of the string, unrolling as I went along. We then twisted at each end with our fingers, doubled it several times, until it was large enough for my purpose; and before the horn called us to dinner the next day I had her completely rigged.

The next difficulty, and by all odds the hardest to overcome, was to obtain material for the sails. I had occasionally thought of this, but how success was to come about I didn't exactly know; yet, like the twine business, I thought it might be obtained somehow or other. All the afternoon I was puzzling my brain as to where the cloth was to come from. At one time I thought I would go to the only store in that section of the country, some two miles distant, get some cotton cloth, and have it charged to father. Then again I thought it was doubtful if the storekeeper would know me, and, if he did, I wasn't sure that he would trust father under the circumstances; so that scheme was given up. Before night, several other projects that suggested themselves were abandoned as not feasible. I went to bed that night discouraged at the prospect, and felt the worse about it because I had got my enterprise so nearly finished. But hope, as she always does, came to my rescue. I thought that I might think of some way to overcome the difficulty, after I got still, and all hands asleep; then I thought of many ways, but upon close inspection found they wouldn't do. At last, when hope had left me for the present, turning over in the bed, I happened to think its sheets would serve my purpose. Instantly the resolution was formed to take them, and make them into sails, and run the risk of getting an extra "thrashing." I expected to get well punished for what I had already done, and concluded that I might as well "be hung for an old sheep as a lamb;" so I firmly resolved to take sheets enough for my purpose. Now, then, I had to calculate how many of them my ship would require, and found need for at least three. Then I matured my plans for getting them into my sail-loft, where the sails could be made up. I think it was past midnight before I closed my eyes to sleep. The plan adopted for getting them away from the house was precisely the same as in the twine business. I was out bright and early the next morning, full of bright anticipations of soon launching my little ship. Of course we all knew that when they made up the beds the sheets would be missed, and that there would be a general inquiry and hunt for their whereabouts. I had instructed the boys what to say when asked about them; they were to give the same answer as they did about the "twine" affair. As it may be asked what came out of purloining the twine, I will merely say, that, before the twine had been made into a rope, Sally Varney, a neighbor, and the only person in that section of the country who understood making twine into loom-harness, called for the twine, which mother had prepared for the purpose, and which she thought was still lying on the shelf where she left it. When she went to get it, it couldn't be found; and, after diligently searching every nook and corner without finding it, mother finally concluded that some one must have stolen it. Of course, when asked, none of us knew any thing about it; and consequently she had to make more, before she could go on with her weaving. When she asked me, I felt so bad I could hardly suppress crying, especially because my act would force her, an invalid, to work so hard, and because she was always so cheerful and pleasant to all, and especially to me. The only excuse I had for myself for taking the twine and sheets was, that *I couldn't help it.* I thought that my ship *must* be built at all hazards; and, to do it, I must have the materials somehow or other. The sheets seemed to be a more serious affair than the twine, and I almost quailed to meet the searching inquiry that I knew would be made. There was only one circumstance which I thought might screen the evidence of my act for a short time. I knew that eventually the secret must come out, and the real culprit be brought to the surface. It was this: My brother Henry, only thirteen months my junior, was in the habit of getting up in his sleep, and hiding things, often his own clothes, where neither he nor any one else could find them. I thought of this at the time I determined on taking the sheets. This was all the hope of avoiding prompt detection I had to lean upon. Like all culprits, I wanted to put off the day of reckoning as long as possible. In addition to taking the sheets, I had taken the shears to cut out my sails with, and the only darning-needle mother had. But these could be returned after I had used them. As I expected, when we went in to dinner that day, there was a most searching inquiry for the sheets, shears, and needle ; there being a large family to mend and sew for, the two latter articles were constantly in use. I had trained my brothers, when asked about them, to merely say, " I don't know," fearing to trust them to say more. Having failed to elicit any satisfactory information from them, mother finally asked me if Henry got up in the night. I said, " Yes." " There," she says, " he has hid them away somewhere ; " and nothing was said about it at that time. But the shears and needle went away so mysteriously, as to puzzle her more than the absence of the sheets. The shears and needle she had been using late the evening before, even after we had all gone to bed up stairs. The next day both were found in an out-of-the-way place, but conspicuous enough to catch the eye of any one passing, as I intended they should be. I almost positively knew I should be severely punished for what I had done, as I had heard father often quote from old Solomon's sayings, " He that spares the rod spoils the child : " yet the pleasure of building a ship myself, and being captain while sailing her over the big pond, quite overcame all dread of getting a " licking," as we used to call a good sound thrashing. That would soon be over; but I should long retain the proud distinction and satisfaction of building and sailing a ship under circumstances most discouraging. This satisfaction would endure as long as my memory should exist.

I had good luck in cutting and making my sails; and in two days she was ready to launch. During the last few days I was in a constant fever of excitement, for fear that father would get home before I got my vessel in the water. Good luck had attended me through the whole affair thus far, and it did not desert me at this critical moment. He omitted to make his appearance until the very day, late in the afternoon, that I got my ship on her element in the morning. We had about a quarter of a mile to haul her across the field to reach the pond, which we did with a yoke of oxen, the vessel being on a large "drag" that was used for hauling stone. About nine, A.M., we launched her. I had some fears that she might not stand up: so before we got in I put some stone in for ballast; and, when we found that she stood up stiff, our exultation knew no bounds. There was a brisk breeze blowing at the time directly across towards where I wanted to go. Henry got in forward, and I aft (or *behind* as I said, not being versed in nautical phraseology). I got the sails up; and, when all was ready, I let go of a bush I was holding on to. She moved slowly at first, I steering; but soon she gathered headway, and we skimmed over the broad expanse of waters as pretty as any ship ever did, whatever pretensions for sailing qualities others might possess. Not even Columbus when he discovered America had feelings to compare with mine, when we were sailing so prettily over the pond for the first time. I realized the important fact, that I had built a vessel, and was sailing captain of her over the tempestuous seas of a pond in the middle of a forest. After we reached the other shore we got out, turned her around, and sailed back again, landing at the very point from where we started on our trial trip. I took another brother as passenger on the next voyage, and followed up, giving each a turn till all had their pleasure-trip. We kept it up all day, going back and forth, changing passengers at every trip, until late in the afternoon when the wind died away. When I was in the middle of the pond on my last voyage for the day, father came in sight of us on what was then called Dudley's Hill. Although we did not see him, or think or care any thing about him or anybody else, our enthusiasm overcoming every other consideration, yet, as I learned afterwards, he watched some of our manœuvres from the top of the hill referred to, which overlooked our farm. He had an old sea-captain in the wagon with him, by the name of Norton, who lived two or three miles above us, and who was coming home with father to see about purchasing a yoke of our oxen. Capt. Norton, in overlooking our farm from the height spoken of, discovered my ship, and, sailor like, sung out "Sail-ho." Father, who was part of a sailor, says, "Where away?" "Over there," said Capt. Norton, pointing towards us. Father stopped his horse when he perceived us, saying, "That's that David's work. The boys haven't done a day's work since I've been gone. I'll pay him for that." Capt. Norton, as he informed us years afterwards, told father that he ought to encourage him (meaning me). "I," he said, "should be proud of such a boy." Father continued, "He's always building mills, dams, and turning-lathes, or something else; any thing but working on the farm." When they reached our home, it was supper-time. At the blowing of the horn we went in to supper, well pleased with our day's pleasure. We hadn't a thought that father had got home, and didn't dream that he had seen our miniature ship. After I found him at supper, I knew that the story would soon be told; and I began to prepare for my flogging. Father asked me how much wood we had cut. I said, " A good lot; " and so we had; I really believe that considerable more was cut than there would have been if I had worked with my brothers. I noticed that father was unusually pleasant. Capt. Norton's talk with him about me cooled him off somewhat.

After supper was over, Henry and I were told to drive the cattle up to the " bars." The pasture where the cattle were kept was a little beyond, and on a line where we had been at work. We started in the direction of the pasture, expecting father and the captain would follow; and, as they would have to pass near where our wood was piled, he could see that there was " a good lot " cut and piled. Instead of going the nearest way, however, they kept to the left, heading directly to the pond where my ship lay moored in the bushes.

I thought, as they were busy talking, that they were not conscious where they were going; not thinking, as before stated, that they had seen my ship; and to call their attention to the right path I hallooed saying, " The oxen are *this* way." They took no notice of my call, but kept on direct towards my ship. I began to feel uneasy at the prospect. Although I knew it was only a matter of a few hours before it would all be known, yet I, like all guilty people, and more especially little boys, desired to defer being found out in misdeeds as long as possible. Directly I heard father call my name. I pretended not to hear him. He bawled out the second time, " David, come here." I kept on pretending again not to hear, when Henry says, " Answer him, David." At this, I stopped, looked round, and saw father beckoning me to him.

I knew now that the " fat was all in the fire." We started slowly towards him, when Henry says, " O David! thee'll get an awful licking," and commenced crying. I said, " I know it, and am ready for it." When we got where they were standing, father says, " What's that ? " pointing to my little ship. I said, " It's a ship." — " That's right, my boy," says the captain, patting me sympathetically on the head. Father then told me to " get in, and sail her." I said, " The wind has gone down, and a vessel won't sail without the wind blows." — " That's right, my boy," again ejaculated the good captain. Father was good to us ; but he had an erroneous idea in that he thought that children had no rights that he was bound to consider, because they were young. If it hadn't been for religious blindness causing him to coerce, instead of using his reason in educating the young, and preparing them to assume the responsibilities of life, he would not have had in after-years so much cause as he did to regret his own lack of wisdom. My object, however, is not to moralize, or tell what parents ought to do to or for their children, but to state facts in my own experience. I couldn't help feeling a flow of sympathy coming from the great heart of the old sailor, and I wished my father was like him. After the above conversation we were told to drive the cattle up, which we did; and after talking, and measuring the oxen, the captain took one yoke, and drove them off. On the evening of that eventful day to me, after the chores were done, and all hands were ready for bed, father told mother about my ship. Mother exclaimed at once, "There's my twine, and there's where my sheets have gone." She continued, "I thought they were remarkably busy." Upon that father said, "I'll settle with him in the morning." Oh, how I dreaded that! If he had thrashed me there and then, I should have got over it before morning; but I had to lie and dread it all night, and then get up in the morning expecting to take it. Father often pursued this course, laboring under the hallucination (for it certainly was such in my case) that old Solomon's suggestion not to spare the rod would be more effective, if he tortured by putting off punishment over night. But he lived up to the best light he had at that time, although I thought then that he might have done far more towards making us good and obedient children by a different course. When I started for bed, mother followed me, and, when out of hearing by father, embraced and hugged me to her bosom, kissing me over and over again, both of us crying; she from sympathy for me, I from dread of the promised thrashing that would come

with dawn of the next day. We had a good though
sad time together; at last she says, " What made thee
do that, David ? " I said, " I *couldn't help it*, mother."
Both of us were still crying. " There, never mind,
darling," she says: " I will coax father not to whip
thee ; " and after kissing me again and again, she
told me to go to bed and to sleep. Whether it was
the hope of her success in influencing father not to
thrash me, or her pure love, that lulled me to sleep,
I do not know: at all events, I was soon in the close
embrace of " nature's sweet restorer," and slept
soundly until morning. When I awoke, the first
thought that greeted me was a " licking." Father
generally would " settle " with us before we were
up, or immediately after; and, as he didn't come, I
got up and dressed, wondering whether he had forgotten it altogether, or was going to torture me still
further by delaying the castigation. I went to work
" doing up the chores " until breakfast was announced. After that was through with, and the
morning devotions were solemnized by mother's first
reading a chapter in the Bible, and then telling how
good and loving God was, followed by a sitting of a
half-hour's length in absolute silence, father and
mother worshipping God in their hearts, I and all
my dear brothers and sisters thinking about the
" licking " in store for me. They all deeply sympa-
thized with me in my sad fate, and I think any one
of them would willingly have suffered for me. By
this time the girls, large and small, knew about my
" ship." After the religious ceremonies were over,
and before we left our seats, father began to talk to

me in a very solemn manner, telling me the "terrible" effects of sin, picturing more vividly than ever the magnitude of that sulphurous lake of fire and brimstone "where the worm dieth not, and the fire is not quenched," repeating what he and darling mother had said hundreds of times before, that into this awful abyss of liquid fire all wicked men and women, and *especially naughty boys* who disobeyed their parents (I knew he meant me), were plunged head and heels, to fry and sizzle for ever and ever. After dilating at some length upon the enormity of my sin, showing as vividly as he could that the evil effects of setting a bad example to the rest, and teaching them to go ahead upon any thing that they had set their hearts upon doing, without first consulting the parents whether it was best or not, was very reprehensible, and that, in the eyes of God's justice, such culprits were sure to find themselves in the awful place, after their bodies were "laid in the cold, cold ground, food for worms," he dismissed us; saying that through the interposition of mother he would defer punishing me at this time, threatening that, if I ever did such a thing again, he "would pay me up for old and new." All through this great preamble my mind was most of the time on my ship. I queried, when he said we ought to consult our parents before entering on any enterprise, how long I should have had to wait before I could show the world that I could build and sail a ship on my own hook, had I consulted him. After all was over, we went about our daily routine of farm-work each succeeding day until it was time for me to again go away from home to work; for such was my custom a part of each year.

Thus ends the account of my first enterprise in shipbuilding, which, considering the discouraging circumstances under which it was brought to a successful termination, fairly eclipses the operations of many a "child of larger growth," no matter how great might be his pretensions to superior constructive skill and business qualifications. It is true that there is no other particular significance in my operation than showing the bent of my faculties in boyhood, and what may be done when one has an object in view, and perseveres unto the end; and also showing, as the reader will see, that this was only one round in the ladder of my progression preparatory for taking a step higher, and so of every succeeding step.

It may be asked how I can reconcile the course I pursued in getting materials for my ship with my fair pretensions to upright and proper behavior. I will only say that at that time I had as much reverence for goodness as I have ever entertained, and was just as anxious then as now to keep myself and all mankind out of the brimstone premises. Every thought was pregnant with doing good: that was natural with me, not acquired, and hence there was no particular merit in it, because I couldn't help it any more than water can help running down an inclined plane. I had no compunctions of conscience for building mills or ships: on the contrary, I felt justified in doing so, because I was told that, when I did any thing not agreeable to or allowable by father, he would "*square*" the account by giving me a thrashing. I was willing to settle in that way, and upon his own terms. I thus bargained with him, and didn't see but that it was as fair as any other trade agreed upon beforehand.

CHAPTER III.

AT SCHOOL IN PROVIDENCE, AND SCHOOL TEACHING.

THE summer following the successful termination of my first operation in shipbuilding, as usual during a few years I worked at a " carding-machine," in the fall at a "fulling-mill," and attended school in winter. In the fall of this year occurred an event which had much to do in determining my future career.

As before stated, my parents, as also we children, belonged to the society of Friends, or Quakers. It is customary to send two children from each monthly meeting to Providence every year, where their tuition, board, and lodging are paid for out of a fund left by an old Quaker by the name of Brown, who founded the institution. Each scholar is allowed six months' schooling *free;* after which, if he remains, he is compelled to pay for his accommodations.

Father determined to avail himself of this privilege, and send me to Providence. His application was successful; he was one of the brightest lights they had, so they couldn't refuse his request. The meeting gave me the necessary papers to secure an entrance into said school. Preparations were com-

menced immediately, to get me ready for the long
journey. Considering the slow mode of travelling
in those days when there were neither railroads nor
steamboats, together with my youth (for I would
not be fourteen years old until the following April),
it was indeed a long journey, and, for one so inex-
perienced with the ways of the world, was a great
undertaking. The stage-coach and sailing-vessels
were the only resources for travellers. Near the
last days of October I was ready for the journey.
A trunk amply filled with suitable clothing was my
only baggage. I shall never forget the eventful
morning that witnessed my departure from the
scenes of my childhood to a distant city.

My brothers and sisters, as also my dear, anxious
mother, were in tears, as well as myself; and when
the wagon that was to convey me to Augusta, where
I was to take passage in a vessel to Boston, was
brought round to the front door, and my trunk
put in, and the last hand-shake and loving kiss
given and taken, the flood-gates of my soul seemed
to burst their bounds, flooding my entire being
with the waters of unfeigned grief. When all was
ready, father said, " Come, David, and get in ; "
he having hard work to suppress his own emotions,
arising from the scenes he was witnessing. At last
we were off; the dear ones at home, with streaming
eyes, watching us, until lost to view by intervening
hills. A couple of hours brought us to Augusta,
where father had previously engaged my passage to
Boston, in the schooner " Eagle," Capt. Blanchard.
Father paid my fare to Boston : from thence I was

to go in a stage to Providence. He also gave me thirteen dollars to pay my way after I left the packet, and have a little pocket-money besides. I mention the amount of money, because it was the first considerable sum I ever had; and when I realized that it was all mine, to be paid out for my own personal necessities, and by myself, it put me in a sort of dignified condition never before experienced. In fact, I felt as though I had arrived at a state bordering on manhood; for now I was left entirely to my own decisions, without the guiding counsel of either father or mother.

When we arrived at Bath, the last important place on the river before we should get out to sea, there was a strong north-east storm raging, and the captain hauled alongside of a wharf to wait for fair weather before proceeding to sea. The storm lasted three days. The sailors employed their time evenings, and sometimes daytime, in amusing themselves in a bowling-alley and drinking-room, on the outskirts of the town, directly abreast of where we were laying. As I had become partially acquainted with the sailors, I used to go with them; and as it was new to me I enjoyed their bowling very much. They employed me to set up the pins for them; they paid me a trifle for this, which went towards replenishing my " pile." One evening, and it proved to be the last that we were to remain there, as usual I went up with the sailors to witness the evening's entertainment, and did not come on board until quite late. Since father left me, at every convenient time, when no one was observing me, I would take out and count my money,

to see if it was all right. Father gave me strict caution not to lose it ; and, besides, it had a sort of charm
for me.   I suppose I did this twenty times after
leaving our place of departure.   When we got on
board this evening, and when about retiring, I took
out my wallet to look at my money ; when, lo ! it was
all gone, not a cent left.   I searched all the open-
ings of my wallet, all the pockets of my pants and
vest, but not a cent could I find.   I knew it was all
right before I went ashore, as I looked at it.   Words
are wanting to describe my feelings at that moment.
I had been nowhere but to the alley ; neither do I
remember taking out my wallet after leaving the
vessel.   Although the sailors drank, I did not.   At
last I concluded that I must ·have fallen asleep,
although I had no such recollections, and that some
one took it, and replaced the wallet.   I crawled into
my berth crying as though my heart would break ;
and no wonder, for I fully comprehended my situation.   Here I was bound on a long voyage, to land
among total strangers in the great city of Boston,
with not one cent to defray my necessary expenses.
Though my passage was paid to Boston, I queried
how was I to get from there to Providence, or pay
for my meals after I landed in Boston.   As all these
serious troubles ahead came bubbling up through my
excited and anxious mind, it seemed as though my
fate was sealed, and my voyage must end with dis-
aster.   After a long while " nature's sweet restorer "
came to my aid, and I fell asleep.

Sometime in the latter part of the night the storm
ceased its fury, and the wind changed ; they got

under way, and when I got up the next morning we were passing Seguin Light. The vessel began rolling and pitching about. I began to be sick, and to "throw up," as sailors call vomiting. To those who know by experience the sensations of seasickness, I have nothing to say; and, to those unacquainted with its deathly sensation, I will merely say it's strictly indescribable. After each throw-up I would have a little respite; but I couldn't go below during the whole passage; for, the moment I would go to the gangway leading into the cabin, the smell of the bilgewater would make me vomit. To make it still worse, the jolly, roguish sailors told me the best remedy for seasickness was to tie a string to a piece of fat pork, souse it in molasses, swallow it, haul it up by the string, replenish it with molasses, swallow it again, and do the same thing for a dozen times, when I could be well. They very thought of it made me vomit then, and almost does now.

With my new but not unexpected troubles, for I was told I should be seasick, I quite forgot about the loss of my money, or in fact any thing else. I felt that I had just as lief be over as on board. It was not until the third day, about ten, A.M., that we got alongside of a wharf in Boston, owing to a constant head-wind the whole distance.

The vessel was a regular packet from Augusta to Boston; and, as it was known at all the hotels that she was due, they were on the lookout for her. It was announced by signals (a sort of telegraphing) that we were coming up the harbor; and, by the time we were fairly tied up alongside the wharf, there were at least a dozen coaches from as many public houses, to take passengers to their favorite places. I was the only passenger; and, if the coachmen had seen the depletion of my wallet, they wouldn't have been so clamorous as they were for my patronage. As it was, I didn't care where I went; but as good luck would have it, somehow or other my trunk was put on a coach belonging to the Marlboro' Hotel on Washington Street. While riding up I kept thinking what I should say or do when the hackman should come for his pay for taking me to the hotel. "What can I tell him?" I kept asking myself. But he didn't call for it. The custom then was, that passengers who stopped at the house that owned the coach were charged nothing for the ride. I saw my trunk deposited in a little room off the office in the hotel. I sat down in the office wondering what would turn up next. I saw folks laughing and talking, seemingly happy; and here I was among total strangers in a great city, half-starved, without a cent to pay for food I very much needed; for now it was over three days since I had tasted a mouthful of any thing. This hunger with my other mishaps filled me with sad forebodings. When the "gong" sounded for dinner, it being the first time I had ever heard such a thundering, outlandish noise, I was half frightened out of my wits: it was sounded only a little distance from my back. As I had nothing to pay with, I didn't dare to go into dinner. At supper-time it was the same; and I went to bed faint, hungry, and discouraged. After I retired I had a good cry, which relieved me: then I dropped into a sweet sleep, and didn't wake until the gong sounded for breakfast the next morning. I had made up my mind, while dressing, that I would tell the landlord my predicament; but, whenever he came near enough, my resolution failed me. When he went into the dining-room to wait upon his guests, one of his daughters came into the office, and waited there until he got through. This morning, when she entered, she looked at me with such a sweet sympathizing smile that my heart leaped into my mouth. It was the first kind look I had seen since leaving my home, and it was with the greatest effort that I could keep my equilibrium; I thought she pitied me, she seemed so homelike. After the landlord got through with his duties in the dining-room, he came into the office, and seeing me sitting there with a woe-begone look, as I suppose, came directly to me, and, putting his hands on my shoulders, said kindly, "Young man, why don't you go in to breakfast? you haven't eat any thing since you came here." He spoke so kind and fatherly, that I burst out crying, and ran into the baggage-room to hide my tears. He followed me in, and so did his beautiful daughter. She was crying, and didn't know for what; probably it was from sympathy for me. He kept asking me what was the matter. When I had recovered my composure sufficiently, I told him the whole story, — where I was going, and how I had lost my money, and ended by telling him, if he would give me something to eat, I would sell him some of my clothes in payment; showing him my trunk, telling him it was chock full of good clothes. He heard me through, and then patted me caressingly on my head, saying, "Never mind about the pay: when the boarders get through, come in and eat with my family;" continuing, "Your father was very reprehensible to let one so young go so far with no one for company; but I will make that all right." I felt as though a mountain had been removed off my back. When the guests had got through with breakfast, he took me into the dining-room, and introduced me to his wife and family. Somehow or other I felt quite easy and at home; they all tried to make me feel so. I had been so long without any thing to eat, they cautioned me about eating too much at first. That afternoon, when the family went on a drive, they took me along with them, and in the evening took me to the theatre, which was all new to me. I saw so many new and fine things in the theatre that I felt as though I was in a new world.

The following morning I got an early breakfast; and, when the stage drove up for passengers to Providence, my trunk was put on, when my new-found father led me to the door, saying to the driver, "This is the son of a friend of mine, on his way to the Quaker school in Providence. I want you to put him down at the door of the institution; do you hear?" says he. He reminded the driver that my fare was all paid; and when I left he gave me seven dollars for pocket-money. After shaking hands with every member of the family, they bade me God-speed, and we were off. Soon after sunset, after a fine day's ride, the driver put me down at the steps of the Quaker college. After examining my credentials, and finding them all right, the principal of the place, Mr. Gould, received me very cordially, and at once assigned me a room for my occupancy. While taking tea with him in the great dining-hall, he asked me my age. I told him I should be fourteen the 10th of next April. "Not *April*," he says, "but next fourth month;" continuing, "we have no *Aprils* here." I mention this little incident to show how very strict they are in adhering to all the rules and regulations of their mode of religious training, also to show how careful I had occasion to be against giving them umbrage by using a word not laid down in their "rules of conduct." To those unacquainted with the peculiarities of this Christian sect, I will say that they do not think it right to employ many of the phrases in common use, because they say it is conforming to the fashionable habits of a sinful and adulterous world: hence, instead of saying "January, February," &c., they say "first and second months;" instead of using the plural, in addressing each other, they use the singular number; that is, instead of saying "you" to one person, they say "thee" or "thou." When the ceremony of introducing me to Mr. Mitchel ("Mokey," as the boys called him) was over, he had my name enrolled on the list of scholars, and, after examining me as to my educational proficiency, selected the proper books for me to peruse after I should be fairly installed in my new home.

My room-mate was a boy about my own age, by the name of George W. Keen, of Lynn, Mass., with whom I soon became on the most familiar terms. He was kind, sympathetic, and genial. We occupied the same room as long as I remained there, each maintaining confidence in and respect for the other through the whole term of my stay.

I made fair progress in all of my studies, and especially in mathematics, in which I excelled; seldom, if ever, needing the aid of teachers in solving our most intricate and most difficult problems, but not always with despatch. Sometimes, when I had puzzled over one during the day without finding its solution, I would dream it out in my sleep, and remember these nocturnal solutions so vividly when I awoke, that I could go to my desk and put down the figures on my slate as I saw them in my dream, without perceiving how the result was reached. I would remember the record so distinctly that I could transfer the figures from my dream slate to my waking one; and not only that, but I sensed the whys and wherefores better than when figuring in the ordinary way. The real facts of the case were, I copied the figures from my *phantom* slate, to the one that I called more material; and the one was just as palpable to my vision as the other.

I will relate a few incidents connected with my stay at the institution, and then shall have done with my scholastic life, and will commence upon the hard realities of an active, and in spots a singularly eventful and fitfully successful business life.

When I arrived at this institution of learning, I was as tall in stature as most boys of my age, but very slim, in fact, almost a shadow compared with many there; and as I was naturally very bashful, timid, and retiring, some of the boys thought they could knock me about just as they took a fancy to, without any fears of my resentment. There was one great lumikin, overgrown, overbearing, confident boy, who was a sort of bulldog among them ; and, no matter what he would do to those less blessed with rounded-out muscles, not one dared to resent his formidable prowess. His name was Samuel Austin. I had not been installed in my new home a day, before he tried it on me. At any and all times when near me he would take hold of my shoulders roughly, and throw me round. Sometimes I would fall to the floor ; then there would be a general guffaw laugh among the boys, and all sorts of derisive names would be hurled at me. I often heard them say, " He's a coward," &c., and, " dasn't dare to take his own part." Some would say, " I guess his mother don't know he's out." But I didn't care what they said, if they didn't touch me. No one but this Sam, up to this time, had attempted that. There being some two hundred of us, and the accommodation for washing being limited to about fifty washbowls, of course one had to wait for another. The custom was, when one was washing for those waiting to say, " I speak next." It seemed to me that Sam was bound to annoy me from the first, as though he had a particular grudge against me. He would wait until I had a basin filled with water, when he would take hold of my shoulders, and slat me round to the infinite amusement of the rest, then take my basin, and wash himself. He had done this every morning since my arrival. The fact was, I was half frightened out of my senses. I tried to keep out of his and

everybody else's way, but it was no use. They were
bound to have me for a laughing-stock any way,
and matters every day growing worse; enhanced, I
thought, by my apparent non-resistance. The fourth
day of my stay was the hardest to put up with; and
although I had never participated in a fight, in fact
never had seen one, never could even witness people
talking hard to each other without trembling all over,
and always tried to get out of hearing of angry
talk, and up to this time never once thought of trying to defend myself from the aggravating, and, as
far as Sam was concerned, malicious assaults. I had
tried to get the sympathy of George, my room-mate;
but he was careful not to say any thing to which
Sam would object, for fear of the consequence if Sam
should hear of it. The fact was, he, with every one
of the set, was afraid of him. Finding I hadn't a
friend among them, or, if so, that their fears of this
master prevented them from showing it, I concluded, after I got to bed, to measure swords with this
taunting Goliath. At first the thought frightened
me; but, the more I harbored it, the less formidable
the conflict appeared; and before daylight I had
firmly resolved to " lick " Sam in the wash-room that
morning if he gave me the least provocation, and I
was sure he would. I scarcely closed my eyes to
sleep all night, but rolled and tumbled, cogitating
upon the conflict that would come off with the
rising sun. I dressed, and went into the wash-room;
this time I waited for Sam, as he had previously
done for me when he arrived first. Directly he
came in, blustering and swaggering in a sort of

shuffling gait.   The moment I saw him enter, I went to a boy washing, and spoke "next."   Standing right behind me, the moment I had filled my basin, as I anticipated, Sam took hold of me to whirl me round.   I was watching his movements, although back to him ; and, instead of his whirling me round as he had previously done, I got him down on the floor, and pounded him with all my might.   I heard a low chuckle from the bystanders at the moment he fell ; and that was the last I heard, or in fact knew about the encounter.   I only recollected a sense of possessing immense strength, and of Sam's fall : the details of the fight I got of those who witnessed it. At first, they said, there was none who thought of interfering, as every one thought Sam could take care of himself ; but finding the-champion was getting the worst of it, as the blood was streaming out of his eyes, nose, and mouth, some of his friends tried to haul me off ; the moment they attempted that, they said, I would hug Sam all the tighter ; and, he being heavy, they had to give it up, and run for some of the officers.   By the time the officers arrived, Sam was lying there senseless.   They got me clear from him, sent for a doctor, and after a while got his face patched up ; but it was near a month before he was able to attend to his studies.   The superintendent had me up for trial before I had got cleaned up ; and after an examination into the details of the case I was reprimanded, and sent to my room to wash up.   The unexpected development of my great pugilistic qualities astonished everybody who witnessed it, but none more than myself.   The officers called in several of the boys, who corroborated what I had said about Sam's abuse and insults, every one of whom fully testified to his insulting conduct towards me. They didn't dare to tell any thing different after witnessing that combat, for fear I would try my hand on them. After this, there was no question as to who was entitled to wear the belt. This was the only incident that occurred through my term, that tended to mar the general harmony among us. I hesitated some time about relating this incident, and should not have done so, but to carry out the general object had in view from the first; viz., to show that I have been controlled in all important matters by unseen influences, who are ever near, watching my intentions, thoughts, and acts, and at all proper times, when the tide of circumstances seemed to press me to the wall, and I had not a ray of hope for escape, they came to my aid. I have no more doubt that I was completely obsessed by some powerful pugilistic spirit, and that through me he gave Sam that awful castigation, than that I am writing this account of it. It may be said that it couldn't have been a very good spirit, who had such fighting proclivities; but if taking the starch out of an overgrown, insulting boy, who made it a rule to insult everybody he dared to, was the direct means of making him, ostensibly at least, respectful and kind, of changing his whole deportment from an overbearing, unscrupulous, insulting course, to one of kind and genial manners, was bad, then I do not know the use of suffering. Thunder and lightning may do some individual harm; but if they serve to purify the atmosphere from poisonous, deadly gases, they become a universal good. I might add other incidents connected with this attempt of adding to my small stock of knowledge, of more or less interest; but, as I intend to relate only the more prominent ones here, I will defer others to another volume I am writing, entitled " Odds and Ends of an Eventful Life."

The time for which I was entitled to stay having expired, I began to make preparations to leave. This was in May, 1828. The superintendent and all the teachers, not excepting Mr. Brown the founder of the institution, and by whose liberality it was kept up, tried to induce me to prolong my stay. Mr. Brown offered to defray all the expenses out of his own private purse. But I had got homesick, and nothing they could say or do had the least influence in changing my determination. All, old and young, with the exception of Sam, seemed heartily to regret my leaving, which was a source of extreme satisfaction to me. Finding that they could not alter my determination to go home, the teachers and superintendents, with their wives, selected such books from their libraries as they thought would be interesting and instructive to me, and offered them to me as tokens of their appreciation of my conduct while an inmate of the school. Everybody seemed to vie with each other in forcing me to accept some little token of regard as a remembrancer. I had so many books and other presents given me, that I was obliged to get an extra trunk to carry them home. I found a vessel at one of the wharves, bound to Augusta, in which I took passage, and, after three days fair weather, landed at the above place. A farmer living near my home, who was in town to market, kindly offered me a passage home, where I arrived quite unexpectedly. I was received with that exuberance of feelings known only to those who have experienced them.

Thus ended one of the very important periods of my early life. I arrived home much improved in looks, and possessing some more scholastic knowledge than when I left many months before.

After having visited my relatives and acquaintances in the neighboring towns, I engaged work of a Mr. Tilden in his carding-machine and fulling-mill, for whom I worked through the summer and fall months several seasons. While working at the above place, father engaged me to teach the town school through the following winter. I commenced the school the 5th of December, and would not attain to my seventeenth year until the April following. The school was large in numbers, and embraced large boys and even men, one of whom was thirty-five. Many, if not all of the eldest, were then going to school for the last time. Somehow or other I had got the reputation of being very learned for one so young, and I was looked upon almost as a paragon of refinement and goodness; which I never claimed to be, and did not envy the distinction with which they honored me. I boarded "round;" that is, each family boarded me in proportion to the number of scholars it sent to the school. The time I was an inmate of the different families varied from one to four weeks. Wherever I was temporarily boarding I was treated with the greatest deference. The parents and their children almost adored me, and expressed unfeigned regret when my time came to take up my abode in another family. I had the best reasons for believing there was not a family in the district but would have esteemed it a privilege, and been pleased, to have boarded me the entire term, without compensation, if they could have afforded it. This was a source of great satisfaction to me; and everybody regretted when the school closed, but none more than myself, as I fully appreciated their kindness, and was loath to leave where I had been so happy. To prove their sincerity, they engaged me for the next winter before I got through with this, there not being one dissenting voice, — pretty good evidence of my popularity. This school lasted five months. Before I had got through here, I engaged another of three months' duration in the same town, some two miles from my first effort at " teaching the young ideas how to shoot," at a place called Deer Hill, making in all eight months' continuous teaching. Here I had the good fortune to please quite as well as in the former place. The following summer and fall I worked for the same man that I did the year previous, and at the same business; the succeeding winter and spring, taught school at the same places as the winter before. It was while teaching here that I became acquainted with a Miss Rebecca F. Chapman, who some six years subsequently became my wife.

CHAPTER IV.

FIRST VOYAGE WHALING.

THERE was living, some three or four miles from my home, an old sea-captain by the name of Moore, with whom father was intimately acquainted. He had followed the whaling business long, and, having procured a competence, purchased a farm, and was now living at his ease. He came from Nantucket, famous in those days for being extensively engaged in carrying on the whaling business. This man was a great talker; and the hearing him often tell his wondrous sea-stories, and about killing the great sea-monsters, well seasoned with hairbreadth escapes, and thrilling events in the hazardous business, so interested my imagination, my sensitive, restless mind and roving disposition, that I determined to try the realities of one whaling voyage at least. After this was firmly fixed in my mind, I began to think how to get father's and mother's consent, expecting that they would veto the thing at once. But after telling father my desires, to my astonishment he made no particular objections, but doubted about getting mother's consent. I asked him to talk with her about it, and see what she would say. Soon after this conversation, as I found out afterwards, he talked the matter over with her, and subsequently broached the subject to me in her presence. She objected *in toto*. But, now that the ice was broken, I urged my suit with vigor. She held out some days; but father, seeing my mind was set upon it, became my solicitor, and between us both we finally got her reluctant consent.

Now, then, we must make the necessary preparations; and, as we were all ignorant of what things were needed, father and I rode over to Capt. Moore's to consult him in the matter. He kindly gave us all necessary information, and gave me a letter to some who were engaged in the business in Nantucket; which latter proved very valuable to me. It was but few days after this, before I was off. We found at Augusta a vessel called " The Nantucket," a regular packet plying between the island and the Kennebeck. She was commanded by a Capt. Hause. I engaged a passage at once, and started immediately on my second voyage, which was of a very different character from the one when I first left home. After a pleasant passage of about one week, I landed upon the island of Nantucket, where, at all of the principal wharves, swarms of men were busily engaged in fitting out whale-ships.

By a strange concurrence of favorable circumstances, I got board with an old Quakeress, Elizabeth Coleman. Of all the places on the island, this was the most agreeable to me, as it not only tallied with my Quaker habits and education, but Elizabeth almost took the place of my own mother. From the first she took as much interest in all my affairs

as my own parents; and, besides having lived so long
amid men who had followed whaling all their lives,
she was capable of giving me some important advice.
When on shore I made her house my home for many
years. Through my new-found mother I procured
an introduction to a Mr. David Joy, who was reared
and educated in the Quaker religion. His father
was an elder in the church. This Mr. Joy was
engaged in the whaling business, owning some three
or four ships and barks employed in the business
in which I was intending to engage. Mr. Joy was
then fitting out the bark " Peru " for a voyage to the
South Atlantic Ocean, on board of which I shipped
to go in pursuit of " right " whales. There are
several species of these sea-animals (they can hardly
be classed with the finny tribe, for their blood is
warm); several species that generate, bring forth, and
nurse their young precisely as land cows do theirs.
The *right* whale is short and thick, producing from
fifty to one hundred and fifty barrels; and sometimes I am told that on the north-west coast they
yield from two hundred to three hundred barrels of
oil, of an inferior quality compared with sperm oil;
which latter species, that is, the sperm whale, is quite
different in several respects; one of which is, they are
from two to three times longer, and proportionately
slimmer, yielding all the way from fifteen barrels to
one hundred, seldom more; and then, again, they have
but one spout-hole, which is on the end of the head,
while the right whale has two, one-third the distance
from the head towards the tail. Right whales congregate at certain seasons of the year in specific

localities, and are never met with elsewhere; whereas sperm whales are found more plenty in some places than in others, yet, unlike the first, are met with in every latitude. Then, again, the right whales are found in shoal-water; and at certain seasons they congregate in bays, where they drop their young; whereas the sperm whale is never seen on soundings. There is the male and female, the same as are seen in a herd of domestic or wild cattle. The cow-whale experiences the same process of gestation that the domestic cow does in producing offspring. Their bags containing milk are constructed precisely as the common cow's; the young getting nourishment by sucking teats, of which there are two, just as do the calves of the farmer's cows. The milk is white, and looks the same as that from cows, but has a strong taste. There are several other kinds, each species varying in habits from all others, which are not sought after by whalemen, and hence I do not deem it necessary to describe them. They are of many species, from the porpoise to the largest-sized whale, and cannot stay under water beyond a limited time without drowning. The sperm whale usually stays down an hour ere he makes his appearance, and then stays on the surface the same length of time, breathing; the right whale, and most others of the whale species, are down from fifteen to thirty minutes, and upon the surface the same.

I have given this imperfect sketch of the habits and characteristics of the leviathan of the deep, thinking it might not be uninteresting to those unacquainted with this department of the animal kingdom.

After shipping on the bark " Peru," Mr. Joy sent me with an order to a Mr. Sturtevant to get my outfit. Of course I didn't know what I wanted for a voyage, any more than any other "greenhorn;" but I found in Mr. Sturtevant a willing adviser. He seemed so very unselfish that I took whatever he said was necessary. To show how *unselfish* were all his pretensions, the articles specified in his bill of a hundred and forty-seven dollars could have been purchased at almost any place where they dealt in such articles, for forty-seven dollars at most, throwing off the hundred. Thus it was then, — and it is no better now, — that land-sharks gobbled up the hard earnings of the storm-tossed sailor.

No sooner than I had got my outfit, than they bundled me and my traps on board the ship, then laying outside of the bar, where the supplies for the voyage were taken in. The crew of twenty-eight men, all told, consisted, with two exceptions, of men and boys belonging on the island. The two exceptions were a man by the name of David Gardner, and myself, both hailing from the State of Maine. When I got on board I found every berth in the forecastle occupied excepting one; the boys knowing the ropes, to use a sailor phrase, after shipping, had picked out their berths before going on board, and, to secure them from the encroachment of others to come after, put their names on them; and, as there was only the complement to accommodate the crew, it was Hobson's choice — that or none — for me. It was the least desirable of any; but, as I couldn't help the matter, I tumbled in upon my straw mattress and straw pillow and bedclothes, and made the best of it.

An amusing incident transpired after I had agreed to go, and while the ship was lying at her wharf rigging and painting, before going over the bar to take in her outfit. I was working on board, assisting the riggers. Of course before night on the first day, my hands became all daubed over with tar. Not knowing how to get it off, I asked some of the riggers how I should remove the sticky substance. Thinking they might get some sport at my expense, they told me to wash them in salt water. So down I go to the water's edge, and commence operations. I washed away, they eying me all the while; but the more I washed the less it was inclined to leave; in fact, it stuck closer. I heard the roguish sailors break out into a coarse laugh at my stupidity. Instantly I saw there was a joke. I relinquished further endeavors in that direction, and went home with my tarred hands uncleansed. Upon meeting Aunt Elizabeth, I asked her how I should get my hands clean. "La, David," she says, "get some slush" (meaning grease), "rub it on well, and it will start the tar; then soap and soft water will do the rest." After this experience I never had any more difficulty in removing tar.

On the day for sailing, when I arrived on board and by the time I had my dunnage stowed away, eight bells was struck, signifying noon, when all hands were told to get their dinners. I went into the forecastle with the rest, to partake of my first meal on shipboard.

Our dinner consisted of salt pork and beef, potatoes, and hard-tack as sailors call sea-bread; and, although the ship was lying perfectly still, a nauseous stench coming up from the lower hold made such an impression upon my sensitive stomach that it was with the greatest difficulty I could force down a particle of it. I managed to swallow a small quantity, and then got on deck as soon as possible. The bill of fare at this first meal was a sample of all on the entire voyage, with the exception that on Thursdays we were allowed either duff or rice, the former a flour pudding boiled in a bag, and both eaten with molasses, of which latter we were each allowed one quart per week ; and Fridays we had salt fish and potatoes, that is, when we had potatoes, if not, then salt fish.

Before going on board I purchased a quadrant and other nautical instruments for determining the ship's position when at sea. These I put in the bottom of my chest. I also bought a fiddle and its accompaniments, thinking if I couldn't use it some of the boys might, and thus while away an hour pleasantly. The fiddle I put in my bunk, and covered it up, thinking no one would see it.

After lying at the bar some two weeks to take in all our outfits, we were ready for sea.

Up to this time I had never seen our captain. He was a great, tall, bulky, broad-shouldered man, hair and beard slightly gray, prominent Roman nose, and great blue eyes ; upon the whole, not a very prepossessing man at first sight, but he proved to be a very good man. His name was Brooks. His home was on the west side of the island, at a place called Cuttyhunk, I think. The chief officer was a Mr.

Smith, rather large physique, pretty good looking, with black piercing eyes, nose aquiline; a man of few words, who always meant what he said, and was a very efficient officer, and a good man generally. He had commanded several ships; but dissipation of one kind or another had caused him to fall from his high estate, and take a step down. He was a native of Nantucket, where he always made his home.

The second officer, or second mate, was a man of very different characteristics from the other two. He was tall and slim, high cheek-bones, gray eyes, reddish hair and whiskers, and about thirty years old. His name was Albert Coffin, and he had always made the island his home, excepting when at sea. The crew were of all temperaments, many of them full of fun, and always playing jokes on each other. In general they were deficient in education, their schooling having been sadly neglected when young. After we cleared the land, the two first officers chose and set their watches, first one selecting a man, and then the other, and so on, until all hands belonged to one or the other's watch. The two watches are called starboard and larboard; the second mate controlling the starboard, the first the larboard or port watch.

The watch is set at eight, when the starboard watch takes the deck, and the other turns in, to be called at twelve. Thus it goes on as regularly as clockwork, four hours on, four off, or what is called in nautical parlance watch and watch. These rules are strictly adhered to the entire voyage, excepting while whaling, when all hands are on duty. From four to eight, P.M., is what is called the dog-watch, when all hands are spinning yarns, singing songs, or telling stories. Now we are past Gay Head, and out on the broad Atlantic, the wind from the north-west, heading to the southward and eastward. Although the sea wasn't very rough, I began to feel qualmish, and soon after to throw up. About ten o'clock, it being somewhat squally, Mr. Coffin began to take in the light sails. I heard him say something which was then quite unintelligible to me, but subsequently found it was an order to clew up the main-top-gallant-sail. I was as sick as death at the time. I heard the men hallooing something, but what it was I didn't comprehend. Directly Mr. Coffin bawled out to me, saying, " Here you d——d Down-East white-head, come and help take in sail." I went where the men were hallooing, and pulling at something. I took hold, and did the best I could; soon after, I heard the officer say " Belay," when they stopped their jargon. Then I heard him say something about doing something else, which also was Greek to me, and was followed by something about " d——d white-head," which was *not* Greek, as I was the only boy in the crew with a " tow-head," as they sometimes called mine ; at least I was the only one that was thus called by this brutish officer, and hence I knew he meant me. As I was very busily engaged just then in giving old Neptune the remaining contents of my agitated stomach, I paid no attention to his gibberish. Directly he came to me while I was leaning over the lee-rail, sick as death, and, taking hold of my shoul-ders, roughly whirled me suddenly round, dragged me to the weather main rigging, saying, " Go up there and help furl that main-top-gallant-sail, and be d——d to you; " accompanying the last word with his foot deposited in my rear and about the middle of my sick body. What he meant by top-gallant-sail I had not the least conception ; and as for going *up*, I didn't know where, that dark night, expecting to do any thing, sick as I was, I couldn't think of it ; but after his swearing and kicking, being too sick to resist, I managed to get into the rigging, and after a while, by dint of great effort, succeeded in getting up to what is called the main-top ; and as I didn't there see any thing to do, nor anybody to help, and being ignorant how much higher I would have to go before I got where the man was bawling out for help, and the officer swearing and cursing to expedite my movements, and as I couldn't get up through the lubber-hole, I concluded that further efforts in " getting up stairs " were useless. As for going out over the top with the ship rolling and tumbling fearfully, that was entirely out of the question. I concluded to remain where I was. When subsequently I was about retracing my steps downwards, still hanging with my arm around the futtock shrouds, throwing up every moment or two, for, being so high up, the motion of the ship made me still sicker than when on deck, and while taking in the true position of affairs the best I could, I felt some sharp-pointed instrument pierce the posterior portion of my hips. I instantly hauled off one foot, and " let go." The pricking proved to be the work of the officer of the deck, Mr. Coffin. I had on a pair of new cowhide boots; and, when I felt I had come in contact with something, I used one of them. After he had received my boot-heel he retreated down, and I followed him. My kick accomplished a good job, as it peeled the skin off his left eye, nose, and under-lip, making a fearful disfigurement of his ugly phiz. I neither heard nor saw any one, but made my way deckward as fast as I could with safety, and landed soon after my tormentor. I was told afterwards, that seeing me hanging in the cat-harpings, as the short shrouds leading from the mast to the rim of the top are called, and after bawling and swearing to the top of his lungs, and I not heeding it, he took out of a pigeon-hole in the binnacle what sailmakers call a marling-needle, some six inches long. It was this sharp-pointed instrument that raised my boot in self-defence; the result of which he carried to his grave. The fact was, he was a coward; and, although he never attempted any thing of the kind afterwards openly, yet he used his influence against me in every possible way, at least for the next five months: then a change occurred which brought his real character to the surface. After I came down, he sent another man up. The next morning while I was at the wheel learning to steer, the old man (the captain of a ship is always designated the "old man") came on deck, and, seeing Mr. Coffin's patched-up face, asked him how he did it. Mr. Coffin told him that "he run afoul of an overhead boat in the night." He being a tall man, and the boats having not yet been secured on chocks, which would put them out of the reach of a man's head, the story seemed plausible, and nothing further was said about it. When I got forward I told the facts to old Jack, an old sailor who had taken me under his charge. He says, " You done just right, but he'll work up your old iron for it before you get home." And he did so. Whenever a shovel was to be used after the hogs or hens, I was always ordered to do it. Without the least provocation, I being entirely ignorant of having done amiss, he would stop my watch below in the daytime, pretending to the captain that I had done something punishable, or had not done my duty. When on my regular watch he would keep me constantly at some menial work, such as scraping and slushing down topmasts; which pleased the men in the forecastle, as they, too, tried to make me a scapegoat for all sorts of funny jokes, and some not so funny, they-taking their cue from Mr. Coffin. This was my first experience in roughing it on shipboard, but not the last by any means, as the sequel will tell.

In the course of a week I got partially over my sickness, and began to regulate things in my chest and bunk. When I looked for my fiddle, it was nowhere to be found; at last I found it on some soap kegs, with the strings gone, a hole burst in the top, and the fiddle filled with what is called salt-water soap, or soap by which clothes can be washed in salt water as easily as with common soap in fresh water. Somehow or other the men took a dislike to me in the first place, although I tried every possible way to please them. I tried to be as near like them as I could, using the slang phrases they did, and joining them in all their boyish, roguish sports ; but, do all I

could, it availed me nothing : they were bound to have
some one to ventilate their hectoring spleen upon;
and as I had incurred the displeasure of the second
officer, with whom they were well acquainted before leaving home, and as apparently my principles
were non-resistant, they thought me a fit subject
for their sport. To begin with, they broke up my
fiddle. It is a saying among such a gang, that there
is always a fool in a company of that kind ; and they
hit upon me for the fool. I, in turn, was decidedly
opposed to their selection. They did every thing
possible to annoy me ; and, the more I tolerated their
insults, the more they tried to plague me ; at last,
finding all my efforts for peace useless, I told them
that I had stood all that I conveniently could, and
that, if they persisted in their annoying habits, I
should certainly take my own part. This warning,
threat, or challenge only brought down the house
with laughter, and immediately they began whispering among themselves. My coolness somewhat daunt-
ed their ardor ; but as there were so many of them,
indirectly backed up, too, by Mr. Coffin, they finally
concluded to try my mettle. So one night in the dog-
watch, soon after my threat, and while I was writing,
by a preconcerted plan, one of the number, when
the ship lurched to leeward, came tumbling down
upon me, tipping over my inkstand, he pretending
that the lurching of the ship was the cause. I knew
he lied, but quietly told him *not* to do it again. Determined to test my prowess, another convenient
lurch of the ship gave the same fellow an excuse for
doing the same thing again, which produced a tre-

mendous laugh and clapping of hands; but, before the gang had proceeded far in their mirth, I had the fellow on the deck punishing him liberally. At first no one interfered; but, finding their chum was getting the worst of it, they came to his rescue: after I had punished him sufficiently, I let him up, with the claret running from his mouth and nose. At once the news was carried aft, and I was hauled up to answer for fighting. After a few inquiries by the captain, I was told to go forward. They didn't give me any more serious annoyance, excepting laughing and making fun of me, until we had left the Western Islands, where we were to recruit with fresh supplies and men, and where I determined to run away if possible. They tried in various ways to annoy me; but, finding that their methods failed to frighten me into submission, they thought of a new plot. One dark night, when the ship was lying to in a gale of wind, one of them thought that I might be frightened through playing the ghost; and he donned a white sheet for the purpose. He came on deck stealthily, and took up a position on the bowsprit, between the knight-heads, enveloped in the white sheet from head to foot, and commenced groaning in a sepulchral tone, loud enough for me to hear; which must have cost his lungs an extra effort, as the wind was howling fearfully, the rigging rattling, and the timbers groaning. I turned my eyes towards where I heard the sound, and perceived the apparition, but thought, the moment I saw it, that it was one of the roguish scamps in the forecastle trying to frighten me. I almost *knew* it was

Bill Fitzgerald, whom it proved to be. The instant he saw that I perceived him, he came slowly down the heel of the bowsprit towards me, groaning all the while. I grasped a handspike, and stood up facing him, determined to give his ghostship a warm reception when within reach. He perceived the manœuvre, and halted about eight or ten feet from me, groaning still; but, as I hauled off ready to let go, he cut and run down into the forecastle. I let fly the handspike, which reached the bottom of the stairs before he did, doing no other injury than hurting his foot and shin so much as to lay him up a few days. Directly I heard a tremendous uproar below, where the boys were laughing and jeering the poor ghost, he being the only one frightened; and he came near being disabled for the rest of the voyage. After this failure they never attempted to spring any more jokes upon me.

By their actions, one would infer their opinion that I felt myself superior to them, which, as far as scholastic education was concerned, was true; but which I tried hard, as before stated, to avert. After a passage of a couple of weeks, we came in sight of the island of Flores, one of the Western Islands so-called, situated midway between America and the Continent of Europe, where we were to make up our complement of men from the natives, and purchase potatoes, onions, chickens, and pigs. On the passage out we fell in with numerous schools of black-fish, one of the whale species, which yield from one to five and sometimes more barrels of oil, according to size. We improved every opportunity to catch them, partly for the oil, and partly to teach us greenhorns the different evolutions in a whale-boat when killing whales. We secured several barrels of this oil, with which the captain intended to pay for his supplies. We made the island early one morning; and when near enough, the old man had his boat lowered, and a barrel of oil put in. I belonged to his boat, and of course I had opportunities of going ashore, getting a look at the natives, and deciding from my own observation whether it would be feasible to put into practice my determination to run away.

As there were no piers or wharves, or safe anchorage, the only alternative was to lay off and on for the two days and nights that we should be occupied in getting our recruits aboard. We landed in a small bay near which the little Portuguese town was located. After hauling the boat up, the oil was deposited near the head of the boat. By this time a large crowd of men and women of all ages had gathered about us, ready to barter off their commodities for oil. After conversing a few minutes with some of the principal natives, the captain selected me for peddling out the oil; another lad was detailed to watch the natives, and prevent them from stealing things out of the boat. I was to give one pint of oil for a pair of chickens, and one quart for a pig. The potatoes, onions, &c., the old man was going to purchase up town. As soon as I got fairly under way in my new occupation, and somewhat used to the outlandish gibberish of the natives, the captain left us. No sooner was he out of sight than my assistant left also; and, as the beach was lined with natives, I was obliged to execute the trading and watching too, which I could not do without neglecting one or the other. However, after waiting a long time for the return of my companion, I went ahead making my purchases. As I bought a brace of chickens, or a pig, I would throw them into the boat, and was doing, I thought, quite a flourishing business. I kept on until my barrel of oil was nearly exhausted, when the old man made his appearance. Coming up to where I was dealing out the oil, he asked me how many I had bought. I answered, " A good many." " Where are they ? " he continued. I said, " In the boat." He says, " I can't see them; " and, to my astonishment, neither could I. The natives, as soon as I put my purchases in the boat, would steal them, and sell them over again; so that when I thought I had at least three or four dozen pairs of chickens, and some half-dozen pigs, only three pairs of chickens and one pig could be found. My chagrin and astonishment defy description. Now, thought I, the boys will have something tangible to taunt me with; besides, I supposed I had incurred the displeasure of the captain. I expected that he would give me a blowing-up, if nothing more. But he said nothing to me then, for he saw how the thing was brought about. Of course I told him of my assistant leaving me as soon as he was out of sight, and that he hadn't yet returned. We finished out the rest of the oil, and got in some things he had purchased up town; and after the men had returned we pushed off. The captain scolded the one he left with me, whom, being his neighbor's son, he let off easily. As I expected, the boys began their "digs" at me by asking one another, in a suppressed tone, while rowing towards the ship, "How much is chickens worth?" &c.; then would follow a low chuckle. Once in a while I would hear them say, "He'll catch it when he gets on board." Whether they meant the old man would punish me, or they tantalize me, I did not know; but after getting on deck they told the news of my day's financiering, and had a merry time over my "*smartness*" as they called it; and until late in the night the roguish scamps were buying and selling poultry and pigs. It was genuinely ludicrous to hear the sallies of wit they exhibited in trying to annoy me. I enjoyed their merriment. This day's operation, added to my experience previously, fully decided me to run away if I got ashore on the morrow. My bad luck this day might induce the captain to take another in my place; that was the only drawback to my hopes.

After breakfast the next morning, I heard the mate say, "Clear away the starboard boat," which was the same that went ashore yesterday, and to which I belonged. When she was hauled along to the gangway, and the oil, two barrels, put in, the crew was told to get in, and I found my place pretty quick. Anticipating a chance for leaving the ship, I had put on two pairs of pants, three shirts, two pairs of socks, also vest and jacket. We landed at the same place as yesterday, and to my utter astonishment I was intrusted with peddling out the oil again. This dampened my hopes of getting away. The captain selected a trustworthy fellow this time, to stay with me, and charged him not to leave a moment on any account. I said to myself, " What shall I do ? " and was thinking, while trading, how I could manage to get away unobserved. After thinking it over and over again, I hit upon a plan which I thought might work. I said to the man who was watching the boat, that I must go away for a few moments, and asked him to watch the oil as well as the boat. No sooner was I out of sight of him than I put for the interior. I was fearful of running afoul of the old man : so I kept a good look-out for him, trusting to luck to get out of it if I should meet him. I travelled a long way, as I thought. At last I came to where some boys were playing marbles, and halted, watching the game ; they all the time were chattering in a language utterly unintelligible to me. To the right of the boys, from where I stood, I noticed an old woman standing in the doorway of her house. As soon as she perceived I was looking towards her, she beckoned me with her hand towards her, saying at the same time, " *Entree, entree*," which signifies in English, as I learned afterwards, " Come in." As I didn't make any signs of compliance, she came towards me, jabbering over something. After getting to where I was standing, she gently pulled my sleeve, and, leading me on, started for the house. After getting there she said over the word " *Entree*," pointing inside the house. I reluctantly entered, not knowing what sort of a place I was getting into. She almost compelled me to take a cup of coffee, and offered me some wine which I refused. However I felt comparatively easy : the old lady and her two daughters — as I took two young ladies to be who were in the house when I entered — did all they could to make me feel so. After I had been there a short time, she said something to the girls, who started off, and were gone but a short time, when they returned with two chickens, " galenas " as they called them. They asked me by signs what I called them : upon being told, they seemed to be satisfied. ˙ They tried a good many times to speak the word " chicken " after me, but failed to give it the right sound ; and, amid laughter at their and my attempts to speak each other's language, they went somewhere to prepare dinner. In due time they came to me, saying, as near as I can spell the words they used, "*Este umbre camis munge?*" which I rendered as meaning in English, " Are you hungry ? " I followed them, and found a nice dinner steaming hot ; and, it being the first time I had seen any thing like a good meal since I left Aunt Elizabeth's house, I enjoyed it hugely. After dinner was disposed of, we entertained each other in teaching one another the names of things in each other's language. Thus time passed until ten o'clock, when they assigned me a hammock to sleep in. By this time I had got quite domesticated, and felt entirely at my ease. I remember, after I got into my hammock, of saying to myself, " By morning the old ' Peru ' will be out of sight," and wondered what they would do with my things. After the day's excitement, with no sleep the night before, I was soon sound sleep, and did not wake up until I heard some one saying, " *Umbra, umbra,*" meaning " man." At first I felt bewildered, forgetting for the moment where I was ; but, Memory unrolling her scroll, I read the doings of the day before. We got our breakfast, and spent subsequent time much the same as yesterday.

Just before dinner was ready, while lazily lounging in the hammock, one of the girls swinging it, all hands laughing at each other's blunders in trying to speak in a strange language, and enjoying ourselves in the pleasantest possible way, and when I thought that the ship was two hundred or more miles away, who should darken the doorway but Capt. Brooks! If the earth had opened, and I knew I was to sink into its yawning cavern, I could not have felt worse. Language baffles a description of my feelings at this moment. After eying me a while, still standing in the doorway, he says, " I have found you at last, you young rascal : here you have kept the ship waiting for a whole day." Hearing him talking so loud, and I looking so pallid, the old lady came forward jabbering in the most piteous tones, seeming to ask what was the matter. Her anxious look, to know what was up, set me weeping ; and this set the two girls crying ; and taken altogether it was quite a scene. At last the old man, being familiar with their language, told them, in their own vernacular, that I was a runaway from his ship. After seeing the true state of the case, the old lady interceded in my behalf, and begged him to let me stay with them, which of course was entirely useless. He didn't talk hard to me, as I had a right to expect, but, on the contrary, was very sociable, and seemed not to take advantage of our different positions. He kept on talking with the good old lady; her daughters, one on each side of the hammock, trying to talk with me. We all took dinner together, the captain as courteous and affable as though nothing unusual had taken place. When we came to take our leave, there was another scene; the old lady and her beautiful daughters crying as though their hearts would break. The old lady and her girls kissed me over and over again. When finally we got away, the old man was much affected, although he tried to keep it to himself. We soon arrived where the boat was waiting to take us on board. Thus ends my first and only attempt at running away.

The boys in the boat kept telling one another, while rowing towards the ship, "He'll get a flogging when he gets aboard;" but the captain never alluded to it in my presence. Not so with the crew: they kept it up awhile, as also the trading business; but, finding I cared nothing for it, at last it died out of itself. There was one consolation I had,—that they didn't dare to touch me, as they found out I was fully able to take care of myself.

I am thus particular in relating this incident; for it may indicate that my friends in the summer land influenced the captain to hunt me up, also show the difficulties one has to contend with in climbing the ladders of promotion and progression, where seemingly every circumstance favorable to success is cut off, and that, if we only knew that such aid was always near at hand, what strength it would give us in the arduous duties of life!

Nothing further worthy of note occurred to

break the every-day monotony of a whaleship making a passage, until we arrived on "whaling ground." This is located in latitude from thirty-eight to forty-two degrees south, between Cape Horn and the Cape of Good Hope, rather nearer the latter. The customary routine of a whaleship when on cruising ground, is, after cruising all day, with a lookout at each masthead for whales, to take in all the light sails, jib and mainsail, and double-reef the topsails, at sunset, and, if the captain wishes to keep in the vicinity, leave orders to wear ship at a certain time. The watches correspond in number to the boats a ship carries. Ours was a three-boat ship; that is, we could man three boats: consequently we had three watches. The night is divided into three equal parts; each boat's crew takes its watch the allotted time, whose boatsteerer is the officer of the deck for the same time. None of the mates stand watch after arriving on whaling ground.

We were nearly three months out before we saw the first right whale, the kind we were after. After breakfast one morning the lookout sung out, "There she blows!" Learning the direction of whereabouts, the captain mounted up the main-yard, and after using his glass pronounced them right whales. He immediately gave orders to put the "tubs" in the boats; that is, the tubs in which three hundred fathoms of towline is coiled, and which are never allowed to remain in the boats when on the "cranes" upon which the boats usually rest. As soon as the whales were visible off deck, the main-yard laid aback to stop the ship's headway, and all things ready, the "old man" sung out, "Lower away the boats." The crews were soon in their places, each one having a particular oar designated for him to pull, to avoid confusion, mine being the tub-oar. While we were getting the boats down, the whales turned flukes, as whalemen say when they go down. We pulled to where they were last seen, and peaked our oars. As this kind of whale usually stops under water some half-hour, we had some time to wait for their re-appearance; the captain standing upon the stern sheets, while the boatsteerer was doing the same thing on the bow of the boat, both looking out for them. While this was going on I was cogitating in my mind what a whale looked like, how big his eyes were; for I imagined that, if they were proportioned like other animals, their eyes must be as large as a good-sized cart-wheel. While thinking of this and other things, the captain jumped down into the boat, and seized the steering oar, saying in a suppressed tone, "Pull three, and stern two," meaning to pull ahead on the three-oared side, and back-water on the other or two-oared side; by doing which the boat would swing almost square round, without going ahead. I looked in every direction, my eyes as big as demijohns. Directly I heard a roaring sound. The whale had come up, and the sound I heard was the noise he made in spouting. The old man had seen him under water, when he gave the above order about pulling three and backing two, which manœuvre brought the head of the boat towards him, and when he broke water he was within striking distance ; and the boatsteerer let fly first one harpoon and then the other. Then came the order, " Stern all," meaning, back-water with all the oars. The whale making his appearance so unexpectedly, and so near us, we, that is the green-horns, got confused, at least I did; for I didn't know whether I was on my head or heels, and never knew whether I pulled ahead or backed-water, or whether I did either. Now came the killing process. The whale was a large one, and seemed decidedly opposed to being interfered with in that unceremonious man-ner. He kicked and thrashed round furiously. While he was thrashing round, trying to get clear, the captain and boatsteerer changed places. The officer of a boat always does the killing; the boat-steerer and crew keeping themselves ready to exe-cute any order the officer may give. Soon after we were " fast," the second mate came up, and got in two harpoons more, " irons " as they are called by whalemen. This second indignity to his whaleship exasperated the monster still more. Finding he couldn't get clear by kicking with his enormous flukes, or tail, he commenced running to windward at a furious rate, dragging the two boats after him. To stop this fun, they carry sharp spades in each boat, attached to small lines. With these, when brought near enough by hauling on the line, and watching a favorable opportunity, they cut the sinews of his tail, which lies horizontally, and when going ahead it is always waving up and down. When the extremity of the tail is down, of course the muscles and sinews are taut on top; this is the time selected to use the spade. When these muscles and sinews are seriously damaged they lose their propelling power, and of course are compelled to stop propulsion; then the officer uses his lance, a long slim shank, with a round steel head made very sharp; with this they pierce the vitals, which sets the whales to bleeding. Nearly an hour elapses before they turn up, as whalemen say when the whale is dead. Our whale was soon checked in his running-away propensity, — quite as suddenly as I was at Flores. In a shorter time than it takes to write this paragraph, Mr. Whale was spouting blood; and in thirty minutes more he was a lifeless mass of bones, muscles, and blubber. After he was spouting blood, the old man cut off his line near to the harpoon, and went on board to get whale alongside. After our boat was on her cranes, we soon had the monster secured alongside the ship. After the other boats were taken up, all hands got dinner. Thus I had witnessed and participated in the capture of the first whale I ever saw.

After dinner was over, we commenced cutting him in, that is to say, getting the blubber off his body and into a room between decks, prepared for the purpose, called the blubber-room. By dark we had his hide off, and his head in on deck: out of the latter comes all the whalebone for umbrella-sticks, ladies' corsets, and a hundred other uses. Now, then, comes the process of extracting oil from the blubber, or boiling-out process. The man in the blubber-room cuts up, with a spade adapted to the purpose, the great blanket-pieces, that is, the strips of blubber taken off the body, about three feet wide, and fifteen to twenty feet long, called blanket-pieces; these he cuts into small pieces, which are called horse-pieces; these latter are again sliced up into one-half-inch slices, by a long, wide, thin-bladed knife, with a handle on each end, and very sharp; this is called a mincing-knife, and is used by the mincer, whose duty I was selected to perform in my watch. The blubber varies from fifteen to six inches in thickness. At the end of the second day, the product of the whale, eighty-five barrels, was in large casks ready for stowing down. The oil is tried out from the scraps; a wood-fire for the first kettle-full, after that scraps are the fuel. Before we had a chance to stow down our first oil, we got another whale, and kept doing so, with varying success, until we made up our voyage, and started for home; where we arrived the following June, safe, sound, and I very much improved in bodily strength, my muscles rounded out and hard; in fact, I had changed from a sickly-looking stripling to a full-grown, healthy man.

The captain had sent letters home, in which he extolled me highly, and wanted the owners to secure me as third mate of the ship the next voyage; that is, if he went in her again. This I was ignorant of. When we anchored outside the bar, and before we had got the sails furled, a boat came alongside in which was the owner, Mr. Joy; the moment he landed on deck he inquired for me, and at once offered me the third mate's berth the next voyage, and was anxious for me to accept, as he said Capt.

Brooks had recommended me very highly; and, as he was going in her again, he wanted me in that capacity. I was astonished at his recommendation, as I had caused him no little trouble by attempting to run away, and very considerable exercise of patience on account of my troubles with the men. Ascertaining that Mr. Coffin, our second mate on the voyage just ended, was going chief officer, and a brother of the captain as second mate, and also that I could go home before the ship would be ready, I agreed to go. When it was found out that I had been lifted over the heads of all the island boys by promotion, there was no little grumbling among them ; but no one was to blame but themselves. Their attempts at bullying me often brought me in contact with the captain, who was not blind as to who was really at fault in all our differences on the voyage.

After settling up the voyage with the owners, I had something over one hundred dollars to carry home to father. My ambition then was great to assist him in clearing off a mortgage on the farm. I took passage for home in the same vessel that brought me to the island one year before. After a passage of four days, I found myself at Augusta, from where I engaged a ride home with a neighbor who lived not a mile from the home of my youth. Our family had all retired to bed before I got to the house. The old house-dog was the first to welcome me; and, when I knocked, I thought he would suffocate me with his caresses. In response to my knock, mother inquired, " Who is there ? " I said, " Come and see." In a moment the news spread through the house like an electric shock, that David had come: in another moment my brothers and sisters came tumbling down stairs, and into the front room, where mother and old Rover were trying their best to see who could express the most feeling. Such a reception, such hugging and caressing, no poor mortal ever had to endure before. All told there were eighteen of us, eleven boys and five girls, besides father and mother; each and all vieing with each other to see who could express the most affection.

Thus ends another important event of my life, in which I had experienced much that tended to develop and bring to the surface many latent forces and propensities, which might otherwise have lain dormant and useless.

I love to go back at this late day, and live over again some happy halcyon days of my youth, and forget for the moment the troubles and cares of the past and present. It makes me feel young and vigorous again, and gives me courage still to endure with added serenity the struggles incident to one, the larger part of whose vital sands have already run to the bottom of life's hour-glass.

CHAPTER V.

SECOND VOYAGE WHALING.

AFTER passing two happy months in visiting friends and relatives, always accompanied by some loving member of our family, my furlough expired, and I commenced preparations for a second voyage. I induced my brother Henry to accompany me, and try the realities of whaling. Getting away from home this time was not so hard as heretofore, partly because I had my brother for a companion, and partly because I had got somewhat used to it. We took passage in the same packet that took me away from home on my first voyage, and after due time landed on the island of Nantucket. I introduced my brother to the owner of the ship, who seemed well pleased to add his name to the shipping articles.

After getting our outfit, we went on board the ship (which was laying outside of the bar, taking in her supplies), to commence the practical realities and active duties that would end only with the voyage.

The ship was fitted out this time for two and a half years. Our instructions were, that after the right-whale season was over we should go into Delagoa Bay (on the east coast of Africa, where the whales resort to rear their young), and whale there through the season; then cruise in the Mozambique Channel and up the Red Sea for sperm whales, until the season for right whaling came round again.

The ship being ready, we sailed the 4th of July, 1832, under very different auspices than on my first voyage. Nothing of importance transpired on the passage to the Western Islands. We were devoted to the common routine of every-day life on shipboard, and the taking of several black-fish, with the proceeds of which we were to recruit ship. We called at the same island as on the voyage before, but I was feeling altogether different than when I landed there the previous year. We filled up our complement of men from the natives, and laid in an ample stock of vegetables, pigs, and poultry, and proceeded on our voyage to the south.

While we were taking in our supplies at the island, I got liberty to spend a day and night with my friends whom I found there the year before. They seemed as much pleased to see me as if I had been a son and brother, returning after a long absence; and when I left the next day, all three, mother and two daughters, accompanied me to the boat. The final parting came at last, the boat's crew witnessing their caresses and tears. They watched us until an intervening promontory hid them from my view forever; I have never since had the pleasure of visiting their island home.

I have always looked back to this little event of my early history with the greatest possible pleasure. It seems like an oasis in the desert of life, giving momentary rest to the weary traveller, and sweet hopes for the future. After we got on board, we shaped our course for the Cape de Verd Islands, where we could leave letters to be forwarded home by the American consul. When these islands passed out of sight, we saw no more land for nine months and ten days. We had a fair passage to our regular whaling ground, where, having procured a fair portion of oil, and the season being up, we started for St. Augustine Bay, on the Island of Madagascar, situated in the Indian Ocean, some two hundred miles from the east coast of Africa, in latitude about twenty-four degrees south; that is, the Bay of St. Augustine, at the head of which is situated a town of the same name, where the officers and men were to recuperate health and strength, all of whom had become more or less debilitated by long continuance at sea. The body of water between this island and the mainland is called Mozambique Channel. About midway of the island, on the west side, is situated the harbor and anchorage of the little thinly settled town referred to above. Into this bay, after a long passage from our whaling ground, we effected an entrance.

The crew, to a man, were down with the scurvy, a loathsome disease, brought on by long exposure at sea, and eating salt junk, as sailors call salt beef and pork. We were aware that we had the disease, but did not know to what extent, until we got in under the land: when the land-breeze came off, many were taken down sick, some worse than others. We had our anchors ready to drop before we got a scent of the land-breeze; else I think we should have been too weak to have got up the chains, and shacked them to the anchors. We anchored near the shore, but, on account of our debility, were unable to furl the sails until the next morning, when we managed to roll them up. We were then sent ashore, to wallow in the dirt and sand, this being the best attainable remedy for this terrible malady. We laid here eight weeks before we got our wood, water, and outfit on board for another cruise. Here first I came in contact with royalty. The day after we anchored, the king and queen, who ruled in this part of the island, with some half-dozen princes and princesses, made us a formal visit. They came on board with all the "pomp and circumstance" of the most favored potentate of any European court; and, although as black as coal-tar, they put on more airs, and assumed more importance, than any white royal pair I ever read about. They had straight glossy hair, regular features, nose aquiline, well-formed chin and mouth, with not a symptom of the African race about them, with the single exception of the color of their skins. As a whole, they had more regular features and were better looking than the average white man; more especially the women, who, if they had a white instead of a black skin, would have been looked upon as models of beauty.

The inhabitants were very kind and hospitable to strangers, and confiding and affectionate among themselves. By a royal mandate issued in this part of the island, all the men, after they arrive at the age of twenty years, carry a long lance made of "iron-wood," about an inch through, with a spear on the end, so as to be ready at all times to repel inhabitants of other parts of the island, who are ruled by other despots, of which there are several: thus all males are constituted into a standing army, to be ever ready to respond to the call of their sovereign.

The royal pair, with their retinue, remained on board all night. I gave up my state-room to two of the princesses, and camped down on deck. The next morning, after partaking of a bountiful breakfast, and after accepting presents of calico, ribbons, beads, &c., from the captain, they went ashore, observing the same ceremony as when they came on board. They were received, on landing from the royal barge (merely a large canoe), with all the pomp and ceremony that the most favored sovereign could wish for. The royal pair passed through long lines of their sable subjects; everybody, large and small, giving demonstration that their loyalty was unadulterated with any party politics, that their love and respect knew no bounds, and that their only desire was to do any thing and every thing to enhance the happiness and well-being of their august majesties.

The day before we went to sea, an incident transpired in my personal experience which was of such thrilling character that I think I will give it in detail. I wish I could never recall it; for it thrills me with sensations impossible to describe. On some accounts, I would gladly pass over its details; but, having undertaken to furnish the marvels of my experience, I will not shrink from going back and living over again these experiences as they follow one another through the ever-varying scenes of life.

It was this: The captain requested me to take one of the men, go ashore, and get some "iron-poles," that is, poles on which harpoons are fitted. They are about six feet long, and the size of a man's wrist. I selected a man by the name of Jim Winslow, a boat-steerer. We took the boat up a small creek, a dozen rods or so, and fastened her to a tree. We then went up into the woods looking for trees of the right size for our purpose. Jim moved off, diverging from my left; and, when we had got fifteen or twenty rods from our boat, I came to a small tree about eight inches through, leaning over at an angle of forty degrees or so. Around this tree I noticed something circling, the circles being about eighteen inches apart. I had often seen, in forests, vines as large as a man's arm, wound round large trees, of a yellowish color, with white spots as large as a thumb-nail; and, as this looked like those, I thought nothing of it until I had got within five or six feet of the tree, when I happened to look higher, and perceived that what I had called a vine grew larger the higher up it went; this excited my curiosity, and my eye followed the coils all the way up: and what I took for a vine proved to be an enormous anaconda. About six feet of the upper end was stretched straight out from the tree, directly over where I was standing. It seemed to be anxiously looking in the distance. The thickest part of the body I should think was at least six inches through; the end, where it joined on to the enormous head, was not larger than the thick part of a man's arm; the head seemed to be over a foot across it, in shape like any other serpent's. I didn't stop long in that vicinity, but started for the boat, with all the speed a frightened man could muster, hallooing as I ran, " Run, Jim, run, Jim ! " Jim thought I had seen some wild animal, as the natives said the woods were full of them: he ran for dear life, trying to catch up with me. We both jumped into the boat, shoved off, paddled down the creek and out into the bay with all our might, neither speaking a word. When I thought we were out of danger I stopped paddling, and told Jim what I had seen. After I had got through, Jim said, if he had been where I was, or even had known the cause of my sudden retreat, he could not have moved out of his tracks.

The snake could not have been less than sixty or seventy feet long, judging from the length of the tree he was circling. No inducement could tempt me to go ashore again, nor any one else out of that ship's crew. I asked some natives who were on board, if any such monster had ever been seen there before. They said there was one seen about a month ago ; but, as it hadn't been seen since, they were in hopes it had left altogether. They seemed very much frightened, and told such extravagant stories about the size of some of the monsters that had been seen in that vicinity, that my snake was a mere child compared to theirs. They said one was seen more than a foot through, and longer than the ship. At all events, I desire never to witness such a sight again ; and even now, when any thing occurs to bring that monster to mind, cold chills run through my body from head to foot.

The next day we went to sea, and shaped our course for Delagoa Bay on the east coast of Africa, in latitude about 24° south. Thus ends our Augustine visit.

A week subsequent to leaving our last port, we entered the bay referred to, where we were to remain the entire whaling season, some three months. The entrance to the bay is through a narrow channel from one-eighth to one-fourh of a mile in width: we had considerable difficulty in finding it by sounding in a boat. To the north of the channel there is a dangerous coral reef, extending some ten miles, submerged only at high water; to the southward is another extending some five miles. The bay is seventeen miles deep and about eight in width. We found two whale-ships already anchored, one French and the other English, both waiting for whales to make their appearance. We selected a place for anchoring, at the southward of the other ships, and nearer in shore. We then sent down top-gallant yards and masts, and double-reefed the topsails, ready to meet a so'wester, if one should put in an appearance, which is not an uncommon event at that season of the year. While one lasts, the wind seems more like a tornado than a common gale, tearing up and demolishing every thing in its path. To meet an emergency of this kind, we used the above precautions; also we reefed the fore and main sails, bent a new fore-staysail, main spencer, and close mizzen; so that, if we lost our anchors, we should be prepared to get under way and go to sea. We had taken extra pains to get the correct bearings from the ship to the entrance of the narrow channel through which we must pass to get to sea. We paid out forty-five fathoms of the largest chain, got the other ready to let go ; both chains were on deck ready for immediate use. So many precautions would have been unnecessary for any other emergency than the occurrence of a gale while the boats were away ; in which case there would not be men enough on board to handle the vessel promptly.

After all was done for the safety of the ship if a sudden gale should come on in the absence of the boats (for gales there come without any warning), we were ready for business.

The custom is to take the land-breeze in early morning, run down to near the reef, then peak our oars, and sail back and forth all day with a man standing up in the bow and stern, looking for whales ; the boats keeping about two miles apart. At noon we partake of a lunch. At about ten, A.M., the sea-breeze sets in ; and at four we sail towards the ship, where we arrive earlier or later, according to the strength of the wind ; this being the every-day routine of bay-whaling.

We had been engaged going and coming from the cruising ground for about ten days, with not one sight of a whale, when one day about noon the chief mate signalled us to go on board. We had noticed all the morning that the atmosphere seemed to be impregnated with something unusual, although no indications of a storm appeared other than a few straggling clouds. The wind had been steadily increasing since morning, and when we were signalled

it was blowing quite strong from the south-west. We
down sail, and pulled to where the mate was waiting, when he told us to hurry on board as fast as
possible, for we were going to have a south-wester.
Instead of having a sea-breeze to help us, we had
the wind almost in our teeth, all the time increasing; and we pulled until dark before some of the
boats got alongside. In ordinary weather we could
have rowed the distance in two or three hours. The
captain had done every thing he could think of for
the safety of the ship before we got on board: so
there was but little for us to do but watch the course
of events. By this time the wind had assumed
fearful velocity. We were anchored in five-fathom
water; and, although the wind had not more than
three or four miles sweep, the seas were tremendous;
and at every jump the ship made it seemed that
every thing forward must go by the board. The best
bower, that is, the large chain, was run out to the
batter end ninety fathoms; while the other anchor
was forty-five fathoms from the ship. After seeing
to every little thing that we thought would add to
our security, we went to supper. I shall never forget
that table-scene as long as Memory holds her sway.
There sat Capt. Brooks looking the picture of
despair, and all the officers exhibiting by their looks
the most intense apprehensions for the safety of the
ship. The feeling was universal throughout the
ship's company, that she would *not* ride the gale out
in safety. Not a word was uttered by any one until
we had nearly completed our meal, when the ship
seemed to stand on end, and, as her bow came down,

a loud report and a crash saluted our listening ears. Before we reached the deck we heard the awful cry, that the large chain had parted. Such consternation as followed this announcement baffles description. The chain had parted at the windlass, and in going out got kinked up, and took out the hawser-pipe, and carried away a considerable portion of the bow. This accounted for the report and crash which we heard in the cabin. Of course the only thing to do next was to pay out the other chain; but, as the ship was nearly side to the wind, we had little hopes of checking her. She was drifting directly foul of the "Duke of Orleans," the large French ship already referred to. If we struck her, no power on earth could prevent both from going ashore. Upon paying out the other chain, the moment it brought up that parted at the anchor, without so much as checking her in the least. It seemed now that our only chance for saving the ship was gone. The captain was running fore and aft like a madman, talking incoherently. The subordinate officers held a hurried consultation to determine what was best to be done. The old man being out of his right mind, we did not consult him, but agreed among ourselves to slip the cable, get what sail on she could bear, and try and go to sea. This was a hazardous undertaking in that dark night in such a furious tornado ; and, to make it still worse, we would have to go seventeen miles, and run our chances of hitting the entrance to the narrow channel, the only passage from the bay to the ocean. It was fortunate for us that the ship swung round to the eastward, and forged ahead far

enough to just clear the French ship. We divided
ourselves into separate squads; some to unshackle the
chain around the foot of the main-mast, which was
no easy job, as the shackle-pin was so completely
rusted in that it took a great deal of work to start
it; others went to close-reef the top-sails, and get
ready, as soon as the chain was clear, to start on our
perilous passage. After a while the news was passed
up, that the chain was clear. We soon had it on
deck, and so arranged that it would run clear. In
less than a minute afterwards it was lying at the
bottom, doing no other damage than cutting the
windlass pretty bad, and carrying away the hawser-
pipe. Every thing being in readiness, we soon had
her under way towards the reef. The course, as
previously ascertained, from where we anchored to
the passage out, was E. by S., $\frac{1}{2}$ south; but, as we
had drifted somewhat to the leeward, we must make
that good by steering E. S. E. I took the wheel by
the special request of the other officers, as I was
thought to be the best wheel-man on board; besides,
I was taking things so coolly, they thought that I
would be the safest in an emergency of that kind.
Although their preference did not excite my vanity,
I partook of the same feeling myself. The soundings were regular, from seven to nine fathoms until
we neared the reef, when they began to diminish
slowly. We could see nothing; but, as we drew
nearer to the dangerous rocks, the roaring of the
breakers both to windward and leeward, amid the
howling tempest, was terrific. This awful sound was
increasing as we advanced, the wind being two or

three points free, the weather top-sail braces well checked in. We were making at least from eight to ten knots per hour. Not a word was spoken the whole passage, except the ominous ones of the man in the chains, giving the depth of water. All hands cuddled close together on the weather side, near the main-mast, expecting at every downward plunge the ship would strike the bottom, which would be the end of all things temporal with us. When the depth of water had diminished to five fathoms, I heard some-one say " Luff." Instantly I rolled the wheel down; and, when she was heading S. W. by S., the same voice rang out plain and distinct, " Steady ! " and, when the soundings indicated $4\frac{1}{2}$ fathoms, the *voice* again said, " Keep her E. by S.," which instruction I obeyed with the same alacrity and promptness that I would an order from an earthly pilot. At the time I received the last " course " from my invisible pilot, I did not know the last cast of the lead, which the man in the chains, having ascertained, threw in on deck, and followed it himself, expecting the next jump we should be on the rocks. When he came aft, I ascertained the above. Finding she didn't strike, I told Jack to see how much water there was. He threw the lead overboard, and ran out the whole line, twenty fathoms, and sung out lustily, " The bottom has dropped out."

At this announcement we all breathed freer: yet there was no demonstration, no congratulation, but a solemn silence was the only expression visible upon the anxious countenances of those hardy, weather-beaten sailors. For the time being we were silently

hopeful.   But this state lasted only a moment : the
danger was not passed ; it had only changed places ;
for, in less than two hours after crossing the bar, the
wind veered suddenly to the south-east, with no
variation in its velocity.   The change set us toward
a lee shore of overhanging mountains, of craggy,
solid, granite bluffs, extending many leagues both to
the north and south, and but a few miles distant.
The sudden change of wind made a tremendous
heavy cross sea, which caused the ship to labor very
heavily.   The heavy press of canvas we were obliged
to carry, to keep her from falling to leeward, strained
every timber and bolt to their utmost tension ; and
although we had preventer topsail braces on, yet we
were under fearful apprehensions lest . the topsail
sheet would be unable to resist the fearful strain ;
and, if it did not, our chances for escape would be
hopeless.   We were on the starboard tack, with Cape
Corientes, a high bluff of black, craggy rocks, only
three points off our lee bow, which we must weather :
upon this all our hopes of escape were centred.   But,
as we neared its almost perpendicular walls, it seemed
impossible to weather it.   When not over one and a
half leagues from its frowning front, we found we
had either to go about or go ashore.   With this as
our only alternative, we made several unsuccessful
attempts to stay ship ; that is, to get on the other
tack without going to leeward.   Failing in this, our
next and only alternative was to wear ship ; and, as
there was not a moment to lose, we set about it
immediately.   Of course every thing was done. that
seamanship could suggest to facilitate the operation ;

for in wearing we knew that she must necessarily go toward the iron-bound coast which we were so anxious to avoid. In due time we had her braced up on the other tack; and, owing to the sudden change of wind as before mentioned, the sea took her on the lee-bow, which prevented her going to leeward as fast as she did on the other tack. If the wind should not change to our disadvantage, which it might do almost instantly, and if nothing of a serious nature occurred to the ship, our chances were becoming favorable; but, as we were not safe in indulging that view of things, we were kept for twenty-three hours in the most anxious suspense. When at last the gale subsided, and all fears of going ashore were dissipated, we repaired damages as far as we could, and headed once more for the bay, to recover our two lost anchors and chains; which, being buoyed, we would have no difficulty in finding. In two days after passing over the bar that fearful night, we again recrossed it, and found the French ship still at anchor. After parting both chain cables, she rode out the gale with an old condemned hemp cable. The English ship, the moment the gale abated, got under way and went to sea. We learned some five months afterward, that the English captain, on going into Cape Town, a port on the southern promontory of Africa, reported the " Peru," with all on board, lost in attempting to get to sea in a gale from the south-west. This false story got into the papers in Nantucket, and was copied into others. Of course all from the island were mourned as dead. Luckily the news failed to reach my folks. We were somewhat surprised, however, when we anchored in Cape Town, to find we were all "dead men."

We got our anchors and chains, and proceeded to sea, and cruised some five months with varying success. On our passage to Simmons Bay, twenty-two miles from Cape Town, a heavy sea boarded us while lying to in a gale on what is called Lagullus Bank, and carried away the rail and bulwarks on the starboard side, fore and aft; what with that and the damages sustained in Delagoa Bay, took some six weeks to repair.

Before dismissing this part of the voyage, I will again refer to the VOICE which told me to luff when nearing the passage out of the bay, on the eventful night referred to, when we were seeking for the channel by which to get to sea. From careful observations by sounding, after the gale, I found that the specific depth of water indicated when Jack threw the lead in on deck was nowhere else to be found; that we were then on the northern side of the channel, and, had I not heeded the *invisible pilot*, we should have most certainly gone on to the rocks to leeward of the channel. As no other one in the ship ever heard these voices, I said nothing about them for fear of unfavorable comments. None of the officers knew but what I was all the time steering the course determined upon when we got sail on; everybody thinking, myself included, that the course east-south-east amply provided for her drifting before we made sail. Thus it was proved beyond a peradventure, that some unseen intelligence, come from what source it might, took upon itself, through my organism, to pilot the ship out through that difficult passage to the deep waters of the ocean. If any should say it was a delusion on my part, that I fancied it, such an assertion does not in the least change the character of the transaction; for it must be evident to all, that, had not something outside of myself and that ship's company told me to change the course, the ship and all hands must inevitably have been lost. If this had been an isolated case in my experience, I myself might have thought little of it; but many times, both before and since, this same VOICE has piloted me out of many difficulties, when every resource at my command had been exhausted. And I *know* from whence this guiding voice emanates. I should feel recreant to every principle of justice if I failed to " give unto Cæsar the things that are Cæsar's, and unto God the things that are God's."

After recruiting and repairing ship, we sailed, the 10th of December, on another cruise for right whales, and, having procured an average quantity of oil, started leisurely for home when the whaling season was over, lying to nights under easy sail, and looking out for whales through the day. On our passage home, we called at the island of St. Helena to recruit ship. The island is nothing but a large jagged, barren rock, as seen on approaching it, inaccessible for landing excepting in one place, where the little town of Jamestown is located, and where all the business of the island is transacted. It is unproductive except in the gorges of the mountains, where small patches are cultivated; it being the only place, as before stated, where a landing could be effected. Jamestown is protected by immense forts, which completely command all approaches to the town. The island belongs to England, but was leased and controlled by the English East India Company, as a rendezvous for their ships going and coming from India, until 1833, when their lease expired. The British Government reserved the right of sending convicts from England to the island, to serve out a penal servitude for misdemeanors committed in the mother country. It was here that the first Napoleon was banished after his disastrous defeat at Waterloo, and where his body was lying at the time of our visit to the island. I made two pilgrimages to his tomb at Longwood before we left the island; and while contemplating the causes of the fall of one of the most ambitious conquerors the world ever knew, whose every movement was watched by all nations with suspicious suspense and anxiety as to what would be his next move, — causes of the fall of the hero of Austerlitz and Lodi, — I could but exclaim, with one of old, " How are the mighty fallen ! "

After remaining here some three weeks, we proceeded to sea on our homeward passage ; and when only a week out, having occasion to replenish the bread-locker and harness-cask, we broke out the after hatch where all reserved provisions were stowed away ; and the first bread-cask we opened was found empty : the next and the next proved to be the same. This alarmed us ; we followed up the examination, and all the bread we could find was one cask about two-thirds full. We next examined the pork and beef barrels; and less than one half-barrel of beef, and not a pound of pork, was the result of the investigation. When it became known how small was our allowance for at least six weeks, and no possible way of getting back to our last port on account of the south-east trade-winds, which blow from that quarter with but little variation the year round, our consternation can be better imagined than described. The mate, in accordance with instructions from the captain, over-hauled all the bread-casks and meat-barrels, soon after we entered the harbor; and, as all were properly marked, he reported accordingly; and the quantity was considered sufficient to last at least three months. Considerable blame was attached to the officer for not unheading them so as to be sure of their contents; but such a circumstance as ours was never known before, and hence he was not so much to blame. I doubt not that those who growled the most would have rested on the same evidence that he did.

The only hope of replenishing our exhausted larder was that we might possibly fall in with some outward-bound West-Indiaman when we should have got far enough north. But it would not be prudent to trust to that; and so, after viewing the situation as it really existed, we came to a sensible conclusion to find out the exact amount of our provisions, and to put our-selves forthwith on allowance, reckoning on a basis of six weeks to either get into St. Thomas, or fall in with some outward-bound vessel. After weighing out all our bread, there was precisely ten ounces per day to each man for six weeks. The course adopted was, to weigh out seventy ounces to each man, as all

he would get for seven days; and then each one would
get the same allowance for another week; and so on
until we could get more. As there was less than a half-
barrel of beef, it was thought best to divide it equally
among all hands, and let each use his share when and
as he pleased. As a strange concomitant, our water
was also short, so that we had to allowance ourselves
on that as well. Although of no great consequence,
upon investigation into the steward's department,
we found that we had tea and coffee for only about
two weeks; but what added more than any thing else
to our inconvenience was, our tobacco failed us in
about three weeks; thus proving the old adage true,
" It never rains but it pours."

One consideration kept our hopes moderately buoyant. We had all the appliances for catching whales;
and, if we failed in capturing them, we had a right to
expect, in fact almost knew, we should be able to get
some black-fish and porpoises, which we had been
accustomed to fall in with almost every day or two;
and then again we might and probably should catch
plenty of dolphin, skip-jacks, and alvicoes, all deep-
water fish, and never eaten but by those compelled
to it by the lack of other and more palatable food;
but, in case of starvation, any thing with a particle of
nutrition in its composition is eagerly sought for, and
as eagerly eaten. But, strange to say, for the five
weeks and three days we were subject to this short
allowance, we did not catch any thing big or small,
although we used every means within our power to
do so, prompted by that most inciting organ, a famish-
ing, empty stomach: yet we failed entirely. Thus

day after day came and went, bringing each morn fresh hopes of better luck, which kept us comparatively easy, although after the second week had passed we began to show our lack of sustenance.

Before the first week was passed, some *unseen intelligence* told me to change my mode of eating. I listened to the suggestions and reasoning with the same interest that I would to any mortal who I had reason to believe was competent to advise in an emergency of the kind I was laboring under; and, as the suggestions seemed reasonable, I determined to adopt them at once. The advice was to eat three days' allowance in one, and nothing the next two days. The VOICE reasoned, that on that day I would not feel any inconvenience from want of food; the second, I would hardly realize that I was limited; and, the third day, I would suffer no more than I did continuously when I eat my small regular allowance every day. I mentioned my determination to the captain and officers, giving my reasons, but kept dark as to the source of suggestion. They all advised me not to do so, arguing that it would be very injurious to my stomach, and, besides, that there would be danger of the small intestines growing together. However, contrary to their well-meaning advice, I adopted and carried out the suggestions to the letter; and after a few days' trial, finding that I was a gainer by it, followed it up until we were finally relieved, some five weeks and three days from the beginning of the famine; at which time, early in the morning, the lookout aloft gave the welcome shout, " Sail ho ! " To make sure of it, I went aloft myself, and with the glass could see the upper sails of a vessel, but, she being so far off, could not see her hull. I got her bearings by compass, and reported the news to the captain; who upon hearing it jumped out of his berth, telling me, at the same time, to get my boat down, and get ready to start, which was soon accomplished; when the captain giving me a purse of money, with a memorandum of what to purchase if they had any thing to sell, and taking what bread we had along with us, we started a little before sunrise, and did not get alongside until twelve o'clock. She proved to be the brig " Nahant " of Boston, loaded with pork, beef, dried codfish, and potatoes, bound for Barbadoes, one of the West India Islands, for a market.

We had made only sixty miles in the last three weeks, being becalmed most of the time; and what seemed the strangest of all was, we were where there usually is the strongest part of the north-east trade-winds. I had passed there several times before with reefs in the topsails; but now it had been calm as a pond for over three weeks.

When I got on the deck of the brig, I told the captain our situation, and what I wanted. He was a genial, good soul, and said he would assist us all that he could; but, says he, " You want something to eat, first of all. Take your crew into the cabin, and get some dinner; and I will set the cook to get some for ourselves." He led the way into the cabin, and waited upon us while we did ample justice to a wholesome, well-cooked dinner. Before I had completed my purchase, a light breeze sprang up from the westward; and, as the vessels were bound in opposite directions, neither went out of her course in approaching the other. The wind continuing, I remained on board the brig until four, P. M., when, with my boat-load of provisions, I hauled alongside of our ship. In a few minutes every thing was on deck, the boat on her cranes, and the " Peru " heading her course once more, with all sail set, the wind by this time having increased to a stiff breeze.

I will mention one incident in connection with this affair, which, to say the least, was remarkably singular; showing that often, when we have plenty, nature and many men are ready to assist us, while, when reverses come, both the courses of Providence and our most intimate friends often pass us by unaided. So it was in our case. The whole time we were suffering for something to eat, not a fish of any kind could we take: when we got one almost on deck, it would wriggle off the hook, and drop into the water; but, while I was gone, dolphin came round the ship in such quantities that the crew actually took them out of the water with boat-hooks, and when I got in on deck they had over half of a beef-barrel full; but as we were now amply supplied with good provisions, and the dolphins being rather unsafe to eat because of their sometimes being poisonous, we consigned them to the ocean.

Nothing further of importance occured during our passage home. We anchored outside the bar of the harbor of Nantucket, where we arrived in August, 1836, having been absent about thirty months.

The voyage, as a whole, was a success. After

settling up, and receiving the compensation agreed
upon, I shipped as second officer in " The Henry," a
new ship commanded by Capt. George Chase, on a
four-years' voyage around Cape Horn, in pursuit of
sperm whales exclusively. After all the preliminaries
were settled as to how long I should be absent, my
brother and self started for the home of our childhood,
where we were received with all the demonstrations
of joy that loving hearts were capable of expressing.
Thus ends the account of my second voyage.

CHAPTER VI.

THIRD VOYAGE WHALING.

WHEN two of my six-weeks furlough had expired, I received a letter from the owners of the ship, saying, that as there was a prospect of war being declared against France, on account of the non-payment of some indemnity due our Government, the ship would be laid up until the difficulty was adjusted. Gen. Jackson, the then president, made declaration, backed by his cabinet, that, if the French would not liquidate their liability, he would whip it out of them. The French, seeing the impossibility of frightening the hero of New Orleans, wisely decided to make a virtue of necessity, and pay up, rather than measure swords with a people who were determined to fight for their rights, if no other course would secure them.

I had kept company with a Miss Rebecca F. Chapman for several years; and it was agreed between ourselves to get married after I had made another voyage. But events transpiring as above related would keep me at home until the next summer, and perhaps longer. We therefore thought best to have the ceremony solemnized at once. This being agreed to all round, preparations were commenced to carry it into immediate consummation. The day fixed for the nuptials was the 5th of September, 1836, at which time the event took place at the home of my bride, amid the congratulations of friends collected to witness the ceremony. We were to be married in the morning; and it was arranged to go on a drive of some ten miles in company with a few friends, take dinner with an old friend of mine who kept a public house, and return in the evening; all of which was carried out as per programme. On our return, I was handed a letter, in which was an order for me to repair at once to Nantucket and join the ship, as the brush with the French had been amicably settled. The ship would go to sea as soon as she could be made ready. I said nothing to any one about the contents of the letter until next morning, when I showed it to my wife. She was somewhat surprised, as well as myself; but as the request was imperative there was no way to avoid it, unless I gave up a first-rate chance. I left on the 13th, thus having had but six days for my honeymoon. When the time came round, I left friends and home once more, this time bound on a long and perilous voyage. My young mate bore up under the separation much better than many of my own family connections. Good sense told her that it was the only thing that could properly be done, and she submitted to her destiny, with the peculiar heroism of her sex; that is to say, she *made the best of it*.

In due time I arrived at the island, where I found the owners driving business, to get the ship to Edgartown on the island of Martha's Vineyard, where she was to take in her supplies, and where she arrived in about ten days after I landed on the island. After we had taken aboard our supplies, we sailed on the 19th of November, 1836, to be absent four years, unless we filled the ship. before. We had an average passage to the Western Islands, where we filled our complement of men from among the natives, and supplied the ship with fresh provisions, and a good stock of poultry, pigs, &c.; after procuring which, we proceeded on our voyage towards the Pacific Ocean. It being in January, we had a remarkably pleasant passage round the Horn, carrying whole topsails and topgallant-sails until we entered the Pacific. Saw several lone whales off the cape, but did not succeed in capturing any. We made our way down the coast until opposite Chili, where we cruised in the vicinity of the island of Juan Fernandez between three and four months; procuring, in the mean time, several hundred barrels of *sperm* oil. Landed on the above-named island, hoping to be able to obtain a supply of fresh water, which we failed to do, on account of the difficulty of landing sufficiently near to a stream or pond. However, we succeeded at the island of Massafurio, some sixty miles distant from Juan; after which we leisurely started for Callao, situated in latitude 12° south, on the coast of Peru, where we intended to recruit both men and ship; which port we entered on the 6th of May, 1837.

After remaining here some four weeks, we got under way, and proceeded to what is called the Offshore Ground, some six hundred miles off the coast of Peru, in latitude about 12° south, where we succeeded, in six months, in procuring about five hundred barrels of oil; when Capt. Chase, who was suffering with indigestion, determined to again visit Callao, to recruit the crew with a run ashore, and the ship's larder with fresh provisions, vegetables, &c.; also to procure, if possible, medical aid to recover his health. In due time we re-entered the above-mentioned port, and he at once consulted the surgeon of the United States ship "Ohio," carrying seventy-four guns, lying at that time at the above-named port. The doctor, after examining the state of his stomach, told him that he would have to stop ashore at least six months, before his disease could be cured. It was hard to submit to this condition; but as there was no other remedy he had to comply. So it was arranged that the ship should go on a cruise without him. After all our recruits were aboard, we proceeded to sea, and, as per instructions, arrived on the Offshore Ground, our last cruising ground, where we were even more successful than in the previous six months. When our time was up, we headed once more for Callao, where we arrived in due time, highly elated with our good luck, but not more so than the captain, who had in the mean time completely recovered his usual health and spirits.

After recruiting both men and the ship, we put to sea again, heading for our old cruising ground, where we cruised the season out, obtaining some four hundred barrels, after which it was time to recruit ship again; and, as our wood and water were getting

short, the old man decided to go to Tombez, a small
Spanish town situated on a river of that name, in
latitude 3° 12′ south, where wood and water could
be procured in abundance. A slightly laughable
incident happened as we were running down the
coast. Not one in the ship had ever been there;
and, although we knew the latitude, there was no
harbor or town near the shore, nor headland, to indicate the entrance to the river. We were told that it
would be difficult to know just where to so anchor, as
to be near the outlet of the stream.

When within twenty or thirty miles of the place,
we saw a whale-ship beating up the coast, and,
rightly judging she had but just left the watering-
place, we concluded to speak her, and ascertain more
particulars than we possessed about where to anchor.
In reply to our question how we should know when
we got to Tombez, the answer was, "Run down the
coast until you get tired, down anchor, and that'll be
Tombez." With the above definite (?) information,
of course we anticipated no great trouble in finding
the anchorage. Looking out sharp to see when our
latitude was run down, we anchored, though uncertain whether we were near the river's mouth, or not.
Soon after coming to, we perceived a sail-boat
coming out of some bushes, as it appeared to us, and
heading towards our ship. From the men in the
boat we ascertained the entrance to the river to be
directly in shore from where the ship was anchored.

We lay here some three weeks; and after getting
wood, water, fresh provisions, and vegetables, also a
live bullock to be killed at sea, we got under way,

bound up the coast to Payta, in latitude 6° south, where we could procure a supply of onions, which could not be procured in the former place, and which, being potent for warding off scurvy, we much wanted: also we wanted to cooper our oil, since by indications from pumping we found it to be leaking out of the casks.

In beating up the coast to Payta (for it must be remembered that the wind there always blows down along shore the year round) an incident transpired, which, if it hadn't been for my guardians giving me timely warning, would have wrecked the ship.

The second night out from Tombez, we tacked off shore just at sunset, with a whole-sail breeze, which continued until two, A.M., our instructions were to tack in shore at that hour. It being my watch from twelve to four, it devolved upon me to execute the order. Soon after we went about, the wind slackened so that the sails flapped against the masts; and by three and a half, A.M., it had become very light. I was suffering with a jumping toothache, and tried every available means to lessen it, but without avail. I walked the deck rapidly, trying to get up a perspiration; failing in that, I laid the aching side of my head in my hand on the cabin gangway. I hadn't been in that position over a minute, when I heard my familiar VOICE say in clear, distinct words, "Get into the lee after boat." I started instantly to obey the summons. When with my hands on the rail, and one foot on a spare topmast lashed to ring-bolts in the stanchions, and I was about to spring into the boat, I happened to look under the foot of the mainsail forward, and saw that we were near the shore, seemingly not a dozen rods off; and large rocks were nearer still. I could see the water dash against them. For a moment I was paralyzed; but it was only momentary. I saw at once the real position of the ship, and that the only chance for escape was to tack at once. As the wind was light, I had serious apprehensions about her coming round; which, if she failed to do, she must inevitably go ashore. I told the man steering, to roll the wheel " hard down," singing out at the same time to the watch to " stand by for stays." The ship was soon hard aback. I watched the vane at mast-head to see when the ship was head to the wind, and thus to know when to haul round the after-yards; although she swung round as fast as could be expected with such a light wind, yet it seemed an eternity to me. When it was time to " topsails haul," in the hurry and confusion, the men forgot to attend to the main tack and bowline; perceiving which, I started across the main hatch to let them go; and, the bullock standing in my way, I made a clean breach over his back without touching him; a feat which under ordinary circumstances would have been impossible. By the time I had her braced up on the offshore tack, it was daylight. I went into the cabin, and got the old man up to look out of the cabin windows; and, although she had been going off shore some time, yet in the dim daylight the land did not appear to be more than a dozen rods off; in fact, the land appeared to be directly under the stern of the ship. The captain was speechless for a moment, and then

asked how they got there. I informed him, what I
have already said, about tacking in at two, A.M., also
in regard to the strength of the wind while on the
offshore tack, &c. It was a mystery then, and has
always remained one; we finally talked about an inshore current not laid down on the charts, and let it
go at that. I will merely add that the excitement
killed my toothache, and I do not remember of ever
having it since. The significance of the above incident will be apparent, when the *fact* is regarded, that
the saving of the ship was attributable entirely to
some invisible intelligence, telling me in clear, distinct
terms, how to avoid it. This intelligence, I claim,
was my guardian spirit, who has been and ever is
watching over my welfare. It might be asked, if this
intelligence can talk to *me* audibly, informing me of
dangers, and how to avoid them, why not to all? In
answer to this, I can simply say, *I do not know*, any
more than if asked, If one cow has horns, why don't
all cows have the same? No reasoning, intelligent
person, can doubt for a single moment, that for every
effect there must be an adequate *cause*, whether they
understand it or not: there must be an adequate
cause for the differences in the cows' horns, and also
for my hearing suggestive, warning words, coming
from some unseen intelligence, while most persons
cannot.

In due time we entered the port of Payta, where
we got a supply of onions, &c., and, after coopering
our oil, put to sea again; this time heading for the
Galapagos Islands, situated on, and both sides of, the
line; that is, in latitude 0°, — where we intended to

spend the next six months in the prosecution of our legitimate business.

We were peculiarly fortunate here, in procuring oil; for in about four months we succeeded in stowing down over five hundred barrels, lacking only about two hundred barrels of filling the ship. Before I leave this part of the voyage, I will relate an incident which happened to myself while killing a large sperm whale, which may not be uninteresting to the general reader, and which I think worthy of recording. It opened up to my mind a new train of thought, in regard to the survival of the acts and thoughts we perform and cherish while gliding down the stream of time; which survival, if heeded, would save us many severe reflections in our more mature years if not after we shall have passed from the material form through the portal of death. Such survival I as fully believe in as in my own existence now. At the time the experience occurred, I had never heard of any thing like it before; but, in relating it to others in after years, I found that such scenes have been the experience of many who have been resuscitated when nearly drowned.

One day in Lee Bay, at the above-named islands, and where we procured the most of our oil on this cruise, having fastened to a large sperm whale in a rough sea, instead of going round to leeward (which would have taken but a few moments), and to gratify a foolish vanity to be thought courageous and brave, I hauled on to windward to lance him. As the whale was lying in the trough of the sea, this brought the boat, by the action of the waves, alongside of him, and so close as to render the oars useless in handling the boat. Perceiving the boat was in danger of shooting ahead on to his jaw, I gave order to the boatsteerer to "lay on," so that the head of the boat would bring up against the whale's side and stop her. He mistook the order, and hove the head off instead. Seeing that the boat would range ahead too far, I ordered the men to "stern all;" at the same time putting my lance against the whale to help stop the boat. As it proved afterwards, I stuck the lance in his eye. The next thing I knew, I was under water, how far down I had no means of knowing. It seems, as I afterwards learned from those looking on, that, the moment the lance touched him, he rolled suddenly, striking the boat directly under my feet, taking the head of the boat off, and throwing me up, some said as high as thirty feet, whence, turning a somersault in the air, I came down head first, and disappeared under water. Those who witnessed it thought I was killed outright. When I came to myself, I felt no inconvenience from having swallowed water, as one would naturally suppose I must, having been made entirely unconscious by the concussion, and remaining so for a time while many fathoms below the surface. The moment I came to consciousness, I saw directly before me, and about twenty feet off, what appeared the front of the stage in a theatre, with a dark-colored screen rolling from right to left, similar to canvas representing panoramic views. On this canvas I saw all my nearest and dearest friends, full size, and dressed precisely as last seen; each one separate and alone, until

they all successively passed in review before me.
Following this exhibition, all my thoughts, from my
earliest childhood, were represented on the rolling
canvas by symbols; and, although I had never seen
or heard of such a thing before, I knew, when the
different symbols were presented, what thought each
was intended to illustrate; and not only that, but I
knew where I was when each particular thought
came into my mind. A great many of those represented I never gave expression to by act or deed;
and yet there they were, plain and distinct, the good
and bad alternately, following each other in regular
order as they came into my mind; those less desirable to contemplate being largely in the majority, I
am obliged to acknowledge. All this could have
occupied but a very brief time; and yet each friend
remained still long enough for me to scan the features and dress before giving place for another; and
so with the thoughts. After viewing one, the screen
rolled to the left, when another presented himself or
herself; and so with the thoughts.

The vision ended the moment I came to full consciousness, and could, as before stated, have occupied
scarcely more than a moment of time. When I
came to myself under water, although I knew nothing of what transpired at the time the whale struck
the boat, I seemed to know all about it, paradoxical
as it may seem. I knew the boat was stoven; and
as I looked up I saw the line, which was coiled in a
tub before the boat rolled over, sprawling round in
the water; and knowing that this was fast to the
whale, and that if I got entangled in its coils and

the whale should start off, it would be all up with
me, I commenced at once to swim towards daylight, heading so as to keep clear of the line. Soon
after I had commenced making my way to the surface, I touched something with my left foot. Thinking it might be a piece of "squid" (a sort of enormous jelly-fish of the squid species, and on which,
with smaller ones of the same kind, the sperm whale
subsists), I pressed my foot suddenly on it, knowing
that if it was what I supposed it to be it would
"give" under the pressure; but my foot brought
up on a hard substance. By this I knew it was Mr.
Whale, who had settled down, but now, like myself,
was seeking the upper air. I bent my legs against
his head, and made a spring upwards, and soon
"broke" water, not in the least unfavorably affected
by the unceremonious bath. Before I had got into
another boat, the whale made his appearance a few
feet from where I came up. The crews of three boats
from the ship "Abigail," of New Bedford, who were
in company with us, and who tried hard to get the
whale, and four boat-crews from our own ship, all
said that I was under water at least five minutes,
and many of them that it was over ten, either of
these estimates was probably too high. When I got
into a boat, I felt no more inconvenience from the
immersion than though I had simply tumbled overboard and been the next minute in the boat again.
I went on, and helped kill the whale, as though
nothing unusual had happened. The most interesting part of the affair, to me, was the vision ; and, if
I had seen only my friends and relatives, I might

have accounted for it (from the fact that they were often in my mind) on the principle of dreams; but when I take into account the different symbols, each representing long-forgotten thoughts, it assumes a phase and interest far transcending all previous knowledge; and to me at that time it was, and is now, mysterious. The lesson it taught far exceeded all that religion ever promulgated from the pulpit; and if heeded, as before suggested, it would save us many serious regrets. For if this is true, — that is, if we *do* write our own autobiography on the escutcheon of our souls, as the vision fairly indicated, — then every act and thought will be in the future known not only by ourselves, but everybody else can see them as well, when we shall have crossed the mystic river that separates this state of being from the one immediately beyond the tomb. How careful, therefore, ought we to be not to harbor a thought, or do an act, that, when Memory unrolls her scroll in the world of causes, shall make us blush, or shall cause our friends and associates unhappiness!

And then again, such things as those above related, coupled with other and more significant facts in the same direction in my own experience, as the reader will see as he peruses these pages, prove to me beyond a peradventure, that we are living and acting every moment of our lives in the presence of near and dear friends, who are cognizant of our every thought, and the real object of all our acts, whatever we may pretend. While here we can cover up and hide away many things that would be distressing to our earthly friends if they were known. Not so can we hide from our dear departed, who are watching over our welfare with as much solicitude and interest as they ever did while in the form. Nothing can be hid from the keen eyes of the spirits: therefore we should be very careful not to pay them for their sympathy and kindness, by doing aught that may cause them to grieve and be unhappy. If we would not do or say any thing to cause our living friends regret, from whom we can cover up many things that we would not wish them to know, how much more careful should we be to do nothing in thought or act that would wound the sensitive, loving spirits, with whom nothing escapes their keen observation! It seems to me, that knowledge of such a state or condition of the spirit after death, if universally believed, would do more towards harmonizing and improving humanity than all the churches of Christendom could ever accomplish by their accustomed teachings.

Soon after the little incident above related, we started for the little town of Tecamus, in latitude 0° 56′ north. Here we succeeded in obtaining a few sweet potatoes, some fresh beef, also wood and water. Some of the crew having become dissatisfied about something, nobody ever knew what, not even themselves, took it into their heads to run away. So one night the boat-steerer of the larboard boat, who with his crew had the watch on deck from two to four, A.M., lowered the bow-boat silently, put in all their traps, and started off, nobody knew where but themselves. The next morning at daylight, news got into the cabin that Chadwick (the boat-steerer referred to) and all his crew were gone. Capt. Chase was nearly frantic with anger, raved like a madman, threatening all sorts of vengeance if he ever caught them; and, as soon as our breakfast was over, he went ashore, and offered the captain of a Peruvian military company stationed there a large bounty to take and deliver them on board the ship. This coming to their ears through some of the natives, they concluded that it would be impossible to elude the vigilance of the soldiers, any of whom would murder a man for ten cents, and that the best thing they could do was to come on board of their own free will. The next night, at about two, A.M., they came alongside. A more dejected, disheartened set of men never lived; and at daylight the captain had every one of them triced up to the main rigging for a thrashing. He gave the ringleader (Chadwick) forty lashes, less one, with the "cat." The others fared much better. That is a most brutal and unmerciful way of correcting the errors of misguided and humble delinquents. It was a heart-sickening scene to witness, but we were all compelled to. That old hardened sea-dog, with one foot in the grave, tied up seven misguided fellow-beings, and laid on to their bare backs, with the whole of his brute force, that cutting cat-o'-nine-tails, until the blood ran down their lacerated bodies in streams. It was the first and last time I ever witnessed such a brutal sight.

Having taken aboard our supplies for another short cruise, we went to sea. This time we cruised in the vicinity of the Cocoa Islands some three months; in which time we succeeded in filling the ship within a few barrels, and then started once more for Tombez, to fit for home, where we arrived in due time. We felt happy and joyous at our successful voyage thus far, and, as soon as we had our supplies on board, made sail for home. This is always cause for rejoicing, after a long and successful campaign, either at sea or ashore. Ninety-three days from the time we left Tombez, we entered the port of Edgartown, from whence we sailed thirty-eight months before.

The only casualties on the passage home were the accidental loss of two of the crew; one a boy by the name of Joseph Coombs, who fell from the mizzen-top, and was killed by the fall; the other, William Berresford, from the North of England, who fell off the jib-boom when assisting to furl the jib, while running before the wind in a heavy squall. After our oil had all been taken to Nantucket, the ship followed. After arriving we were all paid off, and started for our respective homes. I arrived at my home the latter part of February, 1840. Thus ends a long and prosperous voyage.

CHAPTER VII.

I REACHED home the last of February from my last voyage as detailed in the preceding chapter, and was undecided whether to go to sea again, or settle down on *terra firma.*

My previous voyage had been a success, and my friends thought I had better go to farming; they picturing to my verdant mind the enormous profits sure to accrue from such an effort, if properly managed. More to please friends than to fill my coffers, I *reluctantly* consented to abandon the sea altogether, and bend all my energies in tilling the soil. My wife, in fact all my relatives and friends, congratulated me upon my far-seeing business quali- ties; all promising to aid me with their unquestioned wisdom (in their own estimation), if I should need it in my new occupation. Although I had worked on father's farm when a mere lad, — that is, when they could make me, — yet I knew no more about farming details than a child ten years old.

To my question how I could manage a farm, with my inexperience, one said, " Oh, that's easy enough ! You can hire a good steady man to take charge of things for the first year or so, when you can manage it yourself." He suggested a young man by the name of John —— as a suitable person for the responsible station. I did not make a purchase for months after this conversation : yet, through the influence of his friends when I had purchased, this same John got the position, at a monthly salary of twelve dollars the year round. All saw at once that I was a stupid jackass, and that they would have no difficulty in wheedling me into any thing. When it was settled that I was to turn my attention to farming, my friends looked round for a suitable place, and finally hit upon a fifty-acre lot which wasn't worth the gift, as far as getting a living from it was concerned, and advised me to purchase it. They were all good church-members, and I an ignorant infidel to their creeds; and I didn't think it best to provoke their indignation as I should, provided I presumed to differ from their wise judgments about a farm. This being the case, I bought it, or rather they bought for me; for I never saw the man who sold it, until months after it came into my possession. All I had to do was to give them the money; and they, not I, took the deed in my name. As there were no buildings on the land, I commenced at once to put up a barn. My brother Henry, who lived across the road which divided our farms, kindly offered me a home in his house, until I could put up one for myself. I had made no calculations as to the real cost of getting up the necessary buildings for an establishment of that sort, having depended entirely upon the testimony of my officious friends, who were ever on hand with their advice. By the time I had the barn ready for occupancy, I found that it would cost more money than I could spare, or, at any rate, wanted to invest in an enterprise, the success of which was extremely doubtful to my mind. If I had been a little less credulous in the first place, and depended more upon my own figures, instead of listening to the advice of my friends, the barn would never have been built. It cost about three times as much in money as I was told it would, besides my own time and labor.

This revelation was a damper upon my going any farther in the building business, at least until I had ascertained somewhere within a thousand or two dollars how much the building would cost. In fact, when alone I seriously contemplated giving up the whole concern, and going to sea again. For here I was, being all the time tormented to death with Tom, Dick, and Harry giving me unsolicited advice, no two of whom agreed upon any one thing of the slightest importance; each wanting to be thought the wisest and most knowing. Sometimes I hardly knew whether I was on my head or heels, and often went off a half-mile to hide myself amid the foliage of the friendly thicket, where I could have a breathing-spell. I finally concluded to stop just where I was, and let the farm, such as it was, take care of itself; if I didn't, it with my friends would take care of me. This I told my advisers, and in such a way that they could not mistake me. But I wasn't to get off so easy with this experience in farming. After I had got my barn completed, I made the remark, that it would have been much cheaper to have bought a place with buildings on it. This coming to the ears of a Mr. Jones, whose farm joined mine on the north, and he learning my determination not to build any more, and wishing to sell his place, thought this a good opportunity to dispose of it. So he set about the operation in true Yankee style. In the first place, he talked with some of my friends about it, requesting them to induce me to talk with him in relation to a purchase; telling them that it would be cheaper than to build, as he would sell his whole farm, improvements and all, for fifteen hundred dollars, which would be less than the cost of the buildings alone. I was such a poor diplomate, that the "bait" took; and I called upon Mr. Jones in relation to his place, and, without any circumlocution, asked him his price. He pretended at first that he didn't want to sell, but if it would accommodate me he would sell, but doubted whether he could better himself. He also pretended that he had not any price fixed upon it. I told him I understood he offered it for fifteen hundred dollars. " Well, yes," he said, " I did say I would sell it for that amount, but had forgotten it until you brought it to my mind." He knew all the time he was lying on purpose to blind me; and his hanging-back was for the same purpose. However, the bargain was made there and then; and the next day the conveyance was made for fifteen hundred dollars. Now, then, I owned a farm with good well-finished buildings, a well of pure water, and quite a large orchard of grafted fruit, with the exception of a few trees. The next thing to do was to stock it, get farming implements, &c.; and, as I was *non compos* in the art of farming, I was advised to secure the services of the aforesaid John before it was too late. So down I go to his home, and engage him as before related. He knew every thing; at least he succeeded in making me think so, and at once commenced operations. He made out a list of what he said was actually needed, which I procured without even a question; for now I had an *autocrat* for a master, whose word was law and gospel combined, for he was very pious. To doubt his infallibility was to lose his valuable services, which, according to the testimony of my friends, or rightfully *his* friends, could not be replaced on this planet.

In due time every thing was procured, and the farm put in running order. John would be ever telling me to do this or that, and I did it. If he told me not to do a thing, I didn't do it. In fact, I was as patient and docile as the most abject slave. Things went on swimmingly through the summer and fall, with not a particle of friction; and after every thing was harvested, the corn in the cribs, the wheat, oats, apples, and vegetables in their appropriate places, I made out a careful estimate of the products of the farm for the year just closed; and, after deducting John's wages, there was not quite five dollars left to subsist on for a whole year; to say nothing about my own labor, or the wear and tear of the implements, &c.

When I showed the account current to my friends, they made me believe that that was as much as could be expected the first year, and assured me I would at least do one hundred per cent better the succeeding year; but when I told them that even then I would have but ten dollars for a whole year's work, and before that time my money would all be gone, and asked what should I do then, " Oh!" says they, "something will turn up." Something did turn up the next spring, as will presently be seen.

My money failed about the beginning of winter; but by borrowing, begging, and running in debt, I managed to get through until spring. John stuck by as per contract; but by the following spring it got noised all through the neighborhood, that I was out of money, and had hard work to squeeze through the past winter; and the very friends who were so officious in advising and almost compelling me to purchase the farm, under the delusion that I could make a fortune out of it, were the very first ones, as is often the case, to turn round and call me a squanderer. " It's just right for him. I knew it would be so," was bandied from one mouth to another. It was the common talk among my friends, that any one with a particle of sense could have made a good thing of it. Sometimes one would say, " I pity him," " I wish he had a better lookout," &c. At last I got hold of the gossip going round, but found it useless to make any comments as to who was the cause of my failure. Some advised John to leave, but he knew which side his bread was buttered. I wish he had left; for he was nothing but a bill of costs to me, or, in other words, the farm was no better for his services, and I'm sure my pocket was no better. All that winter and spring I had indulged the hope of something better turning up; precisely what it was, if any thing, I hadn't the remotest idea. My money was all gone, and with it my friends. We commenced our spring work as usual, and it had got into the first days of May, when one morning, about ten o'clock, while working alone, some twenty rods from the house, I heard some VOICE say, "Get ready, and start for Boston at once." With the words ringing in my ears, I laid down the hoe I was working with, and started for the house. Arriving there, I told my wife I was going away, and packed into an old leather valise a few shirts, socks, and dickies, and, bidding good-by to my wife, started for father's, some five miles distant. John was at work with the horses, at the farther end of the field when I left. Thus ended my farming operations. I still owned the farm; but, as its disposal properly belongs to the succeeding chapter, I will end this at the moment when I started for Branch Mills, the residence of my father.

12

CHAPTER VIII.

As this chapter will prelude accounts of some of
the quite remarkable scenes in my eventful history,
I am induced to give the details of much which is
of no importance only so far as it is connected with
the more prominent features of the story. Every
incident I shall relate, excepting my hearing the
VOICES, can be vouched for by persons now living,
who participated in all things narrated within these
pages.

Resuming where I left off at the end of the preceding chapter, I state that, after I found father, I
told him I was going away, and wanted him to loan
me thirteen dollars, and also to carry me to Hallowell, where I could take the boat for Boston; that
I was now ready, and wanted to start at once, so as
to get to Hallowell before the steamer left. He said
he hadn't the money by him, but would borrow it.
With this understanding we harnessed the horse to
the wagon, and started off. We arrived in time: he
having got the money from a friend of his on the
way down river.

Passengers for Boston then did not pay their passage-money until after leaving Bath, the last landing on the river. I was anxious to stop at Bath, if time would allow, to pay a bill of three dollars I was owing there. So, when the boat hauled alongside the wharf, I asked the mate if I would have time to go up town, telling him where I wanted to go. "Certainly," he responded: "we shall lay here two hours;" adding, "You could go to Brunswick and back before we shall get away." With this assurance I took my valise, and started up town, found my creditor, a Mr. Hatch, paid him, and started immediately for the wharf. I did not stop a moment after I got through with my business: yet when I first got in sight of the boat her bow was swinging off. I knew it was useless to try to get on board, and stood there, stone still, almost paralyzed; for there was but one boat a week for Boston at that time, and no railroads or other conveyance except sailing vessels. I did not move out of my tracks for a few moments; in the mean time I was running over in my mind the real situation of affairs. Here I was among strangers, with but ten dollars in my pocket. To go home and wait would take all my money, with no chance of getting more; and, if I stopped at a hotel, the consequences would be alike fatal. After a little calm reflection, I concluded to find a cheap boarding-house, and run my chances until the boat was on her next trip.

With this determination I slowly retraced my steps up town, watching for a sign with "*boarding*" on its sides; but found none until I got near the middle of the town, when I came to a little second or third rate tavern, kept, as I found out afterwards, by a Mr. Beals. The moment I saw it, I felt impressed to make application for board, which the landlord said would be seven dollars a week: that would leave me three to get to Boston with, and fifty cents for incidentals, such as tobacco, &c. I engaged to stop one week; and he assigned me a room at once, where I deposited my valise, and then got supper.

After I got through my evening meal, I strolled down around the wharves, among the shipping. It being "knock-off" time with the carpenters and laborers, I met many going to their humble homes, apparently satisfied with their day's work, some carrying home an armful of wood, and by their jolly conversation, intermixed with snatches of favorite songs, appeared perfectly happy. I compared my feelings with theirs, and could but notice the marked difference; but being favored *naturally* with a happy, harmonious disposition, I quelled a momentary feeling of discontent, with the thought that, although things looked a little shaky in my present prospects, yet they might be infinitely worse. This reflection smoothed the momentary waves of adverse circumstances, and all was quiet.

By nine o'clock I had finished my walk, went to the hotel, and immediately to bed. After I had retired, my mind seemed perfectly at ease as to the future; nothing seemed to mar its serenity. Being wide awake, my mind kept running from one thing to another, when suddenly it became, as it were, illuminated. Many things flitted across my vision for a moment, and were gone. Among them was one,

which I had never even thought of, and which came
to me in the form of a question. It was this: " Why
wouldn't this be a good place to carry on the whaling
business?" This question subsequently came into
my mind for a moment while I was walking round
the wharves; but I treated it as we often do any
random thought that may intrude itself upon us for
a moment, which we think may not have any significance whatever, and let it pass away as it came.
At length I began to consider that the business part
of the community there were largely interested in
ship-building, that they were decidedly a commercial
people, largely interested in the freighting business;
and, as the whaling business was a lucrative one, I
could see no reason why it couldn't be adopted as a
part of the commercial business of the place. I concluded that, to start it, only needed some energetic
movement in that direction. Up to this time, I
hadn't thought of having any thing to do in getting it
up. The fact that it required a large capital to begin
with, was sufficient to check any such aspirations,
had they presented themselves. While thinking the
matter over, and weighing the natural advantages
of the place for carrying on the business, and wishing I had the means to start it, I heard a VOICE say,
" Try it."

Although I had been in the habit of considering
favorably any thing suggested from that mysterious
source, here was a case where my judgment rebelled.
What chance will there be of succeeding, supposing
I do try it? was the question I asked myself. I
had no money, nor any visible way of obtaining any.

12*

What few business friends I had would not feel justified in risking their surplus capital in an experiment, the success of which was so questionable. I finally concluded that my VOICE had made a blunder this time; or maybe I had made a mistake myself, and did not hear any thing, and was deluded to put that construction upon some fancy because the VOICE heretofore had always proved itself a real friend to me in tight places. I had no sooner settled in my mind the above explanation, than I heard it say, clear and distinctly, "Raise the means by subscription." This was a new idea; maybe I might, I thought. And straightway I got up, dressed, got some paper out of my valise, and pencil in hand commenced writing out a subscription paper, and wrote and altered more than twenty before I got one to exactly suit me; which I did not accomplish until the next day at about ten, A.M. After I had got it to my liking, what should I do with it? I knew nobody there, and nobody there knew me: it was not likely that people would subscribe to a paper of that kind, much less pay out any money to a person who was a perfect stranger to everybody in the city.

However, when I got the instrument to suit me, as before stated, I started forth with no plan of procedure laid out. Seeing my landlord, Mr. Beals, standing alone on the piazza, without a premeditated thought I involuntarily walked up to him, and asked him who was the richest and most influential man in town. Without a moment's reflection, he answered, "Capt. John Patten." Upon inquiry, I found he lived "up at the North End." Off I started; and, as it was near three miles, I did not arrive at his house until after eleven o'clock. From the servant who answered the bell, I learned that Capt. Patten was in. She showed me into the parlor; and, after waiting a few moments, a large, tall, well-built, splendid-looking man entered, whom I took to be the man I was looking for, which proved true. After ascertaining the above, I took out my paper, and handed it to him, observing that that would explain the object of my visit. He took it, and read it carefully over; after doing which he looked at me with that peculiar expression one exhibits when occasion calls upon him to put a damper upon hopes, and to do it kindly. After looking at me a moment or two, with that strange, sad expression of countenance, as if thinking what words would be most suitable to the occasion, he said, " Young man, I do not like to throw cold water upon any new enterprise, but am obliged to say, that in my opinion it would be impossible for any man, if he was ever so influential, to get up an enterprise of that kind here in the way proposed in your paper. And to present my reasons," he continued, "let me tell you a story. A few years ago, a wealthy business man, who was extensively known as a man of probity and honor, circulating in the best society of the city, and universally loved and respected, got the same idea in regard to the whaling business that you have. He talked it up among his business friends, and tried to get their co-operation, telling them that he had made it in his way to get posted up as to its pecuniary results, which would be highly satisfactory. And although he could have fitted out the expedition with his own money, and, if he lost every dollar invested in the enterprise, it would not interfere with the continuance of his legitimate business, yet he wanted to make it a popular affair by getting the thing up partly by subscription. He drew up a paper not dissimilar to yours, excepting that he obligated himself to furnish funds for one half of the enterprise out of his own private purse, if the business men of the city would the other half by subscription. Some few subscribed small sums, and for one whole year he tried his best to accomplish his object; and at last, finding it would not go, gave it up.

"In less than a year after this, another man, equally popular and responsible, made the same proposition, using every effort his immense influence could suggest; but after six months' trial he too gave it up. Since then, some three years, I have heard nothing more in regard to it until now;" continuing, "As I said in the first place, I do not want to put a damper on your efforts; but I tell you these things to show you the utter impossibility of carrying out your project through the means proposed in your paper."

He looked at me as though trying to see the effect of his story. But, strange as it may appear, it had not the slightest effect upon my mind, that is, of a discouraging nature. Seeing that he was waiting for me to say something, I merely said, "If you will put your name down, I will try;" not caring whether it was one dollar or one thousand, for in real truth I hadn't the remotest idea myself of succeeding: what

I had done was purely mechanical. It served to keep me busy, and that was all I expected. As I was an entire stranger there, I thought it was nobody's business how I occupied my time, as long as I didn't interfere with the rights of others.

After writing his name on the paper, he looked up to me saying, " I was about to put down one thousand dollars; but, if you lack another thousand to insure the enterprise, count on me for it." I said, " Whatever you would do under any circumstances, do it now." So, instead of one, he put down two thousand dollars. My paper called for but eighteen thousand, and his subscription made one-ninth of the entire sum. He told me afterwards, that he should have subscribed that amount if he had no way of meeting it, so sure he was that it would be the last of it. Before leaving, I asked him for the name of the next most influential man. He named Henry Tolman, pointing in the direction where Tolman was building a new house, and where I would be most likely to find him. Off I started, it being some two miles to the south and west of where I then was. After arriving I found Mr. Tolman smoking a cigar, and at the time when I approached him looking up to the top of his house, where some tinmen were at work on the roof, directing them as to how he wanted the work done.

As soon as I saw he was disengaged, I showed him my paper, without saying a word. He took it, and, seeing John Patten's name down for two thousand dollars, immediately put his down for the same, without apparently even reading what he was signing;

obviously thinking, that, as Capt. Patten had subscribed so liberally, he need have no hesitancy in
doing the same.

After he had subscribed, I asked him the same
question I did Capt. Patten when I left him. Mr.
Tolman told me to call upon Capt. James Patten, a
brother of the first subscriber, who with the same
alacrity as the last one put down one thousand dollars; making, in the three, over one-fourth of all I
called for.

Capt. James Patten sent me to a Mr. Hyde, a
hardware dealer, who put down five hundred dollars,
and asked no questions. So I went on, getting directions from the last one whom to apply to next, and I
never made an application that was refused; every
one subscribed according to his means and inclination, seldom even looking very carefully at what he
put his name to, depending entirely upon the well-
known sagacity and business qualifications of those
who subscribed before him.

Thus I went on, and in less than two weeks I had
$19,950 subscribed by responsible men, which, as will
be seen, was nearly two thousand more than I asked
for. I then put up notices in different public places,
requesting the stockholders to meet at Samuel Stinson's counting-room, and organize. This announcement operated like an electric shock among them,
for they never expected to hear from me after they
had put down their names. However, they all met
as per request, and a jollier set of men I never saw.
It seemed a complete surprise to all, with a few
exceptions. When they began to arrive I could

hear the question as acquaintances met, " Why, you here ? You in this ? " Capt. John Patten was one of the first on the ground ; who, after entering the office and not seeing me, asked Mr. Stinson where I was, and said, " I want to see him." I heard the question and answer, being then behind the door blacking my boots. At first I thought he might be dissatisfied about something that I had done, but was soon convinced to the contrary ; for, as Mr. Stinson pointed to where I was, he came to me, holding out his hand in the pleasantest way possible, and said, laughing, "I congratulate you upon your success. I never expected to see you after you left my house, but you have taken us all by surprise. In fact, I doubt whether there was another man in the world, who, under much more favorable circumstances, could have done what we all thought an impossibility ; for our best men had failed in getting one-half the stock taken up after a whole year's effort. At any rate, I heartily congratulate you, and will do all in my power to assist the enterprise."

After a sufficient number had arrived, I called the gentlemen to order, stating in a few words the object of the meeting, and requested them to select one to preside until the officers were chosen. Leaving out all details, the proper officers were selected, a president, vice-president, and five directors, to take charge of the business for the company, which was named " The Bath Whaling Company." At this meeting it was unanimously voted that I should take charge of fitting out the expedition, and command the ship when ready for sea. The affair had been gotten up so quietly, that hardly any outside of those engaged in it knew any thing about it ; and scarcely one, even among the subscribers, until after the meeting, knew my name, or what I had to do with the business. The next day the papers came out with very flattering puffs for me, eulogized me as one endowed with wondrous persuasive powers, because able to get up the expedition entirely by subscription. To say the least, I felt highly flattered. But there was one consideration that gave me many uneasy thoughts. Up to this time, no questions had been asked as to who I was, which I expected would come before they would intrust me with so much property. I thought that as business men they would want to know something about my qualifications to take charge of such an operation. How did they know, excepting from my own lips, that I had ever been a-whaling ? I had no one to refer to nearer than Nantucket; and there, even, I was not known excepting as one who had gone several voyages : the captain and officers with whom I had sailed were most of them at sea. These thoughts haunted me night and day, after the meeting resolved to prosecute the enterprise, until I had my papers from the Custom House, duly signed and countersigned by the proper officials. Strange as it may seem, the question was never asked, and all they knew about me was from myself.

All things being settled, as far as the preliminaries for the voyage were concerned, we set about to find a suitable vessel for our purpose.[1] At last we hit

---

[1] I agreed to take one-eighth of any vessel we might purchase;

upon a large double-decked brig of three hundred and eight tons register, called the "Massasoit," belonging to Samuel Stinson & Co., and Capt. Thomas Trott who commanded her. The purchase was made ; but she was under a charter to carry a load of pine lumber to the Western Islands, which would occupy some two months.

While she was gone on that trip, I was busily engaged in getting the necessary outfit ready on her return. In this I was unusually successful. The ship "Science" of Portland, Me., had made three unsuccessful voyages in the whaling business, which so disheartened the owners, that they determined to give up further efforts in the business, and had advertised to sell all her whaling-gear, boats, &c., at auction. This was most opportune for our enterprise, as we doubtless could purchase for half price, or less, all our whaling-gear, which was a large part of the outfit. When the time fixed for the sale had arrived, attended by one of the directors of the company I went to Portland, and succeeded more favorably than we anticipated. Before this, our vessel had returned, and was undergoing some alterations and repairs. One of the alterations was, in changing her from a brig to a bark, as in the latter "rig" she would be much more serviceable and handy for our purpose, than in the former.

In fitting away an expedition of this kind, in a new place, where every thing has to be manufac-

and with my commissions, and five hundred dollars which I got through a mortgage on my farm, I managed to pay up my interest in her.

13

tured, and everybody is ignorant of the business, it takes much more time than where workmen understand what is wanted, and know how to do it : consequently it was not until the 10th of November that the crew was got on board, and the ship ready to haul into the stream.

I didn't go home, nor let my family know where I was or what I was doing, until the 1st of November, when I had made sure that I should command the ship, by getting papers from the Custom-House, in which I was named as commander of the bark " Massasoit; " then having business connected with the ship, at Augusta, some twelve miles from home, I made my appearance there unexpectedly. Before telling my wife what I had been up to, I went over to brother Henry's, near by, for I wanted to secure him as chief mate, I knowing he was a most efficient officer, and an excellent whaleman; which latter qualification is of more practical importance, in a voyage of this kind, than all others combined. When I told him what I had been doing, that I had a ship almost ready for sea, and that I wanted him for my first officer, he says, " You lie." Producing my papers convinced him ; and we started immediately for father's house, arriving there just as they were sitting down to supper. They making way for us, we joined them at the festive board. After we had submitted to the religious rite of sitting half an hour or so in silence, before partaking of a mouthful, father asked me where I had been, and what I had been doing? I told him I hadn't been far, waiting for Henry to tell them, as agreed upon.

Henry answered for me, telling father that I had bought a ship, and was most ready for sea, and that he was going mate of her. Father says, " I don't believe it." The proof being produced, I saw father lay down his knife and fork ; and after a moment or two he said, " I shouldn't be surprised to hear that David was crossing the Alps with an army of men yet." My farming operation, as before related, was enough to satisfy them of my utter inability to manage any business of the least importance ; and hence the surprise. When news of it got noised through the neighborhood, as I afterwards learned, it only produced ridicule and laughter at my wild experiment. Some said, " If he couldn't manage a farm with a host of friends to assist him, how can he command a large ship? Bah! it's all nonsense." This and much more was the constant gossip of my friends. Some said they didn't believe I was going in a ship at all ; and, if I was, it was in some menial station, &c. The old adage, " They that laugh last, laugh best," proved true in this case ; for I not only commanded for the voyage, but what was more, I made it a lucrative operation for the owners, and myself as well.

One more incident in this connection, before I go to sea, and I am done with operations on the land until the voyage is ended.

It will be recollected that after I bought a piece of land to make a farm of, and finding that to put up buildings would cost more than the farm adjacent, on which was a good house well finished, with barn and outbuildings, &c., and that I could get the land for nothing, I bought this farm, paying what I could, and giving notes for the balance, secured by a mortgage on the whole. One of these notes was already due; and Mr. Jones, of whom I bought the farm, finding I was going to sea, watched for my coming home to bid my folks good-by just before sailing. Finding out after my arrival when I should leave home, he preceded me to Augusta, got out a writ or something else, put it into the hands of a sheriff; and he and the officer watched for me at the bridge spanning the river at Augusta, knowing I should cross there. When I went on to the bridge, the officer served a process on me, saying I was his prisoner. Upon inquiry I found out the author of my new trouble. The officer took me directly into some kind of a court, and there I met Mr. Jones. I had never been arrested before, nor seen a court-house. I felt terribly bad. Here I was a prisoner, while my ship, with her crew on board, was lying in the stream waiting for me. What should I do? These thoughts were weighty ones for me at that particular juncture of my life. The fact was, by the time I got into the court-room, seeing so many lawyers, and every thing so solemn and formal, the judge sitting so dignified and important on the judicial bench, I became so frightened that I hardly knew whether I was on my head or heels. I was completely demoralized.

The case came on soon after I entered. Mr. Jones's lawyer opened the case, talking over something I did not understand. After he got through, the judge asked who was the respondent in this case.

Of course I was; but I felt so confused, I didn't know what he was driving at. Somehow or other, something was said, what I know not, that convinced me that what he said meant, Who is the culprit? At any rate, I ventured to say I was. By this time every thing was confused, at least I was: every thing, court-room, judge, and jury, seemed whirling round. This lasted but a moment, when the judge asked, Have you any counsel? I had sense enough to say, No. I suppose I was looking bad, for the judge asked me very pleasantly to explain matters. His kind words re-assured me, and I went on and told the whole story, — how that I had a ship, with the crew aboard, waiting for me, and that Mr. Jones knew I was going to sea, and that, if he had said a word about it when I was where I had friends, I could have arranged it, if any thing was amiss; but I had thought that, as he was well secured, he had no thought of stopping me. He then asked Mr. Jones if the farm was not worth what it was mortgaged for. "Certainly," says Mr. Jones. "Very well, then. Give me the notes and mortgage, and I will pay you the balance due, and relieve this young man from a position which you ought to blush for putting him into." I was relieved. The business was all fixed up in a few minutes, when Judge Fuller, turning to me said, "Capt. Densmore, I congratulate myself for this accidental acquaintance, also congratulate you on your success; and when you return call and see me." Then taking my hand he said, "Now go, and may you succeed, as I believe you rightly merit, and may old Neptune smile with favor on his young *protégé*."

13*

With this I left, but being too late for the boat concluded to go up home, and report the day's adventure, but more to show up this Quaker Christian.
When I told father the story, he could hardly believe
it, and wondered how " Richard could do such a
mean act." The next day started for Bath with a
light heart, and arrived before night. I found that
some of the men had deserted, which delayed me a
day or two; but on the 19th of November, 1842,
went to sea with light winds from the south-west.

CHAPTER IX.

MY crew all told, including officers, amounted to thirty-four men, mostly foreigners. They represented all grades of society, some having held important positions among their fellows; but dissipation, one way and another, caused them to fall from their high estate. My second officer, Mr. —— ——, had commanded several large ships on foreign voyages, and was a splendid sailor. As a whole, the crew was an average one for a whaler. A large per cent of them were "green hands," who, as soon as we got to sea, were sick; and, the old sailors being drunk, the chances for taking in or making sail were not very flattering.

After we got outside, the wind was light all day from the eastward; the weather looked unsettled and threatening all round the compass. Most of the old sailors being intoxicated, and the "green hands" sea-sick, I took the precaution, just before sunset, to double-reef the topsails, take in the mainsail and jib, and be prepared for a sudden change of wind, which, from appearances, was not unlikely, especially at that time of the year. It was well that I took these precautionary steps; for a little after two, A.M., I was in the cabin looking on the chart to ascertain what course would clear the banks, if, as I expected, the wind should come suddenly from the north-west, and I felt the ship gently careen over to starboard. What wind there had been through the night, thus far, came from the eastward; the ship was braced up on the starboard tack, heading north. Looking at the tell-tale compass overhead, I found the wind came from the north-west. I jumped on deck, and found her hard aback, fore and aft. I allowed her to swing round, until, bracing round the yards, she was going ahead, then settled the topsails on the cap, hauled out the rigging, and kept her before the wind. Although the topsails were double-reefed, it was daylight before the other reef was put in, owing to the intoxication of the crew.

The next morning I sent the mate into the forecastle, with instructions to take every keg or jug that contained liquor of any kind, and bring it aft; which he executed with no difficulty, as most of them were in a sleepy stupor. The gale increased as the night advanced, and the only thing we could do was to keep her before it; and it was not until the third day that the storm abated, after it had carried us clear of the coast. Now we could take our leisure in putting things in order, and getting ready for whaling. The third night out, and while the gale was at its height, the second officer, Mr. ——, came to my state-room, and told me some of the men were in a fit, and he thought dying. I got on deck as soon as possible, and at once divined the cause to be the sudden breaking-off from their grog after long indulgence. The old cooper was the worst off of any; he was on his back sprawling round on deck, muttering incoherent words, and frothing at the mouth like a mad dog. Although I had never seen any one suffering with delirium tremens, yet I seemed to know the remedy. I sent for some liquor, sat down by the side of the old cooper, got his head in my lap, and poured through his set teeth some of the rum. In a few minutes he revived: the snakes and devils, which he persisted in saying were trying to strangle him, left. I served three other affected ones with the same antidote. After this, I served them with liquor every day, gradually tapering off, and in a week or so they became all right. I did not stop at the Western Islands, on account of its being winter, and the difficulty of landing. When we had been at sea about two weeks, I found the vessel did not work well; we couldn't keep her to the wind; when braced sharp up she would constantly fall off, owing to a lack of after-sail. It will be recollected that when we bought the vessel she was a full-rigged brig. In changing her to a bark we had to do away with the large trysail, and substitute in its place a small spanker, less than one-eighth the dimension of the former. Of course this made a vast difference in balancing the sails, when close hauled on a wind. To remedy this defect, one of two things must be done, —either put on a mizzen topsail, or else take out the mizzenmast and put on the trysail again. As I couldn't do the latter, for want of materials, I decided to adopt the former. This being settled, we went to work making the necessary sails, which we soon completed, when, taking a spare topsail-yard for crotchet-yard, and a topgallant-yard for mizzen topsail-yard, we soon effected the needed change, after which the ship worked beautifully. As I was agent for both owners and underwriters, I had the right to make any change for the safety of the ship that I saw necessary; and although this right was not originally questioned, yet, as will be seen further along, the underwriters made a question of it in law, with the hope of getting rid of paying insurance claimed by the owners, because of her getting ashore. As I had determined not to touch at the Western Islands, for reasons before stated, I shaped my course directly to the Cape de Verd Islands, situated near the west coast of Africa, and where we arrived in about three weeks after leaving home. Here we left letters at the American consul's, on one of the principal islands, to be forwarded home.

The next morning, and while some of the islands were still in sight, an incident transpired which I think worthy of recording, as it will be apparent that some unseen power had a hand in quelling what might have proved a serious affair.

Some of the broken down "*has-beens*," after their rum had failed them, and their reason had returned, found out for the first time that they were bound round Cape Horn on a whale-ship. The contemplation of this was more than they could reconcile with their ideas of freedom; and they set about getting up a project, which, if successful, would relieve them of their obligations. Their plan was, as I subsequently learned, to mutinize, dispose of me and the first officer, compel the second mate to take the ship into some port, dispose of the ship and cargo, divide the proceeds among themselves, and live at ease the rest of their lives. The mode of procedure to bring it about, as agreed upon between the conspirators, was for Bill —— the steward, who had free access fore and aft, and who slept in one of the staterooms in the cabin, to get into a wrangle with me or the first mate, when they would hop in, as they termed interfering in Bill's favor, and in the mêlée dispose of me and the mate, and, if they were ever apprehended, would swear that it was accidental when in the general fight. This was all very well; and, if there had been no resistance, would have fulfilled their hopes in getting possession of the ship. But they had " reckoned without their host." They had made all their preparations with a good deal of care; secured all the boarding-pikes and boarding-knives, and taken out both pump-brakes, so that we would have nothing to defend ourselves with when the onslaught was made. They had even got ready an empty sixty-gallon cask, with which to block up the cabin gangway, so that whoever was in the cabin could not come to our relief. All these preparations were made without the slightest knowledge on my part. In fact, I supposed that they were unusually pleased with their treatment, as I had determined before I left home to follow a more sympathizing course than was usual on such voyages, and wished them to consider themselves men in every sense of the word, and that they were just as much entitled to consideration as the officers, also that nothing but more favorable circumstances would have enabled the officers to occupy the positions they filled. I tried every possible means to instil these sentiments into their minds, that would not interfere with the discipline actually necessary for the success of the voyage. Their food was precisely the same as ours. I took extra pains to see that their " grub " was well cooked; and I furnished them every morning with " soft . tack " (hot biscuits) for breakfast, a thing scarcely before heard of in any ship, and more especially a whaleman.   Notwithstanding all this, they made themselves believe that they were a very badly used set of men; and, after talking over their grievances, concluded to carry into effect the foregoing plan, and thus free themselves from further obligations. I had a brother and a cousin in the forecastle, and a brother and a cousin among the officers, first and third mates; hence it required the strictest secrecy among the conspirators to mature their plan.

The steward (Bill ——) belonged to a wealthy, aristocratic family, and but for the continued solicitation of his friends, and especially his father, I would not have taken him. I told him and them, over and over again, what he would have to submit to; and that after the novelty had worn off I feared he would become dissatisfied, discontented, and make trouble for himself and inharmony with all hands, which latter would be very detrimental to the success of the voyage, for that depended much upon the free co-operation of all hands.

On the morning referred to, while walking the deck after breakfast, and after Bill and the cabin-boy had eaten, Bill brought up the table-cloth, as is usual, to shake the crumbs overboard. When he was doing this I heard something rattle like knives and forks; and as he was very careless, having lost overboard knives, forks, and spoons before, I thought the rattling indicated another draft upon our culinary inplements. I spoke to him pleasantly, saying, "Be careful, Bill, or soon we shall have nothing to eat with." Upon hearing this, he turned round, saying in an excited tone, "By G—d, I can pay for them if I do." Up to this moment I hadn't the slightest suspicion that any thing was wrong; but, the moment Bill answered as he did, the whole thing was laid open to my mind as clear as though I had been a listener to all their plans. I was not frightened, but became rather more quiet and decided than usual. He had hardly got the words out, before I had him by the collar, not the least angry nor excited. I laid him down on deck easily, alongside of the main-hatch. I placed his feet side by side, merely observing, "As you value your life, Billy, don't you move a finger." I seemed to be somebody else, as I really was, but didn't know it then. The ship was going along with all sail set, wind light, and smooth sea, when I heard myself issue order after order, one to call up all hands, another to take in sail and haul aback the main-yard. What it all meant I did not know, still I was unable to resist doing so. The moment Bill was laid on deck, the news was passed into the forecastle; and, when the mate called all hands, they all came rushing along aft on the weather-side of the deck. I met them at the try-works, and told them

14

to go back, and come aft to leeward, saying firmly, "This is *my* side of the deck." They all stopped as suddenly as though they had brought up against an impassable barrier, and came aft on the lee-side to haul up the main-sail and back the main-yard. While this was being done, Bill lay there quiet as a lamb, hardly daring to breathe, the conspirators passing and repassing him several times, without apparently noticing him. After these several orders were completed, I told the men to stand side by side with their backs leaning against the lee-rail. I whispered to the mate, telling him to take the wheel, and not to speak, concluding with saying, "I can manage this affair alone." While the men were arranging themselves, I told the cabin-boy Tom Mars, a lad of some ten years, to bring up my pistol, that he would find it in the back side of my berth. The men, observing my whispering something to the mate, and Tom handing me the pistol, which I put in my pocket, began to think that I knew all about their plot, and was prepared to meet it. When all hands were standing side by side, I commenced aft; and, where one foot was not precisely in line with the other, I gently tapped it with the toe of my shoe, all the time talking to them, sometimes stroking them caressingly down. When I had got about two-thirds towards the forward end of the string, I came to a man whose real name was Samuel Austin, hailing from Newport, R.I., but was familiarly called " Tom Pepper," from his habit of telling big stories; there being a legend among sailors, that, once upon a time, a sailor with the above name died, and went straight to hell, but was such a notorious liar that the Devil kicked him out; hence Sam was dubbed *Tom Pepper*. Poor Tom's legs were trembling fearfully. I stroked him down, and asked him what made him tremble so. He made no answer, and I passed on to the next. After I had gone the entire length of the line, I made a stump speech, telling them what they had intended to do, with as much precision as they could themselves. I had never heard that they had said that a man shouldn't be tied up in that ship, until I heard myself say it. I told them they had said thus, and, continuing, I said I had never thought of such a thing, but, "because you have said it shouldn't be done, I will do it." Suiting the action to the word, I said, " Billy, jump up here, my boy, and let your friends see me make a spread-eagle of you," a phrase used by boatswains on men-of-war when they tie a man up for a flogging. I sent Tom the cabin-boy to the boatswain's locker for a ball of spun yarn, cut off two short pieces, made Bill hold up his hands, and I gently tied them to the main rigging; then I turned up his shirt over his shoulders, as would be done if he were to be flogged. After doing that, I called their attention to it, assuring them I couldn't be induced to strike a man unless in self-defence, in which case there was no telling what might be done.

After this speech was over, I set Bill free, dismissed the crew, braced forward, and stood on our course again, as though nothing had happened. Thus ended this threatened mutiny, through the intervention of my spirit-guides, who really managed the whole affair through me; proving, to me at least, that but for such assistance what ended so peacefully might otherwise have been fraught with consequences fearful to contemplate. It proved, without a peradventure, who was the real " boss," and that no scheming or threats could intimidate him; and therefore it was well that it happened.

I was not conscious of any assistance, although I knew I was not in my normal condition; but, as I had been so hundreds of times before, I thought nothing of it. I distinctly remember, that after every thing had got a-going as usual, in thinking over the affair, I compared myself with Gen. Jackson, who, when fighting Indians in Florida, had two regiments of the regular army, with their officers, become disaffected from some cause or other, actually start on their homeward march. The general, hearing of it, jumped upon a horse, galloped in front of the column, and halted it: then taking a pistol out of the holster, he threatened to shoot the first man that advanced a step farther. The general told them to go to their barracks; and they did as quietly as lambs, and there was no more trouble. Now, the general probably thought that it was his own prowess alone, that effected such a marvellous change in the firmly made-up resolution of those two regiments of determined men. What, I ask, could one man do with a single pistol in physical combat with two thousand men, with as many loaded rifles? At most he could have killed scarcely more than one man, before he would have been riddled with rifle-balls. No, it was not Gen. Jackson *per se*. Through him a host of spirits pressed back the mutinous spirit, and restored order. So it was with me, although I didn't know it; and so it has proved many times before and since. They, this band of spirits, influenced both me and the mutineers, — me with undaunted courage, them with fear; because they knew themselves to be in the wrong, while I felt strong in the right, which consideration would tend to dishearten them, especially when they saw so much cool determination on my part.

Nothing more of interest happened on our way towards Cape Horn, until off Rio Janeiro, S.A., when the third mate and one of the crew forward were very sick. As I failed entirely to relieve them, I deemed it best to go in somewhere for medical assistance. At first I thought of going into Rio Janeiro, but upon consideration concluded to go into St. Catharine's instead, some seventy miles to the south of Rio, to save expenses. I did not fully make up my mind to go to St. Catharine's, until we were near the entrance to the former place; then, at about four, P.M., up wheel and started, and about three, P.M., came to anchor under the guns of a fort that commanded the entrance to the regular anchorage on the opposite side of the fort from where we were anchored. At daylight the comidant of the fort came on board, when we got under way, and, with him as pilot, were soon anchored in the proper place. As soon after as possible, I took Mr. Crosman, the third mate, who was very sick, in a boat, and started for the city, some twelve miles distant; there being not sufficient water for any thing but vessels of light draught to get nearer the city than where we lay.

14*

I got to the city about eleven, A.M., and immediately applied to the American consul for a physician. He procured a German, who, after examining the sick man, shook his head, muttering some unintelligible lingo, which I took to mean *a very bad case.* He gave him a dose of medicine as black as tar, which the sick man threw up the moment it entered the stomach. He gave the second dose, which did not come up. Poor Frank walked round with me all the afternoon until four, P.M., when I got him into a good boarding-house, where I left him, and his brother to take care of him. Promising to come to the city on the morrow, I left for the ship. After I got on board, found the other sick man still worse. The next morning the wind was blowing so strong I dared not leave the ship; but, the man was so sick, I felt anxious to get him to the city. I sent the mate, with the man on a mattress in the boat, to get there as soon as possible, and said that I would follow at noon if the wind lessened.

He started; and, before he had pulled half the distance, the man died; and, when he got to town, he found that Mr. Crosman had also died at two o'clock that morning. Through the American consul he procured coffins; and, as it was hot weather, the authorities compelled them to bury the two men at once. The mate made two attempts to get the news to the ship so that we could attend the funeral; but the strong wind rendered the attempts abortive. I was much surprised when they came alongside that night with the sad news that both were buried. I went to town the next day, settled up the bills, procured some fresh provisions and vegetables, got my clearance-papers from the Custom-House, and next day went to sea, heading once more for Cape Horn.

Nothing transpired worthy of recording on our southward voyage, until we were off the mouth of the River La Plata, where we encountered a terrible gale, the ship laboring very hard, her upper works twisting and working like a raft. The decks leaked, and at one time I entertained serious apprehensions whether she would weather it or not.

After the gale subsided I spoke a new whale-ship outward bound. I have forgotten her name. The captain came on board, and spent the day with me. I consulted with him about risking a passage round the cape. He advised me not to risk it, as it would be so late before I could get up with it; and with the unanimous advice of all my officers I determined to come north, and do the best I could in a milder latitude. Accordingly, after parting with him I turned her head towards the north, concluding to cruise the season out off Rio Janeiro, where we succeeded in procuring some three hundred barrels of sperm oil.

We then started north again; this time to cruise a few weeks off Charleston, S. C., where there is good whaling at the season of the year we should probably arrive, then go to Fayal, one of the Western Islands, recruit ship, go another cruise, and then home. Before we left for the north this time, an incident occurred which I will relate; not that there is any real importance attached to it, other than as it shows what an influence for good or evil one can exert over others strongly impregnated with all kinds of vice and dissipation. One night when the ship was heading to the northward, as I was walking the deck, my mind in its usual quiet, happy state, all at once I saw, off north-west from us, stretching across the heavens, a crimson curtain, suspended on a gold rod, with gold rings similar to common curtain rings. Although thousands of miles away, I saw them as distinctly as if they had been only a few feet distant. After looking at the scene a moment, I saw two hands, back to back, thrust out from behind the centre of the curtain, as if getting ready to pull it apart both ways. After waiting long enough for me to see it, the curtain was pushed each way until gathered in graceful folds at the end of the rod. When the curtain was being drawn aside, I could hear the rings rattle on the wire as distinctly as if they had been in a room where I was sitting. Almost instantly after the curtain was drawn aside, twenty-four females stepped out from behind the curtain, and stood as if on *terra firma*, facing me. They were of all ages; their dresses, although each different from the others, yet in colors and general make-up harmonized so beautifully, that the presentation passes all description. After remaining a few moments in the position first seen, the vision vanished from view.

I did not recognize any of the faces, although I knew my sister Esther was one of the number. What it all meant, if any thing, I hadn't the remotest idea; but it opened up a new train of thought, which resulted in changing all hands from their usual habits of profanity and their drinking proclivities. Although I was an infidel, in one sense of that often illy applied word, yet the vision, coupled with the religious teachings of my beloved mother, set me to thinking seriously; and, the more I thought, the more I realized that possibly there might be more in religion than I had given it credit for. At all events, one thing was sure, and that was, it would do no harm to " tack ship " in social habits, and run in an opposite direction. I made up my mind, there and then, to try it, and forthwith spoke to the officers about my cogitations, also my determination to give reform a fair trial. They fell in with my ideas at once; and, it being Saturday night, I called all hands into the cabin, and rehearsed to them the above thoughts. No objection being offered, I requested them to assemble in the cabin the next morning at half-past ten, A.M., and we would inaugurate on the sabbath morning attempts to do better; and dismissed them, requesting them to bring along any hymn-books they might possess.

At the appointed time all hands, with the exception of one man at the wheel, congregated in the cabin; and as the ship was purposely put under easy sail the night before, to remain so through Sunday, there was nothing to disturb the harmony of our first meeting. I talked about what interested me most just then; next all hands joined in singing several pennyroyal hymns; then I read a chapter in the Bible, and dismissed the meeting, all seeming pleased with the new order of things.

Consequent upon my request for hymn-books, I

was astonished to find that every man in the ship, with the exception of myself and relative, and two Portuguese sailors, brought aft an old Methodist "pennyroyal" hymn-book, given them by a mother or sister as a remembrancer. After this, instead of hearing obscene, vulgar songs, the ear was greeted every evening forward with hymns and songs of praise. These exercises were continued through the entire voyage, every Sunday morning and evening, with a very few exceptions. In addition to this, I drew up a pledge to abstain from drinking intoxicating liquor; and every man on the ship, headed by myself, signed it, and to it they rigidly adhered while with me. Though they were subjected to temptation many times, not a drop was taken by one of them to my knowledge.

Although this radical change in our every-day mode of speech and living made not the slightest difference in my belief, as far as being saved from the pangs of hell was concerned, on any other ground than our own individual motives, acts, and sentiments, yet the contemplation that I was the direct means of making others more orderly and happy, was a source of extreme satisfaction.

Some amusing incidents transpired among that hardy set of men before they had got accustomed to the new order of things. They were so used to bolting out hard words when expressing themselves to one another, upon different subjects, that it was some time before they could rid themselves of their profane habits.

One evening soon after our devotions commenced,

an old Scotch sailor and a Portuguese were discussing in an earnest manner what was necessary to be done in order to secure an entrance into heaven. The old Scotchman was telling José, his companion, that "everybody must be born again." — "How can that be done?" says Jo. — "D——d if I know," says Jack; "but it must be done, else we shall all go to hell together. Didn't ye not mind what the old man (meaning me) read out of the Bible only this evening, that unless ye be born again ye cannot enter the kingdom of heaven?" This was a puzzle to poor Jo, in fact to both of them. After a brief silence, says Jo, "Then I'll go to hell as sure as God; for my mother is dead and gone, and I can't be born again." — "So is mine," responded old Jack: "my mother died when I was a little child."

I was a silent listener to the above; and, although they talked in a suppressed tone, I heard every word distinctly. The poor fellows were very much discouraged at this impassable barrier in their way to the Celestial City. At our next meeting, in my remarks, I took occasion to comment upon some mysterious passages, and, among the rest, the one that caused Jack and Jo so much uneasiness.

In due time we arrived off Charleston, S.C., where we cruised some four or five weeks, when we headed for Fayal to recruit ship. Two of the men were sick when we arrived at the island; one a Gayhead Indian, the other an Englishman. I got them both into a hospital, detailing two of the crew to wait upon them. The Indian lived but three days, and was buried; the other recovered. Having secured all our necessaries, and given the men a couple of days ashore, got under way, and went to sea. I had determined to go into the Gulf of Mexico, and finish our voyage there, where we arrived in due time. After cruising here some four months, and our provisions getting short, started for home, arriving on the coast directly off Cape Hatteras the last days of January, 1844. Our provisions allowing us only about half our regular rations, we made the most of every breath of wind to shorten the distance between us and home.

Another proof of the watchfulness of my guardian spirits over my destiny transpired at this time, without which the ship and crew must inevitably have been lost. Facts then gave a significant answer to the oft-repeated question of sceptics and bigots, " What practical good has Spiritualism done ? "

One evening, after partaking of a scanty supper, I came on deck with the officers, and went along in the waist, or midships, to watch the sunset; the sea as smooth as a mirror, not a cloud to be seen, the wind light, with all sail set, close hauled on the port tack, and going along not over two knots per hour. We (the mate and self) were leaning over the weather-rail, watching the bright luminary go down, which to me is always a grand sight, when he looks as though he were going into the sea.

At the moment his lower limb touched the surface of the water, I heard some VOICE say in clear, distinct words, *Take in sail.* As the words seemed to come from a person abaft, and close to where I stood, I instinctively looked in that direction. But seeing no one, and feeling that the words came from some invisible source, as the like had hundreds of times before, also knowing the mate was none the wiser for it, and that I never heard it unless in some critical emergency, and then not until all my own resources were exhausted, instinctively I looked overhead, and followed the entire circuit of the horizon; and, seeing nothing to indicate danger, I thought it might be hallucination. However I felt restless and uneasy, and wanted to follow the mysterious instructions. But as we were threatened with still smaller allowance of grub, and every man knew this as well as myself, if I shortened sail under existing conditions, with an unclouded and remarkably clear sky, all hands would naturally think me luny. I felt fidgety, and could not keep still, but kept moving uneasily. The mate was busy talking about when we should probably get home, little dreaming what was agitating my mind. When the sun became fully submerged in the ocean, as it appeared, I saw a brassy haze shoot up directly over where the sun set; and, the farther the sun went down, the higher those ominous streaks went up. At last, being unable to control my disturbed feelings, I turned my back to the rail to hide from sight the cause of my uneasiness. In turning round I noticed this haze had reflected itself on the lee horizon both ways, as far as I could see. This decided me. Instantly I told the mate to call up the dog-watch, and take in sail. He looked surprised, and for a moment hesitated; but as I sung out, "Clew up topgallant-sails," to the watch on deck, he went forward growling. I heard him say derisively, "Hadn't

15

you better send down topgallant-yards and masts?"
I remember saying in response, "Yes, every thing if
I had time." The men came tumbling up out of the
forecastle at hearing the order from the mate to take
in sail, looking overhead and all round, and, seeing
nothing indicating danger, wondered what was up.
I heard the query from some of them, "What's the
matter with the old man? is he crazy?"

However, they entered into the spirit that animated
the watch on deck, and came up with alacrity. I was
here and there, letting go this and that, and cheering the men on to still greater exertions. Seeing me
so earnest to get sail in, operated on their spirits, as
though they were invigorated with fresh vitality.
Each vied with each to see who could do the most,
although they saw no necessity for such hurrying, in
fact, saw no need of taking in sail at all.

By the time we had the light sails secured, the jib
furled, the courses hauled up, and the topsails ready
for reefing, a tornado struck the ship from the west,
with such force, that at first I thought the masts
would go by the board. She was lying side to the
wind, so that it struck the yards endways; the sails
were hauled up snug, and the ship was almost on her
beam-ends, which saved the sails from being blown
into ribbons.

The wind continued with unabated fury all night,
or until four, A.M., when it lulled sufficiently to let us
close-reef the topsails, which would have been impossible before, on account of the perpendicularity of the
yards, and ferocity of the wind which levelled the sea
as smooth as a pond. Thus the ship lay on her side

all night, with a quivering, trembling sensation, much as would be experienced when one is laboring under some fearful excitement.

It seemed as though the wind took the surface of the sea in its arms, and carried it along; for there was a dense, white, spray-like cloud constantly passing over the quivering hull, which looked not unlike a fierce snowstorm driving before a furious gale. The gale abated about noon the next day, when we made sail, and once more stood on our course.

I have here tried to give, in plain, homely language, the exact details, without a particle of coloring, one of the many remarkable experiences of my life. If any should doubt the reality of some intelligence speaking to me, and call my facts hallucinations, or the result of a morbid, over-sensitive imagination, that will make no difference as to the final result; for the intelligent reader must confess (unless he doubts the whole thing, in which case I have nothing to say) that the VOICE telling me in clear, distinct language, what to do, let it come from what source it might, saved the ship from destruction, and all hands from a premature grave in the domains of old Neptune.

I determined, in order to save pilotage through the Vineyard Sound, to come in through what is called the South Channel, lying between Nantucket and the Georges Banks.

Some five days subsequent to the above peril we entered the channel about the 1st of February; and, leaving out details, I will merely say, that for the entire month we experienced nothing but a succession of head-winds, either from the north-east or north-west, bringing us up first on Nantucket, and then on the Georges, so that in the whole month we made but twenty-eight miles *nothing*, as sailors call northward.

Here follows another evidence of the watchful care of my mysterious unseen friend, as I was wont to call the author of these VOICES, who had so many times before given me most important instructions in cases of eminent peril, and how to avoid the serious results sure to follow if the instructions thus given were unheeded.

One day, at twelve, M., found us in nine fathoms water, in a terrible gale from the north-west, drifting on to the shoals. According to the chart, the water lessened in depth one fathom a mile ; and a ship laying to under bare poles is calculated to drift to leeward about one mile per hour: consequently, if no favorable change in the wind intervened, she must strike the bottom at about four, P.M. I had made several unsuccessful attempts to get her on the other tack, but failed for want of sufficient head-sail, having lost the fore and foretopmast stay-sails, which were indispensable, in the absence of the foresail, to throw her bow off. If I could get her heading the other way, she would drift parallel to, instead of directly on to, the bank.

After consulting with the officers, I determined to make one more effort, by hauling down the weather-clew of the reefed foresail, that is, to secure the bunt of the sail with extra gaskets, and loose the weather-yard-arm only. We set about it at once. As she fell off sometimes three or four points, and in coming to would get considerable headway on, I thought by watching for such an opportunity, and having the after-yards well squared in, with the head ones braced sharp up, that when she began to fall off, by rolling the wheel "hard up," and hauling down the weather-clew of the foresail at the same time, the chances for getting her round were quite flattering.

We made the above preparations with all the care our desperate situation demanded; for all hands were well aware that this was our last chance, and if we failed, unless a favorable change of wind took place, no power we possessed could avert the certain destruction of the ship, and the lives of all hands, and that in a few hours at most.

All things being ready, the ship began to fall off more than usual, and the wheel was rolled hard up. In attempting to haul down the clew of the fragment of the foresail, it went into pieces in a moment. This was about half-past one, P.M. Consequently every visible means had failed of getting her round; thus was cut off the only hope of relief from our perilous situation, unless a favorable change of wind took place, which was not probable, as the gale had steadily increased its ferocity since noon, and must in a few hours at the longest bring to an end all sublunary things with us: yet my mind was never more at its ease; and, if I didn't fear provoking an incredulous smile, I would tell the truth, and say that it *never* was freer from troublesome thoughts. I tried to feel different. I remember saying to myself, " Why don't I feel sad ? " knowing that our last chance for escape was cut off. I rubbed my head, to see if I couldn't wake up to the realities of our hopeless condition. I thought of my

15*

wife and child, and of mother's religious teachings and admonitions about the awful *unknown;* but all I could do or think not only did not wake up the feelings that I thought every sensible man ought to have under such hopeless circumstances, but actually made my mind more calm and easy. I began to think that I must either be dreaming, or else was callous to all the finer feelings of my kind. The only regret I felt at the fate staring me in the face was, that my family would miss getting some presents I had for their use; and, among them, two pair of ivory swifts I had made on the voyage with my own hands, which latter I regretted more than all the rest. And although I had got up a revival in the ship, as before stated, yet I was a more confirmed infidel to prevalent Christianity than even before. That is, if we were immortal beings (I said to myself), which I very much doubted, I didn't believe in the vicarious atonement, or that people were doomed to eternal torments in hell for doing what they were compelled to through the circumstances of birth and a false education. It may be asked why I carried on the meetings when holding such a belief: my answer simply is, because I saw it made others happy, and didn't do me nor anybody else any harm.

I have been thus particular in relating the workings of my mind while going through this trying ordeal, to show that this mysterious influence, often spoken of heretofore, put forth power to keep me in this quiet, harmonious state, so that, when the proper time came, it would be able to give me direct instructions how to get out of our apparently hopeless dilemma; which, if my mind had been in an excited state, would probably have been impossible. With this explanation, I will go back to where we made the last unsuccessful attempt to get the ship's head the other way.

Because I didn't want the crew to know the real danger we were in, I kept the "lead line" in my own possession; for, if they knew the real danger, it would demoralize them to such a degree, that, if at the very last moment there should come a chance to save the ship, the men would be unavailable. And then, again, I thought it was merciful to keep them in ignorance as long as I could, and thus save them an eternity of mental suffering condensed into a few hours.

The wisdom of the deception will be apparent as I go along. When I was asked by any of the officers the depth of water, I added several fathoms; when it was nine fathoms, I told them thirteen; and so on. From half-past one, P.M., until near three, all we could do was to hope and look for a change in the wind. About this time I got a cast of the lead indicating less than seven fathoms (forty-two feet), with the tremendous sea rising mountains high. I should not have been surprised then to feel her strike the bottom at any time. A little after three, P.M., I went into the cabin, as I supposed for the last time. I looked at our position on the chart lying on the table; and knowing it to be exactly correct, and noticing that the depth of the water to the leeward of us began to diminish more rapidly the nearer we approached the partially submerged bank, I resolved to call all the hands aft, and tell them the exact state of things ; which facts I knew would put them all on their knees, soliciting help from the Lord.

I went on deck with this determination ; and as I was in the act of beckoning the officers to me (for the strongest lungs could not be heard six feet) for the purpose of calling all hands aft, a VOICE seeming to come from my right, a little aft from where I stood, said in clear, distinct tones, " Ware ship." I responded, as I usually do when no one is near, " I can't : my head-sails are all gone." Instantly the VOICE again said, " Make a sail of the men ; man the weather fore-rigging." Although I had never heard of such a manœuvre before, its practicability flashed through my brain in an instant, and I determined to try it at once ; going upon the principle, " Better try and fail, than never try at all." Instead of setting them to praying, I called them aft, and told them in as few words as possible what I had determined upon, telling them to go forward, and that I would take the wheel myself, and when I made the signal every man in the ship to get into the weather fore-rigging, and keep close to each other ; and, when she was before the wind, to hustle down below, haul over the scuttles to the gangways, and stay there until she came to the wind on the other tack. This precaution I deemed necessary, as coming to with such a sea, I had been told, was dangerous in the extreme. She might ship a heavy sea, and sweep the decks of every thing ; and sometimes the mast would go by the board.

After squaring the after-yards, and bracing up the head ones, they all went forward, thirty-three of them, laughing and joking as much as the threatening danger permitted, about being made into a storm-staysail, to ware ship under; a feat in seamanship never heard of before, they said among themselves.

I lashed myself to the wheel; and when the proper time came, at the signal from me, the men scrabbled into the rigging, where being packed close together they made quite a large sail. The ship worked beautifully. The moment she began to fall off, she gathered headway, and, with the wheel " hard up," went round, and came to on the opposite tack without taking a spoonful of water on deck.

I shall never forget my sensations as she was going round, I standing there amid the conflicting elements, lashed to the wheel, solitary and alone; the ship now on the crest of a mountain wave, now in the trough between those tremendous seas, at another time standing almost on end, as she mounted the smooth side of another. My mind being in a passive, quiet condition, I took in the grand, magnificent scene, with feelings bordering on the sublime.

Soon after we had her head the other way, the wind veered a little to the eastward, which was most favorable to us; for this change set her drifting directly away from the bank. I took a mainstaysail into the cabin, and with plenty of willing hands had it so altered, that we made it do for the fore staysail; but we had much difficulty to bend it, as the ship, from the after part of the fore-chains, was one block of ice. By dint of hard work, we bent and set it.

While bending this, we got an old patched foresail out of the sail-room, strengthened it with bands, bent and reefed it, bent and close-reefed a new maintopsail in place of one that was split soon after the gale commenced; and by eight, P.M., the wind having subsided a good deal, we had her under three close-reefed topsails.

Thus ends another remarkable answer to the question, " What practical good have spirits done ? " By noon the next day, the gale had abated so far that we carried all sail; and by night the wind had veered to the south-west light.

Three days subsequent to our deliverance, we spoke the brig " President " of Portland, Capt. Sargent, from one of the West India Islands, with a load of molasses, bound to Portland, Me.; and, as we were very short of provisions, I went on board to see if I could replenish our exhausted larder. It being a little after sunrise, I took breakfast with him, and staid on board until after dinner. He was standing along under close-reefed topsails; and, the wind being light, I asked him why he was under such short sail. He said he was expecting a " north-easter," and wanted to be ready to meet it. At twelve, M., by observation, Highland Light, on Cape Cod, bore north-west by north fifty-four miles. When I was about leaving, he asked me which way I was going; in or off shore. I told him inshore by all means; continuing, " If I go ashore, I want to go where there is dry land somewhere near." He understood what I had referred to, as I had told him what a predicament I had got into off the Georges Shoals.

He said if I did, and the wind should come from the north-east, which he thought from present indications would be upon us before night, that I would be high and dry on the cape before twenty-four hours. To strengthen his argument, he said that he had been in the West India trade for twenty-two years, had come on to the coast at all seasons, and had never lost so much as a studdingsail sail-boom. He plead so hard, and appeared so earnest, and being withal an old experienced pilot on the coast, I made up my mind to do as he advised. We were heading off shore when I went on board of my ship, braced forward, and as soon as we had all sail set, and yards trimmed, I heard my familiar VOICE say, " Tack ship." With not a moment's hesitation, I told the mate to get ready for stays, the brig bobbing along on the offshore tack under close-reefed topsails. As I drew into the land, the wind gradually veered to the south-west; and by eight, P.M., we had a " smoking south-wester," and at daylight passed in by Sequin Light off the entrance of the Kennebec River, and anchored at Parker's Flats by ten, A.M.

I subsequently learned that Capt. Sargent was blown to the southward of the gulf twice, and six weeks after I left him went ashore on Monnoi Point, and lost vessel and cargo, which cost him a whole lifetime's hard work; for he owned most of the brig, all the cargo, and, being an experienced pilot, hadn't a cent of insurance on either vessel or cargo. His wreck made a poor man of him in his old age. But, as good a pilot as he was, I had a better. I called upon him the following summer, at his home in

Portland, where he was keeping a small meat-market to eke out a scanty subsistence. In speaking of our meeting at sea, he said, " When I saw your ship in stays, I said to my mate, That young man will be high and dry on the cape before daylight."

When reflecting upon this portion of my history, and taking into account my inexperience in coming upon the coast in the winter months, coupled with Capt. Sargent's anxiety occasioned by the course I stood after leaving him, and my habits which usually were to give heed to age and experience, especially when there existed doubts as to what was best to do in certain emergencies, I class it among the most remarkable manifestations of direct spirit aid I ever experienced.

Soon after we anchored, as before related, a couple of river-pilots came on board, whom I engaged to take the ship up to Bath, some fifteen or twenty miles.

It being ebb-tide, we did not get under way until the next morning; and, although the wind was dead ahead, we got under way to beat up on the flood-tide. When arrived at the narrows, within sight of the city, I went below to get ready to go ashore; but the pilots, standing over to the left shore too far, got into the eddy, which was setting very strong inshore; and the ship, having considerable headway on, forced her bow high up among the rocks. It being then tip-top high water, before we could get out a kedge anchor to haul her off, the tide began to recede, and left her hard and fast on the rocks. Finding it impossible to get her off that tide, as she was listed outward, we did every thing in our power to heel her inshore, but failed. When the tide had all run out, she lay almost high and dry on a rocky bottom heeled off shore about thirty degrees. We made all preparations to haul her off the next high water ; but, as the preceding · tide was the highest of a high course, the following highwater fell off near a foot. There would not be another as high course of tides for months; and the best thing to be done was to discharge her where she lay.

Accordingly I sent to town for lighters, and at the same time commenced dismantling her. I had sent to the underwriters to send an agent to take charge of her. The vessel when cleared and insured was a bark ; for reasons already explained, I changed her rig into a ship while at sea. This was done for the benefit of the underwriters as well as thé owners, and yet I was in hopes to conceal that fact from the agent when he arrived; therefore I used all speed to get her dismantled before he came, and succeeded in doing so. Soon he came, took charge of her, and relieved me from further responsibility. Upon this I went home ; but I had been there only a few days before I received a note from Capt. Gifford, agent for the insurance office, saying that the vessel I had left was not the one they insured. He said, " We insured a bark, but I learn from the testimony of some of the crew that this vessel was a full-rigged ship." He added, " I shall leave her, go home, and wait further development."

It appears that some leaky fellow informed Capt. Gifford of the change in her rig after she was insured. I subsequently learned it was Bill ——, the man who was so officious in getting up the mutiny heretofore detailed. Capt. Gifford knew it was the same vessel that they insured; but the change I had made in her rig he thought was a sufficient cause to make a question in law.

Of course there was nothing left for me to do but take charge of her again, and make the best of it. After considerable trouble in getting her cargo out, and dismantling her, on account of continuous snow and rain storms, and her lying in such a bad place to get at, we at last succeeded in getting the ship and every thing belonging to her up to town; and soon after, by a unanimous vote, the stockholders commenced a suit against the underwriters to recover the insurance for damages sustained by getting ashore. The hull and tackle were sold at auction. After an unsuccessful attempt to get rid of paying the insurance-money, the insurance company settled up with the owners, though it cost them a bill of expenses which might have been avoided, had they settled up without resorting to litigation to get rid of payment.

Every thing having been sold, including the oil, and the proceeds being added to the insurance, a general settlement with the stockholders took place; and each one received back his principal, with a little over twelve per cent interest on his investment.

Thus ended what, considering the circumstances under which the enterprise was gotten up and carried to its termination, may be deemed one of the most remarkable manifestations of direct spirit aid from beginning to end, that has been chronicled in the business experience of this age of wonders.

This voyage ended my nautical career as a business, but did not put me beyond the reach of the " VOICE." My days ashore have found me amid some scenes less exciting, which yet were full to the brim of strange incidents and experiences bordering on the marvellous, as compared with the every-day routine of ordinary business transactions. In my account of them I shall be as brief as the nature of the case will admit consistently with the object of the work in hand.

CHAPTER X.

LUMBERING BUSINESS AT GARDINER, ME.

THOUGH I had made but a poor fist at farming, I had the farm still on my hands, and thought I would try to manage it again. I worked upon it the summer following my arrival home in the "Massasoit," but the result was not a whit better than at my first effort. I stopped on it until the following spring, when I sold out, and left the place. Thus ended my farming career.

My next operation was to buy another lot, containing some thirty acres of the poorest land in all Maine. I knew its quality before making the purchase; but it had good buildings on it, and I got it for a home for my family.

By this time I had become somewhat involved pecuniarily. Having no business by which I could recuperate my exhausted exchequer, I finally became so poor, that I had serious difficulty in procuring sufficient to keep the starving wolf of poverty from entering our humble abode. This fact being known, my friends (?) gave me the cold shoulder; when one's money goes from him, his supposed friends are apt to follow suit. To tell the exact truth, I was completely discouraged. Everybody avoided me, for fear I would solicit aid; my own family joined in a general cry about my incompetency to gain a livelihood. My brother William at this time was engaged in the manufacture of shingles, clapboards, and laths, at Gardiner, Me. I applied to him for work in the mill. He set me at bunching or laying up shingles, at a small compensation, to be paid out of a store where he did his trading. After a while I got promoted to sawing shingles.

The fall before I commenced working for William in the winter, a whole string of mills belonging to old Mr. Robert Gardner caught fire and burned down. I think there were ten in all. They had stood alongside the one I was working in; and when I commenced work they were about half rebuilt.

Associating as I constantly was with folks who talked of nothing but lumber and its manufacture, I learned that there was a large margin left in the operator's favor after all expenses were paid. I often wished I had the means to try it; but, as I had no experience in the business, it was silly to even think about it; and for weeks, whenever the thought came into my mind, I would throw it away. But, in spite of all I could do to the contrary, it *would* intrude itself for my consideration. Finally on waking up one night, after a few hours' sleep, the first thing that I thought of was a saw-mill. I allowed myself to indulge in some extravagant mental calculations as regarded the profits which one might reasonably anticipate if engaged in the business. I don't know how long I humored myself with such thoughts; but, as I was about going to sleep, some

16*

one close to my ear whispered, "*Lease one of the new mills.*" Although spoken in a whisper, the utterance was very clear and distinct. This aroused me to complete wakefulness, and I began to think how it could be brought about. This mysterious, unseen intelligence had often proved competent to put me through under conditions equally bad. I began to speculate in earnest; for I knew, judging from the past, that somehow or other I should become engaged in the lumbering business, although I well knew that it would take thousands of dollars to get it a-going. *How*, I did not know; but my experience with my guide had already been such, that I had a right to expect favorable results in any thing emanating from that source.

Before morning I had made up my mind to try, and that I would go to Mr. Gardner; and if he would give me a three-years' lease, the rent to be paid when due, without security, I would take it for granted that it was right to go ahead. So the next morning about half-past nine o'clock I told my brother I wanted to go away an hour or so. He says rather petulantly, " Where's thee going? " I says, " Not far." Without more ado about it, I went direct to Mr. Gardner's office, found him in and alone. Ascertaining that the person present was Mr. Gardner (for I had never seen him before), I asked him the rent of the mills then being rebuilt. He says, " Seven hundred and fifty dollars a year, payable every three months." This was all I wanted; and I agreed at once to take one. He said he would have the lease ready that afternoon. After he ascertained my name, I left. I

didn't know but he would want reference, which I
could not have given, for I knew scarce one in the
place, and those that knew me in my home neighborhood would not have been of any advantage to me.
However, I went for the lease about five o'clock,
when he handed it to me, with a note for Mr. Littlefield his agent, who was overseeing the rebuilding,
telling him which mill I had taken, and to hurry up
that one, as I was in a hurry to get to work.

After getting the lease in my pocket, I went back
to the mill, and to work, as though nothing had
happened. Now, then, I had a mill, which would be
ready in about two or three weeks; but where was
the lumber to stock it, to come from? Although I
had no valid reason to doubt that some way or
another it would be forthcoming at the proper time,
yet I could but feel not a little anxious about it. I
didn't dare to tell my folks what basis I had to work
from, as they considered me half insane already, in
going into wild-goose chases, as they called my
operations; and if they knew I was depending upon
some unseen being as my adviser, and that the idea
in the first place emanated from such a one, they
would have put me in an insane asylum at once.

When I handed the letter from Mr. Gardner to
Mr. Littlefield, I requested him (Mr. Littlefield) not
to say any thing about it to any one. I wanted to
surprise my friends.

I worked along as usual, but kept up an anxious
thinking about my wild enterprise. Every now and
then, a doubtful thought would present itself, such
as, Supposing I should fail in getting logs to stock

my mill, what will people say, and especially my own
folks ?   Whenever these thoughts would come, my
mind would instinctively go back to the time when
from the same mysterious source I got up a ship, and
made a successful voyage in her, under circumstances,
if any thing, far more discouraging than my present
prospects indicated.   These reflections would re-
assure me, and tended to keep my mind calm.

One of the two weeks before the mill would be
ready came round wondrously quick, and no indications of logs yet, nor in fact, any prospect of any.
Instead of looking brighter, my future looked more
dark and sombre each succeeding day. About this
time Mr. Littlefield told me he couldn't get the mill
ready as soon as was expected by a week or more.
Although I expressed neither regret nor pleasure, I
was greatly pleased at this information, because it
would give me so much more time to get stock to
start, and keep the mill a-going. If asked what good
a prolonging of time would do for me, I could not
have told ; for there was no visible source from which
I could draw in the least hope. Still I couldn't
help thinking that somehow or other time was all I
needed.

I kept on working for my brother as usual, and
said nothing. There being a good many mill-men
out of work, on account of the mills having been
burned down the fall before, who were on the lookout for a job, I noticed many of them inquiring of
Mr. Littlefield whether any of the mills were rented
yet. As per request he kept mum as to my affairs.
One man Mr. Littlefield recommended as a good fore-

man, and advised me to secure his services. Knowing nothing about a mill myself, it was absolutely necessary that I should employ the best man I could find to take charge. Accordingly about a week before the mill was ready, and before I had a log, or any prospect of any, I hired him, and requested him to say nothing about it until the mill was ready for running.

Two days subsequent to the above transaction, a stranger came into the mill inquiring of Mr. Littlefield for me. It appears, that this man, whose name was Wing, of the firm of Wing & Bates, commission merchants in lumber, asked Mr. Littlefield if he knew of any one they could contract with to saw a large " mark " of logs by the thousand. Mr. Littlefield said he didn't unless it was me; adding, " He has rented mill No. 10, but I know nothing further. Come round, and I'll introduce you to him." Mr. Littlefield beckoned me to him, and we were introduced to each other. Mr. Wing at once entered into the object of his visit. In answer to the question, how much per thousand I would ask to saw out five hundred thousand feet, he saying that a large part of them were in a boom a few miles up river, I told him two and a half dollars, if delivered in the boom at the mill. He acceded to the price on the instant. He said that a proviso must be attached to the agreement, viz., that, if a purchaser came along before I commenced upon them, this agreement must be null and void. I said to him, " According to that, I'm not sure of getting the job, as a purchaser may make his appearance before I can get to work." In response he said, "There is hardly a chance for that, as the logs have been for sale some three months, and not an offer has been made. It is getting late, and everybody has made all provision for their stock long ago; and, as you will be ready to cut into them in a week, I don't think it necessary for you to look elsewhere."

The writings were drawn up according to the above; and, although I didn't feel quite sure, yet his reasoning allayed almost all apprehensions in that direction. At any rate, I told brother William what I had been up to unobserved the past month. In the first place, I told him I had a lease of No. 10 for three years. He immediately asked, "Where's thee going to get logs to saw?" I told him of my trade with Mr. Wing. He seemed astounded, but said nothing. I then left off working for him, and attended to getting ready for business, highly elated at my prospects. I had hired all my men to come on when called for: the foreman commenced at once to see that every thing was being done satisfactorily. I all the while was urging on matters as fast as possible. I wrote my family, who were in the country, telling the dash I had made to court the favors of Dame Fortune again, and this time with better prospects of ultimate success than ever before. They all seemed surprised when they heard of it, but said, "It's just like him." An old friend of mine when he heard of it expressed himself thus, "Bime-by he'll be building a fleet of ships: there's no telling what he'll do next."

But I was not to slide into the outstretched arms of beckoning Fortune so easily.

A little over two days before the mill was to start, I saw Mr. Wing coming into the mill near night. As he advanced towards where I was standing, I distinctly felt a cold chill permeate my entire being. The cause of the chill was soon solved. Without any circumlocution, he told me at once, that a purchaser had come to hand, and had bought the whole "mark," thus cutting me off entirely.

One may imagine my feelings at that moment, but they could never be expressed in words. I was paralyzed and speechless, and stood still glaring into Mr. Wing's face, like one deprived of his reason. When Mr. Wing told me about the sale, I only heard the sentence that assured me my hopes were crushed; the rest of his speech I knew nothing about. All that I could remember was a sort of what seemed to me rumbling sound coming from his lips, the whole purport of which I knew in the first sentence. More thoughts passed in rapid succession through my mind in those few brief moments, than I could give expression to in an hour. In the first place, I realized that I was entirely *alone* in the world, as much so as if I was the only living thing on its surface; that is, as far as sympathy was concerned, in regard to what they would call a very "rash and injudicious act." I could seem to hear them say, " The idea of undertaking, single-handed and alone, a business requiring capital to be counted only by thousands, with not a cent in his pocket, with no credit or business friends to assist him, is absolute insanity." And then that awful "I told you so," and, "I knew it would turn so," &c.; these thoughts, and hundreds of others of similar import, went crashing through my excited brain, one following the other, like so many demons intent on dethroning my reason.

This state of things lasted but a few moments. Soon the cloud passed over, and I was myself again. Mr. Wing seemed to feel almost as bad as I did. To encourage me, he said he would do all in his power to assist me, compatible with his business. I said nothing in response to his kind words. Before he left, a sweet, calm feeling of trust, gradually enveloped and permeated my entire being.

About the time I recovered from the shock those few words from Mr. Wing, gave me, the foreman, who was unconscious of what had so recently transpired, came along to ask some questions relating to something about the machinery. I gave him instructions as unconcernedly as though nothing had happened to mar the harmony of my feelings. When I told my brother of the reverse in my present prospects, the poor fellow felt very bad, for several reasons; one of which was, that, now that all our folks had heard about my successful attempt at getting into a business promising success, to fail up before I had even began, he thought, would bring a stigma upon all who bore our name. However, we said but little, and separated. By this time my mind had regained that calm *trust* that always succeeds serious reverses of expectant hopes.

The next morning I went to the mill as usual, my mind having recovered through nature's sweet restorer its wonted serenity. About nine, A.M., I started out for a walk, not having the least idea of where I was going, and mechanically strolled down Main Street, with no object in view. I came abreast of Wing & Bates's office, although I did not know where their office was at the time. All at once I had an indescribable desire to go to their place. Upon inquiry, I found I was standing nearly opposite to it. Instinctively I entered, and, being introduced to Mr. Bates by his partner, sat down and listened to the conversation of an old man who was trying to sell a small "mark" of hemlock logs to them.

They told him they didn't want them. "But," said Mr. Wing, "maybe this gentleman (meaning me) will buy them." Upon this the old man turned round, and addressing me said, " I wish you would." I told him I had no money. He said almost instantly, "I don't want any," and added, "You may have them for three dollars per thousand by Stewart's survey, on three months. After ascertaining that there might not be more than twenty or thirty thousand, and that they would serve to begin with, and thinking that by the time those were used up I might get more, and that, at any rate, these were vastly better than nothing, I told the man I would take them on the conditions he named. After arranging about giving my note to Wing & Bates in accordance with Mr. Stewart's survey-bill, I left, and never saw the seller afterwards.

Although I had made but a small purchase, I went back to the mill comparatively happy, with my small beginning. On my return I met Mr. Littlefield, who asked me if I had any hemlock logs. I told him I
17

had just bought a small mark. He then said that he had a bill of dimension timber for a large building he was going to put up, and as I was just beginning he would offer the job to me. Upon inquiry I found there would be forty-eight thousand feet. He said he was willing to give me seven dollars per thousand delivered at the mill. Of course I accepted the offer at once. He gave me the bill of specifications, which I passed to the foreman, who tacked it upon the gate-post.

The logs were all in the great boom attached to the mills; and before night I had Mr. Stewart's survey-bill, which made of the lot a little less than twenty-four thousand feet. The smallness of the quantity was a damper, since, according to the survey-bill, I had only about half enough to fill the order. Mr. Stewart took the bill to Wing & Bates as agreed upon, and they made a note in accordance therewith. When I went down the next morning to sign the note, I inquired of Wing where I could get more of the same sort, telling him I had but half enough to fill an order I had taken for dimension stuff soon after leaving him yesterday. They didn't know of any this side of Augusta, told me who had them there, and that probably I could get all I wanted. Upon going up to the latter place, I found that I could get any quantity at two days' notice, delivered in my boom. With this I left for home, promising to call when I found out how many I needed.

A day or two subsequent to this we had the mill running; and, when the logs were all together, there seemed to be enough to fill the order. At any rate, I concluded to wait and see how they cut up, before making another purchase. It is customary, in scaling crooked logs, to make deductions sufficient to make it into straight timber. This lot of logs was unusually crooked, but sound; and as the bill of dimensions contained mostly short stuff, by taking advantage of the crooks, the logs sawed up almost as economically as straight timber.

To make a long story short, we sawed out the entire bill of forty-eight thousand feet, and had left what made almost as much more as the survey-bill called for. As soon as the order was completed, Mr. Littlefield gave me his check for the amount, $336. I sawed, out of the same lot, another small order of thirteen thousand feet, for which I was paid $91; making in all $427; deducting from which my note of less than $72 left me a balance of a little over $355 for the mill, besides a few thousand feet of logs left.

After this, I had no further trouble about getting stock for my mill; and, before two months had passed, I bought a mark of logs amounting, according to the survey-bill, to 2,600,000 feet, of a man by the name of Miles Standish, a direct descendant of the Miles Standish who came over in " The Mayflower," and landed on Plymouth Rock in December, 1620. It was agreed between us, that I should pay six dollars per thousand feet, and, after deducting the expenses of sawing and marketing, divide the balance with him, be it more or less. This constituted him a silent partner in the concern. It was also agreed between us, that the business should be carried on wholly in my name. This arrangement made a good thing for him, and a safe business for me; for by it I should be exempted from giving notes, which must be met at maturity, whether I had any thing to take them up with or not. By the above arrangement, I had got into a large and safe business, with no misgivings about the future, at least for a couple of years. In addition to the manufacture of boards, I got machinery a-going for making laths and shingles. I shipped most of my lumber to Fall River, where I found a ready market for all I could manufacture.

I bought out a large grocery store, which I kept well stocked with all kinds of groceries, also on one side a well-assorted stock of dry goods, such as are mostly used in workmen's families. I had no other object in getting the store, than the accommodating my workmen and their families, of which there were some sixty who were working for me. I let them have goods at cost, deducting only the actual expenses, by which they saved from fifteen to twenty-five per cent. To outsiders I charged the same as at other stores. Soon after I got a-going, finding my business increasing, I took the adjoining mill, at the same price as the first one.

It will be seen that, in less than six months from the time I commenced, I had slid gradually and easily, without one extra effort on my part, into a large and lucrative business, increasing in volume each succeeding day; and, taking into account the circumstances as heretofore detailed, mine was, to say the least, a very remarkable change from as low a condition as can well be conceived of, to one approximating its opposite. I attribute the management of the transaction wholly and totally to business heads in spirit life, working, through my organism, the wonderful change in my circumstances in such brief space of time.

The following spring, I effected a contract, through John Hull & Co. of Fall River, with the Fall River Railroad Company, to furnish fence-boards and railroad-ties for an extension of their road. The whole contract amounted to fifteen thousand dollars, out of which I saved three thousand dollars for my services. I did this by re-letting it to other parties, not being able to fill it from my mills, on account of previous engagements.

Thus the work went on, without a particle of friction, until late the next fall, when circumstances transpired which broke up and destroyed my large and flourishing business entirely. Mr. Standish having become heavily involved in his operations, his paper must be protested. Knowing this, and having the entire confidence of a large circle of friends, and his word being as good as his bond, he took ample time to get into his own hands all the spare cash his friends had, and then failed for upwards of forty thousand dollars. As I thought I had a lien on the logs I was at work upon, I felt comparatively safe. I had a bill of sale of them; but another party held a prior claim as collateral security for money advanced in getting them cut and into market.

As he held my paper for a large amount in addition to my indorsements for him, and as every avenue was cut off to raise funds to cancel them, I failed irretrievably.

Mr. Standish left for parts unknown, and I never heard of him afterwards. Thus, when few men living had a more lucrative business, in complete working order, with no liabilities for a dollar that I could not meet at a moment's notice, that is, as far as my own business was concerned, I was crushed and destroyed without a moment's notice, and at a time when I felt absolutely secure. When I learned the real situation of things, my feelings were such that I will not attempt to describe them. Suffice it to say, I went to my room, locked the door, and threw myself on the bed, with a distressed, sickly sensation in my stomach, caused by this sudden reverse in my affairs. The more I thought about it, the worse I felt, and for two hours I feared I would lose my reason; when, all at once, I heard my familiar VOICE say, " Haven't you done the best you could? Wouldn't you do the same again, with the same education?"

The moment I heard the above, my mind seemed filled with a new light; I saw for the first time that the whole experience of my recent rise and fall was simply educational; it showed me as clear as day, that the experience I had just passed through was necessary to show me that " man may propose, but God and angels dispose;" or, in other words, that something other than our immaculate selves is *real* author of circumstances of birth and education, and of all that we may accomplish, either good or bad, all our asseverations to the contrary notwithstanding.

It seemed as though I was bathing in a sea of light,

which entirely removed all traces of excitement; and I lay there a few moments, revelling in these to me new sensations, and quite forgot, for the time being, the proximate causes of all my troubles; after which I got up, as quiet and calm as though nothing unusual had happened. To tell the *exact* truth, I felt happy at the way things had turned.

Thus ends one of the many remarkable chapters in my eventful history, written to show the methods taken to make me a humbler, wiser, and happier man.

CHAPTER XI.

LEARNING THE SHIP-BUILDING TRADE, AND ITS RESULTS.

As soon as it became known among my business friends and acquaintances, that I had gone under, everybody who had an unsettled account sued me; many did who upon comparing accounts were found to owe me a balance, instead of my owing them. One man, a Mr. Stuart, with whom I had not even a passing acquaintance, and with whom I never had any business relations whatever, sued me for seventy dollars. Calling upon him to know what I owed him for, he failed to find any account against me. My name was not on his books. He said it was a mistake, and let it go at that.

Finding, after a fair trial for my rights, that everybody was determined that I should owe them something, whether I did or not, and that I would have to contest every unfair claimant in the petty courts, I left the town disgusted with everybody in general, and some of the business men of Gardiner in particular. One man, with a little more of the milk of human kindness in his heart than the majority, offered to assist me into business again, but under conditions that I didn't feel justified in accepting. What I should do

next, was what interested me more than any thing
else.   My friends were very officious in advising me.
Some proposed one thing, others something else; but
all thought that any regular business was entirely
out of the question.   All advised me to confine myself to simply working for others more capable than
myself to conduct any thing that required tact and
business forethought.

It is not my purpose to give in detail *all* the little
incidents of life: consequently I confine my writing
to the more prominent ones, especially to those relating to *direct spirit aid*, in telling me what to do when
I am about to sink beneath the waves of untoward
circumstances.

During the fall and winter following the reverses
detailed in the last chapter, I stopped at home.   A
Mr. Eldridge Jackson, my brother-in-law, was a shoe-
maker, and lived in part of my house, carrying on his
business in one of the chambers.   As there was nothing better to do, I went into " cobbling," having had
some considerable experience in that line when quite
young, in making shoes for our family, and sometimes
for the neighbors' children.   Being among old acquaintances, I soon got up quite a business, making
from two to three dollars per day.   After I commenced, Mr. Jackson turned over to me all the cobbling business, confining himself entirely to making
new work for a Mr. Joseph Estes.

The following spring, ship-building took a start all
over the country; and, although I had been at sea in
ships, I was entirely ignorant as to their construction; but having a mechanical turn of mind, as before

related, I determined to go into the business as a green hand, and gradually work up where I could command good wages. My plan was, to work in a place until I had got the hang of things pretty well, then leave there, and go to another place, and let myself for better wages, and keep doing so, until I had got as high in the profession as I could go; which, from what I had accomplished when a mere lad, I flattered myself wouldn't take long to do.

Money being very scarce, and hard to get, I was obliged to take, in exchange for my " cobbling," such produce as the farmers who were my patrons could spare, such as corn, potatoes, meat, &c., which answered my purpose just as well as money, as far as our living was concerned. But I couldn't even get money enough of them to pay for the stock used in repairing their old boots and shoes.

I made up my mind to start by the middle or last of April for my new business; and, failing to get money sufficient from my winter's work to get away with, I borrowed five dollars of my uncle Bounds Crosman, and started for Belfast, where, as I learned, they were preparing to build quite a number of vessels the ensuing summer. I hadn't a doubt but that I could get a chance to work as a green hand, until I had made application at every yard in the place. Failing to get a job there, I took passage in a steamboat for Portland.

On the passage to the latter place, in conversation with one of the passengers, I told him what I was in pursuit of, and my hope that I could get a job in Portland, also telling him of my unsuccessful attempt in Belfast. He says, "If you fail in Portland, push right on to Newburyport, where there are near a dozen ship-yards, and you will probably get a chance to work in some of them." After arriving in Portland, I made application at a few yards for work, but was refused ; and as the chances must be more favorable in Newburyport, and my money would barely take me there, I took the four, P.M., train, landing in Newburyport about eight o'clock.

I put up at the American House for the night, not doubting, that, before another day would pass by, I should get a job. Before retiring, I found out by the landlord, that the shipyards were some two miles from the tavern, at a place called Bellville, on the Merrimac River.

After breakfast the next morning, I started out full of sanguine hopes and buoyant expectations of getting a job, at least before night. The first application proved a failure. This damped my ardor; but, as there were many other yards, I didn't lose hope. Every attempt that day failed. I did not go to dinner on account of the long distance. And, although I had serious doubts of getting a job at all, still I did not lose *all* hope, as there were some half-dozen more yards there and a few miles up river. Whenever I applied for work, I noticed they all asked one question, viz., "Are you a regular carpenter?" Upon answering in the negative, they would say at once, "I don't want you." Sometimes I would venture to say that I was handy with tools, and in a short time would become quite proficient. In response to this, they would say, "Oh! I know all about this being *handy with tools;* " continuing, " I have hundreds of applications every day, from folks out of the country towns, who couldn't tell a ship from a pig-pen; every one of them telling how *handy* they were with tools." The next day's effort proved the same. I began to lose hope, but persevered in my endeavors every day, each resulting with the same luck. In going back and forth from the hotel to the yards, I applied at several sail-lofts and one rigging loft, for work, thinking that, if I failed ultimately in the shipyards, I could fall back on them; but got no better encouragement there.

In going towards the yards one day, I passed some Irishmen, filling up a new wharf with dirt carried in wheelbarrows. I applied to the foreman of the gang for a job. He looked me up and down, and turned away without saying a word; evidently suspecting, from my dress (I then had on my best clothes) and address, that I was insulting him. Every day's effort thus far proved like the first. The fourth day I had applied to all but one yard, and had plenty of time to have tried my luck in that; but, feeling sure that I should not succeed, I thought I would leave it until next morning, and face the rebuff I expected, upon a full stomach. After breakfast, I started for the last and only chance. I walked rapidly, feeling that I might as well know my fate at once, as to be dreading it; but when nearing the vicinity of the yard I felt a sort of weakness in my limbs, that almost deprived me of locomotion; and instead of applying at once, as I had determined upon, when I got into the yard I passed directly through it, and sat down on a large oak log, roughed out for a windlass as I afterwards learned, to gather strength to meet the rebuff composedly. I sat there, all doubled up; for, to tell the truth, I felt so weak that I could hardly sit up straight if I had attempted it, thinking what I should do if I failed here, which I felt almost sure would be the result.

After sitting a few moments, I heard my mysterious unseen friend say, "Ship as a full hand." Although I well knew that I could not do it with justice to myself, as I must soon be found out in the deception, the thought flashed through my mind instantly, "They'll keep you a week before discharging you; and by that time you will get enough to pay your bills, and get to Boston." Upon this I jumped off the log as light as ever, determined to try it, let it go which way it might. In answer to my inquiry for the foreman, they said he was inside the ship. I immediately started to find him. They were putting in the lower deck frame; and, upon inquiry again, I found him down aft, overseeing some work. In response to the query, if he wanted any more help, he answered by asking the same question that all the rest had, viz., "Are you a carpenter?" I said, "Yes, sir." — "Well, then, you can go to work at once." Up to this time I hadn't thought of tools: regular carpenters must provide their own tools, while green hands are furnished by their employers. This thought going through my mind, I told him I couldn't go to work to-day, as my tools hadn't got along. He says, "Can't you borrow some?" I said, "No: I know no one to borrow of." He continued, "Can't you come on after dinner?" I told him I would get me a boarding-house, and come on to-morrow (which would be Saturday) or else on Monday. After I had agreed to go to work, I remember thinking what a muss I had got into, with no tools, and even if I had them I didn't know how to use them expertly. As these thoughts coursed rapidly through my mind, for a moment I felt sorry that I had been so rash; but I felt that if I had overleaped the bounds of discretion my desperate situation was an ample excuse, and now there was no other alternative, but to make the best of it, and go ahead. I loitered around among the workmen some half-hour or so, when, upon the recommendation of one of the men, I made application to a Mr. Watson for board, who consented to take me in. This being settled, I went immediately to the American House, to change my clothes, and told the proprietor that I had a job in a shipyard, and that, as I hadn't means to pay my board, I would change my clothes, and leave my trunk as security.

He objected to this, telling me to take my trunk along; he wasn't afraid to trust me. The fact was, he was *too* kind; for I hadn't a cent of money to pay for moving the trunk, and for this reason should have esteemed it a favor if he would let it remain. I had another reason why I didn't want to take it away; and that was, I didn't expect, nor had I the least hope, that they would keep me more than one week, if they did that, and by keeping it where it was I would save two cartage bills. However, I changed my clothes, determined to let it remain, whether he wanted it or not; but in going towards the yard I happened to meet Mr. Watson, with whom I had agreed for board, coming from market with a horse and wagon.   The moment I saw him, I was impressed to ask him to go to the hotel, and get my trunk, which he willingly did.

After getting the trunk into my room, I sat down to take a square look at things as they actually existed. In the first place, I took into account the novel situation in which I found myself, wondering how it would terminate.   From an old superstition instilled into me when a child, "Never to go into any new enterprise the last day of the week or month," I did not quite like the idea of going to work on the morrow, Saturday; and, if I put it off until Monday, that would be the last day of April.   If ever I needed every thing to be favorable, it was now; and that superstition troubled me.   Upon reflection, however, I concluded the day wouldn't make much difference, as I should not probably work over a week, whether I commenced on the first or last day of the week or month: so I determined to commence to-morrow, hit or miss.

After dinner I went into the yard; and as I saw the workmen at their allotted work, doing it with much facility, I wondered what sort of a "fist" I should make of it.   To say the least, my situation was a novel one, and I didn't know but that my courage would fail when the time came to show my skill in shipbuilding.   However, I didn't allow the thoughts of what *might* be the result of to-morrow, to poison the hopeful anticipations of the present.

The next morning I went into the yard with the rest, and, when the bell rang at seven, went into the ship to join the gang working inside. I went down aft, where I saw Mr. Ewell, the foreman, who saluted me cordially, seeming to be pleased that he had another *skilled* workman added to his list. It is customary for ship-carpenters to work in pairs; and he at once told me to work with Mr. Allen, pointing him out. I saw that Allen was a boarder at the house where I was stopping, and also my bedfellow. This was a happy incident, as, from what little I had seen of him, he appeared to have a happy, genial disposition, which proved to be true.

Recognizing me as I approached, he congratulated himself at having me for a partner, little thinking what a green chap I was. I told him at once, that my tools hadn't got along, and I couldn't go to work unless I could borrow some, until they came to hand. " Oh ! " he says, " I guess I can manage that for you." Suiting the action to the word, he started for the shop where his chest was deposited. He took out an old rule in the first place, and then some pretty well worn tools, observing, " I guess you can get along a few days with these, and some I'm at work with." With this we went to work, he on one and I on the opposite side of the ship.

To answer the inquiry, how I managed to get along without betraying my ignorance, I need only to refer the reader to my early history as detailed heretofore, to show that I could always do almost any thing with tools from my earliest boyhood.

This Mr. Allen, my working partner, was a very slow-moving man, and I the opposite. As we were faying knees, they being heavy, we were obliged to assist each other in getting them in their places. I would allow him to make a beginning first, watching him narrowly to see how he "done it." Taking the cue from him, I would commence on my side, and, being much the quicker motioned, often came out ahead. By knocking off time at night, I had got the run of things pretty well, and thought, that, if there was nothing more difficult to do than what I had seen, I didn't apprehend any difficulty in keeping up the delusion until I had earned enough to pay my bills, and get to Boston.

Thus it will be seen, that the first day of my novel undertaking had ended successfully. The next day being Sunday, I spent the most of the time with my partner, the principal topic of conversation running on ships and ship-building, watching myself so as not to say any thing to unmask my total ignorance of ship-building.

After dinner we took a walk to the yard, and went inside the ship. Once, when talking about the business, he asked me where I served my apprenticeship. I simply told him "down in Maine;" and to prevent him from asking me at what town or place (for I didn't know the name of a builder in the State), I purposely changed the conversation to something else.

I went to work Monday with suppressed feelings of pleasure; and as everybody, including the foreman, seemed to look upon me as an extra good workman, I began to feel that somehow or other I had been more fortunate than most mortals, in becoming so suddenly a master-workman at a business in which

18*

I was entirely ignorant, or else those overseeing the work were remarkably stupid in not detecting the fraud. Still I did not feel sure of keeping the favorable impression I had already created. They might not say any thing if they did see things going wrong in my work, and yet might discharge me at any moment. So after I had worked almost five days, to get an indication whether they were satisfied with me or not, I went out into the yard, and seeing Mr. Jackman, the proprietor, moulding out some timber, I told him I wanted to get fifteen dollars. He looked up, saying, " Do I owe it you ? " I said, " No ; but you will." I then said I had occasion to use that amount ; and, if he was willing to risk it, I should feel much obliged to him. Without any ceremony, he took out his wallet, and gave me the money. This satisfied me that I was all right for at least another week ; and, if nothing happened to uncover my deficiencies, I might be kept on for an indefinite period.

That evening I wrote home, enclosing ten dollars, telling of my successful dash in my new occupation, going into all the details as to how it was brought about. With the other five dollars, I bought me a good second-hand axe and adze, which, added to those I borrowed, made quite a respectable " kit." To show how ignorant I was, also how carefully I had to watch myself not to make blunders, it is only necessary to say that I worked two days with my dull adze, not knowing whether to knock the handle out to grind it, or not, though reason and common-sense might have told me that the handle must come out in order to grind it properly ; but, never having seen it done, I dared not risk it until I was sure. A couple of days after it became mine, a man working near me said, " My adze is as dull as a hoe," at the same time knocking out the handle with a mallet, and starting for the grindstone. No sooner than I saw this manœuvre, I had the handle out of mine, and was on the way to the grindstone also.

After this I had no more trouble in that direction. The beginning of the second week, one of the men wanted to sell his chest and a few tools, as he was going out of the carpenter business. Looking at them one day at noon, in company with my mate, in answer to question of price he said fifteen dollars. I told him I hadn't the money, else I'd buy them. My partner offered to loan it to me, which I accepted, and took the key. My tools *had come at last*, and nobody but myself the wiser as to where they came from.

Up to this time I hadn't hinted a word to Mr. Allen about my adventure, although I wanted to do so many times; but, the evening succeeding the day he loaned me the money, I told him the whole story as heretofore detailed. At first he thought I was joking, but I soon convinced him to the contrary; then he burst out into uncontrollable laughter. After this revelation of my fraud, we had the fun all to ourselves. Sometimes when at work, and thinking over the ridiculous and dangerous but successful subterfuge I had resorted to to get work, he would burst out laughing by himself. I asking him the cause of his levity, he would say he got thinking what a long apprenticeship I had to serve to gain the distinction of being one of the best ship-carpenters out. After I made this disclosure, and also that I had commanded a ship in the whaling business, he told me some of his history. He was a sailor also, and had commanded several small vessels coastwise and in the West India trade. Getting tired of that, he left the sea only three years ago, and took up the carpenter trade; continuing, that he thought he was doing a rather smart business to palm himself off as a first-class mechanic, without having learned any trade, and with only three years' experience; but, says he, " You've taken all the wind out of my sails."

In getting in some large timbers for lower-deck stringers, after I had been at work a little over two weeks, I accidentally got my left knee jammed in between two of the timbers, which hurt it very much. At the time I feared I would lose my leg, but upon examination found no bones broken; and, by applying lobelia soaked in rum, took the swelling down, and kept it so, and in a few days could get about on crutches. After laying up three or four days, I hobbled down to the yard one morning, and, seeing Mr. Ewell, asked him if there was nothing I could do in the shop. I told him I could do any light work, and couldn't afford to lose so much time. He said yes, I could " go into the loft, and see to the making a set of moulds for a new ship; " he going upon the idea that I was well versed in all departments of the art of ship-building. This was a poser; for, to begin with, I had never been inside of a drafting or moulding loft, and, what was more, knew positively nothing about it. He very kindly told me I needn't do much, only to see that a man he had working there made no mistakes, and to keep him at work. Here I was being promoted to a boss, to oversee the most complicated and difficult part of the whole business. I was sorry I had said any thing about work; but I had got into it, and had no way of getting out without acknowledging myself a fraud, which would not do, for now I was looked upon as one of the brightest stars that "twinkled" in the "constellation" of ship-carpentry. After seeing to things in the yard, he took me in his wagon, and drove to the loft, some mile or so from the yard.

After getting into the loft he commenced to "run in" what I afterwards learned was one of the 'cants" to the "after-body" of the new ship. The floor was full of pencil-marks crossing each other every which way, neither head nor tail to them that I could see. His talking about "lifts" and "water-lines," "sir-marks," "diagonals," and "horn-poles," with many other like expressions, were all Greek to me. But there was one thing that wasn't Greek; and that was, my head was more muddled up than ever before. I hadn't been in the loft ten minutes, when, if asked how much twice two was, I couldn't have told; for now I had got into a place where no quantity of assurance, backed up with ever so much "cheek," would avail a particle. The fact is, one must *know* for himself, or he can do positively nothing. Mr. Ewell evidently thought I could model and draft a ship's frame as readily as himself. I said nothing, and let him think so; for, if I had ventured to have said a word, I should have exposed my verdancy, and the fat would have been all in the fire, and I would at once sink into the very *insignificant* artisan that I really was. What I had said or done, for everybody to place such an estimate upon my knowledge, I couldn't conceive. They could never have found out by my work: there was not the ghost of an apology for awarding me such superior qualifications because of any thing I had done there. However, I went on the principle, that if we are thought to be something more than we can rightfully claim, and keep our tongues still, few can tell whether we really possess the merit or not. Mr. Ewell was a great talker, and, when looking over his work, could not think without talking about it. By following the sweeps as he traced them out on the floor, I got a sort of an indistinct idea that somehow or other the moulds must be made to correspond to these mysterious and to me incomprehensible lines, the beginning and ending of which were wrapped up in impenetrable mystery. In looking over some of the sweeps run in the day before, and thinking that he detected a mistake, he asked me to hand him the " horn-pole " for the " after-body," by which he could ascertain whether there was an error or not. I knew that a pole was a straight stick, but a " horn-pole " was a " puzzler." I knew cattle's horns were crooked; and whether it was a crooked stick, and from that fact called a " horn-pole," that he wanted, I hadn't the slightest conception.

I noticed that when telling me to get this mysterious pole he looked in a certain direction, indicating by that the direction to them or it, whatever it

might be, from where he stood : so I hobbled along in
that direction, with my crutch, wishing all the time
my leg ten times worse, which would have prevented
me from coming there at all. I saw some straight
sticks, but nothing that looked like a " horn." I
stood there, supported by my crutch, not daring to
select any one, for fear of falling from the lofty
distinction they had forced upon me. Finally, after
looking a moment or two, I ventured to say I
didn't see it. Upon this, he came to where I stood,
and took up a straight stick, instead of a " horny"
looking pole, saying, as he stooped, " Here it is."
" So it is," says I. But, as good luck would have it,
it was partly obscured by other straight " horn "
poles, thus saving my reputation of being a crack
draughtsman. At another time, a few minutes subsequent to the last incident, he had occasion to ascertain the distance, in feet and inches, from one part
of what he was doing, to some other part, as I was
standing near a bench, on which lay the draft on a
very small scale of the whole ship, that is, the water-
lines. These lines give the exact shape of the ship
fore and aft, if submerged in the water, every two
feet from the keel to the gunwale. These water-
lines are called " lifts." So he says, " Just give me
the distance out on the third lift." Here was another
puzzler. What a lift meant, was as much a mystery
to me as the horn-pole business. I had got out of
one dilemma, only to get into another. However, I
took out my rule, knowing, or rather thinking, that,
as there were feet and inches wrapped up in the
mystery, that the rule was the necessary instrument

to determine it. This was a mistake, as far as measuring on that small scale was concerned. I tried to find out what he meant by "third lift," not seeing any thing to indicate the word. I stood there, gazing at the draft, in a sort of dazed stupor, the perspiration pouring out of every pore in my body, caused by my ridiculous position.

Being in a hurry, Mr. Ewell came again to my rescue ; and, taking up a pair of dividers, opened them until the two points rested on the space to be measured, then, applying them to his rule, calculated the feet and inches desired. Thus I saved my unsought reputation again. After seeing him do it, all was simple. Soon after ten, A.M., he left me to "boss" the mould-making, telling the man at work, a Mr. Mitchell, that I would instruct him if any difficulty occurred.

I was never more pleased than to see him close the door behind him. I found Mr. Mitchell an intelligent and well-informed man, also well versed in what he was doing ; and, as he thought me an adept in the business, I had not the least difficulty in keeping up the delusion. I found out, through him, all about those complicated lines crossing each other ; and, with what I got out of him while Mr. Ewell was absent, I began really to know something about the mystery of "laying down" a ship.

I was in the loft about five days, before my leg would allow me to go into the yard again ; in which time I got so well posted, that I could have taken a model, and made moulds from it, without much if any further instruction. Thus, through the accident of hurting my leg, I secured information of vast subsequent importance to me, as will be seen farther on ; also proof that sometimes vast and important results date their significance from a very slight and often seemingly disastrous circumstance.

Because I slid into important knowledge so easily, I do not arrogate to myself superior faculties for acquiring information.   That would be a serious error, which I should sadly deplore.   As will be seen, it all emanated, as did my previous perceptions, from circumstances over which I, as an individual, had not the least control.   I do not expect that each and every boy or grown-up man could go through these exceptional experiences with the same quiet unconcern that has characterized my various proceedings ; and for the reason that all do not possess the same sensitive temperament and natural mediumistic traits that I do.   If they could hear suggestions from unseen sources, telling them how to avoid getting into difficulties, and helping them out when in, then, as a matter of course, they could do precisely as I have done.   Looking at things in that light takes away all vain feeling of superiority, and, in its stead, creates a humble state of mind, unknown to the egotistical, self-sufficient, arrogant.

Nothing else worth recording occurred, until I had worked near a month, when I got it into my head that I could sooner master the business by taking jobs, and employing first-class workmen ; with what I had already acquired, and what I could soon get out of them, I could attain the top round of the ladder much sooner than by working by the day.   The

19

more I thought of it, the more feasible it looked; and I determined to put it into immediate execution. To do this, would necessitate moving to some other place. I made inquiries, and found that ship-building was carried on quite extensively at Damariscotta, Me.; and, that place being nearer my family, I determined to go there.

I said nothing to any one about my anticipated movement, not even to Mr. Allen, my much-esteemed partner. My reputation as a first-rate carpenter had by this time become universally admitted, not only by the foreman and proprietor, but also by the workmen themselves, a class who are generally jealous and chary in admitting the superiority of any over themselves. From this, I had good reason to believe that I should have difficulty in getting away.

To obviate this, I went up town the evening preceding the day I intended to leave, got a ticket to go on the eight, P.M., train the next night, and engaged an expressman to take my trunk and chest at six the following evening to the depot. When I told Mr. Allen, and the folks I boarded with, of my sudden resolve upon departure, they expressed a good deal of regret. After supper, and after my things were on the road to the depot, I went to the office, and told Mr. Jackman that sickness in my family rendered it necessary for me to start for home immediately. (My wife was sick at the time.) He said, " You won't want all your money;" he thinking, if he kept back a part, I would be more likely to return. I told him I should need all I had due me, and more too. He then offered to loan me what I thought

I should need, which of course I refused. I almost
regretted that I had been so precipitate, after I
found out how much confidence he had in me.
However, it was too late then to change the programme. I had worked in all thirty-one days and a
quarter, at two dollars and a quarter per day, the
highest wages paid then; for which he paid me, and
I was off to encounter new scenes, new associations,
and fresh experiences in the humdrum of life. Thus
it will be seen that a wonderful change in my circumstances had been wrought in that short space of
time, all of which emanated from that brief sentence
of my invisible friend, who told me in clear, distinct
words, to "ship as a full hand."

I arrived at Damariscotta in due time, and succeeded, in a day or two, in getting a job of Abner
Stetson, to put in the two deck-frames and finish
the top of a large ship he was building; for this I
received ample compensation. After finishing that
job, I took another, which, having finished, I went
home, where I remained through the winter with my
family. With nothing else I could find to do, I sat
down to cobbling again, and kept it up until spring.

About the middle of March, I went to Rockland
in pursuit of my now legitimate business, ship-building. After a short time I succeeded in getting a small
vessel to build, of a Mr. Rhoades. She measured
only about two hundred tons, and was named Henry
C. Lowell, after a celebrated lawyer of that name.

In May I had my family moved to Rockland, and
in the fall got a job of a Mr. Robert Sweetland of
South Thomaston, where I moved my family late in

the fall. I didn't get to work on my job until the following April, working in the mean time repairing an old vessel for Capt. Israel Snow. The following summer, finished my first job, and took the decks of two other vessels to put in, and finish their tops. One of the two was on the ship " Kate Sweetland," built by James Sweetland and Charles McLoon ; the other was a bark, built by George Thorndike.

These jobs lasted until into the winter months ; and, as I had made up my mind to go to California the ensuing spring, I moved my family back to our own home at Weeks's Mills, South China, where I remained until the following March, when I was ready to start on my contemplated trip to the gold-fields of California ; the details of which will be found in the succeeding chapter.

CHAPTER XII.

INCIDENTS ON A VOYAGE TO THE GOLD-MINES OF CALIFORNIA, AND RETURN, 1849.

As stated in the preceding chapter, I had determined to go to California in the spring following my work in South Thomaston in 1848.

My brother Thomas had gone out there, on the first vessel that left after the gold-fever had broken out; and his writing home wonderful stories about getting gold, telling of the chances for accumulating a competence in most alluring terms, tended to increase my desire, and determined me to try the exciting business, and see what Dame Fortune would vouchsafe me.

As there had been published all over the country, in all the papers, exaggerated accounts of awful murders and daring highway robberies, my family and friends tried to persuade me not to risk myself among such a wild set of desperadoes.

All through the winter, these stories, accumulating more and more each succeeding week, worked upon their excited feelings to such a degree, that they hardly dared to walk on the street in a country town in the night-time, for fear of meeting some more daring ruffians than ever existed except in excited, overwrought, and muddled craniums. As I had been used to roughing it all through life, these stories had no other effect than to strengthen my resolution, and generate stronger desires than ever to mingle in the exciting scenes of a camp-life in the mountain regions of California.

Although I had said nothing about it to any one, not even my wife, I had fixed upon the first day of March to start; and, as I had said little about it, my folks, and especially my mother, thought, or was in hopes, I had given it up altogether. I expected, when I settled up my business the fall before, that I should have means sufficient to get me there, and some to spare; but I was owing some, which I did not expect to be, and yet was, called upon to pay, which, with other unforeseen drafts, reduced my sum-total, by March, to a little over a hundred dollars. The cheapest fare to California was over four hundred dollars; and my folks thought that I wouldn't undertake such an enterprise with my slim purse. But they had reckoned without their host. The 1st of March found me sick abed, which prevented me from going as I had intended. I had contracted a very bad cold, which culminated in a lung-fever. Although they did not want me to suffer, I could see their secret satisfaction at my inability to sit up, all claiming that it was an interposition of the Lord to prevent me from risking my valuable life among thieves, robbers, and murderers. This was very kind and considerate in them, and I fully appreciated their kindly feelings; but it only strengthened my resolve to go ahead at all hazards. The Sunday preceding the 8th, which came on Wednesday, father and mother made me a visit. I still was unable to sit up a moment. After they had been in the house a few minutes, mother came to the bedside with her sweet smiling face, and said, "Now, David, thee can't go to California, because thee has no money to go with." (They all knew about my lack of funds, and couldn't help showing their pleasure.) "Mother," I said, "I leave for California Wednesday." I had not thought of it, until I heard myself speak the words. She says, "How can thee go so soon, even if thee had the money to get thee there, thee's so sick?" She begged me not to think of it. I told her I knew I was very sick, but somehow or other I thought I should start on that day. I didn't dare to tell her that I heard my mysterious friend set the day; for, had I, my friends would certainly have said that I was out of my head. How I should get there I didn't know. I wasn't sure of going there at all. I only heard the words, "Start on Wednesday." I knew I must leave some money at home, which would reduce my meagre pile that much. I thought that I would go to New York, and maybe I could get a chance to work my passage ; or, if I failed in that, I would go to work in a shipyard until I got enough to go with. Monday found me better. I engaged a neighbor by the name of Choate to take my chest, trunk, and self to Augusta early Wednesday morning. When it came round, I left about forty dollars at home, and with sixty-five dollars started on my voyage to California. I pushed on to New York as fast as possible, landing there on the 10th with fifty-eight dollars and a few cents in my pocket.

Having landed near night, I put up at a cheap hotel near the Battery, a resort for countrymen and the rougher part of down-town folks, such as butchers, dairymen, &c. I intended to look round next day, and see what I could do about getting to the Eldorado of the Pacific slope. While sitting in the bar-room after supper, listening to the conversation of a large crowd speculating about the gold region (at that time it was the principal topic of conversation among all parties), I noticed two young men sitting near me, talking in a suppressed tone upon the general subject. By their looks I took them to be brothers. One was encouraging the other to persevere in something, I couldn't hear what, and anticipating that he would come out all right. I noticed them looking at me occasionally; and directly the youngest-looking one asked me if I was going to California. I told him I left home for that purpose, but couldn't tell until I had looked round some. At this they hitched their chairs nearer, when all three of us got into an earnest conversation upon the all-absorbing subject.

At last the youngest said, "I too started for California; but, never having been absent from home a night in my life, I feel somewhat discouraged about going farther;" continuing, "This," pointing to his partner, "is my brother. He came to New York to see me off, and seeing my despondency has been trying to encourage me to go ahead." Then he said, "I wish you was going along, I should feel so much better." From this I concluded that he had formed a favorable estimate of my virtues.

After a while, they both put in for me to go, holding up before my mind, in most extravagant colors, very flattering prospects. What they said didn't in the least increase my ardor, for I had the fever as bad or worse than either. The elder brother said he would have made arrangements to go along, only that he had a family, that both parents were invalids, and there was no one else to take care of them, and run the place. They were farmers from the interior of the State of New York. While they were pleading with all their rustic eloquence to induce me to go, I heard my unseen friend whisper, "Sell your tools, and go along." This I hadn't thought of, until I heard the VOICE speak it. Finally I told them, that I was a little short of funds, but if I could sell my chest of tools, pointing it out, I would go. Upon inquiry how much I asked for them, I said fifty dollars. I told them what the tools were, and the oldest said, "I guess I'll buy them," but, counting his money, found he had only just that amount, and said, "If I buy them, how am I to get home?" The other says, "I will let you have enough for that." Upon this the trade was closed, he handing me over the fifty dollars, remarking, as he did so, "They'll come handy on the farm : I've been long thinking I would like to have such tools."

I said nothing about how much I had before I got this ; and they naturally supposed I had plenty, and only wanted to get rid of my tools. This being settled, we commenced to talk about what sort of fit-out we must get, and continued conversing until bedtime.

The next morning bright and early, we were up and dressed, got breakfast, and started out. In the first place, we must find a conveyance to Chagres. After a little inquiry, ascertained that the steamship "Georgia" would sail for Chagres in about three days. We purchased tickets for the latter place for fifty dollars each; and by the time I had purchased my outfit, and paid my bills at the hotel, I had a ten-dollar gold piece, and an old-fashioned, smooth, Down-East ninepence left. With this I had got to get from Chagres to San Francisco; how, I didn't know; but as I had received instructions to "try it," from a source that had never failed to furnish means in an emergency, I thought some way would turn up by which I could get up the coast.

The "Georgia" was a new ship of over three thousand tons register. All her officers belonged to the United States Navy, and she was commanded by Lieut. Rogers. There were five hundred steerage and three hundred cabin passengers.

When we went on board I hunted for my berth, the number on my ticket being 478; but upon investigation I found that there were only about 250 berths, all told, in the steerage. I will not attempt to describe the scene, among hundreds of passengers, after they had ascertained that there were less than half berths enough for them. Suffice it to say, such swearing and imprecations I never heard before. The officers put up some temporary berths every night, to be taken down in the morning, but not half enough to accommodate the passengers. This was sufficient cause for perpetual murmurings and growling; and, to make things still worse, we stopped off Charleston, S.C., to bury two of the passengers who died from pneumonia on the passage; and learned there that the steamship "Falcon" from New Orleans was on her way to meet us at Havana, and transfer four hundred passengers on to our already overloaded ship, to be carried to Chagres. This news created the greatest excitement imaginable. The passengers got up indignation meetings, appointed a committee to wait upon the captain, and protest against taking on any more passengers.

The committee consisted of three, of which I was one. I told them, while they were talking about it, how it would turn out; that the captain had nothing to do but navigate the ship from place to place as the owners, or their agents, might dictate. But they were very boisterous; and, for one, I didn't *dare* to refuse to comply with their wishes. The captain received us very courteously; but the mission ended precisely as I told them it would. The thirteenth day after leaving New York, we passed in by the Moro Castle, a large and magnificent fort, mounted with the heaviest guns, completely guarding the entrance into the harbor, and commanding the city.

Here the most frothy and disaffected passengers besieged the American consul's office, imploring that functionary to intervene his official influence, and prevent any more passengers coming on board. Their applications proving abortive, they became desperate, and threatened all sorts of things. Some would sue the owners when they got home; others were going to stop the ship; and still others threatened to hang

the captain at the yardarm if another passenger came
on board. While they were talking with the consul, the " Falcon" steamed alongside of our ship, and
transferred four hundred passengers with their luggage. Some of our passengers then left for home:
whether they ever got any satisfaction, I never heard.

As soon as this last instalment of passengers had
been transferred to our ship, we got our anchor, and
steamed out to sea, and four days after anchored in
Chagres, about half-past nine, A.M.; and before night
every passenger and their luggage was out of the
ship.

Some of my friends, unbeknown to me, had succeeded in procuring the services of a Mr. Smith, who
owned a large flat-bottomed rowboat, to take us up
the river to Gorgona situated at the head of naviga-
tion for even boats; the compensation to be thirty-
two dollars each, payable in advance. The boys had
all paid their passage, and taken their places in the
boat, while I lingered on the bank: they were waiting for me to get in. Seeing me hesitate, unconscious
of the cause, they kept saying, " Come, captain, get
in." I made no response, but stood there like a " mum-
chance " (whatever that may mean), in a sort of
stupor. Mr. Smith, who was standing in the stern
near me, said, " If you are going, get in." Upon this I
stepped in, and handed him my " eagle " (ten dollars),
saying at the same time in a suppressed tone, " That
is all I can give." He took it, and said, " Say nothing; " and I didn't say "nothing."

This was four, P.M. The boat was rowed by six
natives: we kept on until sunset, when opposite a

small town, the houses made of large bamboo reeds, roofs thatched with straw. The boat was laid alongside of the bank, and we made preparations for camping out for the first time in our lives. I was well acquainted with all in the boat, with two exceptions; that is, as well as one could be in the time we had been associated: at any rate, they had much confidence in my integrity and honor; and as I was a rare one in the gang, because not addicted to drink, they made me a sort of bank of deposit for their valuables, while they were carousing and drinking among the natives. When the time came to settle the bills, they all agreed that I should pay nothing, as I was their guardian. On account of the low stage of the river, we didn't arrive at our destination by boat until the third day about two, P.M. We were now within twenty-two miles of the city of Panama, from whence we hoped to get a conveyance up the coast.

It was a question with our gang, which would be the best way to get over these twenty-two miles. Some, in fact nearly all, thought it best to purchase mules, or hire some to take us over the road, and dispose of them as best we could at Panama. Finally they appealed to me, to see what method I thought best. Of course to purchase a mule, at even a low price, would make a fearful draft upon my *ninepence*, which I desired to keep intact. As I had more than compensated the company for my grub thus far, I didn't feel beholden to them; further, if the state of my finances had been exactly opposite from what they were, I should not have favored either buying or hiring mules except to carry our trunks, &c. So

20

I told them, that as there were but twenty-two miles to go, and over the best road in the world, the moon being full and the weather hot, by starting at sunset on foot we could make the distance easier and quicker than on mules; and by keeping together should be safe from marauders; also that, if we chose to do so, we could get refreshments and take a short nap at the half-way house. All but two agreed to my proposition, and at sunset started on shanks' mare, for a night's walk. The moon made the night almost as light as day. We took a rest at the half-way house a couple of hours, then proceeded on our way, and entered the city of Panama Sunday morning, April 1, 1849, just as the sun was rising and illuminating the broad expanse of the Pacific.

We found the city filled with people, estimated at 5,000, on their way to the gold-mines, waiting for a chance to get up the coast; consequently every hotel and boarding-house was filled to repletion, and prices for accommodation were raised to fabulous rates. After breakfast we held a consultation about the best course to pursue, and how we should get along until we could get away. As the length of time was uncertain, it was necessary to economize our expenses as much as possible, especially on my part. Finally it was agreed to get some place to stop in, and get our food as best we could. I was appointed to hunt round, and see what I could find; they were to keep together until I could report. In this mission I was remarkably fortunate; for in less than a half-hour I found and hired a hall, large enough to accommodate all hands, at ten cents a day per man. We were not long in taking possession of our new quarters, well pleased at our good fortune.

Assisted by Charlie Mason, a cabinet-maker from Lowell, with whom I had been on intimate terms since we left New York, I took possession of the valuables of the company, he and I taking turns in doing sentinel duty all day; and before night I had got completely rested.

I had been thinking occasionally through the day about how I should get to my destination. I had heard it said that a small amount of gold could be drawn out fine enough to encircle the globe; but how my *ninepence*, which I still had intact, could be stretched out so as to cover five hundred dollars, was an enigma hard to solve; and although the vast multitude waiting to get up the coast, any one of whom could pay almost any amount asked, only tended to enhance the difficulty, still I felt comparatively easy. The thought every now and then would intrude itself, that somehow or other something would turn up by which I could get out of the difficulty; how, I had not the remotest idea. Finally, about six o'clock, P.M., while lying on the floor thinking these things over, I heard my unseen friend say, " Let us take a walk," or, " Take a walk," I do not remember which sentence. However, as I had become so accustomed to heed whatever came from this mysterious source, I jumped up at once, and told Charlie that I was going to take a walk. I sallied out, and intuitively headed for the beach. I supposed, that, as I had been lying round all day, my friend wanted me to exercise for remedial purposes.

I passed down street; and just as I had got to the lower end of the plaza, or square, I saw looming up before me a large, modern-built building, on the end of which were the words, "*Pacific Mail Steamship Company's Office.*" Instantly I thought I could see in this the significance of the invitation to "take a walk." At any rate, I felt that in some way or other here was an end to my difficulty without making a draft upon my ninepence. I retraced my steps with pleasant anticipations of the future, but said nothing to my friend Charlie about my discovery.

The next morning bright and early, after a good night's sleep, I was on my way to find out what would come of my discovery the night before. When crossing the plaza, in looking towards the building, I saw a man come out, tack a paper up on one side of the door-jamb, and retire inside. I kept my eye on the paper until I read its contents, which I found to be an advertisement for twelve carpenters, to go on board the steamship "Oregon," lying at the island of Toboga, twelve miles distant. After perusing its contents, I went into the office to see about a job. I told the agent what I wanted. He first asked if I had any tools. I knew if I said *no*, I couldn't get the place: therefore I said, "*Yes;*" and I had, but not as many as would be required to do the simplest kind of work. Upon this he enrolled my name on the books of the company. My compensation was to be three dollars per day and board, for one month at Toboga, and then the passage up the coast at the same pay, besides throwing in the passage. This was more than I could have asked. I had not only secured

my passage to San Francisco, but was employed for
six weeks, including the passage, at higher wages
than I ever received before, with board and passage
thrown in. After taking my name, he asked me if I
knew of any other carpenters. Upon answering in
the affirmative, he told me to fetch them there. Of
course I made a straight wake to our rendezvous, and,
selecting such as I knew to be carpenters, told them
of the chance I had found for prosecuting our voyage,
and the terms. As it was yet early, we arrived at
the office before there had been another application
since I left. Enrolling their names with mine, the
agent told us to be down at the boat, pointing it out
on the beach, at nine o'clock, when the captain would
take us on board. After getting something to eat,
we took our things, and went to the boat, as happy a
set of fellows as one would meet with in a lifetime.
Instead of nine, A.M., it was near eleven before the
captain made his appearance; and it was after one
o'clock before we got on board the ship.

After getting dinner, the captain sent the purser
with a request for us to select from among ourselves a
foreman to take charge of the work. Then first did we
find out the character of the work. We were to put
in the after lower saloon, near one hundred feet long.
To me this was a stunner, for the reason, that although
I was called, and was in fact, a first-class ship-carpen-
ter, yet I knew positively nothing about ship-joinery.
The trades of ship-carpentry and ship-joinery are as
dissimilar as black and white. So with house-car-
penters and house-joiners: both have regular trades,
which are quite dissimilar. Both, however, go under

20*

the cognomen of carpentry. So it is in other departments of mechanics. When I saw the advertisement was for carpenters, I never thought but what it meant the trade I was familiar with. Not one of us gave it a thought, until we were called upon by the purser. The officers all belonged to the navy, and were commanded by Lieut. Patterson.

Not one of the gang seemed willing to take the responsibility of being boss, after finding out the character of the work. We all pitched upon a Mr. Kimball from Portland, Me., who was a first-class ship-joiner; but he refused, on the score that most of the work ought to be done by cabinet-makers, and said, rather than boss the job, he'd go ashore, and stay there until he got a chance up the coast. I said nothing, being busy with my own thoughts concerning the predicament I had got into without a chance of getting out of it. Failing in getting Mr. Kimball to accept the situation, they next turned to me. Of course it will be seen, that of all the crew, I was perhaps the least qualified. At first I felt surprised at their preference, forgetting, for the time being, that they were ignorant of my incompetency. I was about declining, when I heard my unseen friend say, "Try it." This gave me a little strength; for, to tell the truth, I felt weak from head to foot at the damaging prospects. Thousands of thoughts flashed through my brain in an instant; such as, If somebody don't take it, they'll all go ashore, and you with them, without money or friends. And besides, I thought that if I undertook it, I would not be expected to do more than to see that the work was executed properly; and as I could see no way but to try it, as suggested, and trust to circumstances as to how I should manage, with my small stock of knowledge, to boss the work satisfactorily. All these things rushed through my brain in less time than I can write a short paragraph. At last I said, " Well, gentlemen, although I do not feel competent for the task, as there is no other one willing to take the responsibility, I'll do the best I can."

They all seemed pleased at my acceptance, when I followed the " clerk " to the captain's office; who received me very cordially, talked about the job, asking whether I thought I could get it done by the 1st of May, &c. I assured him that, as far as I could see, there was no difficulty in getting through by that time. At this, he took out the plans from which we were to work. When he handed me the plans, I looked at them carelessly, perceiving which he asked me, " Is it a complicated job? " — " Oh, no! " I said; at the same time, I knew no more about it than he did. The officers, he said, would show me where the lumber and materials could be found. With this, I went forward, while looking at the plans as though I really knew something about them. Mr. Kimball observed, if he had known they were so plain and simple, he should not have objected in taking the responsibility of " bossing " the job. I distinctly remember thinking at the time, that, if they were so very plain to him, they were all Greek to me; but I said nothing. Silence, and waiting for some favorable circumstance to turn up by which my total ignorance might be turned into a

semblance of knowledge, being my only stock in
trade, I had to look out sharp, not draw too liberally upon it, and not lose a reputation that did *not*
belong to me until the work was fairly under way.
As I was "boss," of course the men expected me to
set them at work; and I was puzzling my brain how
I should find out what was to be done. I merely
knew, or rather heard them say, that a saloon was to
be put in the ship somewhere; where, I did not know,
— whether forward or aft, on deck or between decks;
further than this the whole thing was as dark as
Erebus. I did a good deal of bossing in getting the
materials on deck, and wished it would last forever.
I kept busy thinking, while getting the stuff down,
what the d——l I should find for the men to do next.
In addition to our twelve men there were some half-
dozen others who had preceded us, and all looking
up to me for a "job." I was so muddled that what
little I did know of carpentry began to ooze out of
my finger-ends; but, about the time the last stick of
timber was on deck, I happened to overhear one man
say to another, "We shall want two or three benches,
and a half-dozen horses or so." Lucky thought for
me! Here was something to busy some of the men
the remainder of that and probably part of the next
day; and, while racking my brain to find something
to set the rest to work on, Mr. Kimball approached,
saying that he would like to have a "standing job,"
as he was an old man. I says, "Very well, Mr. Kimball: what would you prefer doing?"— "Well," said
he, "there are those pilasters: there are a great
many of them, also the base-blocks. I can take a

man to work with me, and get them all ready by the time the rest will get ready to put them up." All this was as clear as "mud" to me, whatever it might be to him. What a "pilaster" was, was a puzzler. I couldn't remember of ever hearing the word spoken: whether it was long or short, wide or narrow, thin or thick, I hadn't the slightest conception. Then the "base-blocks:" I knew that "base" meant doing some mean, wicked act. I also knew that partly rotten or shaky wood was called bad, unfit for use, but never heard it called "base."

From his conversation I supposed that the "pilasters," "base-blocks," and "capitals" occupied an important place in the prosecution of the work; further than that I couldn't even guess. Getting out the "stuff" for the doors, I had a pretty clear conception of, although I failed to understand what was meant by "stiles," "rails," and "muntings." All I knew about it was, that, when all these things were put together, I supposed a door was the result.

After I had assented to Mr. Kimball's proposition (whatever it meant) he says, "Let me see, how wide are the pilasters?" reaching for the plans, which I held with as much dignity as a "boss" should. I handed him the whole roll, not knowing enough about them to select the drawing needed. "Oh!" said he, "they are six inches wide;" continuing, "let us go down and ascertain their length." Now, I thought, I shall find out what a pilaster means, and where it goes; keeping remarkably reticent, for fear of compromising the high estimation they entertained of my superior ability. There is a sort of instinctive pride with all of us, to impress upon others our superior proficiency in whatever we are doing; and this is a remarkable characteristic with this class of mechanics. When about commencing any new piece of work, and especially if it is complicated, they are prolific with suggestions as to the best way to do it; often saying, "Some do it this way," telling about it, but "I prefer this way," describing it. This was remarkably so with Mr. Kimball; and, by the time he got through telling how to do it two ways, one must be unusually stupid not to get hold of something to his advantage, especially if he is seeking for light upon a mysterious subject, as this was to me. He seemed anxious to impress me with his superior knowledge and skill. I knew just enough to let him do all the talking; and, as I didn't object to his suggestions, he seemed to feel flattered at my acquiescence to his way of doing things, when in real truth I knew positively nothing of what he was talking about. He evidently considered me possessed of superior knowledge and skill in the profession; and I had not the slightest disposition to disabuse him of his misconception. He got two sticks, for what, I didn't know, and started aft. I allowed him to go ahead, following with the plans as a "boss" should; he got aft, and went down the after-hatch. It will be recollected that I didn't even know where the saloon was to be, but Mr. Kimball seemed to know all about it; he obtained his knowledge from a plan of the deck, unnoticed by me.

When we got below, he took another look at the plan of the cabin that was to be, and counted the staterooms as represented on it. Having ascertained by measuring how far forward it would come, he got the distance between decks with the two sticks referred to, after nailing them together; and asked me the height of the " capitals " and " base-blocks," expecting me to ascertain from the working plan. Here was another puzzler; although I knew, from what I had heard him say, that they were somehow or other intimately associated with the " pilasters; " which latter I supposed by his saying they were six inches wide, and by his getting the distance between decks, were to occupy a perpendicular position somewhere in the work; but, how or where, I hadn't the least conception.

Before he made the request, I noticed the captain and some of the officers coming down the gangway. Pretending I wanted to speak to the captain, but really to get away and save myself the trouble of doing something that I couldn't have done to save the world, I left the plans, and went towards them. I hadn't gone a dozen steps, when, in looking back, I saw him overhauling the plans. That was all I wanted; and I came to where he was looking over them, before he had ascertained the desired information. By this I got an inkling of what, up to this time, had been wrapped up in impenetrable mystery. By the plan, the capitals were eight and " base-blocks " ten inches in height, making in both eighteen inches; which, deducting from the height between decks, left the exact length of the " pilasters." I suggested to Mr. Kimball the importance of knowing about what there was to do, in the first place, so that I could have all parts going on at once; my object being more to find out the meaning of *names* used to designate the different parts of a door, so that I could talk to the men intelligently about getting out the stuff, than for any solicitude about how soon the work could be done.

Mr. Kimball said, " Certainly: if one didn't see the last blow before he struck the first one, he would work to disadvantage throughout the whole job," little thinking that his " boss " could take neither the one nor the other. Suffice it to say that through his aid I got the dimension and number of pieces for the whole lot.

Things began to look clearer as I had found out the meaning of terms that a few moments before were totally unintelligible. It would have been laughable to one in the secret, to see how wondrous prolific I had become all at once with my rule; but, as I wasn't out of the woods yet, I had to watch myself carefully, not to upset the whole thing by making any blunders in speech or act.

Mr. Kimball selecting a man to work with him, I set the others making benches and horses, and getting out stuff for the doors; and by noon the next day I had the whole job fairly under way, busying myself in going from one to another to see that they were doing their work *properly*.

When I saw a man doing something I didn't understand, I would say to him, " Why do it so ? " pretending I was dissatisfied, but really intending to find out his reasons for doing so and so, which he would give with all his possible eloquence. After finding out what I wanted, I would say, "Never mind: I guess that'll do." By this process I became proficient in a position forced upon me by sheer force of circumstances, and which I carried out to the satisfaction of all concerned. The first day of May she started up the coast with seven hundred passengers. I worked all the way up. We had a fine passage, stopping at Acapulco a few hours to replenish our coal; and landed in San Francisco on the 20th of May, 1849. Thus ends another quite remarkable experience of my life, considering the untoward circumstances that attended me from the first day when I set out.

To say I had no outside aid in navigating through the intricate channel I was forced into without so much as getting one set-back, would be arrogating to myself properties I did not possess; nor do I wish to be looked upon in that light. There were many other amusing and intensely interesting incidents, and ridiculous anecdotes, directly connected with the part I was compelled to play in the drama, which I might relate; but, to carry out the object of the book, I need not give many, other than the more prominent ones, leaving the rest to appear in another book I'm writing, entitled "Odds and Ends," a continuation of this autobiography in detached pieces, which will be filled to repletion with incidents of a less prominent character, but not a whit less interesting.

I arrived at San Francisco on the 20th of May, and went immediately to the post-office, where I received a letter from my brother Thomas, in answer to one I sent before leaving home, directing me how to find him. While waiting for my turn in the long line of men who had preceded me, I saw a little piece of paper tacked up on the side of the building, on which was written these words, " If D. C. Densmore will call at a certain place (naming it, which I have forgotten), he will hear something to his advantage." Who it was, I couldn't divine; but, on going to the place designated, found Isaac Chapman, my brother-in-law. He had a job of carpenter-work on a new house, which he expected to finish in about a week, after doing which he was going to the mines. This was most opportune for me, as he had a tent on Rincon Point, where he lodged and took his meals, with the exception of dinners, which he obtained at a saloon. As he was going to the mines soon, and it being rather early to go forthwith on account of the swollen condition of the rivers and streams, I concluded to wait for him.

Failing to get a job with him, and anxious to make the most of my time, I tried all the ship, or rather boat yards, some half-dozen or so, for a job, every one of which had all the men they wanted. This was Saturday, the day after my arrival. They were building what were called water-boats, with a large tank in the hold, in which to bring fresh water from up the Sacramento River to supply the city. At that time there was a great scarcity of water for culinary purposes, to say nothing about a supply in case of fires.

Ship-carpenters were getting twelve dollars per day; and I didn't like the idea of laying still, if it was possible to get a job, if only for a week. I told my brother I should get work among some of them on Monday, although I had failed at every place where I had applied.   He said it was hardly possible, as there were thousands who had been there months, waiting to get into the mines, whose funds had become exhausted; and they had been trying all this time to get something to do. I knew the chances were against me; but I sallied out early Monday morning, and the third one I applied to was a Dutchman from Baltimore. I had been refused by him on Saturday, but so many had been applying that he didn't recognize me. When I asked this time if he wanted any more help, he replied very gruffly, "*No.*" I said I was used to work, and I was going to work whether he wanted me or not. He mumbled over something which I took to be, "If you do I won't pay you any thing." At any rate, I hallooed out as loud as I could yell, "I don't care a d——n whether you do or not, but work I will." I borrowed a few tools from some of the chaps, and got to work about half-past nine, and kept at it until Thursday, before the old gruff Teuton condescended to speak to me. When he did speak, I for a while made believe I didn't hear him. Finally I said, "Did you speak?" he says, "*Yes*, many times, but you didn't hear me." I said I was too busy to talk, and asked him to call when I was less engaged. One would think this rather rough language to an employer; but when it is taken into account that he *didn't* employ me, that I went to work on my own hook, not expecting full compensation, if indeed any thing, then it doesn't seem so much out of place. I was bound to have some fun out of it, if nothing else; and, besides, I had much rather work for nothing, than loiter round in such a place as San Francisco was then.

The old fellow saw by my work that I was more profitable than any one of his gang: hence his good feelings. When he paid us off Saturday, he came to me with a lot of money in a handkerchief, some of it loose, the rest in ten-dollar packages, saying, " You may count it, or take my word for it." I said, I didn't care, as long as there was some, continuing, " Now I'm going to the mines." — " No, you hain't," he says: " you forced yourself in; and you must work another week, and help get that boat in the water."

After getting supper, I counted the money received from him; and, sure enough, there was not only full wages, but the one-fourth of a day I didn't work, making $72. As Isaac wasn't ready, I *did* work another week; at the expiration of which he offered me twelve dollars per day until the 20th of December following, payable every week whether he had work, or not, — pretty good proof of his appreciation of my workmanship.

I mention this incident simply to show that perseverance under discouraging prospects sometimes, in fact often, proves most propitious.

As my brother was expecting me, and I also wanted to try my hand at mining, I refused this most liberal offer of the Dutchman, and, in company with my brother-in-law, started for the mining district.

It is not deemed necessary to give details about how we got to Sacramento. Suffice it to say, we took passage from the latter place on a stern-wheel steam-boat for Marysville, situated at the junction of the Uba and Feather Rivers. From here we had to foot it ninety miles to get where my brother was mining. This was too much for Mr. Chapman: so he stopped, hoping to get a chance to ride part of the way, as there were occasionally long Mexican trains of mules loaded with merchandise for some of the interior towns. After waiting a month, he hired a man to take him to Forster's Bar, within forty miles of where my brother was working his claim; from there he was obliged to walk. We arrived at Marysville early in the morning, and finding, as before stated, no conveyance except shanks' mare, there being some twenty miles to traverse over a flat prairie before reaching the foot of the mountain, and the weather being exceedingly hot, I waited until four, P.M., so that the sun would be less oppressive, and then started in company with a Mr. St. John, to cross this wood-less plateau, hoping to reach what was called the Blue Tent, some four miles beyond the prairie, before dark. I had bought a pair of new cowhide boots, being told such were easier to travel in than others. Also I purchased a pint of Medford rum to put into them occasionally, to keep my feet from blistering; but this was a mistake, as it tended to directly the oppo-site, at least it was so in my case; and by the time we reached the Blue Tent, about eight, P.M., my feet were badly blistered. Laid by the next day, and the following made only five miles. After this we made better time; but it was not until the fourth day that we finished the ninety miles. Found my brother

21*

well and hearty, and one of ten who owned the best claim on the river, as everybody said. He gave me. one-half of his claim, on condition that I would help him work. The claim consisted of a certain territory below the falls. To make it available we would have to dig a canal, and turn the water into it. We could dig the canal, but couldn't turn the river into it until it had reached its lowest stage; and this wouldn't occur until the last of August or first of the September following. We worked all summer on the canal, and didn't finish it until the middle of August; at which time we commenced on the dam. Owing to unforseen obstacles, we did not get the dam finished until the fourteenth of September, and that left us but thirteen days to work, for, by a decision of the *alcalde*, we were obliged to leave it on the twenty-eighth of September. The facts were, we had got into a difficulty with a company above us, the latter claiming that we had no right to back the water up so as to prevent them working their claim; and, to end the dispute, both parties agreed to leave it to this functionary to decide the difficulty between us; and although there wasn't a particle of doubt as to our priority, yet, as our neighbors were a hard set of customers, the *alcalde* thought best to decide as above. Without going into all the details as to how we surmounted the formidable obstacles we had to overcome in constructing the dam where the current was running ten miles per hour and ten feet deep, will merely say that we *did* accomplish the herculean task, as before stated, and took out in the thirteen days allowed us over ten thousand dollars; and I haven't the least doubt but that in a month more we could have accumulated ten times that amount; for we had barely got to work before we had to leave.

The time had come when we must decide whether to remain in the mountains all winter, or go to the city; for, in three or four weeks at most, the rainy season would be upon us, when we couldn't get out if we wanted to. If we concluded to stay we had no time to lose in making our preparations, as we were obliged to get our supplies from the city before the rains set in.

After taking every thing into account, concluded to start on our way home on the morrow. The next day disposed of all our mining apparatus to our neighbors who intended remaining through the winter, and that night, at two, A.M., started on our way towards San Francisco. We found some fifteen or twenty besides our gang going out, and agreed to keep together for mutual protection, all being heavily armed with revolvers and rifles, and every one a dead shot but myself. I suppose I might manage to hit a large tree if not over a rod from me; but my ability to hit a man his length off was something I would not want to bet upon.

Leaving out the incidents that happened on our way out (and there were many amusing ones), I will say that after a four days' march we arrived at Marysville, where we took passage in a steamer to Sacramento, from whence took another steamer for San Francisco, where we arrived in due time.

The day succeeding our arrival, we found a bark to start for Panama in a few days, upon which we engaged a passage to the latter place ; or if any of us chose to land at Realejo, and take the overland route through Central America, we could do so. After a passage of near three weeks, some thirty of the passengers, including Thomas and self, were landed at Realejo.

All hands bought mules, and with a guide started, the second day after disembarking, across the country towards Nicaragua, situated at the head of a lake by that name, from where we could take boats down the lake and San Juan River to the Atlantic coast.

We were some fifteen days on the route before we entered the city. Remaining here a couple of weeks, we started down the lake in what the natives call a bungo, a large, flat-bottomed boat, employed to carry mahogany to San Juan del Sud, situated at the foot of the San Juan River. Leaving out all incidents connected with the passage, we landed at the outlet of the river the tenth day after leaving Nicaragua. Finding no conveyance to the States, and it being uncertain how long we should have to remain there, to save expense a few of us hired a shanty, and went to housekeeping. It being the rainy season, we had to use a great deal of caution against contracting the intermittent fever, so prevalent there at that season of the year. We hadn't occupied our quarters but about a week when the English steamship " Tay," a Carthaginian packet from London, came steaming into the harbor to replenish her coal. On board of her we engaged a passage to Chagres, where she was bound. After getting her supply of coal, steamed out to sea, and the third day anchored at Chagres.

The same day we bought tickets for New York, on the steamship " Kingston," which sailed for Kingston, Jamaica, where the ship was to replenish her coal, and where we arrived the third day after leaving Chagres. Here we remained one day and night, when we got under way, and started on our homeward stretch; and, after a rough passage of twelve days from Kingston, hauled into the dock in New York the 18th of December, 1849, about nine months after I left home.

I was sick all the way from Kingston with something, I knew not what to call it. It was the result of exposures on the way from Nicaragua to Chagres in the rainy season, as we were obliged to lay down in the open air in our blankets all the way, with the exception of a few days at San Juan. I was out of my head part of the time; and when we arrived in New York I could hardly stand. We landed early in the morning, and, as I had not eaten much of any thing since leaving the West Indies, I thought I would get a hot oyster-stew, although I had no appetite for it. I thought, if I could get it down, it would warm me up, as I was freezing to death all the time. I took a few spoonfuls, and left it. And, although it was early morning, I got a ticket on a Fall River boat, and got into my berth more dead than alive, and remained there until called upon to take the cars at Fall River for Boston, where I arrived about six, A.M. I was so weak and exhausted that I couldn't walk without staggering. I wanted to go to the Portland boat. I couldn't ride in a carriage, and started off on foot; and, though I knew the way, the farther I went, the less natural things looked. I reeled from one side of the walk to the other, often hearing the remark, " There goes a drunken cuss thus early." I was too sick to notice them; and when near the East Boston ferry I sat down on some cedar timber to rest. I had but just got down, when a man walking very rapidly, as I thought, to catch the boat, noticing me looking so sick, stopped, and asked me if I wanted help. I told him I did not, that I had plenty of time, and should be in season for the boat. " What boat?" he asked. I told him; and he said, " You are a long way from that wharf. Sha'n't I get a carriage? You look very feeble." I told him I couldn't ride in a carriage. He then insisted upon helping me to the boat himself, assisted me up, and then, taking my blankets, I took his arm; and after a long while, for so it seemed to me, we got to the landing. It being low water, the wide gangway stage on which they were taking in freight pitched at an angle of twenty-five degrees; but, being very wide, I refused his offer to assist me on board, as I thought he was in a hurry. Thanking him for his kindness, I started down the gangway; but being so weak, and by this time completely exhausted, I reeled from side to side ; and, although I had not over twenty feet to go, I came near in one of my sideway staggers going into the dock. After I got on deck, I looked back, and there the Good Samaritan was looking at me, it seemed with bated breath, at the narrow chance I had run of getting into the dock. We waved adieus to each other when he started up the wharf.

While making the dangerous passage from the wharf to the boat, I heard one say, " Look out, old fellow, or you'll get cooled off in the ice-water," intimating that he thought I was drunk. Another remarked, " There goes a drunken fool." I thought, if they knew how miserable I felt, they would be more charitable. I purchased my ticket, found my berth, and tumbled into it " all standing," not being able to take even my hat or boots off. Seeing the chambermaid passing, I called her, stating that I was very sick and weak, and asked her to get me a little toast and a cup of strong tea, which she soon brought. After drinking the tea, and eating part of the toast, I felt better, and was soon fast asleep. I have been thus particular in detailing this uninteresting episode, that I may pay a tribute of gratitude to that good, generous, large-souled man, who verified the old adage, that " a friend in need is a friend indeed."

The next morning, long before daylight, the boat was at her wharf in Portland; and, it being Sunday, I was obliged to stop at a hotel until the next morning at six, A.M., when a train would start for Waterville, where I had a brother who kept a hotel. It commenced snowing at the time we started; and before eight we were hard and fast in a snow-drift in one of the deep cuts. All hands belonging to the train were obliged to shovel snow for an hour before the engine could go along. I had felt cold all the morning, although I was well bundled up; and after the train stopped I fell asleep. I woke shaking all over; I thought I should freeze to death. I fairly shook the car; and do what I might, or try as hard as I could

not to shake, I kept on. I thought when I awoke,
that the stopping of the train checked the draught
of the stove, and that my chilly feeling proceeded
from the decline of the fire. The passengers got
alarmed at my shaking; and, upon my telling
them I was freezing to death, the women took off
their shawls, and enveloped me in them. But all
to no use; shake I did, in spite of all efforts to
the contrary. There being a little fire in the stove,
and room enough between it and the side of the car
to squeeze in between, some of the anxious ones
advised me to get in there, and see if I couldn't get
warm. I did so, but with no diminution of the awful
shaking. By this time all hands had become excited
to the highest pitch, as they thought I was going to
die in the cars; and I didn't know myself but their
fears would be realized. I remember thinking, that
dying itself was not so very bad, but that, as I had
got so near home, I would rather get there before the
event took place. While everybody was speculating
as to what was best to do for me, an old sailor came
along, and, after listening to their fears, relieved them
and me by saying, " He's got the fever-and-ager; and
he won't die unless he gets too lazy to shake." The
moment he spoke thus all felt relieved; and I wondered why I hadn't thought the like before, for I had
seen hundreds suffering with that loathsome disease.
After shaking a couple of hours, the chill ceased
altogether, when a burning fever set in, and I felt
burning up with a high fever; the sweat poured in
streams down my body and limbs. The fever affecting
my head made me as crazy as a lunatic; and, although

I knew what I said, yet I couldn't help talking over all sorts of stuff, sometimes about digging gold, then reefing topsails, &c. The kind-hearted conductor, as well as all the rest, thought I was crazy. He was very kind, and seemed to take a great interest in me. The fever not abating when we got as far as Lewiston, he stopped the train long enough to take me to a hotel kept by a friend of his. He told me I would be well cared for; and, after charging the proprietor to look out for me until he came back, left. Somehow or other I believed or thought that this man was the best friend I ever had; and amid my wildest mutterings I watched him with the greatest interest, and whatever he said was to me law and gospel. For instance, when he was leaving I thought I heard him tell me not to leave the *room*, though he was merely telling me not to leave the *house* until his return. They got a fire in one of the front chambers, and when warm enough came for me, saying they had a nice, warm room ready, and told me they would help me up; but I wouldn't budge an inch. I said I was told not to leave that room (the bar-room), and I wouldn't. Failing to get me up stairs, they made a bed for me on a wide bench, where I slept by fits and starts until the next morning. I was burning up with fever all night. I threw off all the clothes they would allow me to, but it seemed as if I was being immolated by fire. The next morning, while the folks were at breakfast, and when the clerk had left the office for a moment, I stripped off all clothing but my shirt, and went out into the hall which was covered with snow, sat down on the stairs, and commenced rubbing myself all over with snow. Oh, how cool and refreshing that snow-bath felt! One of the servants having occasion to come into the hall for something, seeing me in such a plight, ran into the dining-room, saying, "That crazy man is rubbing snow all over his naked body." This brought everybody out. They tried by coaxing to get me into the room again. Failing in that, they undertook to coerce me. This I objected to most decidedly, rubbing snow on my body all the while, and occasionally eating it. Finally the proprietor's wife came along, and said a few words in which she expressed so much sympathy, that I yielded instantly to her persuasions. She remained with me some time, and asked me if I wanted something to eat. I said, " *Yes;* some porridge, if you'll make it." When it was brought in, I couldn't taste it. About noon that day, the conductor called to see how I was getting along, and seemed displeased that I hadn't a better room. After learning the cause, he asked me why I didn't take another room. I told him my reason; when he laughed, and said he didn't mean that, and escorted me to the room they had failed to get me.to enter.

The conductor found out, somehow or other before he left me at Lewiston, that I had a brother who run a hotel at Waterville, and hunted him up, and told him of my indisposition. Another brother (George), happening to be there on a visit, came to me with him, and accompanied me to Waterville, whence, after a couple of days, I went to my home, arriving there the twenty-seventh day of December, having been absent a little over nine months.

Thus ends another epoch in my history; in which I had obtained some valuable experiences, which, connected with a fair pecuniary recompense for my time, made the voyage, as a whole, a good success. In about a week after my arrival home, aided by Dr. Bricket and good nursing, I completely recovered from my disability; and by March was ready to enter again the arena of business, and compete for the prize of fortune's favor.

CHAPTER XIII.

THE following May, I moved with my family to
Rockland, where I engaged in ship-building, in which
I was successful for three or four years; but in 1855
a financial crash came all over the country, swamping
thousands in irretrievable ruin. Ships that for three
or four years, especially the clipper class, readily
brought fabulous prices, now became a drug in the
market. In fact, all kinds of shipping became
almost worthless.

At this time I was building a ship of eight hundred tons, every timber-head of which had been
taken up by purchasers before I struck a blow. She
was to be owned principally by her prospective captain and a Boston firm, and some half a dozen small
owners in Rockland. By a strange fatuity, the captain died in Trieste of yellow fever; the Boston
firm failed about the same time; and this was followed by the small owners annulling their contracts:
consequently the ship was left on my hands.

She was so far along I could do nothing but go on and finish her, and abide the consequences. She was of the clipper class, and nobody wanted to invest their money in her. She was finally sold for seventeen thousand dollars less than her actual cost, which swamped me completely; and from that failure I never fully recovered.

An interesting experience connected with my pecuniary affairs, which gave me more real pleasure than almost any event of my life, because it showed how I stood in the estimation of the inhabitants of Rockland, must have notice here. I question whether, in the history of any other strictly religious community (for everybody there belonged to some of the religious denominations), such a universal exhibition of good feeling and downright sympathy was ever accorded to a *notorious* infidel; for such I was called. I was known to every family in town; if not personally, at least by reputation.

The facts of the case were, that I owned a house, and, after purchasing it, made considerable improvements upon the property. When the insurance which was on the property when it came into my possession had run out, I intended to increase the policy a thousand dollars. The above policy expired on the 28th of December, on which day I went down town to get it renewed; but Mr. Cochran, the agent, being absent, and I suffering myself with a bad cold, I thought *one day* would not make much difference, and put it off, thinking I would attend to it on the morrow. I had the cellar full of vegetables, pork, beef, cider, apples, &c., for a winter supply.

22*

That night about two o'clock, the house took fire, and burned down, with the stable and woodshed, each of which was full of hay or wood; and not a thing was saved, except one old bureau. The fire had such headway on before we discovered it, that we had barely time to get the children out before the house was one mass of flames from garret to cellar; we did not save an article of clothing, with the exception of what we had on.

As before stated, I was suffering with a severe cold; and, after tea was over, it was thought best for me to take a regular sweat. It was extremely cold weather; and, we having no fire in any other part of the house except the kitchen, I concluded to go through the operation there on a large lounge. That she might watch and attend me through the night, my wife put a mattress on the floor; and, after I had got under way in sweating, she with the baby lay down on the mattress without disrobing. Some time in the night, in the vicinity of two o'clock, I awoke with a suffocating sensation. I had great difficulty in getting my breath. After a while I perceived the room was densely filled with smoke, and discovered a dim light through the smoke. The light was from a lamp left burning on a table on the opposite side of the room from where I was lying. At the same moment, I saw, issuing from a cupboard on the right side of the chimney, a blaze of fire. In an instant I comprehended the situation, but I was so overcome with the suffocating smoke that I could not speak; I knew enough, however, to awake my wife, who comprehended the state of affairs on waking, and taking the baby in her arms passed through the dining-room to the front door. I took the other child, who was sleeping in another room, and was soon outside. As soon as my lungs were sufficiently clear to let me sing out "*Fire*," I did so. By this time the fire-fiend had got into the dining-room; and our opening the door to go out made a draught through the house, which expedited the work of the devouring monster. After a few moments we had our neighbors around us; and in less than a half-hour the whole town was there. There was one little hand-engine in town; but there having been a long time of dry, cold weather, the wells were insufficient to furnish a supply of water; and, to crown all, it was *dead low* tide. They tried the engine; but it soon gave out through some defect, and would have been useless if water had been ever so abundant. The weather, which had been extremely cold for a few days, at midnight moderated; and snow commenced falling rapidly. As it was useless to try to save my property, the best thing that could be done was to save the adjacent buildings, which at one time was thought impossible; the thing that did save them was the throwing on snow by thousands of willing hands. Not another building took fire; and by daylight there remained not a vestige of what had cost me much hard labor to obtain.

But the best part is to come. By special invitation we, that is, my family and self, took up our quarters at Capt. William Pendleton's for the time being, or until I could find a house to move into. While partaking breakfast with the captain and his beautiful family, and when nearly through with our morning meal, a Mr. Ingraham, a near neighbor of mine, who carried on the blacksmith business, and with whom I had an unsettled account, came into the dining-room, and deposited a package on the table, saying, " That is for you, captain," meaning me. At first I thought it was his bills for work: he knew I had a little money; and I thought he meant to be on hand, and get his pay before it was all gone. I now remember thinking then how hard-hearted he must be to press his suit while my property was still burning; for by the time I had finished my breakfast I had made myself believe he had made a call for money. I dreaded to look at his package, and took no notice of it, because I didn't want to. I was about leaving the table, when Capt. Pendleton drew my attention to the dreaded bundle. " Oh, yes!" said I, at the same time taking it up. Upon taking off the wrapper, what was my surprise, to find, instead of dunning bills, a large package of bank-bills, of all denominations, from one to fifty dollars, and a note reading thus : " A small token of the high appreciation of a few of your numerous friends, who sympathize with you in your recent great loss." Upon counting it I found $585. All this was contributed after the premises were burned to the ground, and before eight o'clock, A.M. This Mr. Ingraham, of whom I had such ungenerous thoughts, was the very one who started the subscription. Not a name accompanied the donation, so that I never knew how much any one contributed. Nor was this all. They kept the thing going; and every day or two I would get a package of money, so that in less than four days I had received over $900.

Everybody wanted to do something; and those that had no money would send wearing apparel for my family and self; so that, besides the money, we had a larger and better wardrobe than before the fire. At South Thomaston where I had done business for about a year, some four miles from Rockland, they got up a subscription of some two hundred and odd dollars, and sent it to me the next day after the fire. A little village on the outskirts of Rockland, where I was but little acquainted and the people poor, made up a sum of thirteen dollars, and sent it to me: this latter sum, considering the poverty of the place, and my limited acquaintance with its inhabitants, seemed to me the most hearty manifestation of good feelings among all the givers. Those who were so poor that they could contribute nothing else offered to contribute work toward putting me up another house. Never having had any experience in such matters before, and feeling totally unworthy of such universal kindness, I was quite incapable of doing aught but show my gratitude by "expressive silence." I found that no distinct class constituted my friends: all, everybody, was my friend.

A few days subsequent, being down town, I happened into the Hon. Kendall Kimball's store, when in speaking of the conflagration he said playfully, "If you wasn't such a confounded *infidel*, you would have some friends in your calamity." This man, as I subsequently learned, put in one hundred dollars before the fire had finished its work. Does it often occur that what we deem faults of omission prove to be great blessings? If I had effected the insurance I

would never have known that there was no limit to
my personal sympathizers and friends, the knowledge
of which made me stronger and better, and gave me
unbounded confidence in prosecuting my business
affairs subsequently, because I knew that I had the
entire confidence of everybody around me, rich and
poor, and that my credit was unlimited; all of which
gave me facilities for competing successfully in the
arduous struggles of life, rarely if ever vouchsafed to
any one having such limited capital as mine.

In the spring of 1852 I became interested in modern Spiritualism. It had been the theme of conversation all over the country for some three or four
years; and, although I had often heard VOICES as
heretofore stated, yet I hadn't the remotest idea
that they emanated from disembodied spirits, as was
being alleged by those who had given Spiritualism
scrutinizing attention. I was often solicited by
friends to investigate the mystery, but had not a
moment to spare outside of my business; and then,
again, I thought that after a while it would die out
entirely, and cease to be even a "nine-days' wonder."

One morning Mr. John Jameson came to me with
a note from a Mr. John Bird, a young married man
who lived on the outskirts of the city, requesting Mr.
Jameson to invite three or four friends, naming whom
he preferred, to call at his house after dark on that
day, and see what they could make out of some manifestations taking place in the presence of himself
and wife. Although Mr. Bird was a strict church-
member, and his father a deacon and quite wealthy,
yet he selected four noted *infidels* to investigate the

mystery. This Mr. Bird, jun., married his wife in Worcester, Mass., from where he had just returned from a visit to his wife's father, who was a confirmed Spiritualist. John and wife were, while making this visit, urged to attend numerous circles with the old man, whom they both thought demented : out of deference to his childish fancies, as they called his enthusiasm, they did not object, and yet took no other interest in the affair than the pleasure of contributing to the old man's happiness.

After partaking tea one evening, a few days after they arrived home, they were speaking of the old gentleman and his insane delusion, as they termed it, when John said to his wife, " Lizzie, let us get the table out, and see if it won't tip for us."

Suiting the action to the word, they sat down to it ; and, behold, it began to rock about as if instilled with an active existence ! Having attended so many séances with their father, they understood the " *modus-operandi* " of asking questions, &c. They experimented, and found that the table would respond intelligently to their mental questions. This established the fact that one or both of them were mediums. Fearing to remain in their own house with " ghosts " around, they spent the night with old Mr. Bird, a few rods distant. The next day Mr. Bird sent the note to Mr. Jameson above referred to. In the course of the day Mr. Jameson got the promise of the invited ones to attend a sitting at Mr. Bird's house. Their names were, John Jameson, Capt. George Brewster, Capt. Smith, and myself; the three latter old " sea-dogs," and all of us very sceptical, especially in relation to matters of a religious or spiritual nature. The distance from our homes was about three and a half miles, and it was in April; and, as sidewalks extended but a short distance out of town, the walking was very muddy and disagreeable.

On our way, we speculated upon what we should see and hear, concluding at last that it was all " bosh and nonsense." At any rate, we agreed among ourselves, before we got there, that, if the table tipped at all, it should tip *towards* us. It was agreed that we would sit on the side directly opposite Mr. and Mrs. Bird. We never had attended a séance; but we got it from Madam Rumor, that the table always tipped towards the medium; and this fact was to our bigoted minds remarkably suspicious. Our reasons were, that as the law of physics said, and no intelligent man dared dispute, it " takes weight to move weight," and according to the most intelligent investigators a thousand spirits didn't weigh an ounce avoirdupois; and consequently the *medium* must press downward if the table tipped over toward the medium at all, whether conscious of pressing or not. This was a knock-down argument with us; and, as before stated, no one disputed the reasoning. On the road, if I saw any one ahead that I thought would know me, I turned out, and went alongside of the fence, as if judging that I could get along easier there, but really to avoid being known; for I felt ashamed of what we mutually called a wild-goose-chase, and thought everybody whom we met knew what we were up to.

Although we were debarred suspicion that machinery would be used, by both the fact that Mr. Bird was so frightened he didn't dare to sleep in his own house, and that he was above any attempt to practise deception, yet to show our remarkable Yankee skill in detecting fraud, and to acquire a reputation for being keen to detect stupidity in others, we looked under the table, and pushed it over the floor, as if we expected to find cords attached to it in some way, though each one of us knew there was no such thing, and that we were only showing off remarkable (?) detective powers.

After satisfying ourselves, the table was placed in the middle of the floor; and, all things being ready, John took his seat on one side, and, as per agreement, we four sat down on the opposite side. John put his hands on the table: we did the same. The table didn't budge an inch. Then Mr. Bird says to his wife, who was fixing up the room, " Lizzie, come and sit down." She put one hand lightly on the table; and John put the question, " Are there any spirits here? " Instantly the table commenced to rise slowly on our side, we using our united efforts to keep it down. The leaf on our side cracked and snapped as though it was coming off; and, for fear it would break under our pressure, we " let up " a little, though still bearing down all we thought the table would bear. It didn't seem to notice our opposing force, but rose up from the floor, moved up and down easily three times without touching the floor, and then let itself down as gently as we could if trying to see how lightly we could let it down. When the table began to rise with our determination not to allow it to do so, my hair went up with it; for I saw in an instant, that all my vaunted philosophy and pretended knowledge of the law of physics was knocked higher than a kite. I saw that here was actual power "not dreamed of in my philosophy."

I was a medium myself: yet it was some two or three years after this séance before I was fully satisfied of the fact; and I doubt whether, if I had to depend upon others besides myself for tests, I should have ever given it sufficient attention to prove its reality.

But to return to the séance. After the table had answered several questions put by Mr. Bird, he told us we could ask such questions mentally as could be answered by yes or no; yet that one person only should ask at a time. I was requested to try first. I did so; and, without going into details, will say that I asked the table all sorts of mental questions pertaining to things that transpired both in the long ago and in recent days; to all of which the table, or something else, knew how to and did manifest correct answer. All the rest did the same. I noticed that old Capt. Brewster, who sat next to me, after getting through with his questions, looked very sober; and I said to him, "What do you think of it, Capt. George?" He responded, in his rough way, "By G—d, I don't know what to think of it." He had lost his wife; and had been asking questions, and getting as intelligent and appropriate responses as though she had been personally present. After occupying an hour or so with tipping the table, we tried other experiments: for instance, something would hold the table down to the floor so that the strongest man could not raise it more than an inch or two. It seemed as though one was applying his strength to stretch or pull out a strong thick piece of India-rubber; and, when requested to do so, the table would become so light all at once, that all four of us sitting on its top, with the leaves down, couldn't keep it on the floor. Thus we experimented a long while, and got home about midnight, well pleased and much astonished with our wild-goose chase.

After getting to my home, I went into the dining-room, where was a lamp burning on a large dining-table on which were all the plates, pitchers, knives and forks, &c. I placed my fingers lightly on one end; and to my astonishment the farther end began to rise gradually, until the dishes began to slide towards me, when I said aloud, as though some one or more were lifting the farther end, " Oh, don't let the things slide off the table!" when instantly it commenced to lower a little. After a minute or so the table came down as quiet and easy as if some one was trying to see how lightly it could be done. After this manifestation, I went out into the stable in the dark, and upstairs on the hay, where it was totally dark, and waited some time to see a spirit, as I was told that they could be seen in the dark. After waiting a half-hour or so, I came down, and got ready for bed. Thus ended my first night with the spirits; and thus began a work that has engaged my close attention since, in many parts of the world, and which has caused me more real happiness and supreme felicity than all else combined, because it *proved* to me, without a shadow of a shade of doubt, the immortality of man ; proved that death was only a change of residences ; that in this life we were only going though a gestational process, not dissimilar to the embryotic growth of the infant, after which the child is born into the actualities of this mundane existence : so at death we shall be born into the actualities of the life beyond, with all our faculties, dispositions, and peculiarities, loves, likes, and their opposites, unimpaired ; in fact, greatly intensified. To sum it all up, it proved, as Dr. Franklin said in a letter to a friend who was deploring the loss of a beloved sister, among other things in condolence, that " *we are not really born until we die.*"

The above séance also brought possible explanation of what I had all my life considered a mystery ; viz., who gave me audible instructions what to do in trying emergencies, and told how to proceed to get out of difficult dilemmas. I now began to see that this *might* proceed from attendent guides who exercised a watchful care over my career from my earliest infancy. But this remained to be proved. Being naturally a sceptic to every thing relating to the mysterious and marvellous, it took a vast amount of evidence to convince me of its reality. Still this first séance took the starch out of all my preconceived notions, and pompous arrogance of knowledge in matters I knew nothing about, relating to the spiritual part of man ; and it opened up a vast unexplored territory, the nearest confines of which I had not as yet seen, nor believed to exist except in the fertile imagination of the superstitious enthusiast.

The possibilities of what might be concealed at a longer or shorter distance from where I stood excited such a powerful desire in my mind, to know more of this to me greatest wonder of the nineteenth century, that it enlisted all my powers of observation and research, to find out for myself this mystery of mysteries. I reasoned in this wise: "If this is worth any thing, it is worth all things;" and where there seemed to be, or even might be, such a mine of wealth only a few feet and possibly but a few inches below the black soil of superstition and ignorance, I thought that it was worth digging for.

From that time, I used all the means in my power to search out and ascertain the one great fundamental fact; viz., whether our friends that had preceded us to that "bourn from which" it is said "no traveller ever returned," did really come back and tell us of the world beyond.

I soon found that I was not only a medium for tipping the table, but also for writing; that is, my hand, in spite of all exertions to the contrary, would twitch and move about nervously when I sat at a table, either alone, or in company with others. Sometimes these manifestations would be very boisterous, and, it being out of my power to control them, made it very annoying to me. At first I pretended that I was doing it myself, that I was only mimicking others who pretended to be mediums, was trying to prove that anybody could do the same; thus bringing obloquy and disgrace upon all the pretended mediums, by reflecting upon their honesty. But I was brought up with a "round-turn double-

23*

bitted," as sailors say, one morning some two years
subsequent to my first attendance at a circle. It
came about in this way. A Mr. and Mrs. Danforth
being on a lecturing tour, and giving private manifestations in our place, by invitation took up their
abode with us. One Sunday morning, after all had
left the breakfast-table excepting Mrs. Danforth and
myself, we sitting on opposite sides, the conversation,
which had been running upon Spiritualism, was continued by us; I all the time denouncing it as arrant
humbug, and imposition upon the credulity of the
weak-minded. About this time, feeling my arm influenced powerfully, and wishing to conceal the *real*
cause of the manifestation, I said to Mrs. Danforth,
"See my hand thrash about: don't you see that I'm
a medium?" Up to this time, whenever my arm got
cutting up pranks, I could stop it by pressing my
elbow against my side. On this occasion, however,
my hand and arm thrashed around terribly. I tried
to stop it in the usual way; but I couldn't get my
elbow to my side, so that, instead of stopping it as
heretofore, it increased in violence. Finding I
couldn't stop it, I said to Mrs. Danforth, "I guess
the d——l's here." She quietly remarked, "I think
you'll soon find that he is." In a moment I was
fully entranced by a powerful spirit, who assumed
the appearance and gestures, through my organism, of
an Indian. I jumped to my feet with my eyes
closed, and commenced jabbering in some unknown
language, gesticulating as though fighting. I would
advance, seemingly against great odds; then fall
back as if retreating; all the time gesticulating and

seemingly talking to some unseen people. This was kept up near an hour, when all at once I felt something pierce me through the region of the heart; and I fell my whole length backwards with such force that the whole house jarred. It was thought that I had broken a blood-vessel, and had actually died; every appearance of my face indicating death. My lips turned purple, my face assumed an ashen hue, my nostrils drew together precisely as though death had taken place. I lay there a minute or so, when the influence left as suddenly as it came; and I opened my eyes, and found Mary, my second daughter, leaning over me crying, and her tears streaming on my face. When I came to myself, I found the house full of neighbors, attracted by the savage yells of the Indian. All seemed struck with awe at the freaks I cut up, some attributing it to one thing, some another; but none, with the exception of our visitors Mr. and Mrs. Danforth, to the real cause. This was the first time I was fully controlled as far as I knew; although, as the reader is already aware, I had been under some kind of influence many times in my previous life, without knowing it. Not one who witnessed it doubted or questioned that it was some outside power, any more than I did; but what power, or whence it emanated, was the question. Everybody had heard of such things; but few had ever witnessed any such before, and had treated them as the wild vagaries of a madman. Accounts of this tussle with the Indian, or rather of the tussle of the Indian to control me, spread like wildfire; and I, being well known, was bothered to death by the inquisitive to know more of this matter. From this time I began to develop very fast in mechanical writing. At first, and for a long time, nothing came but hieroglyphics perfectly unintelligible to any one; but, after nearly a year of constant practice, long communications would come, treating upon all conceivable subjects, but all of high moral quality. Most of the writing was signed by two or three men who figured high in the political world, holding the highest public positions in the gift of a great nation. As I had noticed that mediums, with hardly an exception, received communications from some great personages of the past, and not feeling worthy myself of such high considerations, and reasoning from analogy that "like generally attracts its like," and knowing that I possessed not one quality that could attract such men to me, although I had not a doubt but that it was somebody out of the material form, I doubted its being whom it purported to be. One of these mysterious personages, and by whom most of the communications were signed, was James Madison. Failing to ascertain to a certainty that it was he, I requested the spirit, if it was really the one it claimed to be, not to sign his full name in the future, but merely *James*. After this request, only James was ever affixed to any communication purporting to be by him. I was very anxious to find out the real truth; but not until the succeeding spring did I become fully convinced that James Madison was really one of the operators through me, although the communicator had said so through my hand thousands of times.

Early the following spring, I went to Boston for the purpose among others of finding out the truth of this. I visited many mediums, but long failed to get what I wanted. Finally, one morning about ten, A.M., a public circle was being held in the back parlor of the Fountain House; and, having a desire to attend, I went in. They had commenced operations before I arrived. When I entered the room, a medium from Cape Cod was speaking in a trance.

He was standing back to the door, about four feet distant, when I entered. I had never seen or heard of him before. The moment I entered the room, he stopped speaking, turned his head partially round, and, lowering his voice, said, "Good morning, *James*." I instantly replied in a pompous manner, " My name is not James, but David," thinking I had him now. He quietly remarked, "I was speaking to James Madison." It proved to be Abner Kneeland, who was a contemporary of Madison before either left the form, who was speaking when I entered. These two possessed similar religious proclivities while living, and they met in friendship when they passed to the other side. To give any thing of an adequate sense of my feelings at that moment, is impossible. To sum all up, here was a perfect stranger to me, and I was a stranger to all present; none but myself in all the world knew of my anxiety to find out whether or not one particular spirit manifested through my organism; and yet I got just what I wanted thus unexpectedly, when I wasn't thinking about it, and through a person who had never yet seen me with his mortal eyes. This was a test that the most incredulous could not gainsay or doubt. I felt mortified and chagrined at the rude, brusque manner, in which I had responded to what I thought was addressed to me personally, and sat down in one corner of the room feeling not far removed from a culprit. After the above encounter with Mr. Kneeland, he resumed his discourse, and having finished it, turned to Dr. Gardner, and said, " There is a spirit waiting for some one at the door of the room *next* to No. 29." This brought to mind an engagement I had with a medium to meet me at my room, No. 28, at that time, and which I had entirely forgotten. Here was another test through the same medium, at the same sitting, and before he had even seen my face. I had never doubted but that some invisible personality wrote through my hand, for I knew the writing was not subject to my will, and was with me purely mechanical, devoid of a particle of volition on my part; but, whether it was the particular person it claimed to be, I didn't know. Now my doubts were entirely removed; and, as if this wasn't enough, Mr. Madison took the medium before he had opened his eyes, and wound his way around through the people, and came to the remote corner where I was sitting. Then stooping down he repeated a communication of about ten lines that had been written through me some two weeks before. After he had repeated it he said, " James Madison : that name was attached to the written communication." Then he said, " Do you remember ? " I told him I did partially ; he again repeated it, and then said, " Do you recollect *now ?* " I told him I did ; after which the medium came to his normal condition, entirely unconscious of what he had been doing ; and yet he had done much to satisfy me that spirits hold converse with earth's children.

After the above experience I rapidly unfolded in writing, and healing by laying-on of hands ; which latter power unfolded in a remarkable degree. I shall specify some of the many cures, farther on. The spirits began to give me tests in writing ; some of them were very marked, and a few of them I will relate.

It had become a custom with me, after the day's work was done, to sit at a table by myself, and solicit spirits to communicate by tipping and writing ; sometimes also raps would come, but the latter were merely slight sounds by which I never could get any thing satisfactory. On the 13th of April, soon after I sat down, the following words were written : " We want you to go to Boston." That was all. And for several evenings nothing else came. Finally one evening I asked, " What do you want me to go to Boston for ? " In response they wrote, " To attend a Spiritual convention." Upon asking the question, when and where it was to be held, they wrote, " It is to be held the 27th of May." Relating to where it was to be held, they wrote, " It is undecided." Up to the 13th of May, nothing else was written but, " Go to Boston." Do all I could, nothing else would come. I had become wearied with the whole thing, and, if in my power, would have cut short all further communication ; for wherever I was, whether talking with a friend on business or any other subject, my hand would often write the few words, " Go to Boston."

Finally on the evening of the 13th of May, just a month since the first direction to go to Boston was written, I asked, "Which way shall I go?" There were three practical ways, — one by stage to Bath, from there by rail; another by boat to Portland, and from there by rail; and still another by boat from Rockland direct to Boston. Instantly they wrote, "Go in 'The Governor.'" "What," I says, "you don't mean the old steamer 'Governor,' that used to run from Bangor to Boston?" My hand immediately wrote, "The same." Now, I thought I had got them for sure, because the old "Governor" had been burned up some three years before in New York; so the papers said, and everybody seemed pleased at it, because she was not considered seaworthy. I then told them these facts with considerable satisfaction, at being able to teach those something, who I had been taught knew every thing. However, this information made no difference in their writing; for every night when I sat down to the table, from the 13th to the 25th of May inclusive; nothing would be written but "Go in 'The Governor.'" The morning following, going up town, I met Mr. Willard Farwell, who I knew was agent for this boat when she ran on the Bangor and Boston route; and I asked him in an off-hand manner, what had become of the steamer "Governor." He responded, "She has gone to h—l: didn't you know that she was burned up three years ago in New York?" I told him I recollected something about it, but was not quite sure it was correct. "Oh, yes!" he continued, "she has gone to her long home, and a good job it was for the travelling public." This boat was never a favorite with travellers, and everybody avoided going in her if they could help it, for she was not considered safe; and hence there was a general rejoicing when the news reached Rockland of her tragic end.

Of course I said nothing to Mr. Farwell as to my object of asking about her. Now I thought I had something tangible by which I could substantiate the oft-repeated saying among sceptics, that, if there were spirits that could communicate with mortals, they were unreliable. Of course there could be no doubt about it in this case, whatever there might be in others.

By this time I had become quite noted as a splendid medium; and, among my friends who were real believers in the philosophy, was a Capt. Israel Snow, who had a daughter who was a good medium, and at whose house I had often sat in circles. On my way home I called upon him, and showed him the communication in relation to "The Governor." He seemed astounded, and asked me if they wrote but that once; I told him that a dozen times the same thing came. "Now," I said, "Capt. Snow, this thing is perfectly unreliable; and let us have nothing more to do with it," continuing, "As far as I'm concerned, if I'm obliged to write (which, as before stated, I could not resist), I shall make no more account of it than I would of the wild ravings of a maniac." The following evening Capt. Snow and family spent with me. He tried every possible way to get my hand to write something in explanation; but "Go in the Governor," was all the response we could get; and for twelve days nothing else would come. In the mean time we had learned

24

through a Spiritual paper, " The New England Spiritualist," that there was to be a Spiritual convention held on the 27th and 28th inst.; and some dozen friends, favorable to the cause, concluded to attend. Among the number was Capt. Israel Snow above alluded to, and family, also my wife. Pressing business prevented me from attending, which I should have been pleased to do, although my faith had waned: still I really hoped that what had proved such a stumbling-block might be removed.

It was agreed to take the boat from Bangor to Boston on its outward trip, on the afternoon of the 25th, which would get along to our place, Rockland, about four, P.M. I attended the party to the wharf, all the while chaffing the deluded ones on their prospective " wild-goose chase." Soon after we got to the place of landing, I saw a boat rounding Ingraham's Point, some four miles distant. I called Capt. Snow's attention to it, saying in a sort of sneering way, " There comes ' The Governor,' Capt. Snow." He paid no attention to my poking fun at his credulity, evidently not a little puzzled himself at the way things had turned. We paid no farther attention to the approaching boat, thinking all the time it was the " Boston," a new boat that had been on the route but a short time. When she was ranging up alongside the wharf, we were all standing with our backs to the water; but, as she came into the wharf, I turned my head partly round, and to my astonishment saw on the wheel-house in large letters, " Governor." For a moment I was paralyzed. Soon I turned Capt. Snow round, pointing to the letters, saying, "*Look!*" Sure enough, there was the identical old "Governor," which everybody thought was burned up three years ago, Capt. S. as well as the rest; for they all knew of the spirits writing through me so much about going in "The Governor," when we all thought there was no "Governor" to go in, at least not the one that used to run on that route. They were dumbfounded, and for a moment no one spoke. At last Capt. Snow says, "I hope you won't doubt any more about spirits being able to communicate to mortals, much less doubt your own mediumship." Although I had received a few convincing tests through a third person, as before related, yet this being the *first real* test through my own mediumship, and under such test conditions, I confess that I felt highly gratified; and, to tell the exact truth, not a little vain at being a favored medium for the transmission of the thoughts of higher intelligences roaming at will through the more rarefied atmosphere of the summer-land.

The illustrative facts of the case were these: The steamer "Boston," on her trip to Boston, became disabled through the breaking of her machinery, repair of which made it necessary for her to lose one trip or more; and "The Governor" lying at one of the wharves, happening to be unemployed, the agent of the "Boston" hired the former to take the place of the disabled boat. She passed up toward Bangor at two or three oclock in the morning, and no one but the agent at Rockland and a very few others knew of the accident; certainly no one of our party did. "The Governor" did get on fire, and burned to the water's edge, but subsequently was rebuilt; and, as she was employed in carrying passengers and freight up the Hudson River, her total loss by fire was never contradicted. How she happened to be in Boston at this particular time, or how she happened to be unemployed, I do not know. But one thing is certain: our party of investigators did go to Boston, and return, in the old " Governor; " and she was never seen East again.

I have been thus particular in giving the details of this case, for two reasons: one of which is, that, if what I had before received had inclined me to credit the reality of spirit-communion, this test removed every lingering doubt that might be lurking in my naturally sceptical mind; the other reason is, or was, that it established beyond all cavil the genuineness of my own mediumship. At the time this occurred, I could see, or rather had seen, enough to convince me that there were spirits so far advanced in the laws of life, that they could see somee vents pertaining to particular mortals, that would transpire in the future, with the same precision that they could those already experienced; but how they could tell about the breaking of a piece of iron, thirteen days before it transpired, was and is a mystery that has thus far eluded all my efforts to unravel. At any rate, this proved, to me at least, that what had all down the ages been called prophesying future events, and was always clouded in mystery and doubt, was now no mystery at all as to the fact; because I could see that our course was all mapped out, and that highly unfolded spirits could discern all the prominent capes and headlands on the voyage of each mortal's life, that must be doubled, with the same precision that the skilful navigator before leaving home can tell precisely what capes and headlands he must inevitably pass before he can reach his port of destination; but the precise moment when he will double any headland or cape depends entirely upon circumstances. If the winds are favorable, and invariable in velocity, and he knows precisely the speed of the ship, he can tell very near at what time he will pass a certain point on his outward voyage. Just so with spirits: they can see, on the chart of one's life, that he must inevitably pass a certain point; but when, as in the case of the ship, depends entirely upon circumstances. I have no doubt there are spirits that could tell precisely any event of any mortal's life, and the precise time any particular event would occur, if it were really useful; but such are extremely rare visitants, or rather are so far advanced in spiritual lore, and so unable to communicate to us, excepting through successive mediums all the way down from their high estate, that, by the time it reaches us, their information is so warped and twisted from the original, that but little semblance of the genuine may reach us: hence so many mistakes as to *when* certain things will transpire. At first, not unlike almost everybody else, I thought spirits were infallible, and that they knew every thing that ever did or would transpire in this whirling, bustling world; and not only that, but that they could tell the very moment when each event would take place. This led me into many wild-goose chases, often resulting in bringing me deep chagrin and humility; but it taught me one grand lesson, viz., to accept nothing that did not comport with my reason and better judgment.

I might rehearse many amusing incidents in the first years of my experience, as to how the spirits tried to make me believe I was the most wonderful man on this planet, and to the marvellous works they were going to do through my wonderful organism. To tickle my fancy, and especially to develop still further my already overgrown vanity, they told me that they had been searching the world over for just such a man as my humble self; and, to crown all, with much dignity and a show of solemn sincerity they named me "the Franklin of the nineteenth century." They told me, among other things, that the vast resources of the spirit-world were at my command, &c. Among the most ridiculous things they were going to accomplish through my wonderful self, was building ships that would go through water with lightning speed, and supersede all other sea-going craft in transporting freight and passengers from one point to another. The propelling power was to be electricity; and this was to be placed in the stern, unlike our ocean-steamers, corresponding to human craniology, thus saving much valuable space for freight and passengers. There was another quality attached to these ships, so ridiculously absurd that I refrain from speaking of it.

Although I could not see in myself a particle of a Franklin either in philosophy or genius, and often told them so, yet reasoning upon the above hypothesis, and taking for granted their explanation, when I expressed a doubt that if my wonderful faculties did not then show themselves, they were only in a torpid condition, and would certainly come to the surface some time, through development, I confess that my reasoning upon the subject gave me a secret apprehension, although I didn't dare to own it, that I was really somebody in embryo, and that some time in the future I should burst the shell of a " know-nothing," and flash upon the world like a brilliant meteor at noonday, eclipsing all others in wisdom, *the veritable " Franklin of the nineteenth century;"* and in my vain imaginings would. fancy hearing people say, " What a bundle of wisdom is this wonderful man!" This condition of things lasted some four or five years, which time, with all the means I could command, was devoted entirely and conscientiously to the behests of the spirit of the great philosopher; I going hither and thither as he directed through his communicator. When the shell *did* burst, instead of becoming the great one that was to be, I found myself still the poor, credulous David C. Densmore, who entered the movement with such bright prospects years before, poor in purse, with entire loss of all the confidence of his most intimate friends, and former business acquaintances; for all of them without an exception considered him a worthy candidate for an insane-asylum. The prophesies which most elated me came through the organism of a man eminent for his goodness. It will probably be asked, since I was such a good medium, why my friends did not, through my own mediumship, post me as to the non-reality of these things. They did so a thousand

times ; but I felt such inferiority in purity and goodness to this great and good man as persuaded me
that I could not myself have as truthful revelations
from the world of causes as he could ; and hence I
totally ignored my own mediumship, and followed
blindly and faithfully what came through this highly
favored mortal. I mention these circumstances in
my experience, not to impeach the truthfulness of
the medium through whom the above and hundreds
of other seemingly non-practical things come, but to
show how careful we ought to be in accepting any
thing that does not tally with our own reason, no
matter how high may be the pretensions of those
through whom it comes. If I had not received
indubitable evidence, through my own mediumship,
of the reality of spirit-commune, these revelations
of seeming duplicity on the part of what purported
to be truthful spirits would have shaken my faith in
every thing outside of my physical senses ; but I
had been, as before stated, favored with so many
instances of special helps in trying emergencies, from
unseen sources, all the way up from childhood,
coupled with my unfolding as a medium for giving
indubitable evidence that guardian spirits constantly
aid and assist when most needed, through my own
mediumship, that faith and belief had become
merged into positive knowledge.

CHAPTER XIV.

HEALING THE SICK BY LAYING-ON OF HANDS, AND OFTEN WITHOUT CONTACT WITH THE PATIENT.

HEALING by laying-on of hands has been successfully practised among all nations from time immemorial; it is as old as the human race itself. Some attribute the efficacy to one thing, some to another. Some think the benefit is produced by psychology, — will-power, — the stronger will overpowering the weaker. There are some who say it is a special interposition of the Almighty through some of his saintly children: notably is this said in the Catholic Church. Then there are others who say that this power, or faculty, comes through prayer direct from God, with no mundane will-power about it. Then there is still another class who maintain that the benefit is produced by neither one nor the other of the above, but that it is emanated from a positive power, independent of either God's or man's will, which power acting through certain mediums, sometimes aided by the galvanic battery, medicated vapor baths, &c., cures all curable diseases flesh is heir to. This last phase often has seemed to be my mode of cure, by which I have been eminently successful in chronic complaints, more especially where the internal organs were diseased; the lungs, throat, stomach, spleen, liver, and kidneys yielding very readily to this treatment, no matter how long they may have been affected, providing there is sufficient vitality left to build upon. Although I may not have a doubt but that the will-power of the operator, if strongly concentrated and powerfully exercised, may contribute to this result, and although he may say and think to the contrary, yet my impressions are that the *real* healing essence in all forms of mediumistic practice emanates from one and the same source; viz., spirits acting through differently constituted organisms, and instruments and medicines employed. I think it is the same with the old-school physicians, where they are most successful; and, although they give the credit of cure to medicines skilfully and scientifically administered, their success, I think, depends much more, if not wholly, upon the healing power working out from within themselves, than upon draughts from the apothecary-shop. It is said that the most successful practitioners in the old school give the least medicine. Dr. Abernethy once said, that, as a whole, the world would have been better off if there never had been a graduate from the mills where they turn out M.D's; continuing, " I have no doubt but that there are isolated cases where the doctor has been practically useful, but these are rare." This is meant to apply to doctors commonly called the " scientists of medicine;" though, in fact, there is no science about their work, it being purely experimental, as any one can see who will give it a moment's reflection. For example: when a member of some family is suddenly taken ill with some of the many diseases affecting mankind, the family physician is sent for; and if the ailment does not prove to be one of the simplest, but is some internal complicated affair, the physician feels the pulse, looks at the tongue, is puzzled to know what to administer, because, as is known by every physician, the greatest difficulty is to diagnose and ascertain the real nature and cause of the disease, and this because many a single symptom may appertain to a dozen diseases or more; he also knows, even if he happens to diagnose correctly, — which is seldom the case where he depends upon symptoms, for reasons above given, — he is as much puzzled as ever as to what to administer, from the fact that "what is one man's meat is another's poison;" or, in other words, what will work favorably with one may work diametrically opposite with another, who manifests precisely the same symptoms. The poor doctor looks as if, and really he is, "at sea," without chart or compass. He can only guess what to do in the premises; finally after a good deal of thinking he makes up his mind, fills out a formula in Latin, and some one starts upon the "double-quick" for an apothecary's shop; the doctor leaving strict injunctions, that, if the medicine don't work so and so, to let him know at once. The medicine proves insufficient; the doctor is recalled; upon entering the sickroom, he finds the patient worse; again he goes over the same roll of pulse and tongue analyzing, and finally changes the medicine entirely; and, upon leaving, gives the same injunctions as upon his first visit. The patient is sinking fast: again the physician is hastily sent for, and upon arrival finds the patient very low. If the sufferer be wealthy, another or two M.D.'s are sent for, and hold a private consultation with the first one, and they conclude that nothing more can be done, that nothing can save the patient; and so report to the anxiously waiting friends of the invalid. Science has failed: the patient dies, and all the consolation the mourning friends have, is that he died by law and gospel; and they charge it all upon God, who baffled the skill of science, and took the poor sufferer to himself. This is a fair representation of many cases occurring every day and hour. Now, is it not hard to find one particle of *real* science in the practice of the old-school physicians? but the easiest thing in the world to see, that the whole system, from beginning to end, is nothing more or less than sheer speculation and unsuccessful experiments. To call it by any milder name than *murder*, would be to stultify reason and common-sense, which is done by those persisting to call things by wrong names, only because backed up by law and common usage.

I am not unaware that this is strong language, and may be looked upon, by those mostly interested in keeping up the delusion, as rank heresy; and who would, if in their power, invoke the strong arm of the law to put it down, as has been done in five States of this free (?) country; that is to say, science has instituted laws in these five States, prohibiting, under heavy penalties, the practice of healing the sick without having obtained a diploma from certain colleges; thus virtually telling the sick, " You must be treated so and so, pay your money, take the consequences, and say nothing." That such a law exists on the statute-books of any State, does not reflect very favorably upon the intelligence of this or any other country; and yet it is so. I do not wish to be understood as discarding medicine by any means: far otherwise; for I believe that the very fact that disease exists, is proof that there is somewhere in Nature's vast domain an antidote for every disease; the difficulty is to find it, and adapt it properly to the sufferers needing it. Until this is known, the whole system of medicine must, to all reflecting minds, rest under the opprobious name "guesswork," or consummate "quackery." The limits of this book preclude the possibility of an extended rehearsal. My purpose calls for no extended specification of the blunders made by the "regulars" in their extensive practice: I must confine myself to a few, coming under my own personal observation, where patients have been given over to die by the old-school practitioners, and afterwards entirely restored to health and usefulness, simply through manipulation with the hands of certain mediums called healers. Well-authenticated cases all down the stream of time, from the remotest ages of antiquity, as well as of more recent date, could be cited to prove that an actual power exists, exercised through certain persons, which arrests disease often instantly, and restores the sufferer to his normal health, after, as before stated, the medical faculty has utterly failed to even relieve the sufferer, much less to cure him. This, as in my own case, is often brought about instantly, without my even

25

knowing at the time that there is any disease in the persons cured; for instance, a person lying speechless, and to all outward appearance dead, my undesigned coming in contact with him has caused him to revive: this proves that there is a positive power existing somewhere, that brings about this wonderful change. The first case of curing without contact that came under my own observation, which I was willing to accept as real (although many had made declarations of like results before), was that of Mr. A. E. Newton, then editor and publisher of the New England Spiritualist newspaper, printed in Boston. I had never met Mr. Newton previously; but, from what I had heard of him, I had a strong desire to make his acquaintance. One rainy morning in the last days of April, I called upon him at his residence in Tyler Street. I found him enveloped in a large shawl, and hovering over a stove, trying to get warm: he had taken a bad cold, and was trying to get up a perspiration. I seated myself on a sofa some eight or ten feet from him, conversing upon various topics, when, after fifteen or twenty minutes, he said, "Do you know what you have been doing?" Thinking I had said something not pleasant, I said, "No: I am not aware I have done any thing." He then said, "You certainly have." In answer to the query what it was, he said, "When you entered the room, I was suffering with a severe cold. I felt as though I would freeze, even over a good fire in the stove, though muffled up with shawl and cloak. The moment you entered, I began to feel better; and soon after, as you may have observed, threw the shawl off, and moved back ; and, though the fire has gone out, I now am sweating profusely from head to foot. Come and make a few passes on my head, and I shall be well." I did so, and he was entirely cured; put on his boots and greatcoat at once, and went down town, and attended to his business all day, returning after sunset, when he told me he never felt better in his life. The stove was made of sheet-iron, heated with pine wood which soon burned up. I selected this case out of a great many, not that there was any thing remarkable about it, excepting that it was the first case coming under my own personal experience and observation, to show that there was not a particle of will-power, or volition, on my part; for I didn't have belief that such a power existed in me, though others had told me of singular effects from me before, which I thought was pure fancy on their part. Mr. Newton printed quite a long article in his paper, relating the whole story in detail as here stated, leaving out my name per request, as I, not unlike many others at that early stage of recognition of healing by this process, did not want my name identified with a subject so unpopular, even if it was true.

At one time, when attending to business not connected with healing, I was called upon one morning by a Dr. Smith, a professor in one of the colleges in the city of Cincinnati, who said he wanted me to go with him, and visit a young man who was dying; for my doing so would, he said, gratify a whim of his distracted mother. I refused to go; but he urged me quite earnestly, saying it would gratify the poor woman if she could see me; continuing, "The young man commenced dying at midnight." This was said about nine, A.M. He said we should probably find him dead when we arrived. He seemed to be so anxious, that I finally concluded to go along. To encourage me he said that nothing could be done, nor did the mother expect any thing could restore her dear boy to life. On our way to the house he related the history of the case, and stated that all the most celebrated physicians in the city had been called in and consulted with, and that himself had been the family physician for the past twenty years. He thought Mrs. Weaver, the mother of the lad, was losing her mind; for, said he, "She came to me an hour or so ago in an excited manner, and asked me if I knew of a magnetizer." I told her, no, but that I knew a man that did. "Well," she says, "I want you to get a magnetizer." — "What for?" said I: "He is dying, and nothing can rescue him from the grim monster." — "I know that," said she; "but I got thinking, as we had tried all the skill in the city, and failed, if we also got a magnetizer, that, after Willie should be buried, I should have nothing to regret, because then I could say we had tried all systems of cure." He continued, "I could not withstand this heart appeal." The family lived at 455 Fifth Street. I found the dying one on a lounge in the back parlor, no pulse, entirely unconscious, surrounded by his anxious friends and relatives; and with Dr. Smith were seven old-school physicians watching the dying moments of the young man.

Everybody was standing up. They took no notice

·of me, a charlatan and impostor. The moment I entered the sickroom, I saw the position I had got into, and for a moment would have given any thing I possessed in the world to get out of the scrape. I took a seat at the head of the lounge, and, for the want of something to divert my distracted feelings from the embarrassing attitude I had involuntary got into, placed my right hand upon the lad's forehead, and with the other took one of his. Thus I sat in perfect silence, looking down on the floor; for, to tell the truth, I couldn't look up. I fancied I saw crimson daggers streaming from the eyes of those scientists, all concentrated upon my vitals. Whether I did or not really, I actually felt their sharp points piercing my heart, and thought I heard them say, " Wonder what he'll attempt to do, after science has failed;" they expecting, as a matter of course, that I would try. To give description of my feelings at that moment is impossible, and I will not attempt it: suffice it to say, that while looking down, regretting my thoughtlessness in being wheedled into such an unenviable position, my eye fell upon the hand I was holding; and to my astonishment I perceived the blood-veins filling up, precisely as I have seen an empty hose fill out when lying irregularly on the ground, and water was let on. For an instant I was almost paralyzed; for here circulation was going on in a person I·thought was near, if not already on, the other side of this life. To me he looked like a corpse; and no one was expected to even attempt to do any thing for him. I had not, up to this time, examined him. After perceiving the circulation, I

25*

gently turned my head, and noticed the muscles of one eye and right side of his mouth twitching slightly; at the same time I perceived that the malady was the congestive chills, which had wrought such fearful havoc with this beautifully developed young man. The symptoms of chills represent so many diseases that, with all their science, the doctors had failed to diagnose correctly the cause of the sad condition of things. Instantly after noticing that the circulation was coming back, and the wheels of motion were again slowly revolving around their normal axes, I beckoned to the mother, who was standing near weeping, and whispered in her ear, " Get them all out of the room." No one perceived any change but myself; for all were intently gazing on me to see what I would do, if any thing. Soon the room was cleared, Dr. Smith being the last. As the latter passed me, he stooped down, and whispered, " May I stay? " I told him " No." He then asked, " What do you call it? " meaning the disease; and to my response, " congestive chills," he expressed great surprise by holding up both hands, knowing, that if I was correct, which now he was perhaps inclined to believe, they had been treating him altogether wrong. When the coast was clear, I got my hand over the region of the stomach, and he showed signs of life, and soon opened his eyes. The first sentence he uttered was, " I wish you would get these plugs out of my nose." I should say, that, in addition to the seven medical doctors, they had employed a surgeon from one of the hospitals, to stop up the nose to prevent the blood from running out. He had been sick so long (some three months), and taken so much medicine, his blood had become so thin it would not coagulate; and hence when he was lying on his side it would run out of his nose like water. I kept him still a few moments, and then removed them; and in twenty-three minutes he was sitting up laughing. He gained so rapidly that Thursday morning (it being Tuesday when I first called), he answered the bell himself, when I rung it; and in a week's time went down town. Of course all the regulars were dismissed; and I attended him some four or five days, when he was as well as myself.

Now, here was a young man, nineteen years old, the only child of a wealthy family, being poisoned to death with the nostrums and drugs of science, and who but for the " foolish crazy whim " of the anxious mother, as Dr. Smith called her singular request, would have been been laid away in the silent tomb, a victim of consummate ignorance in the important principles of pharmacy. Who will say this is not actually murdering by the slow process of poisoning with drugs called, by misnomer, medicine? Medicine, to merit its high name, should *cure* the disease for which it is administered. If it fails to do that, and the patient dies through a misconception of its virtues, then it ought to take the name of poison, which it really is; and the prescriber of it should be dealt with as he would be for administering any admitted deadly poison, because the same result ensues in both cases; the only difference being that the fatal narcotic accomplished its work more rapidly, which, if it makes a difference, is in the poisoner's favor.

At another time, in an inland town, a man was suffering with some obstinate disease, the nature of which the family physician failed to know; it baffled all his skill to arrest it. Finally another physician was called to a private consultation. After due deliberation, they both concluded that nothing could be done to save the man from dying, as he was very low and entirely unconscious. After the doctors had reported the result of their deliberations, the anxious wife and relatives sent for me, because the sick man had, when first taken ill, expressed a desire to have my services. I was living only a short distance away, and was pretty well acquainted with the family. I went immediately to the house; found the man speechless and unconscious. The moment I got to him, I perceived the trouble; and suddenly turning to ask his wife for some herbs, one of the M.D.'s (they were both still present) says, " What do you call it, Mr. Densmore ? " — " Small-pox, *Mr.* H—l," says I. As he chose to call my name without a professional handle preceding it, deriding my simple mode of cure, I paid him in his own coin, by calling him *Mr.* H—l. Leaving out details of this to me interesting case, I will merely say, that in less than one hour the pox came to the surface, covering his entire body from head to foot; so near together were the pustules that scarcely a pin's point could be put on his body without coming in contact with them. The moment the disease left the vitals for the surface, the man was relieved, and came to consciousness. The doctors remained until they heard the man say to me, " I wanted you all the time, but they [meaning his aristocratic relatives] wouldn't send for you." Then the M.D.'s left. Thus it will be seen that the doctors failed in the diagnosis; hence their failure in aiding Nature to cure the disease. If they had known what disease the man was laboring under, they could have administered medicines that would have relieved him in an hour; but, depending altogether upon symptoms, they administered drugs that aggravated instead of lessening the trouble; and but for the timely aid of one who, upon entering the sickroom, instantly comprehended clearly the nature of the disease, and used means to put to rout the insidious and fatal monster, would have been laid away, labelled as usual in such cases, " The Lord has taken the sufferer to himself; " and nobody would ever have been any the wiser as to the nature of the disease that carried him off. The taking immediate measures to prevent the malady from spreading among the healthy denizens of the country village would not have occurred if the nature of the malady had not been detected in time. As it was, the disease did not seize upon any neighbor; and only one member of the family besides the father was attacked with it, and he lightly.

Had I space, I could enumerate numerous cases similar to the foregoing, in my own experience, besides ten times that number by other impressional and intuitive healers all over the wide world; many of whom may have been more successful than myself in arresting disease from the iron grasp of the total incapacity of scientific regulars to detect the nature and cause of disease. Among the most notable and successful of modern healers in our country is Dr. J. R. Newton. Among the many thousands, more or less, that he has treated, not more than one per cent, and probably less, but had been given over by the allopaths as incurable; and all, or nearly all, because of sheer inability to trace effects to the causes that produced them. It is obvious that every disease must any wise have a cause, the detection of which must precede application to ward off its legitimate effect.

Disease generally is but a negative condition of the system; whereas vitality, or the life-giving principle, whether produced from drugs or magnetism, is positive. If this be conceded, and also that no two things can occupy the same space at the same time, it follows, that, if by any process vitality can be forced into the system, the positive must take the place of the negative; and, being superior, convalescence must inevitably be the result. Light brought into a dark room drives out the darkness. Why? Because light is positive, while darkness is negative; hence there can be no darkness where this positive, or light, prevails. So just as far as this positive principle is introduced into the sick or diseased body (call it by what name we may), just so far is disease displaced; and, if continued in the ascendant a sufficient length of time, the sick, distressed body, either speedily or gradually, assumes a healthy condition, and the suffering invalid is restored to health and usefulness.

Sometimes this change is brought about almost

instantly; and then, again, several treatments are necessary to effect a permanent cure. This usually depends more upon the adaptability of the physician and patient to each other, than upon a lack of healing power. Hence any healer may find it needful to act a longer time on one patient than on another. Sometimes he will fail entirely. But it is no proof, because *I* can't effect a cure, that nobody else can. In the case of the young man referred to in Cincinnati, our magnetisms were *completely* adapted to each other; hence the remarkable suddenness of his convalescence. I might operate upon a hundred cases seemingly precisely similar, and not in one of them would success reward the effort as speedily as in that case, and maybe many would be failures altogether; and yet some one else, of magnetisms different from mine, might produce as happy result, where I should fail, as attended the case referred to.

It is a great mistake to conclude, because one is successful in one bad case, that he can succeed equally well in all cases of apparently the same nature and state. It has not been so in my case, and from a long practice I believe the same rule holds good with every one. I fell into the common error near thirty years ago. I did not follow healing as a business at that time: yet, when I saw a fellow being suffering, my sympathetic nature would go out to the sufferer, and, if in my power, I would relieve from the trouble. One day, casually meeting a lady who was suffering with nearly every disease that a female could have imposed upon her, I heard myself say to her, "I can cure you." She took a room in the hotel where I was boarding, and put herself under my treatment. She had been doctoring a dozen years or so, under all the different phases of practice, and was so reduced in flesh that she at this time was merely a skeleton. Every thing she took into her stomach distressed her excessively; even water would become sour the moment she drank it. She had a small chest full of different kinds of medicine; some of which she habitually took immediately after eating, to assist digestion. She was unable to walk around the room, without supporting herself by taking hold of the furniture. Under these conditions I undertook her case, treating her every evening, and attending to my ordinary business daytimes. Without either battery or any other assistance, use of my bare hands in five weeks and three days fitted her to eat a beef-steak, and digest it as readily as myself could; and her powers of locomotion became such that she walked with me five miles, two and a half out and the same back; and upon our return she ran up two flights of stairs with apparently less effort than I did. This to me was wonderful, and I began to build air-castles as to what I might do. The sick everywhere would be healed, for I could not conceive of a case in which there would be less promise of success than in this.

I was in high glee: every thing else seemed to dwindle down into insignificance when compared with this wonderful power of healing the sick without drugs or medicine, or aid of an M.D.

I enjoyed this ecstatic state of feeling but a few days; for an incident soon transpired that fell like a black pall upon the spirit of my dreams. As soon as it got bruited around, what a wonderful healer I was, the halt, lame, and blind put in an appearance. The first case was a lady apparently afflicted with essentially the same difficulties as was the one above described, only not half as bad in extent. I thought I could cure her in a few days; but, after trying nearly a week, she was no better. I gave it up; and I really made myself apprehend that the first one I had tried my skill upon was an impostor, — that, in real truth, nothing of consequence was the matter with her. If I could have got where she was without a good deal of trouble, probably I should have relieved my mind by telling her of my suspicions. At any rate, I gave it up; and if any said, as some had hundreds of times before, that by merely sitting near me they felt better, I would blow them up, often in not very soft language. Suffice it to say, that for a few years I would have nothing more to do with the pawing business, as I then called manipulating. I reasoned in this wise: If invisible healers can cure one of a certain malady, why not another having the same disease? Unseen ones answered my reasonable question by asking another; it was this: "If one cow has horns, why don't all cows have horns?" continuing, "When you can answer that question, you'll be in a condition to comprehend an answer to yours; but at present you could not if we gave it; and for the simple reason, that you are a mere child in the philosophy of life, and knowledge of laws governing it; you might as well expect a child, when commencing the rudiments of mathematics, to comprehend and understand the

26

abstruse problems of Euclid, and the higher branches of the science, as to expect a taller child, before he has mastered the first principles of the science of life and the absolute laws governing them, to comprehend a firm answer to your question." A good deal more in this strain was said, which did not increase my vanity. I had been tenaciously prone from childhood, when told any thing which I did not fully understand, to ask why it was "so and so," and would not be put off with an evasive answer: yet I was often obliged to accept an effect, without even attempting to trace it to its cause. After being taken down a good many pegs, in my vaunted knowledge of phenomena which I knew positively nothing about, I found I was but a mere apology for a scientific man, and contented myself with the fact, that, although my reason and better judgment told me there must be a cause for every effect, I must wait until I had at last got rid of my swaddling-clothes of ignorance before I arrogated to myself knowledge which could be gained only by experience and persevering industry. These questions being disposed of in this summary manner, there was nothing left for me to do, but either become reconciled to my own ignorance in the matter, and take for granted what came through my organism to be genuine, or else repudiate the whole thing, and give it up entirely. After considering the matter in all its bearings, and reflecting, that, if human testimony was good for any thing, I certainly had been the means of actually curing a great many of my suffering fellow-creatures of long-standing chronic complaints, after they had been given over to die by the allopaths,

I concluded to accept the former, and do the best I could. After coming to the above conclusion, although attending to my ordinary business as usual, whenever I saw discouraged sickly-looking invalids, and felt clear impressions that I could benefit them, I would tell them so; always very cautious, however, not to hold out hopes, only to be crushed in the now hopeful sufferer; and I found, that, whenever I followed these impressions implicitly, I seldom failed in producing favorable results; and I might add *never* failed when the patient acceded to the conditions I enjoined at the beginning of treatments. And although I could not see any reason why " one should be taken, and another left," yet, as before stated, I could tell at sight whether I could or could not benefit the patient, thus leaving nothing to speculation or experiment.

After drifting about for a few years, doing but little in healing, I found myself in New York at the corner of Fourteenth Street and Sixth Avenue, where through the commendations of Mrs. and Dr. Hayden I succeeded in a short time in getting quite a reputation as a successful healer. Dr. Hayden and wife had had ocular demonstrations of my healing power years before, in their own family, I having cured Mrs. Hayden and a small child, the latter on the verge of death. One day, while at the above place, two ladies entered. I knew by intuition that they were mother and daughter; I also knew that the daughter was sick, and knew also that I could not cure her. They both came in looking hopeful; the sick one seeming by her appearance to say, "Now I'm going to get well." Knowing I could not effect a cure, I commenced running over in my mind how I should tell them of my inability in such a way as not to blast their sanguine hopes too suddenly. At last I hit upon the following. Both were sitting in front of me, the mother to the right, her daughter to the left. I began by saying, "I do not pretend to cure all that come, do not attempt with more than half who apply, and not more than half the cases attempted result in total cure; but all upon whom I try are benefited. Why this is so, I cannot tell: I only know it is. Now, if *you* were sick [pointing to the mother] I could cure *you;* but if *this* lady [pointing to the daughter] was suffering with a difficult, complicated disease, I couldn't cure her." The appearance to them was, that I didn't know which was sick, if either, nor the relation each bore to the other. "Oh!" says the daughter, "I am the sick one, and I feel better already." I assured her I could never effect a cure of her if I worked on her ten years; but, seeing they were much disappointed at my refusing to treat her at all, I gave them some encouragement by saying, "You must not suppose, that, because I cannot effect you favorably, no one else can." And was I impressed to tell them that a Dr. Scott, living somewhere on Fourth Street, could cure her. I think I had heard of him, but had never seen him, nor did I know where he lived; yet I was compelled to tell them what I did. I was further impressed to tell them to enter Fourth Street at Sixth Avenue, and ride slowly across the city, watching the signs; and that, before they got to the East River, they would find him. They were very favorably impressed towards me, and urged me very hard to try a

few treatments; finding I would not, they followed
my instructions, found Dr. Scott, and in a week's time
he had her as well as ever in her life. After finding
she was gaining rapidly, they came to my office, and
expressed so much gratitude, that I felt ashamed at
the exuberance of their flattering expressions. They
offered me money, which I refused; but they were
determined to do something to show their gratitude.
So they hunted up all their sick friends and relatives,
and brought them to me often in their own carriage.
Almost every day they would bring a fresh instalment; and they kept it up all the time I remained in
the city.

When I was telling them about my inability to
affect some favorably, while others yielded readily, I
had a vision that partly cleared up the mystery. I
saw, a few feet from me and to the right of the
mother, two casks the size of barrels; one was full
of liquid, the other empty; and a siphon connected
the two at the middle. The instant I was enchained
by the vision, the water commenced running through
the siphon into the empty barrel. Soon each barrel
was half full. I perceived that the presentation was
intended to illustrate the *modus operandi* of healing;
the water representing the life-giving fluid, call it
magnetism, or by any other convenient name; the
strong, healthy, magnetism of or through the operator,
going into the invalid, and filling him or her until
both operator and recipient contain equal quantities,
as in the case of the two barrels. But, as I did not
see its application in cases where the magnetizer
failed in benefiting the sufferer, I said mentally,

26*

if the vision was given for instruction I did not understand it. Instantly the scene was changed; and before me was a full and a nearly empty barrel, as at first. Directly the water commenced running into the empty one, with the same velocity as before; but it run out almost as fast as it entered. Before it began to run, I noticed that the water in the receiving barrel seemed about two inches deep, but gradually lessened in depth as the volume from the full one lessened; and, by the time the water had got down to the siphon, every drop had run out of the receiving one, while the other was half full. This, I presumed, was intended to illustrate the healing process; and it explained very clearly to me that this healing balm, or magnetism, could enter into and permeate all alike, and for the time being all might feel better; though from some unexplainable cause some could not retain it, as was illustrated by the leaky barrel, and hence it failed in effecting their cure; whereas those that did retain it would generally get well. This, to me, did more to reconcile and harmonize "why one was taken, and the other left," than all the speculations and theorizing that ever emanated from the pretentious knowledge of those professing to know all about it. The only difficulty was to find out whom it would take, and whom reject: although I somehow could generally tell very correctly, I found many cases extremely difficult; as, for instance, where the patient was, to use a homely phrase, on the fence, — that is, equally poised between life and death, unless they should receive other aid than mine. Where I found this to be the case, I would tell patients so ; and if they would run the risk of one course of treatment (which in all cases indicates the sequel), I would go ahead : otherwise I wouldn't attempt any thing. The foregoing has been my invariable course of procedure since I found out that there were many things the causes of which I could not see. But many such cases as at first I would reject now yield very readily ; and I think nearly all curable diseases come within my reach. Although, as stated before, hardly any one to me as David Densmore solely seems possible, yet, depending entirely upon the perceptions of an intuitive faculty which acts to some extent in all men and animals, I have been eminently successful. Often when there was nothing expected, and even when I did not know any thing was the matter, I have seen the greatest results : thus proving at least in my case, whatever it may be in others, that sometimes there is not a particle of human will-power, or psychology, about mediumistic healing ; hence, whatever is effected through my organism is exerted and guided by intelligence purely spiritual ; that is, the cure results from application of power by spiritual beings, they probably mingling their auras with my own to produce favorable results.

Although I have been familiar with evidences of this occult power for removing disease during many years, yet, up to this hour, the results through my own mediumship seem wonderful, not to say incredible. I can hardly realize the facts, for I only rarely feel any thing, not even a particle of *influence*. It seems strange indeed, that a person who has been suffering for dozens of years, more or less, with scarce a moment's cessation, though at sometimes more than others, by merely having a few passes made over the distressed region outside of the clothes is instantly freed from the pains and aches. I neither see nor feel any thing nowadays, and experience no exhaustion of the physical; therefore it is no wonder that the result looks even more surprising to me than to the recipients of the healing balm.

I have dwelt longer upon this subject from the fact of its beneficence, not only in healing the physical disabilities of mankind, but in causing more real happiness to the struggling spirit while incased in a constantly decaying edifice, than all other things combined. It leads the storm-tossed mariner on life's social and moral seas into closer relations with the infinite, where knowledge gradually tears away the thin partition that separates us from the world of causes, and shows to us in clear distinctness that we are constantly surrounded and watched over by loving friends gone before, who soothe us with hopeful, cheering words when desponding, and assist us when most we need.

CHAPTER XV.

IN the spring of 185–, I went to Buffalo, N.Y., where I engaged in building vessels for use on the lakes. The following August my family joined me. Here we lived about two years, and passed through some trying vicissitudes, owing to hard times, scarcity of work, and impaired health.

In the summer of 1858 I worked in a machine-shop in Boston, and afterwards made two trips to Europe, for the purpose of selling patented boot-crimping machines and air-pressure churns; in which business of purely mundane projection no desired success resulted from my efforts. I came home poor.

My repeated failures caused nearly all my friends and acquaintances to come to the conclusion that I was a total failure, as far as business was concerned; that I was wholly incompetent to manage any thing where tact and a small share of good common-sense were necessary to success; and few took pains to conceal their thoughts. Though, if I chanced to say any thing about business, they might not say so in so many words, by their looks and winks I could plainly see, that, to use a slang phrase, they took no stock in any thing coming from my demented and muddled brain. As I had embraced the great fundamental truths, or rather facts, underlying the Spiritual philosophy, they attributed all my incompetence to that *delusion*, as they were pleased to call it. Even my own family became impregnated with this idea, and rather pitied than blamed me for being deluded with this consummate fraud of the nineteenth century. I overheard my children, when talking of me, whom they loved with all the ardor of devoted hearts, say, " Poor father, how I pity him ! He is evidently in dotage, and no wonder; for he has passed through enough to crush a stronger spirit than he possesses." Thus the little dears would talk for hours. One time I heard darling Helen (the eldest) say, " When father proposes any thing, we mustn't cross him, but pretend to fall in with his ideas; and maybe he will see his error, and give up this awful idea of Spiritualism, and become once more in his right mind." Oh, for their dear sakes how gladly I would have given up all thoughts of what gave them so much misery ! But I was not my own keeper. I had a destiny to fulfil, and could no more get out of the groove I was destined to run in, than could the planets by a freak of fancy get out of their determined orbits : so it will be seen that I was nearly as much alone, even in my own family, as though I had been the only sentient being in existence. My most earnest desire was, to get away from all acquaintances, and be by myself; for, amid all my vicissitudes, I never lost a particle of faith in what had been my solace and chief friend and support for many years. Everybody was prolific with advice as to what was best for me to do, some recommending one thing, some another; all of which I refused to comply with. My wife's mother, dear good soul, wanted me to be placed under the guardianship of her son Ephraim, which met the entire approbation of all, with the exception of my children, who protested against such a course for the reason, that, as I was partially demented already, to restrain my liberty in the slightest degree would complete the wreck of him who once was an honor to society, and one of the most successful business men in the vicinity. This was talked over and over among themselves. I knew what the older ones were driving at, as well as they did, and was prepared to meet it if it was ever proposed; hardly thinking, however, that with the protest of my children, coupled with a dread of how I might receive it, they would ever dare to make the proposition. At last, as I was talking about going away, they determined to make the effort; and, as my wife refused to do it, her mother took the responsibility upon herself to tell me of my incompetency to get a living, which she did in the easiest and most plausible way she could think of. She began by saying that my constant failures had wrought so hard on my brain, that it was the unanimous advice of my friends, that, under the consideration that I had a growing family, it was best for me to put myself under the guardianship of some one; and suggested her son Ephraim, high-minded and strictly honorable in all his dealings, and for whom I always entertained the most profound respect, as the most efficient to assume such a responsibility; continuing, " Ephraim will get you a chance to work, take your earnings, and pay it over to your family."   Of course, knowing all about their little scheme, and not blaming them for it either, I received it with little concern.   Seeing she hesitated what next to say, I relieved her by asking if she had got through.   She answered, " *Yes*."   It appears that she had, and was only waiting for a response from me, which I was not long in making; simply thanking her and her associates for their great solicitude in my behalf, and saying that I fully appreciated their thoughtfulness and great foresight. I respectfully declined to entertain favorably their suggestions, stating that as yet I felt fully competent to navigate the tempest-tossed bark a little longer.   Thus the hopes that inspired their whisperings and calculations for some time past were dashed to the ground, and I left at liberty to roam at my pleasure.   Writing this puts me in mind of a similar proposition coming from a prominent Spiritualist in Boston.   Through this man I had secured a chance to work for the Government in the Charlestown Navy Yard.   After I had got to work, or just before, being in his office one evening, he made the astounding revelation that I was incompetent to take care of my hard earnings, or words to that effect, and wound up by asking me, without any circumlocution, to appoint him my guardian. I was as much unprepared to hear this from him as one would be to hear heavy thunder from a clear sky. For a moment I was paralyzed; but, after seeing he was not joking, a strong impulse moved me to give him a thrashing on the instant, which I always feel amply capable of giving to any one when under the influence that was upon me then; but I resisted, and merely said, trembling with rage, I had all the guardians I wanted, and walked out of the room. I heard him say, "If you have, they don't allow you enough to eat."

If I had remained there five minutes longer, I should have had to answer to a charge of assault and battery in the courts. I had all I could do to keep from knocking him down in his own office. What in part created such a commotion in my mind was, that I had previously had every reason to think that in a business point of view he looked upon me with favor; that is to say, he believed that, if I had a fair chance, I could compete favorably with most successful business men. After looking the matter all over, and considering he had befriended me in many emergencies, in fact had long been among the best friends I ever had, the commotion passed away; and I thought no more about it.

As before stated, I had determined to go away somewhere; where, I didn't care, as long as I was out of the sight of my friends. The difficulty was to procure means to get away with. I knew of none who would trust me with even a few dollars, excepting it might be my youngest brother, who I thought felt more sympathy with me than any one else. The rest of my brothers who were all well off, and some of whom belonged to the Quaker Church, and all believed in its religious tenets, I didn't ask to aid me, as I knew what the result would be. Finally I went to him, and told him what I wanted. After hesitating a moment or two, he coldly and roughly said, " Go to cutting wood at seventy-five cents a cord, as I do, and get the money." I was so disappointed at what he said, and the way it was said, that I was speechless, and turned away without uttering a single word, and have never seen him since. But I didn't blame him, because he was young, and formed his opinion from the older ones. After leaving him I didn't know where to go for aid; but while wending my way towards home, thinking where next to apply, it was whispered into my most sensitive ear, " Try Isaac Clough." This Clough was a cousin of mine, and, although he presents a rough exterior, is full of the milk of human kindness. I immediately made the application as suggested; and he at once told me he hadn't it by him, but would get it, and, as he was going past my home that evening, would call and give it to me. True to his word, he left the money; and before any other one was astir in the house or neighborhood, by daylight the next morning I silently stole out of the village, and on my tiptoes when passing a house, for fear of making a noise, and attracting some one's attention, if I walked with a strong, firm, heavy step. I felt so lonely, and so disgusted with the treatment I had to endure while a sojourner in the place, that I didn't want any one to ever see me again, or know when or how I got away. After I had got clear of the little village, and when on the crest of a hill some miles away, I felt what it was to enjoy freedom more than ever before; and mechanically turning round to take a last look at the place (for I never meant to see it again, and I never have), I saw my three girls on the top of another little hill near the village, beckoning me either to stop or to bid them adieu. Not knowing when I left the house, and finding me gone when they got up, they put on their clothes, and started after me; but I was too far away, and I proceeded on towards the metropolis of the State, and by nine o'clock reached Augusta, where I could take the cars for somewhere.

I concluded finally to go direct to New York, and see what would turn up. By due course I arrived there, flat broke, to use a slang phrase. Put up at the Washington House at the foot of Broadway, where I boarded three or four weeks; then took rooms of Dr. Hayden, corner of Sixth Avenue and Fourteenth Street. Here I remained some six months, having a good business as a healer. After that, I hired a whole house at 1244 Broadway, and let unfurnished rooms for enough to four times pay all the rent, and have what room I needed besides. Here also I did a flourishing business until I got sick; after which I left every thing, and went to Baltimore to recuperate my health, and to work a patent gas regulator; and here I remained all winter, boarding at the Sherwood House. Here I tried to dispose of my patent, but got barely enough out of it to pay expenses.

The following spring, went to Cincinnati to try it
there, but failed to get it introduced on account of the
gas company, a powerful private organization, considered among the wealthiest in the country. They put
on an injunction against its use, under the penalty
of cutting off the gas from those who had the temer-
ity of allowing me to put my appliance on their me-
ters. I was advised to try the law, but refrained,
trusting to the advice of my guides, who told me in
plain, unmistakable language, that if I attempted it
I would only " get my labor for my pains." This
seemed more reasonable and sensible than any other
friend's advice; and I accepted the suggestion of my
spirit friends as the easiest way out of a bad scrape.
I received about five hundred dollars over and above
my expenses, and gave the business up altogether.

After settling up my affairs at the latter place,
started for St. Louis, Mo., arriving there on Christ-
mas Eve; here I remained all winter, doing barely
enough to pay expenses. The following April went
to Carondelet, a small town some seven miles on
the river above St. Louis, where I got work in a ship,
or rather boat yard. Here I worked until late in the
fall, when the rebel Gen. Smith with an army of
forty thousand men encamped some seven miles
above, threatening to sack the place. I got away on
Saturday; and on Sunday a squad of cavalry came
dashing into the town, and carried off every serviceable thing they could lay their hands upon, driving
off cattle, sheep, hogs, and poultry, but did no other
injury. I got on a steamer, and went to Paducah,
Ky., where was a government railway for taking up

government vessels to repair. Here I worked some six weeks, when one afternoon Gen. Forrest came dashing into town with fourteen thousand cavalry, and, there being nothing to resist him, took possession of the place, and held it until the news reached Mound City, where was a navy-yard, and where several gunboats were moored ready to go to any point where their services were needed. After he had held the place a couple of days, a fleet of gun-boats came to the relief of the besieged town, and drove him off. The boats reached their several positions in the darkness of the second night after the rebel army took possession, and at once opened upon the town from all their batteries; and before daylight the rebel foragers were in full retreat. The first thing the rebels did, after entering the town, was to cut all the telegraph-wires, and burn two government boats then on the railway. They did not interfere with any private property, but carried off any quantity of commissary supplies. After the mêlée was over, I went to Mound City, and got a job in the navy-yard, where I worked all winter. The spring following I went to Cincinnati, thinking I could get business there; but I was sick for a considerable time, and when I got better could get nothing to do. Finding my money was slowly oozing out of my purse, took passage on a boat, and went to Paducah again, where I expected to get work; but nothing was being done there; and after remaining idle some three months I went to Metropolis, a small town twelve miles below Paducah, situated on the Ohio River, on the Illinois side. Here I got a job that lasted fourteen days,

27*

when I was again out of work, with my money all but gone. After remaining idle some three weeks, it dwindled down to one dollar; and I owed three dollars for board, which the landlady dunned me for one morning at breakfast time. I told her I couldn't pay her then, but as soon as I got work I would; and, as I was looking for a job all the time, I thought I should succeed. My companion in all my joys and sorrows was with me, and she was trying to get a chance to do housework to save her board; failing to do that, we determined to take a couple of cheap rooms, as we had some furniture at Paducah, and keep house; and if we failed to get any thing to eat it was nobody's business. When I went down town that morning I had but one dollar, and after purchasing some tobacco I had just eighty-five cents left. We found a couple of rooms for seven dollars a month; and it was settled that Jennie should go to Paducah, and get what effects we had, and trust to luck about getting money to pay the freight, and we would go to housekeeping. I was to go up river some two miles, where a man was building two or three boats, and try and get a job. She went to Paducah, and, by selling a clock and a couple of bedsteads, managed to pay up the rent due, and get the things on board a boat, to be left at Metropolis on its way down river.

In detailing the following exceptional business operation, I shall avoid adding any thing to make it look more wonderful and novel than it really was, because simple unvarnished truth will show to a most remarkable extent the capability of spirits who when here were active business men, to plan and carry out large business operations to a successful issue through properly developed business men called mediums, who are still in the body, — schemes which to the normal business man, unacquainted with the help furnished from unseen sources, would be considered the products of a muddled brain, and who would treat them with the same indifference that they would the wild rantings of a monomaniac; and, if induced to notice them at all, would give vent to unqualified ridicule; and yet these things have been done over and over again in my own experience, as has been seen in the foregoing pages. Before going into the details of the operation hinted at, I wish to say, that, seeing the probability of its truthfulness being questioned, I have heretofore been very chary of telling it to any others than those acquainted with my history; and were it not that an object of this book is to show that our spirit-friends can foresee coming events, and guide and impress us often into paths that lead, if not to opulence, at least to bettering our pecuniary condition as well as the spiritual part of our nature, I should not record this, nor some others of a similar character contained in the foregoing pages. As proposed, after seeing my companion on board a boat bound for Paducah, where she was going to get what few household goods we had, I proceeded up river some mile or so, to try and get a job on some boats being built for parties in St. Louis. Questioning some of the workmen before encountering the foreman, they told me that they thought it extremely doubtful about my getting work, as they were overcrowded with men already, and thought that next pay-day, which occurred the following Saturday, some of them would get their discharge. I soon saw Mr. Cutting coming towards where I was standing; and at once I asked if he could give me work, telling him that I was a first-class ship-builder, having constructed many under my own supervision. He said he was sorry he couldn't set me to work. " To tell the truth," said he, " I have more now than I know what to do with; in fact, I am thinking of discharging some Saturday." From what I knew from my own exertions in trying to get work, coupled with what the men told me, I anticipated such an answer. I then tried to enlist his sympathy in my favor, by telling him exactly how I was situated, hoping that somehow or other he might think of a way to employ me, if only for a few days; but all to no purpose. Seeing from my despairing look that I was very much discouraged, he finally told me that I might come on Monday, and he would try and give me a few days' work to help me along. This was Wednesday; and as he only paid off every two weeks, my not beginning until Monday, it would be nearly three weeks before I could get any money; and, unless I could borrow some, I should famish for lack of something to eat. I thought of this, and asked him if, after I had worked a few days, couldn't he let me have some money to live upon. He said it would be impossible to do so, for reasons he did not care to explain. Finding that was the best I could do, I told him I would come on if I couldn't do any better, and turned away to retrace my steps down river. In all severely trying emergencies like these, when every avenue of escape from a perilous position was closed against me, I have been in the habit of questioning myself substantially as follows: "Now, David, can you reconcile this sad condition as being in harmony with a divine object?" and never failed of hearing an affirmative response welling up from the deepest recesses of my soul. In this case, after leaving Mr. Cutting, I walked slowly down the bank of the river, pondering over these things, until I came to where I had to cross a creek, over which was thrown a light pontoon bridge to save going round the head of the creek when the river was high, as it was then; and I distinctly remember asking the above question of myself while going down the bank to the bridge; and my soul then and there responded " *Amen.*"

I felt pleased to experience that this response could come with the same gush and spontaneity, now that I was passing through one of the severest trials of my life, as when the same question was answered affirmatively while passing through much less sadness than I was then experiencing. After the response came, I felt happy that I really cherished a philosophy that could withstand the severest attacks of poverty and its concomitants. I went on to the bridge feeling as light as a feather, and walked quite rapidly, congratulating myself upon the possession of something that never fails to give strength and peace when passing through the severest vicissitudes of life. I have no words that can express the ecstasy of my soul in that happy moment, — happy, though destitution and starvation were staring me in the face. I

had got about midway of the creek, and, while pondering over the above things, all at once I heard a
VOICE say, in clear, distinct tones, "Build a steamboat." I knew it was a spirit, and thought its tone
familiar, but could not think it came from one of those
who had so often come to my rescue in trying times,
and at once decided it must be some wild, rollicking,
mischievous spirit, aping those in whom I trusted, intending to get me into a scrape, and then laugh at my
credulity. At times more will pass through the
mind in a moment than could be given expression to
in an hour; at least, this is the case with me. The
moment I heard the VOICE, I almost came to a stand-
still, thinking what it could mean. At a glance, being
an adept in the business, that is, in the building of a
boat or vessel, I felt that it takes many thousands of
dollars to begin with; and I had but eighty-five cents,
and no way to get a penny more. Being almost a
total stranger in the place, I had no one I could
count upon for any accommodation whatever; and
I finally concluded that the VOICE came from those
who delight in deceiving mortals. Then I started
up faster, and after taking a few steps heard the
same words repeated. This time there was no mis-
taking the peculiar sound of an unseen friend; and I
passed rapidly on, and headed directly for a sawmill
I had often seen before, where they sawed plank and
timber for boat-building, and had, as I afterwards
learned, been working for the Government. From
the workmen I learned that Mr. Kimball the proprietor was up in the mill. Ascending a stationary ladder at the end of the structure, I saw the one who I

supposed was the proprietor, doing something to a large circular saw; waiting until he got through, I approached, and ascertained upon inquiry that Mr. Kimball stood before me. To do justice to myself, I will say, that, from the instant I heard the VOICE the second time, I had but one object or thought; and that was, to see Mr. Kimball. What for, I had no definite idea. I seemed overshadowed by some power that completely controlled not only my physical locomotion, but the mental faculties as well. As far as I was concerned personally, I didn't seem to have one single object in view, and was conscious only of an indescribable desire to see Mr. Kimball. What followed was purely mechanical on my part; that is to say, I didn't know what was going to be said until I heard myself say it, precisely as if I heard it from another party.

To resume: after the first salutation, I heard myself say, without announcing my name, that as I was here and out of business, if I could find any one who would furnish all the wood material for a boat, and wait for pay until a boat could be built and sold, I would build one; continuing, " I have some funds, and fifteen hundred dollars by me." If I had said "some money," without stipulating the amount, I shouldn't have felt so bad; but, as it was, I felt wretched; and all the way I could excuse the falsehood was in thinking, that as I was an adept in the business, and by attending strictly to carrying out all the details of construction, I could build a boat fifteen hundred dollars cheaper than almost any one else; and, although this excuse served somewhat to break off the jagged corners of the falsehood, yet I did not feel easy, because I was arrogating to myself qualities that might not exist. If, after thus misrepresenting my ability to carry on the work, I should lack pecuniary means, the result must be immediate and disgraceful failure. After I had got through with my proposition, he looked me up and down, and then in a drawling sort of way asked me, " Ain't you a Yankee? " Upon my answering in the affirmative, he said, " I thought so."

Relative to my proposition he said, I "have been sawing for the Government; and, not expecting the war would end for years, I stocked so extensively that I have a great many logs on hand; and now that the war is over, and business all unsettled, I don't know what to do with them; however, I will talk with Mr. Lukins [his clerk], who knows more about business than I do, and let you know." — "Well," said I, " I want to know immediately;" which, however, in business parlance, considering the magnitude of the operation, might be a week or ten days, more or less, for it couldn't be expected that any one would enter into an enterprise of that magnitude, involving so much time and material, without giving it due consideration. In the mean time I would get off somewhere else; for I made up my mind, while listening to him, that if possible I would never see him again; though, if I did chance to meet him, it would be the easiest thing in the world to frame an excuse for not entertaining any proposition from him favorably. Even to think about building a boat under such circumstances never entered my own mind; for my knowledge in ship-building precluded the possibility of such a scheme ending but in disgrace and an ignominious failure. Knowledge that my lips had been telling this man a mess of unmitigated falsehoods about the matter made me feel so bad and chagrined, that all I wanted was to get out of his sight; forgetting that he knew nothing about the truth or falsity of what was said. I wanted to go as soon as possible, and, after hearing what he had to say, did start promptly to get out of his sight. To facilitate that object, instead of going down the ladder by which I gained an entrance to the mill, I slid down over a pile of slabs directly in front of the mill. Due south from the mill, was another small one, which was used to saw up stuff for wagons, &c., with circular saws; I thought I would keep the latter building between me and the big mill, so that he would not see me again; but, after going some distance, found I couldn't go where I wanted to, unless I crossed his millyard, which would bring me into his view again. This I much wished to avoid, and had thought, that, by keeping close to a high board fence which skirted the southern extremity of his yard, I might possibly elude his eyes, and get clear unobserved; but when nearing the street, where I should be hid from view by intervening houses, I heard some one halloo. Instinctively knowing it was the man I wished never to see again, I paid no heed to it, but kept on my way; directly I heard two voices hallooing, and turning my head, trembling from head to foot, saw Mr. Kimball and another man beckoning me to them. I reluctantly and slowly walked towards them, planning what I would say to get out of a difficulty that I so

28

much dreaded.   Upon arriving at their office, before which they were standing, Mr. Kimball inquired my name, and then introduced me to Mr. Lukins. After that ceremony was over, he addressed me as follows: " I have been talking to Mr. Lukins about your proposition, and we have concluded that a boat was never built without being sold; and as we have a large quantity of logs on hand, and no market for lumber, we have concluded to accept your proposal: we had rather have our lumber in a boat than rotting on the banks of the river." Here was a crisis: things were culminating rather more rapidly than I dreamed of; something must be done to stop further progress, else the first thing I should know would be that I couldn't get out of the scrape. So I said this building a boat was merely a passing thought to which I had not given much reflection, and I should prefer not to talk about a matter of such a moment until I had weighed well the consequences, and obtained at least the acquiescence of my better judgment before making the first binding move in that direction. In answer to this he said, " The war is over, and there is great scarcity of boats of the freighting class, apparent to the most superficial observer; and there exists not a doubt, if you should build one of that class, it would immediately find a purchaser." I then told him that when I made the proposition to him I didn't take into account, that I was deficient in yard-tools; and, besides, I had no yard to build a boat in. In response to this he said he would supply me with yard-tools; and, as to the latter, he owned the whole bank of the river far above and below his mill, and

I might have room to build twenty boats, and he wouldn't charge me a cent for ground-rent; continuing, " And, besides, you may have the use of the little mill for sawing out such parts of the frame as it is possible to do; and," said he, " that will save you a great deal of hard work, and I won't charge you any thing for the privilege." Certainly here was a great inducement; but my capital, only eighty-five cents, dwindled into insignificance as means to build a boat with, and I looked about me for something else by which I could stop the thing altogether; for to say the least, the situation was getting critical at this juncture of the negotiations.

I remember of thinking, if I should get wheedled into actually beginning an operation which my better judgment told me must inevitably end in humiliating and disastrous failure, what an awful thing it would be; and I trembled with regret that I hadn't broken off the conversation in regard to it before. It must be borne in mind by the patient reader, that I not only didn't want to commence the construction of a boat, but was doing all in my power to keep out of it; and, although I knew it was the work of spirits, I couldn't class them with intelligent, prudent business ones, when I compared my means in hand with what was actually necessary to even begin building, to say nothing of the finishing. Asking pardon for this digression, we will come back to the business. I told him that I couldn't find fault with his generous offer; but there had been nothing said about the price of lumber. " Oh!" said he, " that is twenty-five dollars per thousand, delivered." Knowing that was the customary price, I didn't want to compromise my business qualities by objecting to it; and so I said the price certainly was not objectionable, but, if one should agree to pay only ten dollars a thousand, the survey might bring it up to thirty or forty dollars. "Very true," said he : "Mr. Lukins, take the tape-line, and show the gentleman our manner of surveying lumber." Of course that could be no such test as would induce me to go on with the operation; for they would naturally hold out the best inducement to further their own object. While absent from the office assisting Mr. Lukins to show what good measure they'd give me if I would give them the opportunity, and while thinking what other argument I could produce against closing a bargain, the thought passed through my brain like a flash of lightning, that it was my friends who had so often befriended me in years gone by, that got up this enterprise, and could carry it to a successful issue if I would but trust them. Instantly running over the past, and seeing that every business transaction of my life in which they started me nearly paralleled this in singularity, I felt ashamed at my obstinacy; and on my return told Mr. Kimball that I had made up my mind to go into the enterprise, and that we would make out the necessary writings, and execute them at once. I sat down, and drew up the agreement in accordance with my proposition; and by half-past eleven, A.M., each had a document duly signed, also witnessed by Mr. Lukins, and I was fairly embarked in an enterprise, the bare thought of which, one hour before, sent cold chills coursing through the system, creating a sickening nausea at the stomach and an indescribable weakening in my limbs. After I became imbued with the fact that it was really my spirit-friends who had navigated me through so many similar business transactions, that were managing matters now, I never once thought of my poverty; and only one idea filled my mind, which was, to get the preliminary part— the contract—through with as soon as possible. As soon as that was over, I wanted to be alone, and to cogitate upon how I should begin. As I turned to go away,.I saw the man I had worked for, going down town. Instantly the thought flashed through my mind, that possibly he had the moulds of a boat that I could hire. With this uppermost in my mind, I pushed after him, and soon overtaking him said, that as I couldn't get any thing to do I had concluded to build a boat on my own account, and asked him if he had the moulds of a model he had in his office. He said he had. I then told him that I didn't want to wait to send to St. Louis for materials to make them, and asked if he would loan them to me to mould a frame; and, if so, what would be his price? He said he would, and charge me fifty dollars for their use. Then he called his son, who was near, and told him to hand down from the mould-loft such a set of moulds, naming them. Upon examination I found every one intact, bevel-boards and all. I inwardly felt jubilant at what seemed most opportune; for saying nothing about my inability even to pay the freight on the materials, independent of paying for the purchase of

28*

them, which I should be obliged to do, his demand was a hundred dollars less than I could have got them up for myself, providing I had the materials on hand. Now, then, every want for beginning the enterprise was provided for; and as I had not a doubt but that the authors, or getters-up, of the undertaking would furnish the means in some way to carry it to completion, I entertained no fears for its terminating successfully.

I ought to say here, that moulds must be made of seasoned pine boards; and, as there were none such in this immediate section, there existed necessity of sending to either St. Louis or Chicago for it.

By this time it was noon; and, after getting my dinner, I told the landlady that I should change my boarding-house, also that I had made arrangements to build a boat; this I said more to make her feel easy about her bill than for any thing else. I got an old pass-book, partly blank, in which I could keep an account of what lumber I might use. Finding Mr. Lukins, we went to work surveying such as I wanted, each keeping the amount separately; and, when I finally settled with Mr. Kimball, we differed only two hundred and thirty-seven feet, an amount not worth more than six or seven dollars. I then went to moulding out the frame; and towards night a young man passing on the street, seeing me at work, applied for a job. Upon inquiry I found he was a green hand; that he never worked at carpentering a day in his life. At first, after I had got into it, I thought I would work along alone for a while, till some way opened by which I could get money to pay

off with.   But, finding I couldn't cant over the
heavy timbers alone, I hired this young man for a
dollar and fifty cents per day for a while, with the
promise that if he suited me I would keep him on;
and upon my telling him to be on hand at seven the
next morning, he left congratulating himself upon
his good luck.

About the time to quit work, seeing a boat haul
into the wharf, I went down to it, and found Jennie,
my companion, with our household goods, and a
freight bill of three dollars to pay. Seeing one of
the men who worked for the man I had been working
for, who seemed quite friendly, I borrowed money
enough of him to pay the freight and get the things
to our rooms. I said nothing to her about my day's
operation until we got the scanty furniture into our
rooms. When I told her I was going to build a
steamboat, she looked at me with a strange stare,
thinking of course I was crazy; and well she might.
I assured her that it was a fact, and to prove it
showed her the agreement.   She then said, "What
are you going to do for money?"   I said I didn't
know; that my spirit-friends got up the enterprise,
and I expected them to open a way by which I could
get it; and then told her how it was brought about,
also how hard I had worked to keep out of it. She
had no faith, nor even belief, that spirits existed at
all, much less that they came back here and constructed steamboats; but she had faith in me until
this came up. However, I assured her that it would
come out all right. During nearly two weeks after
we got into our new abode, we had nothing to eat

but dry white stewed beans; not a particle of bread, meat, butter, or grease of any kind, or tea, coffee, sugar, or molasses; and the beans she got from a farmer for whose boys she had made some clothing. We hired two rooms, up one flight, from a brother of Mr. Kimball's clerk. It was deemed necessary to keep our condition to ourselves, especially as I had commenced the construction of a large boat. If our circumstances had been known, the knowledge would d—n the enterprise in the bud. To keep them secret, one of us ate at a time, while the other watched to see if any one was coming up stairs; and if any one was heard on the stairs by either, when the other was eating beans, obedient to a signal agreed upon between us, the bean-eater was to go into the adjoining room, and close the door. We happened to have a cup full of salt, which she brought from Paducah, to season the beans; and, though we had a pretty rough time of it, the subterfuges we used to prevent folks from finding out our real situation were cause of many a merry laugh. The bare thought that I was building, or had commenced building, a large steamboat, with not money enough to buy a loaf of bread, was so supremely ridiculous, that when either of us thought of it, when alone, we could not help breaking out into hearty laughter. As good luck would have it, the other family were very quiet; and we, being unknown, were not annoyed by visitors. The next morning found me, at seven, in the yard with my new hand ready to do any thing. Finding that another man would greatly facilitate matters, and a brother of the one I had set to work coming along about eight o'clock, and wanting a job, I set him to work at the same wages with the other, so that now my expenses were three dollars per day, which by Saturday would amount to nine dollars for both; and I thought, if the money did not come, so that I could pay them off, I would take advantage of the custom of the place, and pay only every two weeks; and I felt sure by that time something would turn up in my favor. Saturday came, but no money; and I felt sorry for the boys, because they needed it. I kept telling my trusting companion, that it would come in good time; and upon my entering the house she asked me about it. She felt very much discouraged, but I managed to keep up good cheer. I was not quite sure, seeing that I was a stranger, whether they would come on Monday or not. When I went into the yard Monday morning, I found them waiting my arrival; and I soon set them at work, thus commencing what proved a most anxious week in my eventful life; for, if at its close I did not get means to go on with the job, the whole thing would end a total failure. I remember saying this to myself while going home Saturday night. I not feeling very well, and having to work hard, it was agreed after this, that to give me a chance to rest at noon Jennie should bring to me my dinner of beans; and, to keep folks from knowing what I had to eat, we used to get into some out-of-the-way place, to partake of the slender repast. Thus it went on through the week until Friday noon, when owing to some indisposition of my patient, trusting companion, I went home for my dinner, which consisted of the same bill of fare; and just as I got opposite to our house, I met a man whom I had seen, and who I learned was the wealthiest man in the place, but I had forgotten his name. I was induced to stop him, and ask him for a loan of some money to pay off my men on the morrow; telling him I was building a boat, and had been disappointed in getting my money, — as much as to say that I had some somewhere; and so I had, but the Lord only knew where it was deposited. He replied by saying that he "hadn't a cent;" but it wasn't so much what he said, as *how* he said it, that gave me to understand that he wouldn't let me have any if he had any amount. Jennie happened to be looking out of the window while I was speaking to him, and upon my entrance asked me who I was talking to. I told her I didn't know his name, but had learned that he was a wealthy man, and thought that maybe he would loan me some money to pay off with to-morrow. She expressed much surprise at my audacity, and wanted to know what he would think at being approached so unceremoniously by a stranger asking of him a loan of money. I told her I didn't know; and ate my repast almost in silence. Friday night came; but not a ray of light penetrated the dark cloud growing more sombre and dense every moment, and seeming to be slowly settling down nearer and more near, threatening to ingulf me in its murky embrace. Although I felt a sweet calm pervading my inner being like the eternal stillness of the deep ocean, yet like its surface my mind was ruffled and in agony;

not so much that I doubted for one single moment that all was right, and that that trial would bring this, like every thing else, out all right. If the enterprise ended in total failure, it would be so only in seeming; some permanent good would be the result, whichever way the tide of affairs might turn. Saturday morning's light came, and with it a renewal of my anxieties; for none but the invisible beings of the Summer Land knew how matters would end with me. On leaving the house I told Jennie that I didn't care for dinner, that she needn't fetch it, and I should be too tired to come for it; and left her in tears. By this time folks had begun to talk about me; in fact, since the middle of the week, my ear attuned to the utterances of the VOICE, I could hear them say, " He's a fraud, he's got no money, he'll never pay them poor fellows," &c. It seemed as though I could hear a whisper at any distance; and such talkers were right. I was a fraud and deceiver, and, according to the established business code, I was a scoundrel in cutting up so much timber upon the strength of what the business world would call an unmitigated deception.

I went to work with a will, the better to tone down my highly wrought up nerves; but at noon I saw my anxious partner approaching with the well-known tin pail. I had got the keel on the blocks, ready for the frames; and we selected a place near the water, out of sight of my two workmen, to eat my dinner; and I can say I never enjoyed a better meal in my life. There was a flavor and sweetness to the beans that I never noticed before. The afternoon passed off

with not a sign of relief from any quarter. I looked
up, as though expecting to see a rift in the blackness
that surrounded me. At last knocking-off time arrived, when the boys put up their tools, and waited
for me to come and pay them. I didn't know what
excuse to make, and kept on at my work at the lower
end of the keel, as though I wanted to finish some
particular thing before I left; but really I was waiting for them to leave, before I should come up the
bank. They showed no signs of leaving. I kept on
steady at my work, while the poor fellows waited;
directly some of their acquaintances came along, and
discussed with them the probabilities of their getting
any money " from that d—d fraud," as they called
me. I heard all of their remarks as clearly and distinctly as themselves. After having worked on an
hour, seeing the crowd increasing, the poor boys in
the centre with downcast faces, and both hands in
their pockets, pictures of despair, — all at once, without a thought, I found myself going rapidly up the
bank towards the crowd, with not an idea what I
should say; but when directly opposite them, slack-
ing my speed a little, I told them to come to the
post-office after supper, and I would pay them; that
I had neglected to get my money this afternoon;
still keeping on towards my humble home. Here
was another muss. If I had passed them without
speaking, it would have been sensible, compared to
what I did say. I don't think I was ever so out of
humor with any thing I said or did, as this foolish
speech; and I kept scolding myself, all the way home,
for my stupidity. However, it was done; and they

would only be the more disappointed by my not paying them. When I entered, my looks told too plainly that I had failed to pay off. I sat in silence and ate my beans, poor Jennie too much absorbed in grief to join me. After getting through supper, if it could be called one, without a thought as to where I was going I seized my hat, and started to go out. Jennie asked me where I was going; and my lips said I was going to see that man I spoke to yesterday in the road, opposite our house. Then I rushed out of doors, leaving my grief-stricken partner in tears, and, as she afterwards told me, fearing I would do away with myself.

I made a straight wake for that man's office, having previously ascertained its location. It being dark, I halted when within three or four rods of the door, which was open, and talked to myself in this wise: Now, David, you have many weak points, and among them this foolish one: you would almost starve before asking a friend for aid, who would be only too glad to serve you. Now be a man: go to the rich one, tell him your wants, and know your fate at once; continuing, It is no disgrace to try and raise money in a legitimate way, &c. Thus I talked to myself for fifteen minutes or so. At last, thinking I had screwed up sufficient courage, I started for the door; but, when within ten feet of it or so, I began to feel weak in my limbs, and hesitated, waited a moment, then retreated to where I had been talking to myself, in order to get a fresh instalment of courage. After recruiting with a fresh lot, started again; this time, when I began to lose strength, I had got so far that those inside could see me, and, not daring to risk my tongue when I felt so weak, I passed by the door altogether, and circled round until I got in my old place, a little chagrined at my timidity, if not actual cowardice. I waited a few minutes, and without saying a word, or promising myself any thing, I quietly walked up to the open door, and, catching Mr. McBane's eye (that was the rich man's name), beckoned him out. He came at my beck; and, taking him two or three rods from his office, I told him that I was the man that asked him the day before for some money to pay off my help with; and that, as he then refused me, he might think it strange that I should make a second application. After hearing what I had to say, he told me that his mother received three hundred dollars that afternoon, and, if she hadn't loaned it, he could get what I needed for me (I had previously told him I wanted to get fifty dollars); and he started upon the run for the house. In a moment or so I saw him coming out almost upon the run; as he advanced he said, "Mother let Mr. Bear [a merchant] have it; but you go to the post-office, and I'll go into Bear's and borrow for you." I told him I didn't want to go to the post-office, as I had told the boys that I would meet them there, and give them their money. "Very well," he says: "go along slowly up Main Street, and I will overtake you." Upon this he left me, and went into the store; and I walked slowly up street. Just as I had passed a knot of men, who I knew were talking about me, for I heard one of them say in a suppressed manner, "There he goes," — just at this moment I heard some one approaching rapidly from behind ; and, when about turning my head to see who it was, Mac came to me, seeming to look and act as if surprised, and looking earnestly in my face said, " Ah, is this you ?" extending his hand at the same time, and shaking mine vigorously, then added, " I'm glad to see you." While shaking my hand he left in it a hard roll which I knew was money. Almost instantly he asked if I was going up town. " No," I says; " I believe I'll go to the post-office, and then home." Everybody knew Mac, and observed his demonstrative action towards me. I heard one of the gang say, " If he is a friend of Mac, he's all right." This was what I call spirit acting ; for invisibles made him do all this to blind the listeners, and keep them from knowing any thing about my business. When going past a store window, I noticed that my package was wrapped in brown paper ; I took that off, put the roll of bills in my waistcoat pocket, and walked rapidly towards the post-office. A more self-satisfied man never breathed. Near the post office was a store, in which was a telegraph-office ; on the counter was a desk facing out, to accommodate for writing messages·; on this desk was a lamp. Seeing the two boys surrounded with their sympathizing friends, I beckoned them to follow me. Not only they, but the whole crowd followed, probably to see whether I had just enough to pay them off, or not. Going up to the desk referred to, I took out the roll of bills, and laid them on the desk. I owed the two brothers twenty-seven dollars in all. The first bill on the top was twenty dollars, which I passed over to the oldest. The next was a ten-dollar bill ; this I passed to the store-keeper to get broken so that I could make the seven dollars change, which I, passing over to Bill, told him they might divide between them. Putting the three dollars with the rest, I rolled all up, and put it carelessly into my waistcoat pocket, much as a man would do when flush with money. As the first two bills were of high denominations, those looking on would naturally suppose that all the roll was twenty, ten, and maybe fifty dollars, and that I might be rotten with money. The real fact was that each bill remaining in the pile was a one. However, the display of bills established my credit, as far as paying my help was concerned. After leaving the store I made a bee-line for home. Entering in a hurry, I threw the package of bills on the table; and, they being old worn bills, they scattered all round, and looked to be as many again as there really were. When Jennie saw so much money sprawled out on the table, and my flushed looks, she thought I had, in my extremity, robbed somebody; and as soon as she could gather sufficient strength to speak said, "Why, David, what have you been doing?" I assured her that I had done nothing that would bring crimson into anybody's cheek; "but first of all," said I, "let's go to market, and get what will furnish us a square meal." We took a market or rather a clothes basket, and as soon as possible returned heavily laden with the best the market afforded, and about twelve o'clock sat down to the first regular meal for the past two weeks nearly. We never slept a wink until near sunrise, but kept talking over my enterprise commenced under such discouraging circumstances, and now bidding fair to end auspiciously. As per agreement, about midday I called upon Mac, and told him the whole story, — under what auspices the project was gotten up, how I tried to keep out of it, and yet was finally obliged to take hold, and how we had so long eaten not a particle of any thing excepting stewed white beans. When I was telling him this part of the story, the tears trickled down his cheeks; and extending his hand he said, "I will stand by you in this thing: tell me Friday how much money you want Saturday, and I'll get it for you if I turn hell over for it." When he lauded me for my unheard-of pluck, I told him it was spirits, and not me, when he said, "Spirits be d—d! You are the smartest man in Illinois." I have been thus particular because of the peculiarity of the operation, and the untoward circumstances it had to pass through before it was fully under way. I have tried to depict exactly my feelings and anxieties, and the almost superhuman faith I had in my spirit-friends being able through me to carry the work to completion; also the utter hopelessness of my poor anxious partner, struggling against all hope of success just to appear cheerful, hoping by so doing to give me courage, when in truth she was slowly dying with fears as to the effect a failure would have upon my already feeble health; but I have succeeded poorly, for no words in our language can fully express the reality of that week's operation.

After this I had no difficulty in getting all the men I wanted, or money to pay them off with. Mr. McBane, true to his voluntary promise, made his arrangements to meet my wants so that I never failed of paying off every Saturday night. From this time until I had completed the boat, every thing went along without the least friction; and long before she was ready to launch I sold her at my own price, and, in fact, subsequently got $2,500 more than I asked for her in the first place. This needs a little explanation. The facts of the sale were these: One day a man in St. Louis, seeing my advertisement in " The St. Louis Democrat," in which was a full description of my steamboat's dimensions, and that she was for sale, came to Metropolis to look at her, disposed, if she answered the advertised description, and the price was not extravagant, to purchase her. He was accompanied by two other interested parties; and after looking her all over, and she being just what he was looking for, and he knowing that she would not remain long unsold, determined to effect a trade at once. Upon consulting me as to the price and terms, he was told that I wanted eight thousand dollars cash. He said that he had only one thousand with him; but if I would give him until the following Tuesday, at six, P.M. (this was Thursday), he would give me the one thousand now, and, if he didn't come to time, that would pay me for waiting; and, if he did, this one thousand dollars should make one of the eight. This I agreed to, and at once drew up and executed writings accordingly; after which he immediately left for St. Louis, to see about getting up owners to float her.

This, so far as I was concerned, was a safe operation; and I felt quite jubilant over the transaction. Soon after he left, a Dutchman came along, and, after looking at her, made proposals to purchase. Upon learning that she was already sold upon conditions, which I explained, he offered me five hundred dollars more. I refused; telling him, if they didn't come to hand at the time specified, that he should have her at his offer. He said that he didn't dare wait, as the probabilities were that the other party would not allow her to pass into other hands. With this he left; and I felt pleased with this proof, that, if one party failed, another stood by to take her. Thus things went on until Saturday, about eight o'clock, when I received a telegram from the first party, stating that, because of death in the family of one of the principal prospective owners, he should be obliged to give up the contract, adding particulars by mail. Although I had not a doubt but that I could sell her, this announcement for a moment almost paralyzed me. Recovering a little, I carried the telegram to McBane, handing it to him without uttering a word. After reading it he looked up, and, seeing my looks indicated anxiety, said with a pleasant smile, " This is nothing to worry about: it will put a thousand dollars in your pocket; " continuing, " You forget for the nonce that you are the luckiest d—l in all the world. Cheer up, man! I should think you had gone safely through too many typhoons to be alarmed at this light cat's-paw, which, at its worst, can but slightly ruffle the surface of the deep ocean of your experience." This re-assured me. The following Monday another party came along, to whom I sold her for fifteen hundred dollars more than I asked the first one, and, with the one thousand dollars already received, made twenty-five hundred dollars more than I asked in the first place. The first party was a poor man; and I refunded the one thousand dollars, being glad to do so. Thus it will be seen, that, from beginning to end, the whole affair was under the direct influence of spirits; that is, everybody that had any thing important to do with it, as well as myself, was influenced by this unseen band of immortals, whether the humans knew it or not.

In writing out my history, I seem to live it all over as I go along; every sensation, whether pleasant or its opposite, I feel precisely as when going through the experience. I write entirely from memory. I put on paper the exact facts, leaving out many of minor importance. If there are mistakes, it is not in overstating or in painting things to make them more sensational than they otherwise would be. Although there were many laughable incidents connected with the matters described in this chapter, I will allude to but a single one. I requested Mr. McBane, after having told him how the thing was got up, not to mention it to any one. He religiously respected the request until I got her almost completed, when one day he told me that Mr. Gray and his wife, seeing us together so much and often merry, surmised that there was something of special interest up between us, and they were all the while teasing him to tell what it was. This Mr. Gray kept the only hotel in the place; and, as Mac owned it, he spent much of his spare time there; and in that house we used to talk over our matters by ourselves. These talks and our manners were what attracted their attention.

Mac asked me if he should relieve their curiosity. I gave my consent, and appointed that evening to be present, and hear him dilate upon my superior executive ability. After exacting a promise from our host and hostess not to tell, Mac gave a full and brilliant account of it all. Being a lawyer, and possessing great descriptive faculties, he decked my achievements in a most glowing array of adjectives; and when speaking of the first two weeks, and especially of our living on nothing but stewed beans, he drew tears from their eyes; and, forgetting for the moment that it was myself he was portraying, I could not prevent tears running down my own cheeks. In describing other scenes in the play, he made things appear so extravagantly absurd, that all hands would be convulsed in uncontrollable laughter. From this scene leaked out what caused it to be said that I built a boat with a pint of beans and a quart of hominy. So ends the account of in some respects the most remarkable experience of my eventful life, and with it this chapter.

CHAPTER XVI.

PUBLISHING A SPIRITUAL NEWSPAPER CALLED THE
"VOICE OF ANGELS," EDITED AND MANAGED BY
SPIRITS — HOW AND BY WHOM IT WAS FIRST
PROJECTED, AND WHY IT WAS GOTTEN UP.

WHEN I narrated the incidents in the last chapter, which occurred some ten years since, I supposed that, as I was getting well up in years, nothing more of a remarkable nature would transpire worthy of recording; and I was about congratulating myself, that as I had no one to look out for but myself, and that as my business (healing the sick) was bringing an income amply sufficient to provide for my few wants, that I could slide down the afternoon of life with comparative ease, when another phase of things occurred, which, taking every thing into account, fairly eclipsed all preceding ones, not so much as to its get-up, as in its power of being useful in opening the eyes of thousands buried in the darkness of the past.

Subsequent to the time I finished the steamboat mentioned in the preceding chapter, up to the middle of October, 1875, I was engaged in various pursuits, — sometimes ship and house building, but principally in healing the sick. It was while practising the latter profession in Philadelphia in 1870, that the enterprise I am about to relate was first projected. Many interesting and instructive incidents transpired in the interim, but the limits of this book preclude their appearance in its pages; they, however, will be set forth in another book that I am writing, to be called "Odds and Ends of an Eventful Life," which will be printed at some future day.

Some time in July of the above year, while practising my profession in the Quaker City, to facilitate my business, I determined to get up a circular in the form of a miniature newspaper, and issue it monthly. When that project had got well fixed in my mind, I sat down to write a prospectus for it. I had written only a few lines when L. Judd Pardee, a former and esteemed friend of mine, who had been in spirit-land then some five years, put in an appearance. I felt not a little pleased and gratified at the friendly call. I asked him what he thought of my paper, and whether it would subserve the purpose intended. Without answering that question directly, he took advantage of my willingness always to allow him the use of my hand whenever he desired, and wrote these words: "Why not get up a paper that I can speak through to the hungry multitude?" Upon reading his question, I jocosely said, "I will, if you'll edit it." After waiting a few minutes, he seemingly thinking the matter over, or talking with his friends about it, wrote, "I accept the offer, will do the best I can; and with the aid of several spirits who when in the mundane condition occupied high positions in the moral and intellectual world [some of whom he named] I have no doubts of its ultimate success." After a pleasant chat of an hour or so, upon various other topics, he left, and I thought no more about the matter for the time being. I supposed it was merely a playful mood we both happened to be in, that brought out what I should have considered very absurd if I thought he had intended in other than mere pleasantry. This was the preliminary step to an enterprise that culminated some five years subsequently in the publication of the VOICE OF ANGELS.

For weeks subsequent to the above conference, the project would flash through my mind occasionally; and, whenever an opportunity offered, Mr. Pardee would write something relating to our "novel enterprise" as he used to characterize it. Whenever it was alluded to, I treated it with as little consideration as I would a thing that I considered of not the slightest practical importance. I thought that even talking about it with him was a waste of time. Whether it was the novelty of the scheme, that caused me to think about it, or whether I was being impressed by Mr. Pardee of its practical importance, I did not know; but, the more I tried to keep it out of my mind, the more it would intrude itself, until at last I could think of nothing else. For weeks I kept it to myself; but eventually the thought occurred to me, that, if I ventilated the matter among my friends, may be I could get rid of it altogether. This ruse did not work as I hoped it would; for, instead of getting rid of it, my mind became more absorbed in it than ever. What tended to bring about such result was, that every one to whom I mentioned the matter gave it unqualified approval, as a move that would culminate in success if once started. I could not see it in that light. At first, as before stated, I thought of it only as a pleasantry on the part of Mr. Pardee; but, when I found that he was in solemn earnest, I expostulated with him, doubting its practicability; telling him what he already knew of my total ignorance of journalism, and that I had never written an article for a paper in my life; also, that I had no pecuniary means to start the enterprise, to say nothing of keeping it afloat long enough to insure its success, even with fair prospects for such a result at the beginning. But, in spite of all arguments to the contrary, its claims for a respectful consideration acquired a monopoly of my thoughts. Mr. Pardee and many other spirits claimed that they could write out their thoughts through my hand with almost the same ease and facility that they could with their own before leaving the material form; but fearing this was a mistake, and the pressure upon me becoming great, I, to test the feasibility and possible success of the scheme, determined to write out a series of questions relating to the subject, enclose them in a closely sealed envelope, and send them to Mr. J. V. Mansfield, to be answered through him; and thus to learn what my business friends in spirit-life, in whose judgment I had the most implicit confidence, had to say about it. Accordingly I wrote the questions, enclosed them in an envelope so secured that it could not be tampered

30

with without instant detection, and sent it off. In less than a week I received a package containing not only the sealed letter intact, but an elaborate answer to each and every question asked, in regular order as propounded from first to last; and without a single exception all replies were in favor of the enterprise, cautioning me, however, about embarking in it without sufficient means to successfully float it until it could sustain itself; hinting that many projects of the kind had been started, and failed for want of sufficient funds; remarking, " We are not bankers, but we can give matter that will elicit favorable criticism."

Not having any personal acquaintance with Mr. Mansfield, I knew there was no common way by which he could have become possessed of even the drift of the questions: therefore the replies through him somewhat staggered my prior doubts as to its practicability, and I began to consider the project more favorably, although with not the vaguest thought that it would ever amount to a practical reality. To ascertain some of the details as to its get-up, if I ever should find myself in a condition to start it, I sent another letter under the same test conditions as the first; and to this also the answers came in the same regular order and preciseness as did the first.

No way being open for carrying the project forward at that time, it gradually passed out of my mind, except that occasionally it would pay me a visit, seemingly to keep our acquaintance fresh and green. Time rolled on until October, 1875, when the subject came knocking at the door of thought again, asking admittance. The subject had lain so long in a dormant state, that I thought it was merely a passing impression, and would soon leave, as it had done hundreds of times since it was first projected. But this time, as it proved, I was not to be let off so easily. One evening, soon after this last draught upon my mind, Mr. Pardee put in an appearance. Ever ready and pleased to receive a friendly call from my dearly beloved spirit. friend, I hastily opened wide the door of my heart, and bid him enter. After the first friendly salutations were over, he at once renewed the subject of the long-ago-talked-of paper, arguing very earnestly the importance of at once starting it; stating that the project had not been absent from his mind since he first made the proposition, also that he had been unremitting in his endeavors to bring it into actuality, that he had ceased not day or night, from that time to this, in developing me for the work.

Although in a pecuniary sense able to give it a fair trial, if once started, I hesitated, as I was totally void of any practical knowledge in the business; I was getting well up in years; most of the matter must come through my hand; and knowing that, once in, there was no retreat, I recoiled from the responsibility with feelings bordering on horror. Thus for weeks it went on; and, as before, the more I tried to rid my mind of thinking about it, the more it troubled and perplexed me. Unable longer to keep it to myself, and with the faint hope, that by ventilating it among my friends as I did once before for the same purpose, in Philadelphia, I might be able to throw off the pressure that was bearing me down, and robbing me of necessary sleep and rest, I did so. Although my friends neither approved nor disapproved of the project, they seemed rather astonished at the announcement. I told them where and when it was first suggested, and the means I had used to ascertain its practicability; and, unlike their course on the former occasion, with two exceptions all gave it unqualified *dis*approval; arguing that the general stagnation of business all over the country, coupled with the great scarcity of money and a hard winter staring all in the face, said, that if it might be ever so feasible under more favorable circumstances, it certainly could not at that time elicit the commendation of the most superficial business observer from a business standpoint. I fully coincided with that sensible mode of reasoning, yet I could not throw off the influence. Each succeeding day it gained a stronger hold upon my now anxious, troubled mind. Thus for weeks the conflict in my mind went on, slowly but steadily gaining in volume and intensity, with no sign of a diminution in its steadily increasing hold upon my rebellious spirit.

In vain I reasoned with Mr. Pardee against its practicability under existing circumstances, even if I were an adept in the business, reiterating over and over again the reasons for my objections. But all to no purpose. He steadily persisted, that if once started it would culminate in success; and he would not listen to any thing I advanced in opposition to

the enterprise.   Up to this time, that is, for three or
four weeks, I had carried on all the correspondence
pro and *con*, in relation to the enterprise with Mr.
Pardee, through my own hand; but, finding the subject matter had assumed such dimensions that something must be done one way or the other, I began to
question my own mediumship.   Not that I doubted
whether any volition on my part produced what my
hand wrote (for that would be a preposterous idea,
since every thought of my mind, as far as I knew,
was diametrically opposed to the project); but to
ascertain whether there might not be some imper-
sonal, occult, psychological power at work which I
did not understand, and which caused my hand to
write what my judgment did not indorse, I determined to have recourse again to my spirit-friends
through Mr. Mansfield.

Leaving out all details as to questions sent and
answers returned, I will say that I received five letters from Mr. Pardee and other valued spirit-friends,
in answer to as many from me.   In every one of
these, the practicability of the scheme had the unqualified indorsement of most of my friends in spirit-
life.   Some, however, thought that, from the de-
pressed condition of business affairs, it was not the
best time to start it; while equally many thought it
was the right time.   All agreed that it was a move
in the right direction; and those who favored its
being started at that time said, that if once started
it would go ahead; it might be slowly at first, but
eventually it would rest upon a solid basis.   Finally,
having exhausted all objections to the scheme that I

30*

could think of, and having become convinced beyond a peradventure, that its practicability under existing circumstances was perceived by practical business minds in spirit-life, whose pre-judgment of things future was not to be ignored with impunity, and that they would not encourage, much less advise, any one to engage in an enterprise of this or any other kind, involving great personal inconvenience, when the chances were not greatly in favor of the scheme, I reluctantly (I am ashamed to confess) consented to enter the lists, and do the best I could in a project gotten up and managed by this band of beneficent spirits, as I had every reason to believe they were.

To put myself in the best possible condition to be used, I abandoned the use of tobacco, which had been a lifelong habit, also tea and coffee, and confined myself to simple nourishing diet, determined that, as far as I was concerned, there should be nothing wanting to insure its success.

This being determined upon, I set myself to work getting up a prospectus; but could not perfect it until I had decided upon a name for the new paper. I have heard it said that of all things in this world to get at satisfactorily was the name for a new paper or book; but had no conception of the difficulty, until I tried to get one for the novel paper I had determined to launch upon the boisterous ocean of newspaper criticism. Unlike any other paper in existence, this was to be edited and managed by denizens of another, and, to say the least, more ethereal world. To get a name that would correspond to and embrace the design of the work, puzzled my brain for weeks. I asked Mr. Pardee to furnish it: he replied that he had rather I would select to suit myself. The nearest I could come to it was " Spirits' Tribune ;" but that didn't exactly suit. I had made a standing offer of ten dollars to any one who would furnish a name that would fit the design of the work, but failed in getting any thing better than the one that suggested itself to my own mind. I finally concluded to consult my spirit-friends through Mansfield, in relation to this also, before I fully decided. I did so. In response, Mr. Pardee said that what I had selected would do ; and so would " Voice of Angels," suggested, he said, by Theodore Parker. The moment I saw *that* name, I was satisfied, and determined at once to adopt it.

The two most important things having been settled, — viz., to go ahead with the enterprise, and what name to designate the work by, — I commenced making preparations for the birth of the little stranger. Although the accouching process would be conducted by skilled physicians, yet I feared at times, that, notwithstanding my confidence in those engineering the operation, it might be still-born, or not born at all. However, I got up a prospectus to suit me, after writing, cutting down, and doing the same numerous times.

Prior to this I had said nothing about my purpose to any outside of those intimate friends, who all tabooed it, with the exception of two. But, now that the thing would soon be known to the public, I first waited upon an old and esteemed friend who holds high position as a sensible man, and is one of our most practical, common-sense thinkers and writers upon Spiritualism, and see what he might say about my novel undertaking. After stating to him what I was about doing, showing him my correspondence with Mr. Pardee in relation to it, also telling him of my incompetency, &c., I asked him for his criticism. He heard me through, questioned me closely on various points, and then said, " If it is projected and shall be carried on *strictly* by the spirit world, I think it may be a success : otherwise it must end in total failure."

Although I should have gone ahead with the publication unaided, yet at my request this gentleman revised the copy, read the proofs, and whatever merit there may be in the general make-up of the early numbers (apart from the *matter*, none of which he furnishes) is due to his kindly aid. He told me at the outset, and continues to say, that on account of his other engagements he can make no promise of aid in the future. Unexpected help from such a source at the outset engendered confidence that at its first appearance the babe would not lack a respectable dress to make his maiden bow in, whatever might be his ability to survive the harsh handlings of critics which I knew he would be forced to endure.

To make widely known in advance the coming of this Voice, was no easy matter. True, the Spiritualistic and other papers in Boston would insert its prospectus as an advertisement under their rules ; but either self-interest or distrust held them back from such editorial notices as were reasonably expected in some cases. Prophets usually get more honor and favor abroad than at home; and in this case the far-off " Religio-Philosophical Journal " of Chicago made greater demonstration in welcoming a new member to the family of Spiritualistic teachers, than did all those combined who dwell near the new one's birth-place. And not only so, but the publisher of that Western paper loaned a list of his subscribers, which permitted the distribution of twenty thousand copies of our first sample number among the liberal-minded throughout North America. A favorable notice of our intended work having appeared in the " Religio-Philosophical Journal " weeks before our first issue, we had, in consequence of the generosity, more than two hundred subscribers when our first number went to press, and have been obtaining others by hundreds weekly ever since. Our success is greater and our prospects are brighter than our most sanguine expectations embraced at a day so early as this.

The final result of this strange work for one like me to be absorbed in is concealed in the wrapped-up scroll of the future, and cannot be read now. My previous trainings and discipline have no doubt been designed to fit me for my present work. One trained to literary pursuits, and to publishing business, would have become wedded to methods which would hold him back from such novel and free courses as the work imposed upon me requires. The old homely saying, that " It is hard to teach an old dog new tricks," expresses a truth which is applicable here.

and in very many other cases, and perhaps indicates a reason why such an one as myself has been pressed into my present position.

Success in my present field of labor may depend much upon myself, upon cheerful and persistent obedience to my employers, and upon my justice and charity towards all men and all spirits.

The special work to which the Voice now calls me differs from any that is generally known to be possible. Spiritualism has been furnishing a commentary upon the statement that Jesus (1 Pet. iii. 19) "went and preached unto *spirits in prison*, which sometime were disobedient." We have been learning that there are myriads of such spirits dwelling in the abodes of *unrest, darkness*, and *degradation;* and that the kindred and friends of such ones, dwelling in higher and brighter spheres, and seeking to enlighten and elevate these lower ones, by whom the brighter are invisible, find great help in their beneficent efforts when they can lure a wretched one into contact with an embodied medium, for in his auras the two classes of spirits, the darker and the brighter, can come into sensible contact, and thus the better can start the worse up the ladder of progression towards heavenly peace and joy. It is mainly as the instrument of spirits in such efforts that I am now employed; and a main purpose of the Voice of Angels seems to be, to furnish our world with statements of their experiences and labors by spirits of all grades, and thus teach mortals both what lies before them in the next life, and how they can now help in the deliverance of "spirits in prison."

Such is my solemn and philanthropic work.   God
and good spirits help me to perform it faithfully and
well, and aid me to become fit day by day for higher
and more efficient service both in the earth-form and
in the realm of spirit!